A GIF...
EYE AND MORE

A GIFT TO THE EYE AND MORE

Leceila Turnage

URBAN BOOKS

http://www.urbanbooks.net

This is a work of fiction. Any references or similarities to actual events, real people, living or dead, or to real locales are intended to give the novel a sense of reality. Any similarity in other names, characters, places, and incidents is entirely coincidental.

URBAN SOUL is published by

Urban Books
1199 Straight Path
West Babylon, NY 11704

ISBN-13: 978-1-59983-064-3
ISBN-10: 1-59983-064-7

First Printing: January 2008

10 9 8 7 6 5 4 3 2 1

Printed in the United States of America

1

Misgivings

I can see the headline now: BRIDESMAID GOES BERSERK! I've got PMS, so it won't take much more to send me over the edge. Another look of pity cast my way, or another annoying question or comment about my lingering state of singleness, and I'm liable to become a bouquet-wielding fiend. I cried for three days after seeing the wedding announcement in the *Fairview Herald*, and I'm on the verge of bawling right now. Dear God, give me strength!

It's only been twenty minutes into the reception, and I've been—like I expected—pelted with questions about my sad love life. "You next?" "You're such a sweet, pretty thang. I don't understand why some man hasn't stolen you away. What's the problem, baby?" "Eva, it's time you got married! What you waitin' on?" "I hope I'll still be living to see you get married *someday*. Don't you want to change your last name one time?"

Outspoken, mothball-smelling, hairy-lipped Cordelia Weeks, the oldest mother in the church, pinched me on the right arm and whispered, with raised eyebrows, "You ain't

that way, are you? Now that would be a shame 'fore God!"
As I nursed my bruised arm, I assured Mother Weeks, with a
big smile, that I wasn't "funny."

Her sidekick, bushy-browed Reather Upchurch, shot me a
toothless grin and said quite loudly, "Old maids don't go to
heaven, Eva. You know why?"

Regrettably, I asked, "Why not?"

She chuckled and said, "'Cause *Peter* up there!" The crude
joke generated an outbreak of laughter around me. I laughed,
too, despite my embarrassment.

If someone had told me twenty years ago that I would be
single and childless at forty, I wouldn't have believed it. According to Mama and the ladies at Community Baptist, it's
my fault I'm not married. I'm "too picky" they say. I don't
think wanting a tall, handsome, Christian man who is college-
educated, financially secure, and romantic is being "too
picky," considering this is somebody I intend to love and
cherish for the rest of my life. And I *refuse* to lower my standards and settle for less, no matter how much Mama and the
others get on my case about being single.

"Smile, ladies!" the groom's aunt from San Diego exclaims.

I lean close to the bridesmaid next to me and smile at the
camera.

Maybe I should move out West—leave itty-bitty, three
stoplights Fairview for San Diego. I might get lucky there.
Naw, on second thought, I might not, if I'm to believe what
the fine folks at *Forbes* magazine say. San Diego didn't make
their annual list of the best places for singles. Shoot! I don't
see how Raleigh did for a second time. I've worked in
Raleigh sixteen years now, and I find the pickings to be *quite*
slim. I haven't been on a date in eight months! The depressing reality for college-educated Black women like me is
there's a shortage everywhere of decent, desirable Black men.

I grip my bouquet, a miniature version of the bride's, my
cousin, and try real hard to continue looking elated and "dig-
nified." To appear any other way will surely cause a few

tongues to start wagging, and I can't have that. One thing Rose Campbell Liles Allen expects of my two sisters and me is that when distressed, publicly we be as cool as cucumbers. Despite my sunny disposition, I feel like the biggest fool in town, and if I could turn back the hands of time, I would.

Two years ago, the handsome groom doggedly sought *my* affections. To get him off my back, I introduced him to Willnetta, and to my surprise, good-looking, bald-headed Joel fell in love with my homely, gap-toothed cousin. I'll be the first to admit that my lack of interest in him was for all the wrong reasons. He was living in a tiny, one-bedroom apartment, driving a two-door Ford Escort, and working as a correctional officer at the minimum-security prison in nearby Hayesfield. He wasn't making much money as a correctional officer, and I've never found blue-collar wage-earning men attractive. I don't consider myself a gold digger, but if a brotha intends to woo me, he must have money to fuel the romance.

Now here I stand, beset with regret, remembering something my daddy told my baby sister, Stephanie, and me. "How a man starts out in life is not always how he'll end up," he had said in response to my refusal to date men who weren't "degreed" and making more money than me.

Joel has proven that Daddy's words were true. In less than two years, he's completed a criminal justice degree and landed a detective position with the sheriff's department. He's reaping lucrative profits renovating and renting houses, and he recently entered into a partnership to open what will be Fairview's first church supply store. The ambitious Mr. Alexander has made my cousin the envy of every single, dying-to-be-married woman at Community Baptist. He's built Willnetta the house of her dreams—a four-bedroom, three-and-a-half bath, brick, traditional two-story—and given her a white Mercedes E430 for a wedding present.

There're not enough words to describe how miserable I feel right now. That warm spring afternoon, as I cried and stared at Willnetta and Joel's picture in the "Impending Nuptials" section of the newspaper, Mama screamed over and over again at me, "Eva, you let a good one get away!"

"Oh, Eva, the wedding was so lovely!" Mrs. McKnight says, grabbing my hands.

I flash a smile at the pastor's bubbly wife and give her hands a firm squeeze.

"You and the other bridesmaids look so *lovely*!" she adds.

Now how could she stand there and say that with a smile? These *ugly*, botched-up dresses? I don't think so. I smile again and shift the weight on my aching feet. My white satin pumps are a half size too small. If someone were to brush up against my feet, I'd screech out in pain. I'm an emotional and physical mess. Oh, Father! Here comes Mama.

"Rose," Mrs. McKnight turns and says to Mama, "it was a beautiful wedding! Wasn't it?"

"Yes, it was," Mama says, eyeing me sharply. Her nose is covered with beads of perspiration, and she's breathing like she just finished running a marathon.

"Rose! Mrs. McKnight!" Aunt Della Mae yells out.

We all look down toward the blushing bride and handsome groom, at Aunt Della Mae, who is waving to us. She has been beside herself with excitement all day. Her shouts of "Thank you, Lord!" during the wedding ceremony were downright embarrassing. But she's happy; the family has to make allowances for that. She's lived to see what Mama, her only sister, said would never happen: Willnetta jumping the broom before Stephanie and me.

"Rose! Mrs. McKnight!" Aunt Della Mae yells again. "Come meet my in-laws from California!"

Mama nods and shoos Mrs. McKnight on down the receiving line to Aunt Della Mae. I brace myself for another tongue-lashing. Mama has not let up yet about my allowing Joel to slip through my fingers.

"You see that," she whispers up in my face. "That could've been *you* standing down there next to Joel with that"—she holds up three yellow-gloved fingers—"three-carat diamond ring on your finger. But noooo, here you stand, once more a bridesmaid, dressed like you on your way to Bozo the Clown's wedding!"

The tears I've been fighting all day fill my eyes.

"You blink them tears back and smile!" says Mama.

I look down at my fifty-nine-year-old, petite mother and wish I had the courage to shout, "Give it a rest, Mama!"

Mama takes several deep breaths and wipes the perspiration from her nose. "Let me get down there," she says, turning to leave, "before Della Mae starts yelling like a fool again. I can only imagine what them snooty-looking folks from California are thinking."

"Don't you move, Miss Rose!"

Through my tears, I see the flirtatious, gray-haired photographer with the *Fairview Herald* rush over to us. "Please, may I take a picture of you and your *lovely* daughter?" he asks Mama, while giving me the once-over.

Mama throws her head back and smiles broadly. "Of course, you may."

"Eva's the prettiest bridesmaid here," he whispers.

"How observant you are," Mama replies, with a wink and nod. "She gets her good looks from me."

My mother is a very attractive woman. Resembling the ageless beauty Diahann Carroll, she has fair skin that is smooth and flawless. She maintains her perfect size six figure by walking four miles every day. Sporting a layered, classy cut like Oprah, she's aging slowly and gracefully.

The photographer takes three pictures and promises to give both of us an eight-by-ten. Before walking away, he shoots me a sexy grin and blows me a kiss.

"C'mon, Rose!" Aunt Della Mae yells, much louder this time.

Mama sighs, runs her hands down her yellow, silk suit, and swishes down the receiving line, toward the bride and groom.

I hear Willnetta tell well-wishers that Joel has surprised her with a honeymoon in the Virgin Islands. I stare at handsome, sweet Joel, in his black, double-breasted tux, and wonder if I will regret dissing him for the rest of my life.

"Thou shalt not covet. Exodus twenty, seventeen," someone whispers softly behind me.

The whisper admonishing me sounds like my oldest sister, Geraldine. She's an evangelist who is committed to keeping the family on the straight and narrow, but she and her husband, Cleveland, left right after the wedding ceremony to attend a funeral. I turn and face my petite and spunky baby sister, Stephanie, who is the spitting image of Mama. A paralegal in Washington, D.C., she's a second-year law student at George Washington University. "I know. I've got some repenting to do."

"I'm so happy for Willnetta," she says. "And she's beautiful!"

"Yeah, she is."

Despite Mama's assertion that Willnetta is the ugliest girl in the family, my cousin is radiating sheer beauty today in a beautiful ivory, chiffon, beaded Vera Wang gown. A nylon fingertip-length veil attached to a headpiece made of satin rosettes and simulated pearls along with Grandma's pearl and diamond earrings and necklace, complete her ensemble. As tears of joy flow down her rouged cheeks, Joel kisses her forehead and gently wipes the tears away.

Stephanie and I are staring covetously at the newlyweds when Mama walks up. "Stop gawking at your cousin like a pair of lovesick monkeys!" she grumbles, hitting both of us.

"Mama! Hey, honey!" Stephanie exclaims, embracing Mama and kissing her on the cheek. "Don't you look like a million bucks?"

Clearly not fazed by the sugary compliment, Mama places her hands on her hips and glares at Stephanie. "You planning to come see me while you home?"

"Now, Mama, what kind of question is that?" Stephanie asks, embracing Mama again. "Of course, I am!"

Mama is pissed at Stephanie because she's staying at Daddy and Miss Elsie's house. She dislikes Daddy's wife and tries in vain to discourage us from having a relationship with her. She has this crazy notion that Miss Elsie, who has no children, is trying to steal us from her.

"I just thought I'd ask," Mama replies curtly.

"I would've stopped by last night, but it was real late when I got in town, and I slept in this morning," says Stephanie. "I'll be by later this evening. Where's Leon?"

"He had to leave and go to work," says Mama.

"To work? Dang! He works all the time! What you doing, Mama?" Stephanie asks, laughing. "Working that young husband of yours to death?"

I laugh, too.

Mama tosses a piece of hair out of her face and glares at both of us. "Husbands work to take care of their wives. When you two get one, and I pray it's *real* soon, you'll understand that."

"Let's not go there, okay?" Stephanie sings.

"You don't tell me where to gooo," Mama sings back, jabbing Stephanie in the chest. "At the rate you and your sister here are going, you both gone end up spinsters!"

Stephanie gasps. "Spinsters!"

"Spinsters!" Mama spits out. "*Old maids*! Eva has let a prime catch slip through her fingers, and every time I look at you, I feel like crying. For the life of me, I don't understand why you cut off your hair!"

"I wanted it *short*," Stephanie says, running a hand across her one-inch, curly Afro.

"Men like women with hair on their heads, Stephanie! You look like a li'l boy!" yells Mama.

A "why" mingled with a "what" flies out of Stephanie's mouth.

The bridesmaid standing next to me bursts out laughing.

I put a finger to my mouth. "Shhh, Mama!"

Mama ignores me and steps closer to Stephanie. "You and Eva better hurry up and get yourselves some husbands while you still got your good looks and girlish figures!" She taps Stephanie on the head. "And you either let your hair grow back or go get yourself a weave!"

It's a no-win situation when Mama gets excited like she is now. My sisters and I learned early that it's best, especially in public settings, not to quarrel with her. Unlike us, she doesn't mind engaging in public verbal brawls.

"Okay, Mama. Calm down. I hear you," Stephanie says softly, with outstretched hands. "Eva and I realize we need to get serious about settling down now. We know you want more grandkids."

Mamas exhales loudly and clasps her hands together. "Thank you, Lord!"

Stephanie and I cut our eyes at each other.

"You staying with James and *Elsie* again tonight?" Mama asks.

"Yes," replies Stephanie.

Mama grunts and shakes her head.

Daddy has never tried to discourage us from having a relationship with Leon. When Mama divorced Daddy fifteen years ago, Stephanie, Geraldine, and I cried like babies. We didn't want our parents to divorce. Mama said she wasn't happy, hadn't been happy in a long time, and felt it best that she and Daddy go their separate ways. I still believe Geraldine preached her first sermon during that time. However, neither our tears nor Geraldine's sermon, "Until Death Do Us Part," convinced Mama to stay in the marriage. A year after the divorce, she shocked us all when she married Leon, who is thirteen years her junior. The produce manager at Fairview Foods, the only supermarket in town, he's a quiet, hardworking, affectionate man. My sisters and I love him no less and no more than we do Miss Elsie.

"Stephanie stayed with you the last time she was home—"

Mama cuts me off with a wave of her hand. "I'm not talking to you, Miss Bridesmaid."

Stephanie lets out an exasperated sigh and rolls her eyes. I wonder if she truly realizes how blessed she is. She only gets a dose of our overbearing mother when she comes home from DC. I got Mama riding my back 24-7.

"You know Elsie can't cook! There's plenty food at my house," says Mama.

"I'll keep that in mind, *Mother*," Stephanie replies, with a slight smile. "Eva," she says, turning to leave, "Teresa and I are in the back, near the exit."

"Okay," I reply.

Teresa Long is my best friend. We've known each other since second grade. She, like Stephanie and me, is a single, professional woman longing to be married. She drives a 911 Carrera Coupe Porsche, owns a three-bedroom town house, and earns eighty-five thousand dollars a year as a program analyst with the Department of Labor. She celebrated her fortieth birthday this past Valentine's Day.

Stephanie looks back at Mama. "See you later, Mama."

Mama dismisses Stephanie with a grunt and then struts over to Pastor McKnight and whispers in his ear. He looks back and smiles at me. I bet she asked him to pray for me again. I take a deep breath and close my eyes. "Dear God," I pray, "help me get through the rest of this day! And, Father, forgive me for breaking the Tenth Commandment."

"When will I get lucky at love and dress in a beautiful white gown and say, 'I do,' to the man of my dreams?" I ask.

"Me, Stephanie, and every unmarried woman over thirty here are wondering the same thing," Teresa says, fingering a minibraid.

"And everybody at Community Baptist knows Joel had a thing for me before Willnetta," I say.

"Anybody remind you of that today?" Teresa asks, with raised eyebrows.

"Excluding Mama?" I ask.

Stephanie laughs.

"Yeah, *excluding* Miss Rose," Teresa replies, laughing.

I shake my head.

"Good. Because I would hate to have to tell somebody off

on Willnetta's wedding day," says Teresa. Not one to take much from anybody, Teresa always has my back.

"What was Aunt Della Mae thinking?" Stephanie whispers, scowling. "Those dresses are hideous!"

"Please, don't remind me," I moan, kicking the satin pumps off my aching feet.

Aunt Della Mae, determined to have a hand in every aspect of Willnetta's wedding, had taken it upon herself to make all twelve bridesmaid dresses. What were to have been silk, V-necked powder blue gowns evolved into swing dresses, with simulated pearls and rhinestones adorning the front and a row of tiny, white, magnolia-shaped buttons down the back. Willnetta cried when she saw the first dress; I did, too, because it was mine. But she didn't dare voice her disapproval to Aunt Della Mae. Her mama is just as overbearing as mine; they're used to having things their way.

Stephanie's stomach growls. "I could eat a bear!" she says, reaching for a chocolate-covered strawberry.

At each place setting is a small, oval-shaped, monogrammed silver tray—one of three gifts from the bride and groom—bearing an assortment of mouthwatering appetizers: finger sandwiches, shrimp, drumettes, chocolate-covered strawberries, cheese, crackers, and party nuts. Stephanie and Teresa have almost finished their appetizers. I start in on mine.

Sparing no expense in their only daughter's fairy-tale wedding, Aunt Della Mae and Uncle Lee hired interior designers from Raleigh to beautify the banquet room at D & L Barbecue—their soul-food restaurant. Joel and Willnetta are seated under an archway of ivy and yellow and white roses, flanked by gauze-draped columns. Baby's breath and multicolored orchids, lilies, roses, and carnations make up the centerpiece at their table. A miniature version of the centerpiece is on each candlelit guest table, and with the floral chandeliers, they provide breathtaking beauty throughout the room. The tables are covered in powder blue tablecloths and adorned further with gold-rimmed crystal stemware and gold-accented stainless flatware, resting on ivory linen nap-kins. In one corner of the room is a cherub fountain emitting a gentle stream of water onto a bed of floating candles. Across from that are two huge candelabrums flanking the seven-tier lemon wedding cake. And to top it all off, a tuxedo-clad, five-member band plays soft instrumental music, while members of the church youth choir, dressed in crisp white shirts, black bow ties, and black pants, serve as table attendants. Everything is so lovely. I mentally add it all to my wedding must-do list.

"I'd give anything and everything to fall in love," Teresa sings. "Just this one time, I'd like to find what I've been dreaming of. Well—"

"According to this article I read not long ago in *Essence*," Stephanie says, interrupting Teresa's rendition of "I'd Give Anything," by Gerald Levert, "Black folks are the most 'un-partnered' group of people in the world."

"That's depressing," I reply. "We may end up just like Mama said. Spinsters!"

Teresa bursts out laughing. "Miss Rose called y'all spinsters?"

"Yes, and it ain't funny," I say.

"I disagree," Teresa mumbles back, laughing. "That is funny!"

Stephanie and I burst out laughing, too. The three of us laugh until tears roll down our faces.

"O-okay," Teresa finally says. "I believe with all my heart that our Prince Charmings are out there somewhere."

"Where?" I ask, wiping my eyes.

"In them fairy-tale novels y'all love to read," Stephanie replies offhandedly.

"Ooooh! Naw, she didn't! You hear your sister?" Teresa asks me in a high-pitched voice.

"C'mon, Stephanie. What woman doesn't have a fairy-tale notion about love?" I ask.

"Like most, if not all, single women, we're suffering from what's called The Cinderella Syndrome," Stephanie says, looking from me to Teresa. "We're longing and waiting for a tall, handsome, *rich* man to sweep us off our feet and take us to a happily ever after."

"And what's wrong with that? Huh?" Teresa asks, leaning forward, egging on Stephanie for a debate. The two of them can go at each other for hours sometimes.

"It's not likely to happen," replies Stephanie.

"Don't be so pessimistic," Teresa argues.

"Girl, I'm trying to keep it real," says Stephanie. "Brothas like that are *scarce*. When was the last time you went out with somebody like that?"

Teresa sits back and cuts her eyes at me. Her last date—five months ago—was with a high school gym teacher, a far cry from the six-figure-income, suit-wearing brotha she longs for.

"But it *might* happen. Some fairy tales do come true," I hear myself say weakly.

"We, Black women *especially*," Stephanie says emphatically, "have to become open to expanding our options. We may discover love where we least expect it."

"Ain't too much out there," Teresa says bitterly, "but players, jailbirds, substance abusers, psychos, bisexuals, and men with no money!"

Stephanie shakes her head. "I disagree."

"Teresa, I don't want to believe that, either, because if that's true, then we have no chance or hope of finding love," I say. "I want to believe my soul mate is out there somewhere."

"Well, Eva, I don't mean to sound like Mother Dearest," Stephanie says, lowering her voice, "but if you had given Joel a chance, you wouldn't be sitting back here having this conversation with us."

"I know," I mutter, glancing over at the head table.

"We should consider dating blue-collar brothas," says Stephanie.

Teresa gasps and looks at Stephanie like she'd just cursed her.

"They could end up like Joel," Stephanie says, hunching up her shoulders.

"And could not! I'm not settling," Teresa says quite dramatically. "I want it *all*, and that includes a man making at least six figures."

Stephanie lets out an exasperated sigh and shakes her head.

I pray that my baby sister does not find herself like Teresa and me: forty years old and lonely. At thirty-five, she's not "over the hill," like we feel we are, nor is her biological clock winding down as rapidly as ours. She has plenty of time to date, marry, and have at least one child before reaching forty. And while the logical part of me agrees with what she's said, I can't deny what's in my heart. I feel like Teresa. I don't want to settle.

"I read not long ago that women forty and older have less than a ten percent chance of getting married," Stephanie says, cutting her eyes at Teresa.

"Enough already!" Teresa grumbles. "Must you depress us with more facts?"

Stephanie laughs. "I wouldn't have you ig'nant."

Teresa laughs and throws a peanut at her.

"Willnetta has decided, she's gonna try to have a baby," I say.

"At forty-four?" Teresa shrieks.

"So?" I reply.

"I think that's great!" Stephanie says, with a big smile.

Teresa rolls her eyes. "You would. I think she's too old."

"She's not," I say defensively. "We have the same gynecologist, and she says it's medically safe for women in their early forties to have children."

Teresa rolls her eyes again. "Whatever! I hope Willnetta don't end up having an old-looking baby."

Stephanie bursts out laughing. "Girl! You crazy!"

I shake my head and try not to laugh. Teresa can say some of the most ridiculous things sometimes.

"Since I don't have a man in my life, you know what I'd *love* to have right now?" Teresa asks, with a big grin.

"I'm afraid to ask," I say, giggling.

"Some barbecue! I'm hungry!" cries Teresa.

The aroma of Uncle Lee's barbecue is beginning to permeate the place now. He and Aunt Della Mae own the only soul food restaurant for miles around, and they have been blessed with a thriving business for thirty years. Their barbecue is regarded as some of the best in eastern North Carolina. The restaurant is closed for business today because of the wedding.

Willnetta, or should I say Aunt Della Mae, settled on soul food for the reception. There's plenty of barbecue, ribs, ham, chicken, collard greens, string beans, butterbeans, candied yams, slaw, potato salad, macaroni and cheese, and hush puppies to feed the four hundred folks in attendance. And for dessert, each guest will receive a miniature, three-tier version of the wedding cake, another gift from the bride and groom.

"Before this afternoon is over, we'll be asked a zillion times, 'When you gone get married, baby?'" Teresa says, mimicking Cordelia Weeks.

"Y'all don't have to worry about Mother Weeks trekking back here on her arthritic knees," I say. I tell them what Cordelia Weeks said to me in the receiving line; they double over laughing. "But this is kinda sad," I say, shaking my head. "We're sitting way back here, hoping to dodge 'When you gone get married?' questions."

"Let's not lose hope," Stephanie says, raising her goblet. "Our Prince Charmings are out there somewhere."

Teresa and I raise our goblets and click Stephanie's.

"Soooo, which one of you girls is goin' down the aisle next? Huh?" a raspy voice female asks loudly.

We all gasp out loud and lower our goblets.

Hurrying over to our table, smiling and waving a disposable camera, is none other than Miss Ghetto Fabulous herself, Jo Ann Outerbridge, a nosy, gossipy, backstabbing fellow church member. As usual, she's wearing too much make-up, too much jewelry, and too much hair weave. Her lethal lips are covered in gold lipstick and outlined with way too much black lip liner. Her hair, always an unsightly wonder, is finger waved back into a long, platinum blond, curly ponytail to accessorize, I assume, her gold sequin dress.

Teresa and Stephanie, like most people at Community Baptist, don't like Jo Ann. In spite of the rumor Jo Ann started about me sleeping with Joel behind Willnetta's back, I, Miss Try-To-Get-Along-With-Everybody, remain cordial to her.

"Don't y'all answer at the same time!" Jo Ann sings, waving her camera at us. "Get close so I can get a picture."

No one moves. We're too shocked to move; I know I am. Jo Ann wasn't invited to the reception.

"Wh-what're you do-doing here?" Stephanie stammers.

"I don't believe you!" Teresa yells. You're so *uncouth*!"

Jo Ann doesn't answer Stephanie's question, nor does she seem offended by Teresa's comment. "It's some kinda pretty in here," she says, slowly looking around the room. "I know this weddin' put a *serious* dent in Mr. Lee and Miss Delia Mae's wallet! Can't nobody tell me it didn't! And Willnetta's dress! I heard it cost eight thousand dollars!"

"What're you doing here?" Stephanie asks again.

Jo Ann laughs. "I sneaked in to take a few pictures," she whispers hurriedly. "So get close so I can get outta here. My sister's double-parked on the street!"

I ease toward Teresa and Stephanie. They don't budge. They are both giving Jo Ann hard stares.

"Teresa, Stephanie, scoot over to Eva. By the way, Teresa, I love your hair!" says Jo Ann. "Now that suits you. Did you get it done at African World of Braids?"

Teresa doesn't answer Jo Ann. Her slanted eyes have narrowed to slits. Still, neither she nor Stephanie moves in close for a snapshot.

"Aw right!" Jo Ann exclaims, with a heavy sigh. "Smile, Eva!"

I smile, wishing I could bat my eyes and make Jo Ann disappear.

"Girrrl, I must say, you and the other bridesmaids look *festive* in those dresses," says Jo Ann. "Are those real magnolias in y'all's hair?"

I refuse to answer Jo Ann, because I know she's picking.

"Did you look in the mirror before you left home?" Stephanie asks Jo Ann.

"But tell me, Eva," Jo Ann says, ignoring Stephanie and taking more pictures. "How you managin' to keep it together? To think, this coulda been *yo'* weddin' day."

That does it. Not only is Jo Ann a troublemaker, but it seems she's always a glutton for punishment. I pity her. As a social worker, I am constantly analyzing people, trying to figure out the motives behind what they say and do. My assessment of Jo Ann is she's unhappy and *insane*. Because if she were happy and sane, she wouldn't constantly hurt people with malicious gossip and lies and risk enduring the wrath of those she victimizes. I haven't forgotten the time she was physically assaulted at church for spreading a choir member's personal business. It took Pastor McKnight, the drummer, and one of the deacons to pull the woman off her.

"You garish heifer!" Teresa mutters.

Jo Ann opens her bug eyes wide and rolls them at Teresa. "Maybe you'll catch the bouquet this time, Eva," she says, creasing her brows. "'Cause I know this has been a bitter-sweet day for you."

Stephanie starts humming loudly and tapping the table with her knuckles. She and Teresa are looking at Jo Ann like they could rip her to pieces. If looks could kill, Jo Ann would be stretched out on the floor now, stiff as a board. My stomach muscles tighten; I pray a scene doesn't break out back here.

"But don't feel too bad," Jo Ann says, bending down close to me. "Joel *had* to marry Willnetta."

"Huh?" I hear myself blurt out.

"Now, we all know, Willnetta has gained a *lotta* weight in the last three months," Jo Ann whispers. "So don't be surprised," she says, tapping the table with a one-inch, gold, air-brushed nail, "when a little Joel or Willnetta shows up six months from now."

"You're pathetic!" Stephanie yells. "On the happiest day of my cousin's life, you have the audacity to tarnish her reputation with a lie!"

Teresa throws some party nuts in Jo Ann's face. "Leave, now!" she says through clenched teeth.

Jo Ann straightens up and has the nerve to look offended. She turns and abruptly walks away.

My blood boils as I watch her strut around for ten minutes, taking pictures. I exhale loudly when she finally exits the room. In spite of how despicable I think Jo Ann is, I still feel an enormous amount of pity for her.

Six months ago, when the rumor started snaking its way through the church about Joel and me, I went to Willnetta and apologized profusely for any pain the lie had caused her. She wasn't the least bit upset and told me not to worry, either. Mama, on the other hand, was livid. She wanted to bring Jo Ann before the church. I pleaded with her not to do that, for fear it would only make matters worse. She, being bullheaded like she is, along with Teresa, confronted Jo Ann in the church fellowship hall one Sunday morning. I didn't witness the confrontation, but all three ended up in Pastor McKnight's office for engaging in what he called "unbecoming behavior for Christians."

"Family and dear, dear friends!" Aunt Della Mae's shrill voice fills the banquet room. "It's time for us to eat, drink, and be mer-ry! But before you are served dinner, the bride and groom will take to the floor for their first dance."

As the lights grow dim and cheers and applause ring out, Willnetta and Joel make their way to the center of the banquet room. When Joel takes Willnetta in his arms, a hush fills the room and then a mounting chorus of "ahhhs."

A male soloist from the church steps up to the mike, next to Aunt Della Mae, who is weeping and waving her hands above her head. I expect her to holler, "Thank you, Lord!" any second. Before she does, Uncle Lee hurries up front and leads her to a seat. The soloist then nods to the band and begins serenading the newlyweds with Luther Vandross's "Here and Now."

I close my eyes and pretend it is I dressed in a beautiful white gown, smiling up into my lover's eyes as he tells me over and over again how much he loves me. A "Thank you, Lord!" from Aunt Della Mae quickly brings me back to reality. I look over at misty-eyed Teresa and Stephanie. "Let's do something tonight."

"What?" Teresa asks dryly.

"Something fun, something to lift our spirits!" I reply.

"Don't count me in," Stephanie says. "I'm going to visit Mama and then hit the sack. I'm leaving first thing in the morning. I got two papers due Monday morning."

"Eva, I know what'll lift our spirits," Teresa says excitedly.

"What?" I ask.

"Something we haven't done in years!" cries Teresa.

"What?" I ask again.

"Let's go clubbing!" says Teresa.

"Clubbing?" I reply.

"Yeah! There's this new club in Raleigh. Sapphires. I hear it's *crawling* with single, professional brothas!" says Teresa.

"Girl, have you bumped your head? Lost your mind?" I ask.

"No," replies Teresa.

"You're serious?" I ask.

"Yes," says Teresa.

Stephanie laughs. "Stop frowning, Eva."

"I don't want to go to a club! No! And I can't believe you do either, Teresa!" I exclaim.

"Maybe I'm taking"—she cuts her eyes at Stephanie—"the lawyer's advice. Expanding my options."

"She didn't say anything about going to a club!" I retort.

"Why not go, Eva?" asks Stephanie.

"Because, Stephanie, that's no place to meet a decent guy. Clubs are full of horny men on the prowl."

Stephanie exhales loudly and rolls her eyes. "Don't make a blanket statement like that. This place may be different."

"My coworker says it's a really classy place," Teresa interjects. "The owners cater to professionals thirty-five and older, *and* the ratio of men to women is good."

"Has this lady been?" Stephanie asks, with raised eyebrows.

"Uh-huh," mumbles Teresa.

"You trust her judgment?" says Stephanie.

"Yeah," replies Teresa.

"Good. It's settled. Eva's going," Stephanie says, sounding like bossy Mama. "What time you picking her up?"

"Excuse me?" I say.

Stephanie throws up a hand at me. "You're going. Girl, you might get lucky!"

"Yeah, Eva. Let's go. What we got to lose?" says Teresa.

"Move out of your comfort zone," Stephanie sings. "And who knows, you could debut perhaps as early as next summer in your very own fairy-tale wedding."

The possibility of that happening excites me and makes me feel good for the first time in days. I exhale and, against my better judgment, agree to go.

People start clapping and cheering as Willnetta and Joel take their seats. At Aunt Della Mae's cue, the youth attendants proceed to the tables to take food orders. Our attendant is my niece and Geraldine's oldest child, Jalisa. A straight A high school sophomore, she aspires to become the first doctor in the family. Twenty years from now, I pray she doesn't end up in the same predicament as me: a lonely careerist wishing for love.

When I get inside Mama's Lincoln, I kick off my shoes, remove the magnolia from my hair, and breathe a sigh of relief. The wedding is *over*, and my mood has changed for the better. As soon as I get home, my nines are going in a pail of warm water with Epsom salt. I can't be hobbling into Sapphires. I intend to strut in there, in those black, four-inch, leather stilettos I bought at Nordstrom last weekend.

"That wedding was *too* long!" cries Mama.

We haven't even exited the church grounds, and Mama has commenced with the put-downs. I look in the rearview mirror at seventy-three-year-old Mrs. Ida Truelove, a church mother, family friend, and neighbor to Mama. She's looking out the window, waving at people in the parking lot. I often pity her for having to put up with my cantankerous mama.

"Ida, you hear me?" Mama asks, looking back at Miss Ida.

"I thought everything was real nice," Miss Ida says soft and slow.

"Umph!" Mama grunts.

"Miss Ida, I planted those gladiolus bulbs you gave me the other day," I say in an effort to change the topic of conversation from another wedding that did not feature me as the bride.

"They'll bloom in June," Miss Ida replies cheerfully.

Mama hits the dashboard just as I open my mouth to ask Miss Ida, who is blessed with a green thumb, if I need to water the bulbs. "Della Mae ought to be ashamed of herself!" she says, pounding the dashboard. "She acted like a fool today! Whoever heard of folks shouting at a wedding?"

I look over at Mama. "She's happy. Can't you understand that?"

"I know she's happy *somebody* finally married Willnetta. But that"—Mama wags her finger—"doesn't change the fact that her behavior was embarrassing, unbecoming."

I insert one of the music CDs Willnetta and Joel gave each guest into the disc player and press down my window button. The noises from the outside invade the car. Mama doesn't attempt to talk over the honking horns and revving car engines. When the police officer directing traffic gives me the signal to exit the parking lot, I hit the gas.

"My sister got some ugly children," Mama says the second we're out on the street.

"Mama, please!"

"Rose, don't talk like that about Della Mae's children," Miss Ida says. "Your niece was a pretty bride."

"She sure was!" I say, glancing over at Mama.

"I don't care what either one of you say," Mama says, putting emphasis on each word. "Sure, Willnetta was fixed up pretty today. But all those beautiful trimmings don't hide the fact that she's ugly."

"Mama! That's enough!"

Mama turns and yells at me. "Hush and drive!"

I hit the gas. Lord, let me hurry up and get Mama home before she gives me a headache!

"If they do have any babies, I hope the children get their looks from Joel," says Mama.

Miss Ida leans across the seat and taps Mama on the shoulder. I guess she's had enough. "Rose, it's not nice to say such things."

I press on the gas pedal some more. The posted speed limit is thirty-five. I accelerate to fifty.

"Speaking of *ugly*," Mama says, grimacing as if she's in pain, "did y'all see Elsie?"

Neither Miss Ida nor I answer. I wish Stephanie were with us. She would have told Mama to zip it by now.

"My ex-husband's homely wife looks like she's gone up three dress sizes," adds Mama.

"I don't think Elsie has gained that much weight," Miss Ida says.

"I don't think she has, either," I say defensively.

"Y'all need to have your eyes checked," Mama replies.

"I see just fine, thank you," Miss Ida says.

I put my hand over my mouth to keep from laughing out loud. *That's telling her, Miss Ida!*

"Eva, stop and run in the Mini Mart at the corner and get me some antacid. I got indigestion," says Mama.

I take a deep breath and exhale. Mama is really working my nerves now. "I think I have some at home."

"But you're not sure, so stop!" cries Mama.

"Can't Leon bring you some?" I ask.

"You're going right by the store, Eva!" exclaims Mama.

"Mama, I'm ready to go home! My feet hurt, and I wanna get out of this ugly dress!"

"That dress is not ugly," Miss Ida says softly.

Mama looks back at Miss Ida. "Don't lie, Ida. The dress is ugly."

I swing into the Mini Mart parking lot so fast, we all sway over to the right side of the car. Mama looks at me and rolls her eyes.

"Eva, the Lord gone bless you for taking up time with your mama," Miss Ida says warmly.

I throw open the car door, cram my aching feet in my shoes, and hop out.

"Get me a ginger ale, too!" Mama yells.

"You want anything, Miss Ida?" I manage to ask, with a smile.

"No thank you, baby," replies Miss Ida.

I slam the door shut. With each step I take, pain shoots up my legs.

The store is crowded, and I start feeling self-conscious when the two cashiers look at me, then at each other, and burst out laughing. I quickly make my purchases, avoiding eye contact with anybody. As I'm heading out of the store, I run into one of my girlfriends, Gina Williams, and her mouthy nine-year-old daughter, A'Kyah.

"Hey!" Gina yells.

"Ewwww!" A'Kyah exclaims, turning up her nose. "That's an ugly dress!"

Gina bursts out laughing.

I narrow my eyes at Gina. "Stop laughing, okay?"

"S-sorry," Gina replies, giggling.

"What're you two up to?" I ask.

Gina sighs and rolls her eyes.

"I'm making brownies for my daddy," A'Kyah says, with a big smile. "We're going to see him tomorrow. We ran outta eggs."

A'Kyah's father, Gina's ex-boyfriend Tony Roberts, is incarcerated at Hayesfield Correctional Center, a minimum-security prison in the neighboring town of Hayesfield. He's serving a four-year sentence for possession of crack cocaine and petty larceny. He is what the criminal justice system calls a recidivist—a repeat offender, a career criminal. Tony's been in prison three times in the last ten years. Despite his waywardness, Gina makes a point of taking A'Kyah to see him once a month. She believes in fostering a father-daughter relationship between the two of them.

"Yum, yum," I say. "I'm sure Tony is going to love those brownies."

"Mama, don't forget the car oil this time," A'Kyah says, darting inside the store.

What Gina needs is another car, but she says she can't afford one right now on her bank teller's salary. Her '92 Pontiac Grand Am is forever conking out on her. If it's not in a mechanic's shop, it's parked on the side of the road, broken down.

"So how much longer does Tony have in there now?" I ask.

"I don't know," Gina says, hunching up her shoulders. "He had us thinking he'd be out by now. But you know Tony, Eva. He's a big, big liar, so it's no telling when he's getting out. He can stay in *forever* as far as I'm concerned."

"Yeah, right," I reply.

"I'm serious, girl. Like I told you, I've finally got Tony's lying ass outta my system."

If I had a thousand dollars for every time I've heard her say that, I'd be a millionaire. "Have you?"

"Yes!" she snaps.

From the corner of my eye, I see Mama glaring at me from the car. "Gina, I gotta go. I'll talk with you later."

"What Gina talking 'bout?" Mama asks as soon as I open the car door.

"Nothing."

"She still fooling around with that *convict*?"

"She says she isn't," I reply.

"Hallelujah!" Mama says, clapping her hands. "The girl has finally come to her senses."

I nod, hoping Mama is right, because it's past time Gina kicked Tony's butt to the curb. As long as she's known him, he's been nothing more than a financial burden and unrelenting source of anxiety for her, and me. In addition to the money I've loaned and given her for bail and lawyers for Tony, I've had the burdensome task of listening to her moan and groan over Mr. Won't Do Right.

I shake my head in an effort to clear it of the problems that the Ginas of the world bring upon themselves. I got problems of my own. Besides, I need to de-stress so I can have a re-freshing, come-hither look when I step inside the club tonight. I can't believe I'm going to a *nightclub*! But, I've got to do something about my lackluster love life, and this will be a start.

I pull into my mother's pink azalea–lined driveway, hop out of the car in my stocking feet, and hobble to my Lexus LX470.

"I'm cooking ribs tomorrow!" Mama yells.

"Okay!" I yell back. If things go well tonight, instead of feasting at Mama's tomorrow, I'll be having dinner with the man of my dreams. Mama will understand; nothing would make her happier.

2

Divas! Divas! Divas!

Sapphires' parking lot looks like a luxury-car dealership. Every high-end model from Acura to Volvo is parked in the narrow spaces in front of and alongside the posh-looking club. Teresa and I were hoping to beat the crowd, but it seems the crowd has beaten us getting here, and it's only nine thirty.

"Girrrl! Check out these cars!" Teresa exclaims as she cruises through the lot in search of a parking space.

"I see," I mumble, hoping this excursion doesn't end up being unpleasant and a waste of our time.

"Eva! There's got to be some successful brothas inside to be driving *these* fine rides," Teresa says breathlessly. She barks when we pass a Hummer with an Omega Psi Phi front plate.

"Don't bark too loud, dog," I say, with a chuckle. "I saw a coupla Delta plates a few cars back."

Teresa laughs and parks her Porsche between a black Mercedes S500 sedan and a silver Jaguar XK coupe.

My stomach muscles tighten and dread overcomes me

when she turns off her engine. "You remember what happened to me the last time we went clubbing?"

"What?" she asks, narrowing her eyes. "You're gonna have to refresh my memory. It's been almost ten years since we were last at a club."

"No one asked me to dance. I was humiliated!"

"Oh yeah, I remember. No one asked you to dance, Eva, because you were giving off don't-bother-me vibes."

"I was trying to be cool."

"You were too cool, okay?"

I take a deep breath and run a hand over my queasy stomach.

"You ready?" Teresa asks.

Without giving me time to answer, Teresa opens her door and steps outside. It's a warm, starlit spring night, ideal for a romantic stroll along the beach. If I'm lucky tonight, maybe the next warm, starry Saturday night, I'll be doing just that.

Before joining Teresa, I peek in my compact. I smile at myself. Blessed with my mother's good looks and my father's almond-colored complexion, my skin is still flawless. Tall and slender like my father, with long, shapely legs, I'm often told I look a lot younger than forty. I apply a little more lip gloss and powder my nose.

"C'mon, Eva!" Teresa yells, hitting the hood of her car.

Two inches taller than me, Teresa is small-breasted and hippy. Dressed in an eggshell-colored, two-piece, silk pantsuit that compliments her coffee-colored skin, she, unlike me, is extremely confident that she'll meet someone tonight. I'm still not fully convinced that we will find the kind of men we want in a nightclub.

I exit the car and follow Teresa to the club entrance. The Epsom salt and warm water soak did wonders for my feet. They aren't aching anymore, and I step with ease in my stilettos.

The cover charge for ladies is twenty dollars and includes one free drink. We pay the lady at the door and enter a small lobby. The soothing sounds of Frankie Beverly and Maze's "Southern Girl," along with the strong aroma of male cologne, relax me. Three handsome, well-dressed Black men standing in the lobby stop talking and turn to us.

"Good evening, ladies," one says as he eyeballs us, along with the other two men.

We nod hellos and strut past, giggling like teenagers. When the double doors separating the lobby from the club floor close behind us, our giggling abruptly ceases.

"Well, now we know who's driving the majority of those fine rides out front," I mutter.

"Ain't this nothing!" Teresa mutters back.

Sitting at small, candlelit tables throughout the room are women! The room is *packed* with women, mostly Black, with the exception of five White women sitting at a table near the DJ's booth. The men, few in number, are standing along the walls and sitting at the bar. There're a few couples on the dance floor.

"I thought your coworker said the place was crawling with men?" I say.

Teresa moans. "That's what she said. You wanna leave?"

"No. We're here now. Let's stay and try to make the best of it."

We spot empty seats at a table near the dance floor and at the bar. The last impression I want to give tonight is that I'm a lush, so I insist on sitting at the table. As soon as we're seated, a waitress comes over to take our drink orders. Teresa orders a glass of red wine; I order a strawberry daiquiri. While waiting for our drinks, we size up the competition as "Sweet Love," by Anita Baker, resonates around us.

Many of the women are dressed seductively in outfits that run the gamut from tasteless to tasteful. I can't be too judgmental. Big sis, Geraldine, would consider the blue, stretch, plunging neckline, satin sheath that I'm wearing "slutty." I wonder as I look from table to table how many of us will find our "sweet love" here tonight.

The waitress returns with our drinks and a bowl of mixed nuts and places a flyer on the table. The flyer is from WLUV, Raleigh's popular Black gospel station. It's an advertisement for the station's dating service, Finally. I've never consid-

ered joining a singles club, because I've always thought
weirdos and desperate, unattractive people joined them. But,
hey, I need to rethink that, because if I don't meet anyone
tonight—and from the looks of it, I probably won't—I may
give Finally a try. I can't afford any longer to leave any stone
unturned in my quest for love.

The DJ plays "Got to Give It Up," by Marvin Gaye, and the
mood in the room livens up. People throw up their hands and
bob their heads to the music. Several women make a beeline
over to where the men are and pull them onto the dance floor.
Before Marvin belts out, "I'm having a ball!" adults, holler-
ing and dancing like teens in raunchy music videos, have
packed the dance floor.

I look over at Teresa. Her mouth is slightly ajar, and her
eyes are big and round. A soft, warm hand on my shoulder
startles me. I look up; it's one of the men from the lobby, the
tall, bald, buff one. He resembles a guy I dated two years ago,
a psychiatrist who was commitment-phobic.

"Miss Diva, would you care to dance?" he asks, extending
his hand.

Teresa kicks me under the table.

I place my hand in this wonderfully smelling man's hand
and stand up.

Instead of finding a spot for us to dance outside the sexu-
ally charged crowd, Mr. Smell Good weaves his way to the
center of the dance floor. I duck swinging elbows and hips
in order to follow him. Once in an enclave of sweating, bumping, grinding merrymakers, he turns, faces me, and starts
dancing. I smile up at him and, despite the tight quarters, start
dancing, too. A hard bump from behind sends me into Mr.
Smell Good's chest. He wraps his long, muscular arms tightly
around me. I try to free myself. The more I wiggle, the tighter
Mr. Smell Good holds me. I tilt my head back to protest, and
my lips graze his Adam's apple. He laughs, and I manage to
wiggle free.

"You okay?" he asks.

I nod.

"Good," he says, kissing me on the forehead.

I don't appreciate the kiss one bit. Still, I look up into his big brown eyes and smile like a fool.

"What's your name, Slim?"

Slim? I haven't had a grown man call me Slim since the eighties! "Vanessa," I lie.

"I'm Dexter," he says seductively.

Oh, brother.

"I haven't seen you here before. Your first time?" he says.

I smile and nod.

"Well, all right!" he yells, laughing.

Loud barking rings out to the left of me; I look over and can't believe my eyes. A sista and a White woman are dancing with guys who are barking loudly and humping them from behind. The sista's black spandex skirt has inched up her thighs, exposing part of her buttocks, and the White girl's large breasts are spilling over the top of her gold, sequined bustier top. The more the horny men bark, hump, and fondle the women, the more X-rated the women dance. I pity them and look away.

"Super freaks! Super freaks!" Dexter yells.

I look up at him. He's grinning and watching the "super freaks" with glee. I bet he wishes I would dance like those women. It'll never happen. And when this song ends, I'm walking off this floor, with no intention of returning.

I see Teresa on the dance floor, I think. It's hard to tell with so many heads bobbing up and down. I get bumped again and turn around to look at the assailant.

Dexter presses up against me and grips my hips. "Awww yeah! Now this what I'm talking 'bout!" he yells, laughing.

I try to turn back around and am unable to do so.

"Uh-uh, work it, baby! Work it! Drop it like it's hot!" he moans, nibbling my right ear and grinding up against me.

I freeze and claw at his hands.

"C'mon, Slim! Give it up! Give it up!" he cries.

I lift my right foot and slam the heel of my stiletto onto

Dexter's foot. He jumps back. I turn and attempt to leave; he embraces me.

"It's awfully hot out here," I moan. "I need to sit down. I'm dizzy!" I lie.

Dexter mouths, "Okay", releases me, and turns around and starts dancing with a group of women.

Whaaat? He's not gone see me to my seat? Louse! I rush off the floor, bumping into people along the way. Teresa is not on the dance floor; she's sitting at the table, staring down into her drink. I grab my purse. She looks up.

"Hey! Where're you going?" she asks.

"To the bathroom. I feel *nasty*! And I could kick myself for letting you and Stephanie talk me into coming here!"

Teresa presses her lips together and looks back down.

I haven't been here thirty minutes, and I'm ready to go! Oh, I hate that I came.

I smell Romance as soon as I push open the bathroom door. Two attractive, heavily perfumed, well-dressed Black women are at the sink, applying make-up and more perfume. They look to be in their mid-forties.

"Girl, I spent three hundred dollars on this dress!" the older-looking one of the two says to the other. "And for *what*?"

"Honey, you shoulda kept your money in your wallet," says her friend.

"I'm not coming back here any more!" the older woman bellows. "You hear me?"

"Loud and clear."

"This is my fifth and last time," the older woman says, with an outstretched hand.

"What happened to that lawyer you met two weeks ago?" asks her friend.

The older woman sighs loudly and places her hands on her hips. "He told me, he didn't want to be in a serious relationship with anyone right now."

"Naw, he didn't!" exclaims her friend.

"Yes, he did. Can you believe that crap?"

"Men!" the friend exclaims.

I go inside a stall and lean up against the door. I'm getting depressed again. I don't intend to end up like the frustrated sista at the sink, back at Sapphires, trying to outdress and "outsmell" a bunch of women in my search for Mr. Right. *Lord, what am I going to do?* Knocks on the stall door interrupt my distressing thoughts and petition to the Lord.

"Anyone in there?" someone asks.

I flush the commode and open the door. A young, pretty, brown-skinned woman smiles at me. I smile back and walk over to the paper towel dispenser. Two White women enter the bathroom, giggling and giving each other high fives. The women at the sink turn and stare at them. The White women seem oblivious to the lethal stares and dance over to an empty stall. The disgruntled divas throw their make-up and perfume vials in their purses and head for the door. I follow.

Teresa is not at our table; I see her chatting with a woman at the bar. The dance floor is still crowded as people groove to the "Power of Love," by Luther Vandross. I pick up the flyer about the singles club and hope I'm giving off don't-bother-me vibes.

On the front of the flyer is a Black couple enclosed in a large heart. They are smiling and embracing each other. Underneath their picture are the words *Looking for love? Look no further! At Finally, you will find your soul mate. Finally is a Christian-sponsored singles club that caters to a professional clientele. It is where Black Christian singles meet and fall in love. Members' information is strictly confidential. The only thing joining will cost you is a little bit of your time. Come join us! Don't spend another moment alone.* There are gushy testimonials from "real people" who "finally" found love on the back of the flyer.

"You still mad at me?" Teresa asks, plopping down in the seat across from me.

"Kinda."

"I'm sorry. This was a *big* mistake," she says, sighing.

"Who was that you were talking to?"

"Someone from the office."

"Not the person that told you about this place?"

Teresa nods. "She says she's not coming back."

"I overheard someone else say the very same thing."

"Who?"

"Someone in the bathroom."

"What you think?" she asks, pointing at the flyer.

"I think we ought to check it out."

"You serious?"

"Yeah. We gave this a try."

"I'm game if you are."

"Does this mean we're *desperate*?" I whisper, giggling.

Teresa laughs. "Can't speak for you, but I'm getting there, girl!"

"There's a meeting next Friday night. You busy?"

"Real funny."

"Let's go then. I'll drive."

Teresa gives me a thumbs-up.

I place the flyer in my purse and look at my watch. It's 10:17. "Let's get outta here and go get some ice cream. My treat."

"No," Teresa says, grabbing her purse and jumping up. "My treat!"

3

Hayesfield
Correctional Center

The sun is peeking through the bedroom shutters; it's time to get on out of bed. Worship Service starts in forty-five minutes, and I can't pull myself together to make it to church. Geraldine would severely admonish me if she knew I went last night to what she calls a "den of sin" and was forgoing fellowship with the saints at Community Baptist this morning. I'm skipping dinner at Mama's today, too. My period came on as soon as I got home last night, and I'm cramping like a big dog.

Stephanie woke me at seven. She was finishing up breakfast with Daddy and Miss Elsie and was getting ready to head back to DC. I told her about Teresa's and my failed efforts at love last night and our plans to check out a singles club. She said if that didn't work out, we should try the Internet next.

I roll over and turn on the radio to Gospel 680 AM, the local gospel station, just in time to hear Geraldine wrap up her Sunday morning radio show: *Geraldine's Gospel Hour*.

The gospel hour is actually just forty-five minutes long. During her "radio ministry," Geraldine prays, interviews church personalities, discusses the weekly lesson in *The Missionary Helper*, makes local church announcements, and plays music. She's strictly old school; she plays nothing but traditional gospel music. Her favorite artists are Mahalia Jackson and Shirley Caesar.

After "Heaven," by Shirley Caesar, plays, Geraldine bids her listeners farewell until next Sunday. I turn the dial to 88.9 FM to catch some of Shaw University's Sunday morning gospel. "He'll Welcome Me!" by John P. Kee, is playing. I turn up the volume and roll out of bed. The flyer from the singles club is lying on the floor next to my stilettos. I pick it up and place it on my vanity. I hope Finally, as its name implies, *finally* leads me to Mr. Right. If it doesn't, then what? One thing I do know: I'm not surfing the Internet for a man.

After two bowls of Frosted Flakes and a pain pill, I throw on a pair of shorts and an oversized tee shirt, slip on an old pair of sneakers, and head outside. It's going to be another warm spring day, much too pretty to be spent inside. Since the arrival of spring—my favorite season of the year—I've spent a lot of time outdoors, working in the yard. I welcome singing birds and blooming flowers after months of cold, drab weather. Since moving back into the three-bedroom, brick rancher where I grew up, I've become an avid gardener. My yard comes alive in spring and summer with an array of blooming perennials and annuals. It rivals the yard of my neighbor Beulah Jennings as one of the prettiest on the street.

I water the potted petunias, pansies, and geraniums on the deck and front porch; refill the bird feeder and bird baths; and clean out the small goldfish pond. I am deciding whether to sprinkle the wildflower seeds I got from Wal-Mart two weeks ago in the gladiolus bed or to put more mulch around my rose bushes when a motorist passes by, honking the horn. Oh, goodness! It's one of the members of my church. Worship Service has ended. I quickly reel in the hoses, gather up my gardening supplies, and hurry inside. I don't want or need

Geraldine, who lives two streets over, to ride by and catch me working in the yard on the Lord's day.

When the phone rings at 3:23, I'm lying on the bed, finishing off a bag of double-dipped, chocolate-covered peanuts and watching *A Soldier's Story* on HBO. I pick up without looking at the caller ID display, expecting to hear Mama or Geraldine ask why I didn't come to church.

"E-va?" the sniffling caller asks, barely audible.

I sit bolt upright and press MUTE on the TV remote. "Yes, this is Eva."

"It's me, girl. Gina."

"Gina, what's wrong?"

"My car has let me down *again*!" she cries. "Me and A'Kyah"—there's a long pause, followed by more sniffles—"are stranded at the prison. I called AAA. It's gone be a coupla hours before someone gets here. I can't wait that long. Can you come get us?"

I roll off the bed. "Yes, Gina. I'll come get you."

"Thank you, Eva. I-I'll pay you for coming out here," she cries.

"No, that's not necessary. Now stop crying. I'll be there as soon as I can, okay?"

"Okay. Bye."

I've never known Gina to be this distraught over car problems before. I wonder if she and Tony had another fight.

I make what is typically a twenty-minute ride to Hayesfield in half the time. It's a small, rural town like Fairview. In addition to the prison, there are poultry, undergarment, and paper plants in the town. Those industries, along with the prison, employ many residents from Hayesfield and Fairview who don't farm or commute fifteen minutes or more to jobs in or near Raleigh. I don't mind my twenty-minute commute to work, nor do I care to move back to Raleigh, seeing that I live rent free in the family house. This allows me to save and invest a good chuck of the sixty-five thousand dollars I earn a year as family support supervisor with the county Department of Social Services. My life is good, I must say. The only things missing in it right now are a husband and children.

When I turn off the highway and onto the prison road, I don't meet any cars. The land is flat, and to the right and left are acres and acres of farmland. Hayesfield Correctional Center is primarily a prison farm comprised of eight thousand acres of land. Inmates grow and harvest year-round cotton and a variety of edible crops—peanuts, squash, broccoli, corn, collards, tomatoes, sweet potatoes, cabbage, strawberries, watermelons, and cantaloupes. It's been almost a year since I was last at the correctional center. I rode out here with Willnetta one Friday afternoon to bring Joel dinner. It was an eye-opening experience, as it was my first time ever at a prison. The highlight of the trip was the bags of fresh fruits and vegetables the director of farming operations gave us. What blew my mind was the large number of Black inmates I saw in the recreation yard, playing basketball and lifting weights. Joel relayed some staggering statistics to me that afternoon about the makeup of the inmate population at Hayesfield. Of the two hundred fifty men incarcerated there at that time, eight out of ten were Black men, and the majority of them were serving short-term, nonviolent or drug-related sentences.

When the weather is warm, the rec yard, which is sandwiched between the brick administration building and the inmate-housing unit, serves as the visitation area on Saturday and Sunday afternoons from 1:00 to 3:00. And during this time, inmates are allowed picnic lunches with their family. A nineteen-foot chain-link perimeter fence surrounds both the housing unit and the rec yard. There are three Black men and one White man, dressed alike in dark denim pants; sky blue, short-sleeved shirts; and burgundy brogans—prison attire—in the rec yard, picking up trash. I spot Gina's heap in the parking lot but don't see her or A'Kyah anywhere. I pull into the lot and park beside Gina's car. After a minute of waiting, I turn off my engine, get out, and head for the administration building.

"Psst! Psst!"

I look over toward the rec yard. The inmates have stopped working and are leaning up against the fence, staring at me. They smile and wave. I wave back and quickly enter the building.

"Eva!" A'Kyah yells, running up to me the instant I step inside. "Ooooh, you smell good!" she says, wrapping her arms around my waist.

"I haven't seen you in ages!" a husky voice yells from behind me.

I turn around. Scar-faced, bony Tony Roberts is standing behind me, donning a black knit kufi. The last time I saw him, A'Kyah was celebrating her sixth birthday at Chuck E. Cheese's. "I don't frequent prisons," I want to say, but smile instead. "Hello, Tony," I say pleasantly. "It has been awhile, hasn't it?"

Tony gives me the once-over, like the men in the lobby of the club last night, and flashes what once drove Gina wild, his infamous gold-toothed grin. "Gina's in the bathroom," he says, with a nod of his head.

There's a tall, mahogany-complexioned man in the room, sweeping the floor. He's dressed like Tony and the men out-side. Unlike Tony and the other men, he's drop-dead gor-geous. A gift to the eye.

"Xavier, this is Gina's girlfriend Eva," Tony says, making introductions. "Eva, this is Xavier."

Xavier smiles, and a dimple appears in his left cheek. "Hello," he says, with a nod.

I smile and nod back. *Oh, my, my, my, my, my! What is this gorgeous creature doing in here?* I'm trying not to stare, but I can't stop looking at him. He is the finest thing I've laid eyes on in a long time. Nothing like scrawny, scruffy Tony, who is still grinning in my face, Xavier is broad-shouldered, muscu-lar, and well groomed. *Why, Lord, is this man locked up?*

"So, Eva," Tony says, folding his tattooed arms across his chest, "you still single, I see."

Please get out of my face!

"A fine woman like you *still* single." Tony shakes his head and laughs. "I guess you still holding out, huh?"

I don't reply to Tony's inquiry. He's told me more than once, not that I've ever asked him for his opinion on anything related to my life, that the man I'm pining for doesn't exist, never has.

"So what if she is, nigga?" says Gina, who suddenly appears.

Oh, Lord! Gina brushes past me, scowling and dabbing at her eyes.

"She's better off," she says, walking up to Tony. "It's better than wasting her time with some broke lowlife like you!"

"Mama, chill before the lieutenant comes back in here!" cries A'Kyah.

"Yeah, keep it down!" Tony whispers hoarsely.

"You shut the hell up!" says Gina.

Handsome Xavier is now emptying trash cans into a large black trash bag. He looks back and catches me eyeing him. I look away.

"Didn't the lieutenant tell you to take care of the trash, Inmate 992714?" Gina asks, glaring at Tony.

"Don't worry 'bout what the lieutenant told me," Tony replies coolly. "My man"—he motions with his head in Xavier's direction—"got things covered."

"Since when does Xavier take orders from you?" Gina asks, then turns to Xavier. "Don't do his work, Xavier. He's doing time, just like you!"

"I, uh—"

Gina cuts Xavier off with a wave of her hand. "Tony's lazy and sor-ry as hell!"

"Mama! Daddy ain't lazy and sorry," says A'Kyah.

"You shut up!" Gina yells down at A'Kyah. "I'm not talking to you! Now say one more thing!"

A'Kyah rolls her eyes and buries her head in Tony's chest. Honey-colored like her trifling father, with the same expressive eyes and broad nose, she idolizes her daddy and is quick to jump to his defense.

"I'm ready, Eva," Gina says, sighing. "A'Kyah, tell your

daddy good-bye, because it'll be a long while before you see him again!"

"Gina, come on now. I tried," Tony says, hunching up his shoulders. "What mo' can I do?"

Gina shoves A'Kyah aside and smacks Tony in the face. "For starters, keep your ass outta prison so if I'm ever in a bind again, you can take care of your daughter!"

Tony sighs heavily and rubs his right cheek.

I've known Gina for eighteen years. She's quick-tempered and has poor impulse control. At least thirty pounds heavier than Tony, she's apt to deck him now if he breathes too loud. That ugly, long scar above his right eye comes from her hitting him in the face with a hot curling iron. Despite how much I dislike Tony, I don't care to see Gina beat the crap out of him, so I head back outside. When I reach behind me to close the door, I discover that Xavier is following me.

"What's going on?" I ask when he closes the door behind us.

"Gina's mother is in the hospital."

"Lord, no! The hospital? For what?"

"She's in a coma."

My heart flip-flops in my chest. "Mrs. Williams is in a coma?"

Xavier nods.

"What happened?"

"She had a stroke earlier this afternoon."

I close my tear-filled eyes and clasp my hands together. "Dear God," I pray, "please don't let Mrs. Williams die!"

"Amen," Xavier says softly.

During the two years I spent in St. Louis, earning my master's in social work, Mrs. Williams was my mother away from home. A custodian in the social work department at Washington University, she befriended me the second we met and invited me to her home that same day for supper—fried fish and spaghetti. That was the first time I'd ever had fish and spaghetti together for dinner, which according to Mrs. Williams, is a customary meal prepared by Black folks in St. Louis. It was delicious, and I spent many more evenings after that breaking bread with the lovable and rowdy Williamses. The memories bring more tears to my eyes.

"The family wants Gina home right away," says Xavier.

"Of course! She needs to be on the next plane to St. Louis. Poor Gina!"

Xavier sighs and rubs his hands together. "She doesn't want to pull A'Kyah out of school. She was hoping Tony's mother or sister would keep her."

"They won't?"

"No."

Even as I listen to this awful news, I can't stop marveling at how good-looking Xavier is! As my watery eyes travel across his broad chest and up to his handsome face, my body temperature rises. Have mercy!

"They won't?"

"No, they will not."

Did I just ask the same question twice? *Oh, Lord!*

Xavier parts the most luscious-looking lips I've ever seen gracing a man's face and smiles at me. "You like honeysuckle?"

"Ex-excuse me?" I hear myself stammer.

"Do you like honeysuckle? I detect a hint of it in your perfume. A'Kyah is right," he says, with a bigger smile. "You smell nice."

What a keen sense of smell he has. I'm not wearing perfume; the shower gel I used earlier is honeysuckle scented. *Hold up!* This is an inmate, a *convict*, towering over me, staring so sweetly down in my face and making a rather personal inquiry. Should he even be out here talking to me? "I'm not wearing perfume," I reply dryly.

"I haven't offended you, have I?" he asks, frowning. "Because I didn't mean to."

"No, you haven't."

"You make me sick, sick, sick!"

Xavier and I glance back at the door. Gina has gone off now. *Help her, Lord.*

"So, if I'm not being too forward, what's a fine-looking man like yourself doing here?" I ask.

Sadness veils Xavier's handsome face, and his broad shoulders drop. "Serving a five-year sentence for being naïve and foolish."

"For what? Selling drugs?"

"No. Receiving and selling stolen goods."

He's a thief!

"I'm no thief," he says, as if reading my thoughts. "I have not willfully committed *any* crime."

I look away. *Yeah, right! Whatever! Another innocent person locked up!*

The door to the administration building flies open, and Gina, A'Kyah, and Tony step outside. Tears are streaming down Gina's cheeks. She looks so pitiful.

"Gina, I'll be praying for your mother," Xavier says compassionately.

"Thank you, Xavier," replies Gina.

I follow Gina and A'Kyah to their car. Gina retrieves her purse and A'Kyah's book bag from the trunk. The instant she gets inside my SUV, I reach over and hug her.

"Gina, I'm so sorry about your mom."

"Eva, I need to get home and see about my mama," Gina cries, sobbing loudly.

"Mama, I can stay with Ebony," says A'Kyah.

"No!"

"Why can't I stay with Ebony?" A'Kyah whines.

"Because I said so!" says Gina.

I open the dash and retrieve a tissue for Gina. "Who is Ebony?"

"One of A'Kyah's *fast* friends," replies Gina. "She's in the after-school program at the Y with her. Her mother works crazy hours, and Ebony's often home alone, doing whatever she pleases."

"So why won't Mrs. Roberts keep A'Kyah for you?" I ask.

Gina exhales and dries her eyes. "I guess she is still mad at us."

"For what?" I say.

Gina sighs heavily and shakes her head. "The last time A'Kyah stayed with them, she and Tony's sister's daughter got into a fight. Girl, they fought from one end of Miss Roberts's house to the other. When they finished, it looked like a hurricane had gone through the place. Miss Roberts was *fit* to be tied." Gina throws up her hands. "And I got to pay for half the stuff A'Kyah and that girl broke."

"That's only fair," I say, glancing back at A'Kyah. She's bobbing her head to the music blaring from her CD player. I start the SUV and pull out of the parking lot. Tony and Xavier are still standing outside. Two male correctional officers have joined them.

A'Kyah lowers her window. "Bye, Daddy!"

Gina sticks her hands through the sunroof, waving her middle fingers. "Sorry bastard!"

I hit the gas. *Lord, have mercy!*

"And with only four more weeks in school," Gina says, buckling up, "I really don't want A'Kyah to miss any days. My baby's trying to get a Perfect Attendance Award this year."

"It wouldn't be practical for A'Kyah to go, anyway, Gina," I say. "You'll have enough to deal with when you get to St. Louis."

"Eva"—Gina sighs and places a hand on my shoulder—"if my mother's condition improves, I'll be back by next Sunday. Would you, could you keep A'Kyah for me?"

"Sure," flies right out of my mouth. "You know I'll help any way I can." What could I say otherwise? Gina's a dear friend, and I'm a softy, a sucker for sob stories.

"Thank you, thank you!" Gina cries, hugging me. "Girl, you're so good to me. I don't know what I'd do without you."

I feel confident that A'Kyah and I will get along fine. So she's a little insolent. What kid isn't to some degree?

Gina is able to get a 7:55 flight out of Raleigh-Durham International to St. Louis. I drop her off at Terminal C at 7:10.

She hands me a note to give to A'Kyah's teacher and reminds A'Kyah that she'll be calling every night to check up on her. A'Kyah hugs Gina and promises to be a good girl.

Instead of riding home up front with me, A'Kyah chooses to stay in the back and listen to her music. I'm glad. She talked nonstop during the forty-minute ride to the airport; it was nerve-racking. I glance back at her and pray that everything goes smoothly between us.

When I pull into my driveway, A'Kyah is asleep. She looks so peaceful; I hate to wake her. I call out to her. She doesn't budge. I remove the headphones from her ears, and she stirs. "We're home," I say softly.

"Has my mama's plane taken off yet?"

I glance at my watch. "It should be taking off any second now."

A'Kyah opens her eyes and yawns. "Can I have a snack before going to bed?"

"Sure. You like ice cream?"

"Uh-huh. Who don't?"

I laugh. "You can have some after you shower, okay?"

"Okay."

I take A'Kyah's things into the bedroom that was once Stephanie's and my old room. Down the hall from the master bedroom, where I sleep, it's the second largest bedroom in the rancher and serves as the guest room. Shortly after Daddy moved out of the house and I moved in, I gave Geraldine the pine bunk beds that were in the room for her kids and put a cherry, queen-sized sleigh bed with matching nightstands and dresser in the room. I've since finished off the room with a Queen Anne chair and ottoman upholstered in gold- and lime-colored fabric. The window accessories are made out of the same material, all ideas straight from *B. Smith With Style*.

While A'Kyah showers, I put away her things and call Teresa, who has left two messages on my answering machine. She picks up during the first ring.

"Where have you been?" she says.

I give Teresa the details of my eventful afternoon.

"Poor, Gina. I hope her mother pulls through, and in the meantime, you get to play Mommy."

"Yeah, something like that."

Teresa laughs.

"Oh, hush up. She's a delightful little girl," I say.

"I'm sure Miss Twenty-One is."

"Oh, Teresa! Girl, let me tell you what I saw this afternoon!"

"What?" she asks excitedly.

"Girl, no lie. I saw the *fi-nest* man—"

"Where? Where?"

"Would you believe at the prison?"

"Who? The warden?"

"No."

"An officer?"

"No! An inmate."

"An inmate?"

"An inmate, girl."

"Damn! What I tell you?" Teresa says, sighing. "They in prison, they broke, bisexual—"

"Slow your roll, girl." I cut Teresa off before she starts in with her litany of grievances about why we're still single. "I heard you yesterday."

"Fine, huh?"

"Melt-in-your-mouth chocola-ty fine! Girl, the man is Denzel, Haysbert, Fishburne, Chestnut all rolled into one. I'm not kidding."

"For real?"

"For real. Pretty white teeth; sexy voice; big, broad shoulders—"

"Okay, stop! I'm getting hot!"

I burst out laughing.

Teresa laughs and then sighs heavily. "What a waste."

"Yep, a waste. I still find it hard to believe that something that gorgeous is a criminal, like that trifling Tony Roberts."

"What you say 'bout my daddy?"

I jump and almost drop the phone. A'Kyah is standing in

the doorway, eyeing me sharply, draped in my purple silk robe, smelling like a honeysuckle vine. I ease off the bed. "I was just telling Teresa that Tony is a Muslim now."

"Oh," A'Kyah says slowly.

"Teresa, let me go. I have to put A'Kyah to bed."

"You don't have to put me in bed," A'Kyah says curtly. "I'm not a two-year-old."

Teresa gasps. "Naw, she didn't?"

"I didn't mean, I was actually going to put you into bed, A'Kyah," I say.

"Why are you explaining yourself?" Teresa asks.

"A'Kyah, go put on your pajamas," I order.

A'Kyah sighs softly and exits the room.

"Teresa, I'll talk to you later."

"Bye, Mommy," Teresa says, laughing.

"Bye."

"Eva! Can I watch TV?" calls A'Kyah.

I step into the hallway. "No. Gina said you're to be in bed at nine sharp. It's almost nine now."

"I'm not sleepy! I took a nap in your truck."

"I'm not changing the rules, okay?"

"Can I call my friend Ebony? I need to ask her something."

"It's too late for a phone call to your friend's house."

"No, it's not. She stays up late."

"Not tonight, okay?"

A'Kyah makes an irritating smacking noise with her lips and mumbles something I can't make out.

I grit my teeth, exhale, and walk away.

I go into the kitchen and fix A'Kyah a bowl of strawberry ice cream. When she shuffles into the kitchen ten minutes later, she doesn't seem to mind that her ice cream has melted. She plops down at the table with her CD player; the music is blaring through the earphones. I leave her to her milkshake in a bowl and go clean up any mess she may have left behind in the guest bathroom.

I'm relieved to see that there are no wet towels or clothes on the bathroom floor. A'Kyah has placed her dirty clothes in the hamper and neatly folded her washcloth and bath towel across the towel rack. And from the looks of it, she's been in my bathroom. The top to my forty-dollar bottle of honey-suckle bath gel is lying on the floor next to the bathtub. I jerk back the shower curtain. The bath gel bottle is lying in the bathtub—empty. Doggonit! I just bought that gel! I toss the bottle and top in the trash can and go to my bathroom. After gathering up my pricey toiletries and hiding them behind a stack of towels on the top linen-closet shelf, I take a partially used bottle of lilac-scented shower gel from Bath & Body Works into the guest bathroom. A'Kyah can use just as much of this as she likes.

At 9:25, A'Kyah is still sitting at the kitchen table. I turn off the kitchen light and say softly, "Bedtime," and leave the room. She moans and slowly makes her way to the guest bed-room. At 9:41, I hear her praying to God to watch over Gina, Mrs. Williams, and Tony. When she says, "Amen," I go into the room, say good night, and turn off the light.

"Dear Lord, please," I pray, stumbling back up the hall, "let this arrangement, however long it may be, be problem free."

4

School Daze

"Summer, summer, summertime! Time to sit back and unwind! Summer, summer, summertime!"

The ceiling light flicks on, off, and back on again. I pull the bedcovers over my head. "I'm awake! So you and Will Smith keep it down!"

"Well, get up then! I don't want to be late for school," says A'Kyah.

I throw back the covers and look over at the clock radio on my nightstand. It's 6:00. I prop myself up in bed, on my elbows. "I'll get you to school by eight thirty, A'Kyah. Don't worry."

"Uh-uh!" she exclaims, rolling her eyes. "You need to get me there by eight o'clock."

"Eight o'clock?"

"Yeah."

"For what?"

A'Kyah glares at me as if I asked a stupid question. "So I can eat breakfast."

"I have cereal, bagels—"

"I eat breakfast at school. Didn't Mama tell you that?"

"No."

"I don't know why she didn't! I *always* eat breakfast at school."

"Hey, it's not a problem, so calm down."

A'Kyah exhales, looking relieved. "And I need these ironed," she says, tossing a pair of jeans on the bed.

"Will do. Anything else?"

"Did Mama call last night?"

"Yes."

"How's my grandma?"

"She's still very sick."

A'Kyah sighs and looks down at the floor.

"Wanna know what I dreamed last night?" I ask.

"What?" she asks, looking up.

"I dreamed that you, Gina, and I were in St. Louis, at your grandma's. She was frying fish and cooking spaghetti for us. Girl, we ate so much food, we ended up having bellyaches."

A'Kyah laughs. "My grandma makes the best spaghetti, don't she?"

I nod.

"Is Mama gone call tonight?"

"Yes, just like she promised."

A'Kyah smiles broadly and turns to leave the room. She stops and looks back. "You got any more of that pink shower gel?"

"If you're referring to the gel you used last night, no, I don't."

"Man!"

"I put a bottle of gel in your bath—"

"I saw it. That stuff stinks!"

I laugh. "I'm sorry. I'll get you some that smells better, okay?"

"Okay," she replies, with another smile. She then turns and leaves the room.

I fall back on the bed, roll over, and close my eyes.

* * *

I get A'Kyah to Carver Elementary twenty minutes before the tardy bell rings, and as she hurries off to the cafeteria, she points me in the direction of her classroom. When I enter room 309, Lossie Hodges is writing math problems on the dry-erase board. The buxom, gray-haired woman is undoubtedly a proud African American. Her walls are covered with pictures of George Washington Carver, the renowned scientist after whom the school was named, and other historic and contemporary Black heroes and heroines. I introduce myself and inform her of A'Kyah's family emergency.

"I'm so sorry to hear about A'Kyah's grandmother," she says compassionately, removing her eyeglasses.

"Gina asked me to give you this. My home and work numbers are written on the back."

Mrs. Hodges takes Gina's note from me, reads it, and sighs heavily. "I'll inform the counselor and principal of the matter, Miss Liles. I hope this hasn't been too upsetting for A'Kyah. It doesn't take much sometimes to upset her," she says, her big chest rising and falling with each breath.

"She appears to be handling the situation pretty good," I reply. "I talked with her some this morning. But if there're any problems, just call me."

"Don't worry, I will," Mrs. Hodges says, flipping the note over and looking at the phone numbers. "I'll ask Mrs. Owens, our guidance counselor, to speak to A'Kyah first thing this morning."

"That sounds like a good idea."

God bless teachers, and anyone, for that matter, that works in a public school. I have a ton of empathy for them. Willnetta, a middle school assistant principal at Fairview Middle, bemoans often the day-to-day challenges of her underpaid, overworked colleagues.

A bell rings, and students begin to file into the classroom. Mrs. Hodges reads my work number back to me two times, thanks me for stopping by, and wishes me a good day. I say good-bye and leave.

After a 10:00 meeting at the Mental Health Center, a quick

trip to the mall, and lunch with Teresa, I return to my office to prepare for a 1:30 staff meeting. The message display light on my phone is blinking; I press the SPEAKER button and then the MESSAGE button.

"There are three new messages in your mailbox," the voice messenger announces. "To review your messages, press one."

I press the number one key.

"9:53 a.m.," the voice-activated messenger announces.

"Miss Liles, this is Mrs. Hodges. I, I'll try to reach you a little later."

I lean across my desk and stare at my phone.

"To delete this message, press—"

I reach over and press three.

I replay Mrs. Hodges's message two more times. She doesn't sound upset, and if something was wrong, surely, she would have said so, I hope, and asked me to call her back.

Feeling confident that A'Kyah is okay, I decide against calling the school and proceed to hear the remaining messages in my mailbox.

"10:35 a.m."

A heavy sigh, silence, and then a click. The caller hangs up without leaving a message.

I press number one to hear the last message, wondering if that was Mrs. Hodges who called and hung up.

"11:41 a.m."

"Miss Liles, this is Preston Cooper, principal at Carver Elementary. Please call me as soon as you get this message. The number here is 454-0907."

Oh, Lord! Something is wrong! I snatch up the receiver and punch in the numbers.

"Good afternoon, Carver Elementary," a woman says pleasantly.

I state my name and, without taking a breath explain that I'm returning the principal's call.

"Hold on, Miss Liles. I'll get Dr. Cooper for you," the woman says, quickly.

My heart races, and tears fill my eyes as I imagine A'Kyah

in distress, worried, and crying over her grandmother. I grab the cross around my neck. "Dear Lord, please—"

"Miss Liles?"

"Yes!"

"This is Dr. Cooper. Thanks for calling me back."

"Is A'Kyah okay?" I ask hurriedly.

"A'Kyah isn't hurt or sick, if that's what you're asking. But"—Dr. Cooper pauses and then clears his throat—"she has been removed from class—"

"Where is she?" I yell.

"In detention."

"Detention?"

"Yes, Miss Liles," he says calmly. "I've placed A'Kyah in detention for the remainder of the day."

"For what?"

"Disrespectful behavior towards Mrs. Hodges. Mrs. Hodges asked her to stop talking on numerous occasions, and she refused. She became argumentative and also refused to complete two assignments."

If this don't beat all! Here I was all worked up, thinking this girl was in crisis, and she's acting like a fool at school! "I-I'm sorry, Dr. Cooper."

"I've been made aware of the family emergency, and because of that, I won't suspend A'Kyah from school."

From the sound of Dr. Cooper's voice and the R & B music I hear playing softly in the background, I figure him to be Black. I wonder if he's also attractive and single.

"But please, if you will, Miss Liles," he says earnestly, "impress upon A'Kyah that she's expected to follow her teacher's directives. I will not allow her or *any* student at this school to disrespect Lossie Hodges, a veteran teacher of thirty-five years."

"Yes, sir," I say, sounding like a little kid. "And thank you, Dr. Cooper, for being understanding."

I grab a legal pad and pen and hurry to the staff meeting, with two questions running through my mind. What am I going to do with A'Kyah if she becomes a problem? And, who is this Dr. Cooper?

When I arrive at the Y to pick up A'Kyah, she and a young Latino boy are engrossed in a game of chess. She looks up at me, then back down at the chessboard. "You're early," she says.

"I know. Let's go."

"I want to finish this game."

"You're done. Let's go."

A'Kyah sighs heavily and grabs her book bag. She tells the boy, "Later," and that she'll play him again tomorrow.

"I got a phone call from Dr. Cooper this afternoon," I say once we're outside. "What's going on? Are you worried about your grandma?"

"No," she says, walking ahead of me to my SUV.

I unlock the SUV doors, and we get inside.

"So what's going on?"

A'Kyah buckles up her seat belt, then looks out her window.

"What's going on, A'Kyah?" I ask again.

"Nothing," she replies, still looking out the window.

"So, you were sent to detention for nothing?"

"Yep."

"That's not what Dr. Cooper told me."

A'Kyah sighs and rolls her eyes.

I start the engine; she reaches for the radio and turns it on. I turn it off.

"Whatcha do that for?" she asks, scowling at me.

"You need to talk to me."

"I don't feel like talking."

I turn off the engine. "Well, we will sit here until you do."

"I had to ask Ebony something, okay? And Mrs. Hodges told me to stop talking."

"Did you stop?"

A'Kyah rolls her eyes and looks back out the window.

"I take that as a no," I say.

No response.

"A'Kyah, that was disrespectful, *very* disrespectful."

"Uh-huh," she says, cutting her eyes at me.

"And it was also wrong of you to talk back to Mrs. Hodges and refuse to complete schoolwork. Tomorrow morning you will apologize—"

"Mrs. Hodges needs to take her big old butt home!"

"A'Kyah! That's not nice!"

"Well, she does," A'Kyah mutters. "She's mean! She's strict! And she gives us way too much work! Mama asked stupid, old Dr. Cooper at the beginning of the year to put me in another teacher's class, and he wouldn't!"

"We don't always get what we want, A'Kyah. Like it or not, you're stuck with Mrs. Hodges for the remainder of the school year. That's only three more weeks, so make the best of it, okay? Don't talk in her class when you're not supposed to, don't argue with her, and when she gives you work to do, do it."

A'Kyah yawns and starts humming.

"Are you *listening* to me?" I ask loudly.

"Yes, Eva. I hear you," she replies dryly, with an eye roll.

I grip the steering wheel, take a deep breath, and start the engine again. *Jesus, give me strength!* "If you get suspended from school," I say calmly, "you won't get that Perfect Attendance Award. Do you realize that?"

"Yes, Eva. Can I listen to the radio?"

"No."

A'Kyah mumbles something I can't make out and slides down in her seat.

I take another deep breath, count slowly to five, and pull out of the parking lot. "Gina is not going to be happy when she hears about this."

"Please don't tell Mama, Eva!" she cries, springing up in her seat, turning toward me.

I shake my head.

"Pretty please!" she whines. "I won't get in any more trouble. I promise!"

"So I can count on you behaving in school?"

"Uh-huh."

"Don't grunt at me."

"Yesss, I will behave in class. Can I listen to the radio now?"

"Nooo, you may not. And as a consequence for your misbehavior today, no TV tonight."

"What?"

"You heard me. No TV."

A'Kyah smacks her lips and glares back out the window.

"Have you forgotten that I'm doing you a *big* favor by not telling Gina about this?"

"No," she replies real nasty-like.

"Then act like it. Check your attitude, and watch how you talk to me, okay?"

"Uh-huh."

This girl is a trip! If my sisters or I had ever gotten in trouble at school or spoken to my mother the way A'Kyah has spoken to me, we would be denture-wearing cripples. And to think I made a special trip this morning to the mall for her. She won't get a thing of what I bought. Man, she has a nasty disposition! I pray Mrs. Williams has a speedy recovery so Gina can come back home to her mouthy, insolent child.

When I pull into my driveway and park, A'Kyah jumps out and stalks to the front door. When I unlock the door, she runs down the hall to the guest bedroom and slams the door shut. My head starts throbbing. I fight the urge to charge in behind her. Instead, I go to my bedroom and plop down on the bed. The number one is blinking on my answering machine; I press play.

"Eva, it's me, Mama. Missed you yesterday. Maybe you were out on a date. Were you? I hope so. Can't wait to hear about it. I got plenty food here, so come over for dinner."

Thank God for Mama! I could use some prayer right now. I hope big sister is home. I press the SPEAKER button on the phone and hear breathing and rap music. Who's on my line?

There's nobody in the house but me and, ooooh! I snatch up the receiver. "A'Kyah! Who're you calling?"

Silence.

"A'Kyah!"

"I'm calling Ebony."

"Hang up the phone."

"Why can't I call my friend?"

"No TV *or* phone calls to Ebony or any of your friends tonight."

"It ain't night yet."

"Hang up that phone!"

Slam!

The noise momentarily deafens me and intensifies the throbbing in my head. I take several deep breaths and speed-dial Geraldine.

"Ealey residence. Praise the Lord!"

"Geraldine."

"Eva?"

"Yeah, it's me."

"Girl, what's wrong with you? Rough day?"

"A *taxing* afternoon," I whine. I give Geraldine the low-down on my temporary stint as babysitter.

"It's going to be all right," she says reassuringly.

"I hope I haven't taken on more than I can handle."

"You can do *all* things through Christ, who strengthens you. You believe that, don't you?"

"Yes."

"God will supply you with what you need to manage this situation, and He's going to bless you. Everything will turn out fine. You'll see!"

I hear the guest bedroom door open, followed by footsteps in the hallway. "Pray for me and Gina's mom," I whisper into the phone.

"I will."

A'Kyah walks slowly into my bedroom. The anger that was etched minutes ago in her beautiful face is no longer there;

she looks sorrowful now. She hands me a sheet of pink paper along with three pieces of grape Laffy Taffy candy.

"I gotta go, Geraldine. I'll call you later."

"Okay. Bye-bye."

I look down at the words written in blue ink on the pink stationery.

Dear Eva, I apologize for getting in trouble. I am sorry. I won't get into any more trouble. I promise. And I love you. A'Kyah

Tears fill my eyes. I think I see tears in A'Kyah's. I hug her. The doubt that I have gives way to hope. A'Kyah and I are going to get along just fine.

"I was calling Ebony," she says softly, "to remind her to bring my library book to school tomorrow. It's overdue."

"Okay," I say, releasing her. "You can call her back."

"Eva," she whines, "can I watch *The Proud Family* and *Sister, Sister* tonight? Pretty please? They're my favorite TV shows."

I nod.

"Thank you," she says, with a big smile.

"Here." I hand A'Kyah my SUV keys. "There's something in the backseat I think you'll like."

A'Kyah's eyes light up, and she dashes out of the room. Minutes later, she runs back in and throws her arms around my neck. "Thank you, thank you, Eva! I love all of it! Can I take my shower now?"

I laugh. "Nooo. It's too early."

"Okay," she says, slowly releasing me. "I'm going to call Ebony then and tell her what I got!"

A'Kyah runs out of the room. Minutes later, on the way to my home office, adjacent to the guest bedroom, I hear her over the rap music blaring from her boom box, on the telephone talking to Ebony not about an overdue library book or the bathrobe and bottles of shower gel and lotion I got her from Bath & Body Works, but about a girl in her classroom that she can't stand.

Dinner at Mama's is always a finger-licking, lip-smacking affair. She is an *exceptional* cook. Her dining-room table is covered with Sunday leftovers: turkey, beef ribs, potato salad, cabbage, peas, and homemade coconut cake. I have hearty helpings of everything and fix a doggie bag for lunch tomorrow. It surprises me sometimes when I think about how much food I eat. For a child, A'Kyah has a hearty appetite, too. Mama beams with joy when she asks for seconds and compliments her on how good the food is. After dinner, she goes into the den to watch *The Proud Family*. I join Mama in the kitchen.

"Eva," Mama says, pointing to two grocery bags brimming with food on the kitchen counter, "take that home."

"I'm getting groceries tomorrow, Mama."

"You don't have to now. Take the food home. I want that child to eat well-balanced meals while in your care."

"All she wants is pizza and cheeseburgers."

"That's not nutritious!"

"That's what her mama feeds her, and she looks healthy to me."

"Did you notice," Mama asks loudly, "how she was gobbling down that food in there? Huh? I betcha she couldn't tell you when she last had a decent home-cooked meal!"

"We'll just come over here every night."

Mama shakes her head. "As much as you love to eat, I can't understand why you don't like to cook! I'm giving you food. Cook it!"

"All right!"

"Besides, the practice will be good for you. You'll have to cook when you get married. Your husband's not gonna want *pizza* and *cheeseburgers* every night. Leon was eating that junk when I met him. You think he eats that now? Noooo," she says, shaking her head. "Girl, I got to cook for that man."

It's time to say good night. Mama has brought up the husband thing. I reach for the grocery bags; she stops me.

"Guess who was at the church Sunday?" she asks, smiling and raising her eyebrows.

The sly grin on her face lets me know exactly whom she's referring to: her current prospect for son-in-law, Otis Reid. Still, I act like I have no idea. "I don't know. Who?"

"Otis, girl. He told me to tell you hel-lo."

I've told Mama a countless number of times that I'm not interested in potbellied Otis Reid. Lord, when is she going to get that? Since my fortieth birthday, she's been relentless in her pursuit of a husband for me. Despite my passionate protests and our arguments over my not wanting her meddling in such matters, she still forges ahead, playing matchmaker.

"He had that baby yet?" I ask, laughing.

"Laugh. Hee, hee!" she says sarcastically. "That's a good man, Eva. A good man! I hope you'll soon realize that."

A'Kyah runs into the kitchen. "Miss Rose, may I *please* have another piece of cake?" she asks, with a big, shiny-lips smile.

"Sure, baby. Get what you want," says Mama.

"Thank you!" she yells, running back to the dining room.

"What you want me to tell Otis?" asks Mama.

"Nothing, Mama."

"You gone let him slip through your fingers, too?" she asks, narrowing her eyes. "Don't be so quick to write him off before you get to know him. I thought you'd learned how *foolish* that can be."

I look off.

"So Otis has a big belly. Couldn't you learn to live with that? Huh? Nobody's perfect!"

Otis, owner and operator of Reid Funeral Homes and Crematory, has been hounding me by way of Mama for two months. I'd hoped by now, the pregnant-looking, Jheri-Curl-shag-wearing thing would have lost interest in me. Lord knows, I have no intention of ever going out with him.

"Mama, thanks for dinner and the groceries. We need to

head home. A'Kyah has homework, and Gina wants her in bed by nine."

"Will you at least go out with him one time? Please?"

Oh, this is so sad. She's begging now! "I'll think about it. How's that?"

"It'll do for now," she says, smiling.

"A'Kyah! Let's go!" I grab the grocery bags and kiss Mama on the forehead. "Love you."

"Love you, too," she says, with a big smile.

I head outside, figuring out dinner plans for A'Kyah and me for the rest of the week. We can stop by Miss Elsie and Daddy's two nights for sure. Miss Elsie's cooking is nothing to rave about, but it is edible. And, whatever night Geraldine takes off from spreading the gospel, we'll break bread with her. Friday we'll be right back at Mama's! Cooking just ain't my thang. But what will I do when I get married? Surely, I'm going to have to cook then.

A'Kyah reaches for the radio as soon as I start the SUV. I don't care to listen to any hip-hop music, but I don't want to upset her; I don't need her mad at me right now. I need some information.

"A'Kyah."

"Huh."

"I want to ask you about somebody."

"Who?" she asks, tuning into FM 97.5, Raleigh's hip-hop R & B station.

"Dr. Cooper, your principal."

"What about him?" she asks, turning up her nose.

"Is he Black?"

"Uh-huh."

"Do his children go to Carver Elementary?"

A'Kyah smacks her shiny lips. "He ain't got no kids. He ain't even married."

My main question was answered, and I didn't have to ask it. *Thank you, Lord!* But does A'Kyah really know what she's talking about? "How do you know he's not married?"

"I heard him say so."

"How'd you manage to hear that?"

"I was in his office, and I heard him tell somebody on the phone that he wasn't."

"Did you see pictures in his office, on his desk?"

"Pictures? What kinda pictures?"

"Of people. A woman."

"No."

"No pictures of anybody on his desk?"

"Uh-uh."

"What does he look like? Is he old?"

"Naw." A'Kyah giggles. "Mama thinks he's fine."

That's not saying much, because Gina's definition of fine and mine greatly differ. "You realize Dr. Cooper gave you a break today. He could have suspended you."

"I know," she says softly.

"Tomorrow morning we're going to stop by his office and thank him for not doing that. Okay?"

"Okay."

Work it, girl! Work it! I can't wait till Willnetta gets her butt back home, so I can find out what she knows about *Dr.* Preston Cooper. I wonder why she hasn't mentioned him to me? A single brotha with a PhD right here under my nose!

Now, let's see. What do I wear to Carver Elementary tomorrow? I'll call Teresa and Stephanie; they can help me with that. You only get one chance to make a first impression, and I want to make an unforgettable one. Who knows, this could be it, my chance at love! I would have never thought this baby-sitting gig would lead me into the arms of Mr. Right. Doing good deeds does bring blessings. Amen! Hallelujah!

After watching *Sister, Sister* and making another telephone call to Ebony, A'Kyah showers and voluntarily gets into bed; it's not even nine. I ask her as she climbs into bed if she completed her homework and those classroom assignments she refused to do this morning, and she assures me she has.

Gina calls at 8:45, and I listen as A'Kyah lies about the

"great day" she had at school. I repeat the same lie and tell
Gina that A'Kyah has not given me one minute of trouble. I
feel bad about lying, but in light of the situation, it seems like
the right thing to do. I don't want to worry Gina any more than
she already is, and A'Kyah did promise to stay out of trouble.
Besides, what could Gina do 850 miles away if she knew the
truth? Nothing but yell at A'Kyah and get her upset, and I in
turn end up with my second tension headache for the day.

I stop feeling bad about lying when Gina says she's relieved to hear that things are going well. When I ask about
Mrs. Williams, she bursts into tears and tells me to keep praying for her mother, because the doctor has said that it's touch
and go. I tell Gina before she hangs up not to worry about
A'Kyah and that I will continue to pray for her mother.

I peek in on A'Kyah before calling Teresa and Stephanie;
she's asleep, snoring softly. I wrap my hair and place my
three-way phone call.

Teresa and Stephanie both suggest that I wear my Tracy
Reese lime-colored, linen suit to school tomorrow. Teresa
wonders, like I do, why Willnetta hasn't mentioned Preston
to me, or to her for that matter. Stephanie says maybe it's because he's dating someone. Teresa surmises that it's probably because he's a dog, or is unattractive or gay. Anticipation
is about to get the best of me. Sunday can't come fast enough,
and that's six days away! Willnetta will be back home then.

It's nearing midnight when I turn off the light in my bedroom and tell Teresa and Stephanie good night. I crawl under
the covers, fantasizing about a fairy-tale romance with a man
I've never laid eyes on.

5

SOS

I'm up at the crack of dawn. I dreamed last night that Preston Cooper was fine, and he fell head over heels in love with me. I look down at my left ring finger and imagine a four-carat, platinum, emerald-cut diamond ring on it. I hope A'Kyah is right about him not being married.

During the ten-minute drive to school, I remind A'Kyah of her goal to get a Perfect Attendance Award and how a further act of misbehavior on her part could jeopardize that. We even rehearse her apologies to Mrs. Hodges and Dr. Cooper.

When I pull into the school's parking lot, I'm a bundle of nerves. I almost sideswipe a lady driving a minivan full of children. Before I can get myself together, A'Kyah hops out of the SUV and heads for the school building. I open my door and take off behind her.

The school office is a flurry of activity as students, parents, and teachers rush in and out. The young, plump, brown-skinned receptionist attends to all with patience and courtesy. The door with the word PRINCIPAL on it is closed. Sitting in a love seat across from the receptionist's desk are a middle-aged Black woman dressed in a postal uniform and a young boy that resembles her, dressed in FUBU gear from head to toe. The woman looks as if she could bite through nails. The boy looks as cool as a cucumber. A'Kyah whispers to me that he is a fifth grader who is constantly in trouble.

The receptionist turns her attention to two elderly women—one White, the other Latino—who state that they're volunteering for the morning. After instructing them to write their names in a red notebook with the words VOLUNTEER SIGN-IN BOOK written on it, the receptionist issues them visitor passes and gives them the names and room numbers of teachers needing volunteers. Before they leave the office, she thanks them on behalf of Dr. Cooper for the "invaluable service" they render to the school and reminds them of the appreciation dinner with Dr. Cooper and the PTA board next week. When the women exit, A'Kyah and I approach the desk. The receptionist greets A'Kyah by name and compliments me on my suit. I thank her, introduce myself, and inform her of our wish to see Dr. Cooper. The receptionist's lips form a nice round O, and she slowly shakes her head.

"I'm so sorry, Miss Liles. Dr. Cooper is unavailable at the moment and will be tied up most of the morning, I'm afraid."

Rats!

"Would you like to leave him a message?" asks the receptionist.

I consider leaving a message and decide against it and tell the receptionist I'll try to contact Dr. Cooper later. I thank her and unhappily follow A'Kyah out of the office.

Mrs. Hodges accepts A'Kyah's apology with a half smile and tells her she will not tolerate any of her sass today. I hug A'Kyah, remind her to behave, and leave. I strut my Vera Wang–smelling, chic-looking self back down the hallway and spot one of the lady volunteers. Hey! Maybe I should do that: volunteer! What better way to get next to Dr. Cooper than to be a volunteer at his school!

I hurry back to the school office; the principal's door is still closed, and the woman and child are still seated out front. I tell the receptionist I'm interested in volunteering.

"O-kay," she says slowly.

"Is there a problem?"

"Noooo. Well, school ends in a matter of weeks. There may not be a need for *new* volunteers now, Miss Liles."

Shoot! I hadn't thought about that.

"But I'll take your name, anyway," she says, smiling, "and forward it to Dr. Cooper and the PTA president."

"Thank you. Tell them I'm willing to do anything."

"Yes, ma'am. I will."

After writing my name and home and work numbers down, I glance over at Dr. Cooper's closed office door and leave.

Meetings keep me out of my office until 2:20. After I step through my office door, the first thing that catches my eye is the message display light blinking on my phone. I take a deep breath and slowly walk over to my desk. I pause for a moment before pressing the SPEAKER and MESSAGE buttons.

"Miss Liles, this is Robert from the service department at Johnson Lexus. Our records indicate your SUV is due for a fifteen-thousand-mile service. Give me a call at 555-4497, and I'll be glad to schedule a service appointment for you. And, remember, we do provide shuttle service from the dealership to your office. Thank you."

I exhale and throw up my hands. There are no other messages in my voice mailbox. I scoot to the lounge for a soft drink and return to my office to eat the slice of cake from Mama's and check e-mails. I'm e-mailing Stephanie when my phone rings. I pick up on the third ring. "Eva Liles."

"Good afternoon, Miss Liles. This is Dr. Cooper."

I sit straight up in my chair. "Yes, Dr. Cooper. How are you?"

"I'm fine. Thanks for asking. I understand you and A'Kyah stopped by the office this morning."

"Yes, Dr. Cooper we did," I reply warmly. The receptionist told him I came by! Bless her heart. "I'm interested in volunteering at the school."

"Oh," he says. "Well, thank you for that. I will certainly pass your name on to our PTA president."

"I realize the school year is almost over. You may not even need new volunteers at this time, but I want to do something. Help out in the library, the office, the cafeteria. I don't care where."

Dr. Cooper laughs. "We never turn away volunteers, Miss Liles. Someone will be in touch with you."

"Great!" The doctor and I are chatting! I'm gone volunteer at the school! *Yip-pee!*

"Miss Liles, I want to talk to you about A'Kyah."

"Dr. Cooper, A'Kyah wanted to apologize to you this morning for yesterday. She's learned her lesson. You shouldn't have *any more* problems with her."

"Mmmm, how I wish that was so," he says, with a heavy sigh.

"Excuse me?"

Dr. Cooper sighs again, and I hear what sounds like crying in the background. "Miss Liles, A'Kyah is in my office."

"No."

"Oh yes."

"Is she in trouble?"

"I'm afraid she *is*," he says, with another sigh.

"For what?"

"Fighting on the playground."

I fall back into my chair and close my eyes. A'Kyah is sobbing loudly now, and I feel a headache coming on.

"She will be suspended from school for the remainder of the week."

"Huh? I mean, excuse me?"

"A'Kyah will be suspended for the remainder of the week."

"That's three days!"

"Fighting carries a three-day suspension, Miss Liles. Just last month, I told A'Kyah and her mother that if she was involved in another fight at school, she would incur a suspension."

Wait a minute. Did he say "another fight"? I don't recall

Gina telling me A'Kyah was involved in a fight at school. "Dr. Cooper, I don't know what to say. I talked with A'Kyah yesterday, like you asked me, and she promised to behave. She was hoping to get a Perfect Attendance Award this year."

"That will not be the case now. We've been lenient with A'Kyah all year long. The counselor has worked with her extensively on ways to control her behavior. And today this! She *will* be suspended for the remainder of the week."

I can hear A'Kyah still crying in the background. I feel like crying, too. What am I going to do with that girl? My head starts throbbing. "Dr. Cooper, I know there's only so much you can do at the school. I'm appreciative of all that you've done for A'Kyah, and I'm sure her mother is, too."

"She won't be going to the Y this afternoon. You'll have to pick her up from school."

"Yes, sir."

"Good-bye."

I hang up the phone. What am I going to do? I can't sit home *three* days with A'Kyah. I have a ton of work to do! Case files to review and employee evaluations to complete. Everybody I know works, except Daddy and Miss Elsie, and I don't want to impose on them, but I'm in a bind! Since their retirement from the undergarment plant two years ago, they've been at everybody's beck and call. I feel people take advantage of them, and now, here I go imposing. They'll jump at the chance to help me; I know they will. Bless their hearts.

Daddy married sweet, soft-spoken Miss Elsie five years after Mama divorced him. She had been a widow for over twenty years. A hard worker and faithful churchgoer, she's liked by all that know her, except Mama. I feel sorry for Miss Elsie whenever we're all together, because Mama is not nice to her. It still brings tears to my eyes when I recall how Mama humiliated her at Geraldine and Cleveland's twentieth wedding anniversary dinner three years ago.

The dinner was held at D & L Barbecue, financed by Mama, Stephanie, and me. Several family members, including Miss Elsie, volunteered to bring desserts. Mama had heard from one of the members at Miss Elsie's church that she was a "lousy cook," so she told us not to eat anything Miss Elsie brought to the dinner. No one knows what caused Stephanie to become violently ill shortly after a trip to the dessert bar. Mama fingered Miss Elsie's banana pudding as the culprit, since Stephanie had a small serving of it on her dessert plate. As Stephanie heaved and vomited in the bathroom, Mama screamed down at her, "Didn't I tell you not to eat Elsie's nasty food?" Miss Elsie overheard Mama and started crying. Daddy and Geraldine told Mama to apologize. Mama responded by rolling a big trash can up to the dessert bar and tossing the banana pudding in it. Poor Miss Elsie collapsed into a blubbering heap in Geraldine's and my arms.

It's almost three. I was hoping to complete several reports and one employee evaluation this afternoon. I can forget that. Dismissal time at Carver Elementary is 3:15.

I retrieve a bottle of Motrin from my desk drawer and pop two tablets in my mouth. I really hate to call Daddy and Miss Elsie, but I have nowhere else to turn. And Miss A'Kyah can count on me telling Gina all about her antics tonight. Maybe if I had told Gina the truth last night, I wouldn't be in this predicament. I have to stop lying; even when it seems like the best thing to do, it never is.

I pick up the receiver and dial Daddy's number.

"Hello."

"Hi, Miss Elsie. It's me, Eva."

"Hey, baby. How you?"

"Oh, I could be better."

"You having a bad day?"

I laugh. "You can say that."

"I'm so sorry to hear that."

"Miss Elsie, is Daddy there? I need to ask the two of you a *big* favor."

"James is at the church, helping paint the fellowship hall. What you need, honey? You know we'll help you."

I inform Miss Elsie of my surrogate-parent role and pressing need for a babysitter. She agrees—like I figured—to help. Too bad she never had children. She would make a wonderful mother. That's a nice thing to say about a woman. I wonder if anyone has ever said that about me.

It's almost four when I pull into an empty visitor space at Carver Elementary. There are three Black adults, two women and a tall, slim, pecan-complexioned man, standing in front of the school. My heart starts racing. Could that be Dr. Cooper? I turn off the engine, run my fingers through my hair, make sure no food is lodged between my teeth, and get out.

The trio greets me with smiles and hellos.

"Hello," I reply cordially.

Upon close inspection, I find the tall, slim man to be quite attractive. Dressed neatly in a navy suit, he looks as if he stepped off the pages of *GQ*. His wavy hair is cut close and parted to the side. That, along with his goatee and wire-framed glasses, makes him look scholarly and distinguished. I glance at his left hand. No wedding band. Even if this isn't Preston Cooper, I know this brotha has women hounding him. On my Best-Looking Brothers Scale, he scores a solid eight. He would score higher if he had a li'l more meat on his bones.

"Are you here to pick up someone?" one of the ladies asks.

"Yes. A'Kyah Williams. I believe she's in the office."

"Miss Liles?" the man asks, opening his eyes wider.

"Yes," I say, with a nod.

"I'm Dr. Cooper," he says, extending his hand. "Pleased to meet you."

Oh, my goodness! Be still my racing heart! I remove my sunglasses and shake Dr. Cooper's hand. "Pleased to meet you," I say as pleasantly as I can.

"A'Kyah is in the office," he says.

"Thank you," I reply.

I turn and head inside. From the glass doors, I see Dr. Cooper turn and watch me. I throw my head back and put an extra wiggle in my step before entering the building.

The school office is not crowded, like it was this morning. The receptionist and A'Kyah are the only people inside. A'Kyah is asleep on the love seat. The receptionist hands me a large manila envelope, which she says contains the suspension notice and homework, including the assignments A'Kyah failed to complete yesterday. I glance over at A'Kyah. The little liar told me she completed that work! I thank the receptionist, go over to A'Kyah, and nudge her. She opens her eyes and yawns. "Let's go," I say softly.

A'Kyah grabs her book bag and slowly rises to her feet. A tube of lip gloss rolls across her lap and onto the floor.

Uh-uh! My eyes must be deceiving me, because I know that ain't my fifteen-dollar tube of sheer gold Fashion Fair lip gloss. I snatch the lip gloss up from the floor. It *is* my sheer gold lip gloss. I narrow my eyes at A'Kyah. "Move it!" I whisper hoarsely.

When A'Kyah and I exit the building, my heart starts racing again. Dr. Cooper is still out front. He turns and tells A'Kyah to come over. She groans and shuffles over.

"I expect you," he says, glaring down into her face, "to return to school on Monday with the proper attitude. I do *not* want to see you in my office any more this school year."

A'Kyah's bottom lip quivers. "Yes, sir," she says as tears fill her eyes.

"I mean it!" says Dr. Cooper.

"Yes, sir," A'Kyah murmurs.

"We're going to work on her attitude while she's home," I say.

Dr. Cooper looks up and smiles at me. "I appreciate your cooperation, Miss Liles," he says softly, while giving me the once-over.

I like the way he said, "Miss Liles." It sounded as if he was flirting with me on the sly.

"And if you have any questions about anything"—he points to the manila envelope in my hand—"please feel free to call me or Mrs. Hodges this evening. We're both listed in the phone book."

"Thank you, Dr. Cooper," I say.

"You're welcome," he says, giving me the once-over again.

When I pull out of the parking lot, I look over at Dr. Cooper and wave; he waves back. If I knew how to reach Willnetta, I would call her now. Oh, I can't wait till she gets home!

"I won't be staying home with you, A'Kyah. I have to work. You'll be at my dad and stepmom's while I'm at work."

A'Kyah folds her arms across her chest and slumps down in the seat.

I continue. "I'm so upset with you. You gave me your word that you would behave, and you turn around and get into a *fight* today."

"She was talking 'bout my daddy!"

"What?"

"This stupid, ugly girl in my class was talking 'bout my daddy! She called him a crackhead."

"A'Kyah, you can't let what people say about Tony upset you to the point of violence. Fighting never solves anything."

"I betcha she won't say nothing else 'bout my daddy."

"Really? You so sure about that?"

A'Kyah smacks her lips.

"You should have ignored the girl or told the teacher she was bothering you. You accomplished nothing, absolutely *nothing* from fighting, other than a suspension, which will result in you not getting a Perfect Attendance Award."

"I don't care 'bout that dumb award!"

"I don't believe you."

"Believe what you want," she mumbles, looking out of the corner of her eye at me.

"Well, you can believe *this*. When Gina calls tonight, she will hear all about—"

"Noooo, Eva!" she cries.

"Save the tears. I'm telling! And please tell me what possessed you to go into my bedroom and remove my lip gloss off my vanity."

"I didn't think you'd mind."

"I do mind."

"You saw me with it on last night and didn't say nothing!"

"What?" Oooh, so that's why her lips were so shiny last night. "You're not old enough to wear make-up, okay?"

Silence.

"A'Kyah?"

"I heard you! I'm not deaf! Dog!"

I hit the steering wheel. "I've had enough of your sass! You will *not* talk to me in that manner!"

"I'll be glad when my mama comes home!" she growls.

"Me, too!" I growl back and regret saying the instant it comes flying out of my mouth.

When we get home, A'Kyah runs into the guest bedroom and slams the door shut. I charge in behind her and remove the telephone and her boom box and tell her she'd better not slam another door in my house. I don't wait for Gina to call; I dial her mother's number, praying she's there.

Gina answers on the first ring. I blurt out that A'Kyah has been disrespectful and in major trouble at school. Gina cries and apologizes for A'Kyah's behavior. I cry, too, and ask her to forgive me for lying last night. She does and then tells me to take A'Kyah to the prison on Saturday so Tony can chastise her for misbehaving. She'll make arrangements for me to do that, by requesting special visitation privileges through Tony's counselor. After Gina takes down my vitals, my DOB and Social Security number, she asks to speak to A'Kyah.

While Gina lays down the law to A'Kyah, I lie back on my bed and cover my head with a pillow to drown out A'Kyah's loud sobbing. As bad as I loathe the thought of having to go to Hayesfield Correctional Center, I welcome any help I can get with A'Kyah. If it has to come from her daddy, the convict, so be it.

6

Finally?

TGIF! A'Kyah and I have survived the week as roomies, and in spite of the strict punishment that Gina meted out, A'Kyah has actually been pleasant to be around. Poor kid can't watch TV, play outside with the neighborhood children, talk on the phone to her friends, or listen to her boom box. And in addition to that, she has to be in bed every night by eight. I feel sorry for her, but not sorry enough to amend any of her punishment in light of the glowing reports from Daddy and Miss Elsie. She was "a joy to have around," they said. Tomorrow my pint-size charge faces the wrath of her father. She's thanked me five times since leaving the salon for getting her hair done. We're both looking cute, she with box braids and me with a bouncy doobie.

I can smell the fish cooking when I pull into Mama's driveway. Leon is in the yard, waxing the Lincoln. Mama volunteered to keep A'Kyah tonight, while Teresa and I, once more, search for love. I pray this Christian singles social doesn't end up like the trip to the nightclub.

I park my dusty Lexus beside Leon's shiny white Navigator, and A'Kyah and I get out. Leon looks at my SUV and shakes his head.

"Yeah, yeah. I know it's dirty," I mumble.

"You got time for me to wash it?" asks Leon.

"Yeah!" I say.

"Can I help?" A'Kyah asks.

"Sure can," Leon says.

Granted Mama doesn't look her age and is one of the prettiest women I know, my sisters and I still wonder how our overbearing, nagging mother managed to snag this hunky, handsome, sweet man.

I trek to the back of the house. Mama is on the patio, battering fish in an aluminum pan. Provided it's not raining or frigid cold, without fail, she and Leon fry fish every Friday afternoon.

"Why is the food not ready, Mama? I'm hungry," I say.

"And good afternoon to you," she says, looking back at me. "Where's A'Kyah?"

"Around front with Leon. She's gone help him wash my ride."

"She needs to eat something first. Poor child probably ain't had nothing fit to eat all day."

"Don't start."

"What your *stepmother* feed her today?"

"Don't know," I lie. "But I would sure love for my mother to hurry up and give me something to eat."

"What you want? Perch or trout?"

"Both."

"What time's your date?"

"I don't have a date."

I explain to Mama once more that Teresa and I are going to a singles club, hoping to meet someone *to date*.

"You don't have to go there!" she protests, removing fish from the deep fryer. "Okay, so you let Joel get away. I'm over that. There's still O-tis."

"Please."

"He stopped by the nursing home yesterday morning."

Unlike me, who commutes outside of Fairview to work every morning, Mama and Geraldine work in town, at the Nursing and Convalescent Center. Mama's the housekeeping supervisor, and Geraldine, an RN, is a nursing supervisor. Otis often stops there, I jokingly say, scavenging for bodies.

"Who died?" I ask, trying not to laugh.

Mama rolls her eyes at me. "Nobody. And I pray you don't meet no *psycho* tonight."

I laugh. I would never admit it to Mama, because I wouldn't want her to worry, but the thought of crossing paths with a lunatic has crossed my mind. These singles clubs, I'm sure, are magnets for all types of people, and that would include psychos, too. *Oh, Lord, please keep Teresa and me from danger!*

There aren't many cars in the West Raleigh Country Club parking lot. A banner with FINALLY SINGLES CLUB SOCIAL in red letters is stretched across the club entrance. When I park, Teresa mutters that she hopes she doesn't end up wishing she'd stayed home.

We enter a well-lit lobby and are warmly greeted by an attractive middle-aged man and woman. In response, I'm sure, to the apathetic expression on Teresa's face, the man stands and goes into a spiel about how Finally is the premier singles club in the area catering to the needs of African American Christian professionals. He then assures us that we made the right choice by coming tonight. The lady issues us ink pens; HELLO MY NAME IS adhesive labels, on which to print our first names; and short questionnaires to complete. The merry duo explains that the information we provide will be available for interested males to review.

The first part of the questionnaire asks for biographical information and what I hope to accomplish by joining the singles club. I write: *A friendship that will lead to marriage.* In the second section of the questionnaire, I indicate what I'm looking for in a soul mate. I repeat the same attributes I listed in section one about myself: thirty-five to forty-five years old, nonsmoker, college educated, professionally employed, annual income of $60,000 to $79,999, attractive, good physical health, Christian, and diversified cultural interests. After Teresa and I complete our questionnaires, the woman ushers us off to what we're now psyched up to believe will be our chance at love.

"Ooooh!" Teresa exclaims, stopping dead in her tracks.

Déjà vu! Milling about in a tastefully decorated large room are five men. The room, unfortunately, is partially filled with women. Gospel jazz, along with the chatter and giggles of the few in high spirits, fills the air. I feel like crying. I got dressed up again for nothing!

I spot a table covered with food and take off for it. Teresa follows. We pass a well-dressed, despondent-looking group of women. From the corner of my eye, I catch them eyeing us. I'm going to be optimistic and hope for their sake, Teresa's, and mine that more men will show up. *Lord, please send more men. Oh, let me be specific: men like Dr. Preston Cooper.* Since meeting him, I haven't been able to stop thinking or dreaming about him.

"Teresa?" I say.

"What?" replies Teresa.

"What you think Preston is doing tonight?"

"Call him and find out. I dare you!" she says, laughing.

"Oh, you're funny!"

"Chicken."

"Whatever."

After filling small plates with meatballs, drumettes, fruit, vegetables, and dip, Teresa and I head over to the bar. The male bartender greets us, with a big smile, and explains that it's a nonalcoholic bar. I order a glass of Sprite; Teresa orders iced tea. A light-skinned, modestly dressed lady sitting at the bar says hello and compliments us on our outfits. She looks to be about the same age as Teresa and me. I sit down next to Plain Jane to quiz her about Finally.

Teresa gasps out loud and nudges me in my side so hard I almost topple off the barstool. "Check out the entrance!

Check out the entrance!" she whispers excitedly. "More brothas in the house!"

I look back, blink, and open my unbelieving eyes wide. Three attractive, well-dressed men are standing in the entrance. One of them happens to be Preston Cooper.

"There's Preston, Teresa!" I squeal.

"Whaaaat? Which one?" she yells.

"In the gray suit!"

"Stop lying!"

"I'm not! It's him!"

"He's fine!" Plain Jane exclaims. "You know him?"

"Uh-huh, kinda, sorta," I murmur.

"He's fine!" Plain Jane exclaims again.

"How do I look, Teresa? Do I look okay?" I ask.

"You look fine, Eva."

"Yeah, girl. You're sharp," Plain Jane adds. "I *love* that dress."

I'm wearing a DKNY, black, V-necked knit dress with ruffle edging at the neckline. This sexy number has a lattice hem and three-quarter-length sleeves. And my nines are in my new stilettos.

"Is my hair okay? Do I have on enough lipstick?" I ask.

"Yes, yes!" Teresa replies. "Now calm down."

I take several deep breaths to calm myself.

Preston and the men head to the hors d'oeuvres table.

Teresa nudges me. "Get up and go over there!"

"You better move, girl!" Plain Jane says, still all in the Kool-Aid.

How I wish I could. My heart is racing. This is my chance to hook up with Preston, and I'm afraid to move. I stare at him longingly as he piles food on a plate. When he turns and heads to the bar, desire overpowers anxiety. I hop off the stool and stroll over. "Hi, Dr. Cooper."

Preston looks at me, smiles, and gives me that I-know-you-from-somewhere-but-can't-recall-where look.

I smile and point to my name tag. "I'm Eva Liles, A'Kyah—"

"Oh, yes, yes, Miss Liles. How are you?" he asks, extending his hand.

"I'm fine," I say, shaking his hand. "And please call me Eva."

Preston nods and smiles.

Teresa walks by, looks back, and winks at me. I hope she meets someone and feels what I'm feeling right now—unadulterated joy! The guy in the lobby is right: I did make the "right choice" by coming here.

"Would you care to sit down?" I ask Preston. "There're seats at the bar."

Preston nods again. "Thank you."

"So tell me," he asks once we're seated, "what's someone as *lovely* as you doing here?"

I cross my legs and smile. "Well, Dr. Cooper—"

"Please," he says, ogling my legs, "call me Preston."

"Okay, Preston. I could ask you the same thing."

Preston smiles and pops a meatball in his mouth.

"Have you been here before?" I ask.

He shakes his head.

"My first time, too." I take a sip of my Sprite and catch Plain Jane stealing glances at us.

"Eva, I'm trying not to stare at you," Preston says, reaching into his plate for another meatball. "But"—he smiles and looks over at me—"you're one *gorgeous* woman. And, I must confess, you've crossed my mind several times this week."

Hot dang! Yippee! He's thought about me! He's thought about me! Should I tell him that I've thought about him, too? No, I better not. I read somewhere that women should never let men know how they feel about them right off the bat. Then again, maybe I should be candid with him, like he's being with me. We'll see.

I gently toss my hair and smile. "No kidding?"

"No kidding. For the life of me, I can't understand why you're here. You're beautiful, and you smell"—he takes a deep breath and exhales—"*wonderful*."

"Thank you."

"I know guys are knocking down your door. Don't tell me they aren't."

Yeah, right! I sigh softly and toss my hair again. "Let's just say"—I laugh—"the right one hasn't knocked."

"Describe him to me?" he asks, leaning close to me. "Who knows, tonight may be your lucky night."

My heart starts racing, and my body temperature skyrockets. No, no, no! Yes, yes, yes! He's making a move on me! The man I've been fantasizing about since I first heard his voice is making a move on me! *Oh, Lord, please don't let me blow it.*

I run my fingers through my hair and take a deep breath.

"I'm waiting," Preston says, smiling.

I open my mouth to run down my Brotha Must Have List for Preston, and a chesty, brown-skinned woman rushes up to him and throws an arm around his shoulders. He flinches and looks back.

"Diane! Hey! How are you?" he says.

The woman plants a long, hard kiss on Preston's right cheek. So hard, she leaves the imprint of her ruby-colored lips there. "Much better now," she says.

Preston laughs.

"I thought we were supposed to get together last week and play a round of golf?" she whines seductively.

My exuberance plummets. This can't be happening! This woman—this *Diane*—surely isn't making a move on Preston right in front of me. The nerve of her!

Plain Jane looks at me and shakes her head.

To quell my mounting anxiety, I begin to compare myself to Diane. For starters, she needs a touch-up, and some pressed powder for that oily, blotchy face of hers. *And,* she could stand a visit from the fashion patrol. That black, beaded, fringe sweater and leopard-print stretch pants outfit she's wearing is tac-ky, and so are those ugly leopard-print mules. She's a step from being ghetto fabulous, and I can't see Preston choosing her over me.

Wait! Hold up! What am I doing? I shake my head in disbelief at myself. I'm playa hating. I shouldn't be hating on

Catwoman. Like the saying goes, "Don't hate the playa; hate the game."

I sip my soda, try to look cool, and glance around the room. I look for Teresa; I don't see her. Women have flanked the guys that came in with Preston. I pity the women, and myself. Our chances of snagging men like Preston and his affluent-looking friends are not good, not good at all.

Diane tells Preston about a principals' conference she's planning to attend next month in Atlanta and asks if he's heard about it. He tells her he has but isn't going.

From the corner of my eye, I watch her reach into Preston's plate, pick up a meatball, and pop it in her mouth.

"It's going to be a *great* conference," she says, licking her fingers. "So come on and go."

I'm pissed now, not just with Diane, but with Preston, too. Why won't he tell her to go away?

Diane starts massaging Preston's shoulders and asks if he's available this weekend for that game of golf he promised her. He laughs and tells her he's leaving for Miami in the morning. She asks if she can go. I cough. Preston looks over at me and stands up.

"Diane, let me get back to you, okay?" he says.

"I've heard that before," she moans, pressing her double Ds into his chest.

Preston chuckles and steps back.

I don't see a doggone funny thing!

Diane laughs and runs a hand across Preston's wavy hair. "You smell gooood."

Plain Jane grunts loudly.

Diane cuts her eyes at Plain Jane and then me. "Preston, may I speak to you in private? Please?" she asks, pouting and tugging on his arm.

Preston lets out an exasperated sigh and turns to me. "Can I call you?"

"Sure," I say, with a wink and smile.

He winks back. "Good."

Diane sighs softly and rolls her eyes.

"It was good seeing you again, Preston," I say, hoping to piss Diane off further.

He winks again. "Likewise."

I sadly watch Diane lead Preston out of the room.

"Can you believe that hussy?" Plain Jane mutters angrily.

"Girlfriend, I'm not the least bit bothered by that," I lie, with a wave of my hand. If Plain Jane only knew. I'm humiliated! My pride, however, won't let me say that to her. I look around the room again for Teresa.

"It's a shame how some women are so low-down! I would never do something like that," says Plain Jane.

"Me neither," I say, sliding off the stool.

"You leaving?"

"Yeah, I'm outta here."

"Um, before you leave, could you tell me the name of that perfume you're wearing?"

"It's Allure, by Chanel."

"Thanks. I have to get some of that!" she says, opening her eyes wide. "It smells good."

I smile and wave good-bye.

I'm humiliated, angry, and depressed. But somehow, I manage to walk out of the room with my head high and a big smile on my face. I spot Teresa in the lobby, talking to a light-skinned, stocky, bearded, bald-headed guy. Neither Preston nor Diane is anywhere to be seen. The duo that greeted Teresa and me earlier is standing at their table, arranging materials. I go over and pick up Preston's questionnaire.

Dr. Preston Cooper is a forty-four-year-old divorcé with no children, looking to remarry and have kids. His earnings fall in the $80,000 to $99,999 income bracket. A Christian, romantic, and sports enthusiast, he enjoys traveling, listening to jazz music, watching movies, and attending concerts and plays. He's just what I'm looking for. *Lord, I want him. Can I have him, please?*

"He's quite a catch," the lady says, eyeing Preston's information from across the table. She hands me a pen and a piece of paper. "Feel free to jot down his e-mail address."

I shake my head. "We talked earlier. He's going to contact me."

"Great!" she says, clapping her hands. "See. You did make the *right* choice by coming out tonight. And your friend"— she looks over at Teresa—"isn't doing bad, either."

I hand the lady Preston's information and walk over to Teresa. The guy she's laughing and chatting with is fairly attractive. He looks to be in his midforties. Dressed neatly in black slacks and a beige, short-sleeved shirt, he has only one strike against him—his height. He looks to be about five feet eight. Teresa is five feet ten in her bare feet.

"Eva," Teresa says, with a big smile, "meet professor *and* author William Carter. William teaches anatomy at NC State. William, this is my best friend, Eva Liles."

The professor and I exchange hellos. Teresa appears to be enjoying his company, but I know her. She's not going to date him, because of his height. I catch her eye and mouth, "Let's go." She acknowledges my gesture with a slight nod.

"William," she says, reaching for his hand, "I thoroughly enjoyed talking with you."

"Don't tell me you're leaving?" he asks, grabbing her out-stretched hand.

"I'm afraid so," says Teresa.

"May I call you?" he asks.

I make my exit outside before Teresa shoots William down. Anxiety mounts with each step I take. Where is Preston? Did he leave with Diane?

A Mercedes pulls into the parking lot. The headlights sweep over two figures standing between an Escalade and a minivan. I hurry to my SUV as quietly as possible, wondering if it's Diane and Preston and hoping that it's not. Once inside my vehicle, I slide down in the driver's seat, lower the windows, and try to make out the figures between the Escalade and van. A BMW pulls into an empty parking space behind me. Three women get out. As they approach the country club's entrance, the guys that were with Preston exit and head in the direction of the Escalade and van. My heart starts pounding in my chest, and I ease farther down in the seat.

When the Escalade's exterior and interior lights pop on, the figures emerge from between the vehicles. It is Preston and Diane. I groan out loud. Preston gives Diane a quick hug and hops inside the Escalade, along with the men. Diane places her hands on her narrow hips and watches the SUV pull out of the lot. For a split second, I feel sorry for her. When she turns and stalks back toward the club, I laugh.

Teresa exits the club, glowing. She surprises me when she says she gave William her phone number and will go out with him if he calls. She's not going to let his height be an issue.

I give her a high five and head to Baskin Robbins, hoping and praying that I get a call from Preston.

7

Intrigue

I don't want to move. Oh, this feeeels soooo goood! I add more jasmine and lavender to my bathwater, lie back, and think about Preston again. I wish we could have spent more time together last night. Teresa has called me five times this morning. Lucky wench is at the mall, dancing up and down the aisles at Saks in search of a "boating" outfit. The professor called; they're going sailing this afternoon. Gina beeped in while I was telling Stephanie about Teresa's date and asked if I would keep A'Kyah a little longer. Even though her mother's condition has been downgraded from critical to guarded, she doesn't want to leave St. Louis right now. I told her I understood and would keep A'Kyah as long as she needed me to.

A'Kyah took the news of Gina's extended absence well. She's out shopping with Mama and my niece Jalisa. When she returns—which should be any minute now—we're off to Hayesfield.

My thoughts return to Preston. I wonder what he's doing in Miami, and who with. Shrilling horn blasts in the driveway end my mini-spa treatment and whimsical thoughts of romance. I climb out of the tub, grab a towel, and run to the front door. A'Kyah is on the porch, anxiously waiting for me to let her in. I open the door, and she runs past with shopping bags from JCPenney and Old Navy, announcing that she's wearing one of her new outfits to the prison.

"You heard from the doctor yet?" Mama yells, backing out of the driveway. She was wide awake when I picked up A'Kyah last night, eager to hear all about my evening.

I shake my head.

"Maybe he'll call today!" she yells, speeding off.

While A'Kyah showers, I dry off and dress in a white T-shirt, light gray, stretch workout pants, and sneakers. After pulling my hair back into a ponytail, I go outside.

Sixty-eight-year-old Beulah Jennings, a widow who has lived next door for as long as I can remember, is unloading groceries from her minivan, with two of the five rambunctious grandchildren she's raising. She waves hello to me; I wave back.

I look up and bask in the sunlight. It's another beautiful spring day. I wonder if it's sunny in Miami and if Preston has once thought of me. *Lord, is romance on the horizon for me this year?* For some reason, I feel it is. I hope I'm right.

"We gonna stay for the entire visit, right, Eva?"

Ugh! I do not want to spend two minutes, let alone two hours, at Hayesfield Correctional Center. But I can't say that to A'Kyah. She's looking forward to spending time with her father, and I of all people—a social worker—should be sympathetic to that. *Dear Lord, give me strength.*

"Huh, Eva?"

I take a deep breath, look over at A'Kyah, and smile. "Yes, we are."

Her exuberance nose-dives when I turn into the parking lot of D & L Barbecue. I haven't had anything to eat, and I'm starving. I don't feel like getting out, so I pull into the long drive-through line.

"I'll go inside for you. The line's too long," A'Kyah offers.

"That's okay. It's moving."

"We're going to be late," she mumbles, looking at her new watch.

"We're not going to be that late. You want anything?"

"No!"

With each passing second, tension mounts in the SUV. From the corner of my eye, I see that A'Kyah is scowling. "We're almost there," I say cheerfully when I'm one car away from placing my order. Unfortunately, I'm behind a car packed with people.

"And I bet they all got separate orders!" she grumbles. She follows up her comment with a lip smack.

"Stop it!" I yell. "Don't start that lip-smacking crap again! Like I said, we're not going to be *that* late. Besides, Tony's not going anywhere!" Oops. That slipped out, and it wasn't nice, either.

A'Kyah rolls her eyes and glares out her window.

When I place my order—a barbecue sandwich, a dozen hush puppies and a large lemonade—I hear A'Kyah grunt. The tension between us diminishes once I speed out of the parking lot en route to Hayesfield.

The sandwich and hush puppies do not sufficiently abate my hunger. I'm craving peanut M&M's and potato chips like a big dog, but I dare not make another stop for fear of ticking off A'Kyah again. She's humming away and eating Laffy Taffy. Her sun yellow shorts set with sunflower buttons and her white platform sneakers contrast sharply with my outfit. When she came outside to tell me she was ready, she asked when was I getting dressed. When I told her I already was, she gave me a disapproving look and walked off the porch. I hate to disappoint the kid, but I'm not dressing up for her daddy.

"See, see that sign that got Hayesfield Correctional Center on it?" she asks, pointing. "Turn there."

I was just out here not quite a week ago. I remember how to get to the prison. "I see it. Thank you," I reply softly.

I turn onto the prison road, and a string of cars file in behind me. A Black woman driving a Mercedes roadster is directly behind me. She's practically on my bumper.

"I can't wait to see my daddy," A'Kyah sings, dancing in her seat. "When he gets out, he's says I can live with him if I want to."

Ha! Live with him? Where? Tony has never had a place of his own in the ten years that I've known him. When he's not locked up, he's freeloading off his mother and sister, or shacking up with Gina or one of his other babies' mamas. A deadbeat father of five, who is forty thousand dollars in arrears on child support, he's a shameless, irresponsible individual, and I can't stand him.

It's 1:12 when I pull into the prison parking lot. The lady driving the roadster speeds around me and into a space. The second I park, A'Kyah throws open her door, hops out, and sprints across the busy parking lot, toward the administration building. Miss Roadster is right behind her, with a picnic basket.

I enter the administration building and follow people, mostly women and children, through a door that has the words VISITATION CHECK-IN over it. Inside the large room are two officers—one male and the other female—sitting at a table that has a five-by-seven file box, a telephone, and a clipboard on it. A'Kyah is standing at the table, waving me over. When I approach, she tells the female officer, whose name badge identifies her as Lt. Rivers, that I'm here to see Tony Roberts also. The lieutenant, a petite, attractive, brown-skinned woman, asks to see my driver's license, while the White male officer thumbs through the file box. I pull my license out of my T-shirt pocket and accidentally drop it. A'Kyah grunts loudly and picks it up. She hands it to the lieutenant, who looks at it and then at the card—Tony's visitation information, I assume—that the male officer has in his hand.

"Okay, Miss Liles," the lieutenant says, handing back my license. "You and A'Kyah may sign in now."

I write my name on the visitor sign-in sheet affixed to the clipboard. While A'Kyah does a messy job of printing her name, the lieutenant tells the male officer to inform housing that Tony Roberts has two visitors.

When A'Kyah and I step out into the rec yard, I see that a few inmates are already engaged in visits. They're sitting under large green umbrellas at wooden picnic tables. I spot Miss Roadster and hurry over to an unoccupied table near her. Curiosity has gotten the best of me. I'm eager to see who she's visiting.

Sista girl is a very attractive, well-dressed, cocoa-colored woman who looks to be in her late thirties. Decked out in peach-colored, linen pants; a white, short-sleeved knit top; and white, high-heel mules, she is sharp! Her hair is neatly braided back into a bun, and her jewelry sparkles in the sunlight as she moves about. The best-dressed woman on the yard, sista girl looks like she's got it going on. I can't imagine her here to visit a husband or boyfriend.

A'Kyah busies herself by arranging her math and literature books, along with her homework folder, on our table. She declined my repeated offers to check over her homework; she wants Tony to do it instead.

As more women and children file out of the administration building, more inmates pour out of the housing unit. Like a year ago, when I rode out here with Willnetta to bring Joel dinner, the men I see in prison attire are mostly Black. I count four White inmates so far out of about twenty Black men. Why do our men continue to make choices that lead to prison? As bad as I want a boyfriend, I could easily get one here. But I'm not *desperate*. In my opinion, any woman that does become romantically involved with a man who would rather break laws than uphold them is *desperate* and suffering from low self-esteem. Gina was one such woman. I hope she meant it when she said it was over between her and Tony, and I pray the next man she falls in love with scores high marks in character.

From her picnic basket, Miss Roadster pulls out a KFC chicken box.

My mouth waters. "A'Kyah," I whisper. "You know"—I point with my head—"that lady?"

"Uh-huh. That's Freda."

"Who does she visit?"

"Clarence, her boyfriend."

I don't want to believe what I heard. "Who did you say?"

"Clarence, her boyfriend."

Her boyfriend? Dang! I look over at the woman and wonder why a sophisticated-looking woman like that would be romantically involved with a convict.

A young, stout Black woman and three chubby children— two boys and a girl—trudge over to the table next to us. "Hey, Freda! Girl, I missed you last week," the woman says loudly. The children place three large Papa John pizza boxes and two bags of Wise potato chips on their picnic table.

My mouth waters again.

"I was out of town last week at a business expo," Freda says, fanning herself with her hands.

"Still makin' the money. Go 'head, girl!" the woman replies heartily.

Freda laughs. "It's not because I don't try."

"I didn't see that phat Lexus of yours in the parkin' lot. You drivin' somethin' else?"

"Yes. Something I got for my boo."

"Oh! What?" the woman asks excitedly.

"A little sports car."

"What kind?"

"A roadster."

The woman frowns. "A who?"

I turn to ask A'Kyah about the bubbly woman conversing with Freda. A'Kyah is looking over at the housing unit. When she sees Tony, she jumps up and runs toward the gated fence separating the housing unit from the rec yard. There are three male correctional officers standing there. One unlocks the gate, and a large group of inmates swaggers onto the yard.

"Eva!" Tony yells, hurrying over to the picnic table. "I really 'preciate what you doing for me and Gina, girl. And, I apologize," he says sheepishly, "for A'Kyah's behavior."

I smile. "Apology accepted."

"You taking care of *my* kid, somethin' my *own* folks wouldn't do, and she gone mind you. I thank you," he says, patting his bird chest, "from the bottom of my heart."

"You're welcome, Tony," I say.

Tony sits down next to me and pulls A'Kyah to him. "And I want *you*," he says, tapping her on the nose, "to apologize to Eva for—"

"I already have!" A'Kyah blurts out.

"Don't interrupt me!" says Tony.

Tears well up in A'Kyah's eyes. "I'm sorry, Daddy."

"Tell Eva you sorry for misbehaving at school, and for talking ugly to her," Tony orders.

"Tony, she has apologized to me," I interject.

"I want her to do it again," replies Tony.

Tears trickle down A'Kyah's face, and she drops her head. "I-I'm s-sorry, E-Eva," she stammers, "for actin' up."

"Apology accepted," I say, smiling.

Tony gives A'Kyah a hard swat to the butt. "And you gone write Mrs. Hodges a letter of apology. You hear me?"

"Yes," whimpers A'Kyah.

"And if I hear of you cuttin' up *one* mo' time at school, I'm comin'!" says Tony.

A'Kyah's watery eyes grow large and round.

"That's right. You heard me. I'm comin' straight to your classroom, shackled up in a black-and-white striped jump-suit," says Tony.

A'Kyah gasps and starts shaking her head.

"And I'm gone deal with you right in front of your li'l friends. Let's see how you like that!" Tony adds.

"You won't have to do that, Daddy! I'm not gonna get in any more trouble. I promise!" cries A'Kyah.

I'm glad to see that Tony is upset about A'Kyah's misbehavior. Given his propensity for misconduct, I surely didn't expect this. Gina said he would get on A'Kyah. I'm impressed.

Tony pleads with A'Kyah to master self-control and paints a vivid picture of where she could end up if she fails to do so. After his impassioned talk with his penitent-looking daughter, they get up and stroll hand in hand around the rec yard.

I turn my attention to the people around me and wonder about their life stories. All of the picnic tables are occupied now, and people continue to file out of the administration building and housing unit. Five male correctional officers positioned along the fence monitor activity in the yard. The steamy kisses taking place under the green umbrellas clearly indicate that many of the women are romantically involved with the men they're visiting. I wonder if these women, including Freda, are concerned at all about the possibility of their lovers engaging in clandestine affairs with fellow inmates.

According to Joel, homosexual behavior is common practice among inmates, and the willing participants aren't just gay men, but so-called straight men as well. Many of these men become infected with HIV and AIDS, and when released from prison, pass these life-threatening conditions on to unsuspecting wives or girlfriends.

After first hearing this dreadful news, I rushed over to Gina's and questioned her about the possibility of Tony being on the "down low"—having sex with men and keeping it a secret from her. She was still madly in love with him at the time and refused to believe he would engage in such behavior. She eventually confronted him about *my* concerns only because I kept nagging her. He cursed her out and sent a nasty message to me to kiss his ass and mind my own damn business. Three months later, Gina was on the outs with Tony, and I was able to talk her into taking an AIDS test.

I accompanied her to the health department and while in the waiting room, we read a disturbing article in *Ebony* about the rise of HIV/AIDS in the Black community. The article noted that Black women account for nearly two-thirds of

HIV/AIDS cases among women in this country, and that the majority of the infections stem from us having sex unknowingly with bisexual men and men previously incarcerated who had engaged in homosexual activity behind bars.

Gina was scared to get tested after reading the article. I had to drag her into the lab. Her test came back negative, thank God, and she's been tested two more times since then, and those tests were negative also. I look at Freda and the other women and pray they aren't playing Russian roulette with their lives and the lives of any children they plan to have.

The bubbly woman and children are sharing their pizza dinner with a short, chunky inmate who two of the children resemble. Unlike his family, he's neat and clean. The woman and children could be a poster family for a relief agency soliciting donations for the poor. My heart goes out to them. They're dressed in shabby clothing, and it doesn't look as if anyone's hair has been combed in days. The woman tells the inmate that she still hasn't found a job, and her aunt wants her and the kids out by the first of next month. The inmate grunts loudly and crams a slice of pepperoni pizza in his mouth.

Freda jumps up when a slim, bowlegged, light-skinned man pimps over to her. He's good-looking—a pretty boy with wavy black hair and long lashes shading big brown eyes. He doesn't look like he's done a day of hard work in his life. And, I guess he doesn't have to, since Freda seems to be rolling in the dough. Pretty Boy gives Freda a

long, passionate kiss that curls my toes.

"You seem in deep thought," says a voice.

I look over to the left of me. Standing at the end of the picnic table is that handsome inmate that was working with Tony last Sunday. A brown-skinned elderly woman wearing a straw hat is standing next to him.

"Hello, Eva," he says pleasantly.

"Hi," I reply.

"Do you mind if my mother and I sit here?"

"No," I say. He remembers my name. *Oh, my, what is his? Alex? Alexander? Is that it?*

"Thank you, sweetheart," the lady says, sitting down across from me. She is tall like her son and modestly dressed in a white blouse and black skirt. There are dark circles and bags under her hound-dog eyes, and strands of gray and black hair hang from underneath the straw hat, down into her face.

"Mother, this is the lady I was telling you about who is keeping A'Kyah."

The lady gasps and throws up her hands. "Oh yes! My, how sweet!"

"Eva, this is my mother, Ann-Marie Dupree," Alex, or whatever his name is, says, sitting down.

"It's a pleasure to meet you, Eva," Mrs. Dupree says, with a nod. "Xavier!" she exclaims.

Oh yeah, that's his name. Xavier.

"She bears a striking resemblance to the McCoys who stay down the road from your daddy and me," says Mrs. Dupree.

"She sure does," Xavier says slowly, looking at me sideways.

"Eva, do you know Novella McCoy?" Mrs. Dupree asks.

"No, ma'am," I reply.

"You could pass for one of her granddaughters," Mrs. Dupree says, smiling.

"She's very pretty, isn't she?" Xavier asks, staring at me.

"Uh-huh," Mrs. Dupree says, bobbing her head.

I smile back, then look over at the family finishing up their pizza. From the corner of my eye, I can see that Xavier is still staring at me.

"Xavier, have you heard anything about your parole hearing?" Mrs. Dupree asks.

Xavier sighs heavily. "Not yet, Mother."

Mrs. Dupree moans.

I tune out the noise around me and turn my full attention to the Duprees.

"Did Dad keep that appointment at the VA hospital?" asks Xavier.

"No," answers Mrs. Dupree.

Xavier sighs again and hits the table with his fist.

Mrs. Dupree grabs his hand. "He says he's feeling much better."

"He needs to go see that cardiologist, Mother. Chest pain is not to be taken lightly," says Xavier.

"You know how Samuel is, Xavier. I can talk till I'm hoarse and blue in the face. If he doesn't see the need to do a thing, he's not going to do it!" says Mrs. Dupree.

Xavier squeezes his mother's hand and drops his head.

"He wants you to stop worrying about him," she says softly, with a smile.

If Inmate Dupree has a conscience, he can't help but worry about his elderly parents and feel an enormous amount of guilt over how his incarceration may have affected them. I'm sure those dark circles and sandbags under his mother's eyes come from her crying and worrying over him.

Freda and Clarence stroll over to the fence and look out into the parking lot. The roadster, a white convertible, is glistening in the sun. Two correctional officers walk over and admire the car, too.

I pick up A'Kyah's literature book. On the back cover is a group of animals reading books and eating ice cream. My stomach growls. I clear my throat, hoping no one heard it.

Mrs. Dupree chuckles. "I'm hungry, too, Eva."

I look up. Xavier is staring at me, smiling. I look down and start flipping through the book. I sense that he's still looking at me but don't look up to see.

"Son, I can't stay too long today," says Mrs. Dupree. "I've got choir rehearsal at two. Samuel will be here tomorrow. Oh my, lookahere!"

I look up. Tony and A'Kyah are hurrying back to the table.

"Mama Dupree! How's my girl?" cries Tony.

"I'm fine, Tony," Mrs. Dupree replies.

"A'Kyah," Tony says, nudging her toward Mrs. Dupree, "say hello to Xavier's mom."

"Hello," A'Kyah whispers, throwing up her hand.

"Good to see you again, A'Kyah," Mrs. Dupree says. "How are you?"

"Fine," whispers A'Kyah.

"That's a pretty outfit you have on. Yellow happens to be one of my favorite colors," says Mrs. Dupree.

A'Kyah smiles.

"You gonna make your grade?" asks Mrs. Dupree.

A'Kyah nods.

"Open your mouth!" Tony yells.

"Yes, ma'am," says A'Kyah.

"She's a pretty smart kid," Tony says, with pride. "Her only problem at school is her behavior. We got to work on that temper of hers. She got that from her mama."

Xavier is staring at me again. I wish he would stop that.

"Daddy, I've done all my homework. I need you to check it," says A'Kyah.

"Yeah, yeah," Tony says boastfully. "No problem, no problem. Daddy gone make sure you straight."

This should be real interesting, considering *Daddy* dropped out of school in the ninth grade.

"I feel bad about not bringing y'all something to eat," Mrs. Dupree says.

"Awwww, don't worry 'bout that," Tony says, with a wave of his hands.

"I wish I had," Mrs. Dupree says, chuckling. "'Cause Eva and I are hungry."

A'Kyah abruptly turns to me. "You hungry?" she asks loudly, with a big frown. "I don't see how! You had that big ole nasty barbecue sandwich and *all* them hush puppies on the way here!"

"Swine?" Tony asks, scowling monstrously.

"Swine!" A'Kyah replies, with a nod.

Help me, Lord!

"Oh, baby girl, no, no, no," Tony says, shaking his head at me. "Don't eat that garbage. You defiling your body! Your body is a temple, girl. You pollute it when you put filth like pork inside it. I see I got to school you on what pork does to the body."

No, this crackhead, petty thief, in-and-out-of-the-penitentiary thug didn't just say he needs to school me. How dare *he*, of all people, sit in judgment of me and accuse me of defiling my body! I'm glad I got my father's complexion, because if I were light-skinned like Mama, I'd be beet red. I take a deep breath and look away, hoping Tony gets the message that I don't care to hear anything he has to say.

"Eva, do you know what's fed to hogs?" Tony asks.

I yawn. *Help me, Lord!* I deal with taxing people all week long; I can't fraternize with them on the weekend, too. *Gina! Hurry back home!*

"Huh, Eva?" Tony asks, tapping me on the shoulder.

"Slop!" A'Kyah answers loudly.

"Baby, you had any swine since you been at Eva's?" Tony asks.

"No, Daddy."

"What Eva been feeding you?" asks Tony.

I look at Tony and want to say, "More than you ever have."

A'Kyah smacks her lips. "Eva don't cook. I don't think she really know how," she says, giggling. "We eat at her mama, daddy, and sister's houses."

Tony throws his head back and laughs. "That's why she ain't got no man. Ain't *no* man gone marry a woman that can't cook. The way to a man's heart is through his stomach. Ain't that right, Mama Dupree?"

Ahhhhh! Give me strength now, Lord!

"I don't know about that," Mrs. Dupree says slowly. "I wasn't much of a cook when I first got married, and I still can't cook some things. Xavier can tell you that."

"I personally like to fool around in the kitchen every now and then," Xavier says, with a chuckle. "So it won't be a problem if my wife is not a great cook."

Tony smirks. "Yeah, right."

"And as far as pork goes," Xavier says, with a big, dimple-cheek grin, "pork chops smothered in gravy, honey-baked ham, pork roast, crispy fried bacon . . . mm-mm, now that's some good eating." Rubbing his stomach, he adds, "And don't forget the chitlins!"

Tony and A'Kyah both gasp out loud. I don't know who is making the ugliest face of the two: the goon or his mouthy daughter. They're both looking at Xavier as if he's a big, stinking chitlin. I burst out laughing.

Xavier laughs, too, and winks at me.

"Man, y'all ignorant!" Tony says gruffly.

What? Uh-uh. I know that scrawny thug didn't just call me *ignorant*! I'm not about to let him get away with that!

"Tony, pork does not defile a person's body," I say.

"Amen!" Mrs. Dupree says, clapping her hands. "You need to read the Bible, Tony."

Tony grunts and makes another ugly face. "That's what the White man's religion would have you believe."

"And what is the White man's religion?" Mrs. Dupree asks.

"Christianity!" cries Tony.

I wish he would shut up and look over his daughter's homework. "Christianity is not the White man's religion," I say defensively.

"That's right!" Mrs. Dupree exclaims, waving her hands. "Christianity is for everybody!"

"Since I became a Muslim, my eyes have been opened to a lot of things," Tony says somberly. "I can get y'all some literature on what pork does to the body, and on how Christianity ain't nothing mo' than a tool of the White man to enslave Black people."

Help him, Lord. I wonder how much Islamic literature he actually reads. I bet he'd be hard pressed to find any promoting a lifestyle of crime and drug use. "No thank you, Tony," I say quite dryly. "I'm *not* interested."

"Me either," Mrs. Dupree says, rising to her feet. "I'm gonna pray for you, Tony," she says, patting him on the back. "In the meantime, have a good visit with your daughter."

"Okay, Mama Dupree," says Tony.

"It was nice meeting you, Eva," Mrs. Dupree says, extending her hand.

"It was nice meeting you, too, Mrs. Dupree," I say, standing to shake her hand.

I watch Xavier and his mother disappear into the administration building and wonder about the story there. I find handsome, articulate Xavier intriguing. He seems so out of place here. There's something about him that sets him apart from Tony and the other inmates in the yard. I'm a pretty good judge of character, and my gut tells me he's not what he appears. Maybe, he's not an inmate after all, but an undercover agent of some kind *posing* as an inmate.

"Eva, I'm serious," Tony says, interrupting my feverish thoughts of espionage at Hayesfield Correctional Center. "You need to leave that pork alone."

I sit back down and look Tony dead in the eye. "Don't worry about my health, okay? The things that truly defile a person's body are banned by the FDA."

He squints. "FDA?"

"Food and *Drug* Administration," I say.

"Um, ye-yeah, right, right," he says, looking embarrassed.

"Daddy, can we get started on my schoolwork?" A'Kyah asks, rolling her eyes at me on the sly.

"Yeah, baby," he says, pulling on his kufi. "Let's get to work."

A'Kyah gets up and moves over to the other side of the picnic table, where Mrs. Dupree and Xavier had been sitting. Tony follows her.

I look at my watch; it's 2:11. Another forty-nine minutes to go! *Lord, please don't let Tony say anything else to me today.*

The bubbly woman's children run over to one of the water coolers up near the entrance to the administration building. I get up to go get a cup of water, and the door to the administration building opens. Xavier steps outside. I sit back down. Mm-mm, he is some kinda fine, all six feet four of him.

Xavier goes over to one of the water coolers, fills a Styrofoam cup with water, and returns to the picnic table where A'Kyah, Tony, and I are sitting.

"I wish I could offer you something to eat," Xavier says, smiling down at me. "This is the best I can do," he says, extending his hand with the Styrofoam cup in it.

"Thank you," I reply, taking the cup from his hand.

"You're quite welcome, Eva. And I'll get you more if you like," Xavier says, with a big smile.

"Thanks," I reply.

"May I sit down?" asks Xavier.

You sure can, Undercover Brotha. "I don't care," I say.

"I don't want to bother you," says Xavier.

"Man, she said she didn't care. Sit down!" Tony says, laughing.

I grit my teeth and exhale.

Xavier sits down next to me and leans in close. "Don't pay him any attention," he whispers.

"I'm not," I whisper back.

Xavier laughs.

"Are you expecting another visitor?" I ask.

"No," Xavier says.

"No?" I ask.

Xavier shakes his head.

No more visitors today for Undercover Brotha. Is my imagination getting the best of me? Is he an agent or another lowlife like Tony? I take a couple sips of water, try to check him out on the sly, and catch him eyeing me. "So, tell me something about yourself, Xavier."

"What would you like to know?" Xavier asks.

I look at my watch; it's 2:13 now. "Anything you want to tell me."

Xavier smiles and clasps his hands together. "Well, I was born and raised right here in good old Hayesfield. My father's a farmer, his father was a farmer, and as fate would have it, I'm destined to follow in their footsteps."

"No kidding?" I say. Is he feeding me a bunch of malarkey to guard his *true* identity?

"My father is the largest Black landowner in Hayesfield," Xavier says proudly. "He owns fifteen hundred acres of land, which have been in our family for more than sixty years."

"Is that right?" I say.

"Uh-huh. And I plan to add to that when I get out of here."

"You don't say?" I reply.

"My father is actually in negotiations right now with several small landowners wanting to sell their farms. There's an elderly gentlemen in Fairview." Xavier smiles at me. "Hunter Exum. Do you know him?"

I swallow dryly. "Not personally."

"He has one hundred acres that he wants to sell. My father met with him last week," says Xavier.

Oh, my goodness! I think he is an inmate.

"Eva?" says Xavier.

"Huh?" I mumble.

"Are you all right?" asks Xavier.

"Oh"—I fan myself with my hands—"I'm fine."

"You need more water?" asks Xavier.

"No, no. Thank you," I reply.

Xavier smiles. "I went to college at—"

I got to know if I am sitting here conversing with an inmate. What he's told me sounds believable. But he would have to tell a believable story of some kind to conceal his identity if he is indeed an undercover agent.

"Listen," I whisper, leaning close to him. "I can keep a secret."

Xavier frowns and looks puzzled.

"Are you really an inmate?" I whisper.

He shoots me a surprised look. "Huh?"

"Are you *really* an inmate?" I whisper again.

"Eva," he says, laughing, "why do you ask?"

I catch Tony stealing glances in our direction, so I hold the Styrofoam cup up to my mouth. "You don't look like you belong here. You're a police officer or federal agent doing undercover work, right?"

Xavier bursts out laughing.

"What y'all talking 'bout?" Tony asks. "What's so funny?"

Xavier laughs louder.

"Shhhhh!" A'Kyah says loudly.

"I-I'm sorry, A'Kyah," Xavier says, collecting himself.

"Yeah, keep it down, man. We trying to work over here," Tony says, rubbing his forehead.

I almost burst out laughing at Tony. It's obvious from the pained expression on his face that A'Kyah's math work is proving to be quite difficult for him. I hope he doesn't make the mistake of changing her right answers to wrong answers.

"I don't mean to laugh at you, Eva," Xavier says, looking deeply into my eyes. "Thank you. That's the nicest thing I've heard in a long time. I wish it were true."

"It's not?" I ask.

Xavier shakes his head.

"It's not?" I repeat.

"No, it's not," murmurs Xavier.

I was wrong! He's an inmate, a convict, a criminal like Tony! "For real?" I hear myself ask.

Xavier sighs and looks off.

"So, you really are an inmate?" I say.

"Yes," replies Xavier.

Poor thing. No, uh-uh. I can't feel sorry for him; he committed a crime, and like Tony, he's where he's supposed to be, in prison.

"It's a beautiful day, isn't it?" Xavier asks, looking skyward.

"Yeah," I say, still trying to process the horrible truth about this handsome creature sitting next to me.

"Forgive me for staring at you earlier," Xavier says, flashing that adorable dimple-cheek grin of his. "I couldn't help myself. You're a beautiful woman."

Okay, now he's hitting on me. I recall what Joel told me and Willnetta about the lines and con games inmates run on women in an effort to charm their way into women's hearts and homes. "They are master manipulators," Joel said, "and pros at eliciting sympathy and female companionship."

Handsome Xavier can cease with his flattering come-ons. I might be lonely, but I'll be doggone if I'm lonely to the point of wanting affection from a man behind prison bars, regardless of how fine he is.

"Save the line, okay?" I say.

The dimple disappears, and a puzzled look crosses Xavier's face. "Line?"

"Yes, line. I've heard all about the *lines* and con games y'all run on women," I say.

"No, no," Xavier says rather gravely. "I'm not running a line on you, Eva. Please believe that."

Man, he's good. He sounds sincere and actually looks offended.

"Ooooh!" A'Kyah exclaims, giggling and pointing at Freda and Clarence. They're French-kissing up a storm.

"Shhhh!" Tony says, laughing.

My eyes drift to Xavier's full, luscious-looking lips. I wonder who he French-kisses out here in the rec yard. From the comment he made earlier about not caring if his wife was a great cook, I gather he's not married, but it's not wise to assume things.

"No wife or girlfriend, Xavier?" I say.

"No," he replies.

"I find that hard to believe," I say.

"It's the truth," he replies, with a slight smile. "I was married once. I married my college sweetheart. The marriage ended in divorce eleven years ago. And, as far as a girlfriend goes, my fiancée broke up with me two months into my sentence."

How awful! But then again, I can't blame her or any woman for not wanting to be engaged to a jailbird!

Xavier hunches up his shoulders. "Never in a million years," he says, looking off in the distance, "would I have thought that I would end up in prison."

"How did you end up here? If you don't mind me asking," I say.

The broad shoulders drop, and Xavier presses his lips together.

"I'm sorry. I don't mean to pry," I add hastily.

"No, no," he says, smiling at me. "I don't mind you asking. It's a story I've told so many times, and not many people believe me."

Could it be because it's a lie? I hope he doesn't think he's gone sway me with it. I smile at him. "What happened?" I ask.

"Two years ago, I engaged in a business transaction that turned out to be a sham." Xavier shakes his head and sighs heavily. "I purchased what turned out to be stolen merchandise, valued at seventy-five thousand dollars, for a clothing store a frat brother and I were on the verge of opening in Raleigh."

"Whaaat?" I say.

"It was a set up, Eva, and I blindly walked into it," says Xavier.

He really is an inmate! "What type of clothing store were you two opening?" I ask.

"It was going to be a men's apparel store, just like our stores in Charlotte," replies Xavier.

"Stores?" I ask.

"We owned two," says Xavier.

"Business must have been good for you to be opening a third," I say.

"Business was very good," says Xavier. "The stores were a success from the time we opened them five years ago. And because of that, we decided to open a third one, in Raleigh. With my parents getting older, and me wanting to move back home to help out more on the farm and start up some new ventures with my father, I thought Raleigh would be the ideal location for the new store." Xavier drops his head, sighs, and then looks back up at me. "You have no idea how many times I wish I had taken things slower and looked more closely at *who* I was doing business with."

"Is your frat brother locked up, too?" I ask.

"Yes," replies Xavier.

"Here?" I ask.

"No, he's serving his sentence up in the mountains," says Xavier.

He really is an inmate!

"I've ruined his life," Xavier says sadly. "He was running for a city council position at the time and had a very good chance at being elected. He and his wife were also expecting their second child. She almost miscarried."

"So you really *are* an inmate?" I hear myself ask.

"Yes, Eva. I'm a *convicted* felon," mumbles Xavier.

What a shame that this handsome, college-educated, articulate Black man resorted to a life of crime! I don't buy for one minute his story of being an innocent party to larcenous conduct. Inmates lie; Joel said they do.

"Is this the first time you've been arrested and convicted of anything?" I ask.

"Yes," Xavier whispers.

"I'm surprised you didn't get probation," I reply.

Xavier scoffs. "The ADA offered me probation, if I would confess to willful criminal misconduct. I couldn't do that."

I look over at Tony and A'Kyah. They're working on the apology letter to Mrs. Hodges. "When will you be eligible for parole?"

"This July," says Xavier.

I look back at Xavier. "Do you think the parole board is going to buy that *story* you just told me?"

"It's not a lie, Eva. It's the truth," says Xavier.

"Not many inmates own up to their crimes, Xavier," I say and look over at Tony, who has yet to fess up to his criminal wrongdoing.

"That may be true. But I'm no criminal. I would never steal or take something that didn't belong to me," Xavier says quite convincingly.

Maybe he's telling the truth. The social worker in me wants to believe he is. Now I feel sorry for him. If he's telling the truth, then he, like an increasing number of people across the state, the country even, has gotten a bum rap. *How awful!*

"God knows," he says softly, "I'm no criminal. I pray daily that I make parole so I can get home and help my father. He needs me now more than ever."

"You sound like a dutiful son," I say.

"I *love* my parents, and this has been so hard on them, especially my father. I don't know what I'll do if"—he pauses and shakes his head—"he becomes ill while I'm locked up."

"Try not to think that way. If that were to happen, you would need to pray for strength. Are you a Christian?" I ask.

"Yes," murmurs Xavier.

"Then God will help you through the difficulty," I say softly.

"My father wanted me to stay in the military and be a career officer. That was his dream for me. He's a Vietnam vet. But after twelve years of service, I'd had enough. I wanted to do something with my business degree."

"So you feel you've disappointed your father?" I ask.

"I do."

"Sometimes the choices we make in order to live the lives we envision for ourselves meet with disapproval from others."

"Mine have caused me many sleepless nights. When I leave this awful place, I have to live with the stigma of being an ex-convict for the rest of my life. My life will *never* be as it was before, Eva. People may never, ever respect me again."

"Time is a healer. It will allow you to redeem yourself in the eyes of those dear to you, I assure you."

"I hope so."

"Believe so."

"Thanks for that," Xavier says, looking deeply into my eyes.

"You don't have to thank me."

"Yes, I do. What you've said is very encouraging. Not only are you beautiful, you're also very kind."

"Stop with the come-ons, okay?"

Xavier laughs.

Good gosh! What a sexy laugh!

"Do you like flowers?" Xavier asks, with a big smile.

"Yes! I'm an avid gardener."

"What's your favorite flower?"

"I have several favorites. But, if I had to choose one, it would be the lily," I reply.

"Visitation is over! All visitors exit the rec yard! Inmates remain seated!" a burly correctional officer yells.

I glance at my watch; it's three o'clock sharp. I finish my water and stand.

"I'll take that for you," Xavier says.

I hand him the empty cup. "Thanks, and I wish you the best, Xavier."

Six more correctional officers have joined the others already on the rec yard. Women, children, and inmates are embracing each other. A'Kyah has her arms wrapped tightly around Tony's waist.

"All visitors exit the rec yard! Inmates remain seated!" the officer yells again.

"A'Kyah, it's time to go," I say.

"It's really nice of you, Eva, to take care of A'Kyah," Xavier says.

"It's the least I can do for a friend," I say.

"From what I've been told, you're a very generous woman," says Xavier.

I don't bother to respond to Xavier's comment. "A'Kyah, let's go," I say.

"Go on," Tony says, prying A'Kyah's arms from around his waist.

"Daddy, I'll see you next Saturday," says A'Kyah.

"Okay, baby. Remember, be good," replies Tony.

"I will," she promises.

"I'll write you tonight," Tony says.

"You can call me, Daddy. I'll give you Eva's number," replies A'Kyah.

"No!" I cry. Ooops. That came out a little too loud. I take a deep breath. "It's best that you write, Tony, okay?"

"Sure, sure," Tony says, bobbing his head. "No problem."

A'Kyah cuts her eyes up at me.

Sorry, kid. I ain't about to incur a phone bill on your daddy's account. I file in behind the women and children heading into the administration building, look back to see if A'Kyah is behind me, and see Xavier staring at me, smiling.

"Yo, yo, Eva!" Tony yells.

What do you want? "Yes, Tony," I shout.

"How long you had that Lexus?" yells Tony.

"Awhile," I say.

"Is that metallic gray or black?" Tony shouts.

"Black," I reply.

"It's sweet, girl! Sweet! I want an Escalade," he says, sounding like a kid. "Top of the line!"

I wave good-bye and shove A'Kyah inside the administration building. When I pull out of the parking lot, I see that the inmates have gathered at the fence and are looking out at the road. I find myself searching the crowd for Xavier; I don't see him. When Pastor McKnight leads us in altar prayer tomorrow and petitions God on behalf of the prison bound, I will remember him and the other inmates at Hayesfield Correctional Center.

8

Sunday Joy

"There's a balm in Gilead! Hallelujah! Thank you, Lord! And it's healing for your soul!" proclaims Mr. T, Gospel 680's multitalented radio personality, kicking off his Sunday morning gospel program. "Now, saints, let's pray." While Mr. T. prays, "Keep Looking Up," a cut from his quartet group's latest CD, plays softly in the background.

I'll be "in the house" at Community Baptist this Sunday morning, and A'Kyah, too, despite her protests about not having anything to wear. The Spring Carnival is in town for a week, and if she weren't on punishment, we'd be heading there after the service. I love carnivals and really want to go. William is taking Teresa this afternoon. I wonder if Preston likes carnivals. I hope so. Maybe he'll take me when he gets back. Boy, I would love to be snuggled up next to him on the Ferris wheel.

I turn off the radio. "A'Kyah! Let's go!"

"Okay," she whines, shuffling into the kitchen.

"Now what's wrong with that dress? It's pretty."

"No, it's not," she says, smacking her lips.

"I disagree."

After leaving the prison yesterday, I stopped by Gina's apartment so A'Kyah could get more school clothes and a dress for church. She's wearing the lavender sundress that Tony's mother gave her for Easter.

"I don't have money to put in the collection plate."

I reach into my purse and retrieve two dollars. "Here."

"Thank you," she mumbles.

I take one last peek at my puffy eyes in the mirror by the door, then follow her outside.

Gina phoned late last night with news that she's decided to move back to St. Louis. Provided Mrs. Williams's condition doesn't worsen, she'll be home Saturday to tell A'Kyah and clean out her apartment. I'm going to miss Gina, but I understand and fully support her decision to be near her aged, ailing mother. Still, every time I think about how much I'm going to miss her worrisome butt, tears fill my eyes. We talked and cried last night for two hours as we reminisced about our friendship.

Gina made her first trip to Fairview on my thirtieth birthday. Her second day in town, she meets Tony. She had gone to the supermarket to get ice cream and ingredients for a cream cheese pound cake, and was accosted by him in front of the Chinese takeout, where he was loitering with his "boyz," selling imitation Coach bags. He wooed her with his "sexy grin" and rendition of Michael Jackson's "Pretty Young Thing." She returned to my house an hour later, love struck, with two new pocketbooks and a half gallon of melted Neapolitan ice cream, babbling about moving to North Carolina. True to her word, she flew back to St. Louis, packed her belongings in her Grand AM, and hit the road to Fairview. Returning home will be easier for her now, since her ten-year, on-and-off, tempestuous love affair with Tony has finally ended. I hope the news is not too devastating for A'Kyah. I glance over at her as a tear slips out of the corner of my eye. I wipe it away and head to church.

* * *

"Ooooh, that's so pretty!" A'Kyah exclaims, pointing to the painting in the choir loft.

I smile down at her. The twenty-by-thirty serene painting of the Jordan River always generates oohs and ahhs from visitors to our church.

Mama is standing up front, talking to some members of the Pastor's Aid Committee, a committee she's chaired for the last two years. She motions for us to come sit up front with her. I shake my head and lead A'Kyah to seats in the middle of the church. Mama has a tendency to make funny comments about fellow parishioners, and I don't want A'Kyah, or me for that matter, giggling throughout the service, only to be chastised later by Geraldine for "ungodly conduct."

A junior usher hands us programs, which have inserts inside about the upcoming annual Summer Bazaar. The bazaar, the Thanksgiving food drive, and the Christmas cheer program are Pastor and Mrs. McKnight's pet projects and are very successful fund-raisers. All monies raised at the bazaar fund summer activities for children at a nearby orphanage, where Mrs. McKnight serves as board member. Since being at Community Baptist, she and Pastor McKnight have adopted two children from the orphanage.

In the eight years that the McKnights have been at Community Baptist, the membership has soared from two hundred active members to nearly five hundred. I naturally clicked with the kindhearted, on-fire-for-the-Lord couple and have been a staunch supporter of their kingdom-building efforts. Under Pastor McKnight's leadership, the church has truly become one that ministers to people locally and abroad. It provides remedial and wellness programs for children and adults, as well as clothing, food, and financial aid for needy residents. AA and NA meetings are held weekly at the church, and a free dinner is provided to the public every second and fourth Wednesday night, before bible study. I'm proud to call Community Baptist my church, and I serve dutifully on the missionary board and as vice president of the hospitality committee. My parents were married here, and my sisters and

I grew up here, singing in the youth choir. Since Mama and Daddy's divorce, Daddy has moved his membership to Miss Elsie's church, a smaller Baptist church across town.

Teresa grew up in Community Baptist along with me and is one of the lead soloists in the gospel choir. Nobody at the church can sing "He's Sweet, I Know" like her. When she starts in on the third verse of that hymn, there's not a dry eye in the sanctuary. Sweet Singing Sister Tee, as pastor calls her, won't be at church today; she's home chirping love songs and getting ready for her second date with William.

Geraldine smiles at me when she takes a seat beside Mrs. McKnight, on the front pew in the Deaconess and Mothers Corner. Tall, slender, and almond-colored, with shoulder-length hair like me, my big sister is a human dynamo. Since entering the ministry as an evangelist four years ago, she's been a relentless disciple in God's vineyard. I glance over at the Deacons and Trustees Corner, at her better half, Cleveland. A doting husband, father, son-in-law, and brother-in-law, he's a trustee and Sunday school teacher. Together, he and Geraldine counsel couples through the church's couples' ministry and oversee the foreign missionary department. Every summer they spend two weeks in an African country, spreading the gospel and assisting with relief projects.

A'Kyah is asleep when Pastor McKnight stands in the pulpit to feed us "manna from on high." Small in stature, with a booming voice, he thanks God for allowing us to fellowship with one another "one mo' time" and then instructs us to open our Bibles to 1 Corinthians 13.

Pastor McKnight delivers a soul-stirring message on charity. It's a timely message for me and empowers me to patiently and lovingly attend to A'Kyah for however long she's in my care. Not only a charismatic and dynamic speaker, Community Baptist's undershepherd is a gifted soloist, too. He ends his sermon by singing "Precious Lord."

A chorus of "hallelujah" and "glory" rings out from the Deaconess and Mothers Corner. The shouters in that corner are typically the mothers. Two junior ushers and the church nurse run over and stand guard with paper fans just in case Aunt Della Mae and the other church mothers become faint from praising God.

When the shouting wanes, Pastor McKnight extends the invitation for Christian discipleship. A family of five and a young woman accept the invitation, and praises to God ring out again. As the second round of "hallelujah" and "glory" dies down, the congregation is summoned to the altar for prayer. I wake A'Kyah and lead her up front.

With uplifted hands, Pastor McKnight prays for the new converts and then petitions the Lord to heal and comfort the sick, weary, and troubled across the land. "Please Lord," I pray, thinking of Mrs. Williams, Gina, and A'Kyah. When Pastor McKnight asks God to have mercy on the prison bound, I hear A'Kyah say, "Please, Jesus." I give her hand a gentle squeeze and say, "Please, Jesus," too.

After the prayer and benediction, I hightail it over to Aunt Della Mae, who is still caught up in the spirit. Miss Ida is fanning her and patting her face with a lacy white handkerchief. Between a "thank you, Jesus!" and "hallelujah!" she manages to tell me that Willnetta will be home around four.

After saying good-bye to Mama, Geraldine, and a host of other folks, A'Kyah and I exit the church and skip across the parking lot, singing "This Little Light of Mine."

"Eva!"

A'Kyah and I stop skipping and singing and look back.

"Hold up, girl!" Jo Ann yells, waving at me. "I'm parked right next to you." Walking alongside the notorious gossip is her sister and two women who stood up when the secretary acknowledged visitors.

I turn back around. Jo Ann's red GEO Tracker, with her nickname, Delicious, airbrushed on a vanity plate, is backed in the parking space next to mine. I groan out loud.

"Who's that?" A'Kyah asks.

"Walk fast!" I say, shoving her ahead of me.

"Wait!" Jo Ann hollers.

Jo Ann's heels clicking rapidly on the pavement as she runs

to catch up with us makes me quicken my step. As I approach my SUV, I press the keyless entry button twice and tell A'Kyah to get inside and buckle up.

"Whew!" Jo Ann says, falling onto the Tracker, with a thud. "I'm outta shape!"

I flash a phony smile at her.

"Uh, isn't that your friend Gina's li'l girl?" Jo Ann asks, peering into my SUV.

"Yes."

"I told my sister that's who she was. Ain't her daddy locked up *again*?" she asks softly, turning up her nose. "He stay in trouble. For the life of me, I don't know what your friend sees in that sorry man."

I open the car door and step up on the running board. "They aren't dating anymore," I say before Jo Ann fires off another question or comment. I want to tell her who Gina dates is none of her business, but I don't.

"Oh, that's good. Where your sidekick? It ain't like Teresa to miss service. Willnetta comin' home today, right?"

I don't answer Jo Ann's nosy questions. I hand A'Kyah my pocketbook, sit down in the driver's seat, and reach to close the door. Jo Ann grabs it. I stare at her gaudy hand. Flashy rings are on every finger, and her one-inch fingernails are polished a bright orange. I imagine myself pounding away at the hand with one of my pumps.

"Eva, I know," she says, shaking her head, "Willnetta's weddin' just 'bout bankrupt Miss Della Mae and Mr. Lee."

I grit my teeth.

Jo Ann continues. "That reception had to have cost a fortune. All that food! *And* them fancy decorations!"

I put the key in the ignition and start the engine.

Jo Ann's sister and the two women come over and stand next to her.

"I still can't get over how much Willnetta's dress cost," Jo Ann says, opening her bug eyes wide. "And I bet Miss Della Mae jack up prices at D & L and make customers, loyal customers like me," she says, jabbing herself in the chest, "who didn't even get invited to that *extravagant* reception, foot that bill and pay for that eight-thousand-dollar wedding dress. And that ain't right!"

"Naw, it ain't!" her sister mutters.

I tug at the car door. "Jo Ann, we have to go."

"Your aunt may find herself in the po' house!" Jo Ann says, snapping her fingers. "'Cause if she and Mr. Lee couldn't afford that big weddin' and *extravagant* reception, they shouldna had it!" Jo Ann looks over at her sister.

"That's right!" her sister yells, bobbing her head.

It's hot outside, and Jo Ann is making me sick and hotter. Perspiration starts trickling down my face; I turn on the air-conditioning. *Jesus, give me strength!* I just left a wonderfully inspiring service, and before I can get off the church grounds, this ignoramus is trying my patience. But I will not, no, I *will not*, let her rob me of my joy or get away with her unfair criticism of Aunt Della Mae.

"For your information," I hear myself say calmly, "my aunt is a long, long way from being *bankrupt*. She's still"—I snap my fingers—"rolling in dough. And I haven't heard anything about the prices at the restaurant going up. But if that's true, it's about time. They haven't changed in years. And if *you* or anyone else chooses to stop patronizing the business because of that, so be it. My aunt will, however, continue to make money hand over fist."

Jo Ann and her sister shoot me a naw-she-didn't-go-there look.

"And Willnetta's dress didn't cost eight thousand dollars. It was eighteen thousand," I add.

Jo Ann gasps, clutches her chest, and falls back onto her Tracker. Her eyes look like they're about to pop out of their sockets.

I close the car door, wave good-bye, put my SUV in reverse, and speed out of the parking lot.

"You don't like her do you?"

I look over at A'Kyah and shake my head.

* * *

A'Kyah and I are singing "Jesus Loves Me" when I pull into my driveway. Mrs. Jennings and her grandchildren are exiting their minivan, dressed in their Sunday best.

"Miss Eva! Can A'Kyah come out and play?" one of the six-year-old twin girls asks, running into the yard.

A'Kyah shoots me a pitiful, pleading look.

"No, she can't," I reply.

"You still on lockdown, girl?" sixteen-year-old Keisha, the oldest grandchild, asks, grinning.

A'Kyah nods and slowly walks up on the porch. I unlock the door, and she heads inside, down the hall, to her eleven-by-twelve cell. Now I feel like a correctional officer. When I look in on A'Kyah later, she's reading a library book.

I change into jeans and a T-shirt. A'Kyah's comment about me not being able to cook has made me want to prove her wrong. I'm going to fix her a spaghetti dinner that rivals her grandmother's. I call Willnetta's house and leave a message welcoming her home, with a request that she call me as soon as she puts her bags down.

A'Kyah and I are having dinner when the phone rings at 5:20. I dash to it, hoping it's Willnetta, but I see from caller ID that it's Teresa.

"Hey, girl," I say into the receiver.

"Hey."

"You still at the carnival?"

"Yeah."

"Don't forget our candy apples."

"I won't."

"You having fun?"

"Nope!"

"What's wrong?"

"Oh, Eva! It's not going to work out."

"Teresaaa!"

"William has too many personal problems. His cell phone has rung ten times since he's picked me up. If it's not an *ex-wife* or one of his children, it's his *ex-girlfriend*."

"What?"

"Drama, girl!" she says, sighing.

"I'm sorry, Teresa."

"And to think, I spent three hundred dollars yesterday on two pairs of low-heel shoes!"

"Where is William now? On the phone again?"

"Gone to get us some roasted corn. Oh! Here he comes! I'll stop by later. Bye!"

Poor Teresa. I rejoin A'Kyah at the dining table and pick at my food. I've lost my appetite now. A'Kyah appears to be enjoying her dinner. She's having a third serving of spaghetti and looking out the window at Mrs. Jennings's grandchildren. They're splashing around in their pool.

"You want me to clean up?" she asks.

"Yes, and thanks for asking."

I toss my half-eaten dinner in the trash and go to my bedroom and stare at the clock. When is Willnetta going to call? I fear that her flight has been delayed, or worse, that she's tied up with Aunt Della Mae. All I need is a few minutes of her time.

I dial Geraldine's number and tell Jalisa I'll need her to come watch A'Kyah while I run over to Willnetta's. When the phone rings at 6:11, I jump off the bed. Caller ID shows that it's Willnetta calling.

"Willnetta!"

"Hey!"

"How are you?"

"Fabulous!" she says breathlessly.

I laugh. "How was the honeymoon?"

"Great!"

"Can't wait to hear about it."

"I brought you a souvenir back."

"Thanks!"

"You're welcome. So what's up?"

"I know the last thing you probably want right now is company, but I really need to see you. I won't stay long, I *promise*."

"Are you okay?"

"I'm fine. I want to ask you about somebody that works in the school system with you."

"Who?"

"I'll tell you when I see you."

"All right. Come on over. Mama's on her way!"

"Okay, bye!" *Lord, please don't let Aunt Della Mae beat me to Willnetta's.*

I call Jalisa. When she pulls into the driveway two minutes later, I'm outside, raring to go.

It's a beautiful, pricey subdivision on the outskirts of town where Willnetta lives. The homes, which start at three hundred thousand dollars, all sit on one acre of land off wide streets. Lush green lawns and breathtaking landscaping surround the huge two- and three-story brick homes. Willnetta looks up and smiles broadly when I pull into her circular driveway. She's on the front porch, watering a pot of pink petunias. Her warm, copper-colored skin has darkened, tanned undoubtedly by the Caribbean sun. I park, run up on the porch, and embrace her.

"Where's Joel?" I whisper, releasing her.

"Gone to check on his grandparents. Ain't nobody here but me."

"What do you know about Preston Cooper?" I ask quickly.

A smile forms at Willnetta's mouth. "Ooooh, him."

"Why you say, 'Ooooh, him'?"

"Well, uh—"

"What is it, Willnetta?"

"What you want to know?"

"What you think?"

Willnetta laughs. "Okay, okay, hold up. Why this interest in Preston Cooper? Have you two met?"

"Yes!" I give Willnetta a rundown on my adventures in baby-sitting, which led to Preston and me meeting, followed by our chance encounter at the singles social.

"Girl, you've been busy!" she says.

"Yes, I have. Now stop asking me questions, and answer mine. What do you know about the doctor? Is he seeing anyone?"

"I've heard that women are running him down."

"I don't doubt that," I say, thinking about that woman Diane. "So why haven't you mentioned him to me?"

"He's kinda thin, and you don't like slim men."

"Girl, I'm forty years old. I can't afford to be that picky anymore, okay?"

Willnetta laughs.

I'm telling her about Teresa's short-lived fling when a blue Volvo Sedan speeds into the driveway. It's Aunt Della Mae, grinning like a child on Christmas morning.

"Welcome home, baby!" Aunt Della Mae yells, throwing open her car door.

It's time for me to go. Aunt Della Mae will be here a long time, and I'm not about to risk her overhearing me query Willnetta about a man. She wouldn't waste any time phoning Mama, telling her she believes I got a boyfriend.

"Eva! You couldn't wait till Willnetta got home, either, could you?" Aunt Della Mae cries, hugging Willnetta.

"No, Auntie, I couldn't," I reply.

"My baby's got herself a tan. Look at her!" Aunt Della Mae says, admiring Willnetta like she's a prized doll.

Willnetta cuts her eyes at me and then rolls them skyward.

I laugh and hug her again. "Welcome back. I'll talk to you later."

"You leaving?" Aunt Della Mae asks.

"Yeah. I just stopped by to welcome Willnetta home," I say.

"Okay, all right," replies Aunt Della Mae.

"Mama, let me say good-bye to Eva. You go inside. I'll be right in."

"Okay, baby. Bye, Eva," calls Aunt Della Mae.

"Bye," I reply.

When Aunt Della enters the house, Willnetta tells me she'll get the 4-1-1 on Preston. I give her a parting hug and leave, praying that the romantic sparks that flew between Preston and me the other night ignite into a steamy, fiery romance.

9

Lilies

The letter from Hayesfield Correctional Center is the first thing I pull out of the mailbox. I hand A'Kyah the letter from Tony and hustle inside to see if there's a message on the answering machine from Preston. It's been four days since the singles social, and he has not called me. And I know he's back from Miami. The first thing I asked A'Kyah yesterday when I picked her up from school was if she saw him; she said she did. And I caught a glimpse of him this morning, when I dropped her off at school.

I stare at the big, fat red zero on the answering machine display until the tears in my eyes make it a blur.

"Eva! I got something for you!" A'Kyah yells, running into the room. She hands me a small piece of white paper that's folded in half and stapled. *To Eva* is written on the outside. I pull the staples out.

10:09 p.m.
Sunday

May 5th
Dear Eva,

May God bless you for the unselfish act of love you've given Gina and Tony by caring for A'Kyah. It is the generosity of people like you that makes the world a wonderful place to live in.

I enjoyed talking with you yesterday. Thanks for listening and offering words of encouragement. You truly are a lovely lady, and that's no come-on.

God Bless,
Xavier

Yeah, yeah, yeah, whatever! I throw the note in the trash can, kick off my shoes, and fall back on the bed. I'm so depressed. A'Kyah, on the other hand, is happy as a lark. She's singing and dancing up a storm in the hall.

"A'Kyah!"

"Yes!"

"What you want for dinner?" *Lord, please don't let it be anything I'll have to cook.*

"Pepperoni pizza!"

"You got it!" I roll over, pick up the phone, and speed-dial Pizza Hut.

After helping A'Kyah with homework, I call Stephanie to unload. Baby sis is cramming for two exams. I wish her good luck on her finals, say bye, and speed-dial Teresa. The phone rings four times before she picks up. She's moping over things not working out with William and drowning her sorrows in a box of Godiva chocolates. I let her vent for thirty minutes before bidding her good night.

When Gina calls at 7:30, I'm in my nightshirt. She tells A'Kyah and me that she'll be back late Saturday afternoon for sure. A'Kyah shouts for joy. When Gina says good-bye to us at 7:52, I turn out my bedroom light and dive under the covers.

* * *

"What's that on the porch?" A'Kyah asks as I pull into my driveway.

I peer over my sunglasses. There's a large bouquet of pink flowers beside the front door. My heart flip-flops in my chest. "Flowers," I hear myself say breathlessly. I turn off the engine, fling open the car door, and sprint to the porch.

The flowers are lilies, beautiful pink lilies. The small white envelope sticking in the card caddy has my name on it; I remove the envelope and pull out the card.

> *These lilies symbolize your beauty and grace. A Secret Admirer*

"I got another letter from my daddy!" A'Kyah yells from the mailbox.

I read the card again, savoring each word. He sent me lilies! Lilies! I could just scream and do cartwheels across the yard! And just when I thought he'd forgotten all about me, he does this! *Oh, Dr. Cooper, you're full of surprises!*

"Pretty flowers," A'Kyah says, walking up on the porch. "What the card say?" she asks, smiling.

Now I can't tell her what Preston has written; she'd blab that all over school.

"Never mind!" she says, giggling.

I make a funny face at her. "Go get my keys and pocket-book, okay?"

A'Kyah runs off the porch, laughing.

I carefully pick up the bouquet and wait anxiously for her to return and unlock the front door. I can't wait to get inside and call the girls!

"C'mon, A'Kyah! You're moving like a snail!"

"Eva's got a boyfriend!" she sings, running up on the porch. She unlocks the front door, and I head straight to my bedroom. The lilies are going on my vanity. I want them to be the first things I see when I wake in the morning.

After finding a spot for the lilies on my crowded vanity, I call Teresa. She doesn't answer at home; I dial her mobile. She picks up during the first ring.

"What's up, girl?"

"Hold on! Let me get Willnetta on the line." I press the FLASH button and speed-dial Willnetta. Joel answers. I tell him to put Willnetta on the phone immediately.

Willnetta answers the phone, sounding like somebody having an asthma attack. I press the FLASH button and scream.

"What's wrong with you?" Teresa asks. "Ooooh! The doctor called?"

"No! He sent me flowers! And guess what kind!" I exclaim.

"Roses?" Teresa yells.

"No! My favorite, lilies!" I shriek.

"S-say whaaat?" Willnetta asks, still sounding like an asthmatic.

"Girl, what's wrong with you?" Teresa asks before I do.

Willnetta exhales and starts giggling.

"Ooooh!" Teresa and I exclaim.

Willnetta giggles some more.

"I can call you back," I say.

"No, go ahead. We're finished," Willnetta whispers, "for now."

"Oh, you so nasty!" Teresa says playfully.

"Nasty girrrl, oh you nasty girl!" I sing, sounding like Janet Jackson.

Willnetta laughs. "Oh, hush! Now tell me about these lilies you got today."

"Okay, okay. Y'all listen to this!" I read out loud the card that came with the lilies.

"Oh, how romantic!" Teresa cries.

"This looks *promising*, cousin," says Willnetta.

"So when is he going to call me?" I ask.

Willnetta clears her throat. "When he can give you his un-divided attention, so be patient. This is a busy time for school principals. They're administering end-of-the-year tests, planning year-end celebrations, making decisions about student retention and promotion—"

"Yeah, yeah, whatever!" Teresa says, interrupting. "Principal Cooper doesn't work twenty-four/seven."

Willnetta sighs. "No, he doesn't."

"Eva needs to dress up again and make another trip to the school office," says Teresa.

"No, she doesn't need to do that," replies Willnetta.

"Why not? She hasn't heard from the PTA president about volunteering. That could be her reason for going," says Teresa.

"The PTA president is not going to call her," Willnetta insists. "School is almost over. They don't need any more volunteers. Eva just needs to be patient. Patient. Preston sent the lilies, and he's gone call, sooner or later."

"But then again, we're not certain he sent the flowers, now are we?" says Teresa.

"Preston sent the flowers, Teresa. Who else?" I say.

"Otis Reid," Teresa replies, laughing.

Willnetta bursts out laughing.

"Uh-uh! As long as Otis has been sweating me, if he was going to send me flowers, I think he would have done it by now," I say.

"I'm just joking," Teresa says, laughing. "I believe they're from Preston."

"I believe so, too," Willnetta says softly.

I look over at the lilies. "Eva Liles-Cooper. That has a nice ring to it, doesn't it?"

"Yeah, it does," Teresa says.

I chat with Teresa and Willnetta for ten more minutes, hang up, and scurry into the kitchen to fix dinner. When Gina calls, I'm soaking in the bathtub, fantasizing about Preston. I tell her about my flowers. She suggests I put on a sexy outfit— sexy to her is hoochie mama—and strut into the school office tomorrow, demanding to see Preston, and not leave until I do. Now she would do something like that.

I crawl into bed at midnight. Unlike last night, I lie down

with a smile on my face. I can't sleep, because I'm still keyed up about the lilies. I turn on the TV and tune into *Midnight Love* on BET.

A'Kyah wakes me, waving a piece of paper in my face. "Eva, look over my math homework, please!"

"Marla and her six children need your help. Will you help them?" It's Larry Jones with *Feed The Children* on BET.

Oh no! I've overslept! I kick back the covers, jump out of bed, kiss the lilies, click off the TV, check over A'Kyah's homework, shower, dress, and still manage to get A'Kyah to school by eight. When I pull into the car-pool lane at Carver Elementary, Preston is curbside. He's smiling and chatting with a tall, well-dressed White woman. I want so badly to get out and walk over to him, but I'm too chicken to do it; I blow my horn instead. He looks over, smiles, and waves. I wave back. When I pull off, I look in the rearview mirror and see that he's looking in my direction. Yessss! I pray this passing encounter results in me *finally* getting a phone call tonight.

"Where've you been?" A'Kyah asks, scowling.

It's 6:11, and she's the only kid waiting to be picked up from the Y. I left work an hour early and met Teresa at Gold's Gym. After forty-five minutes on the treadmill, I did aerobics for an hour and fifteen minutes. I feel great.

"You gonna have to pay a late fee if you pick me up late again."

"Sorry. I won't be late anymore. What you want for dinner?"

"Pizza!"

"Noooo! No more pizza this week."

"Awww, c'mon, Eva!"

"No! How about hot dogs and baked beans?"

"We had that for lunch today."

Shoot!

"Oh, I almost forgot," she says matter-of-factly while reaching for the radio dial. "Dr. Cooper asked about you."

"He did!" I hear myself squeal.

A'Kyah scoffs and looks over at me. "Why you so happy 'bout that?"

"No reason," I lie. "So, what did he ask you?"

"How you were and if I was still staying with you."

"What did you say?"

"I told him you were fine and that I was still at your house."

"When did the two of you have this conversation?"

"This morning. Right after you dropped me off," she says, tuning into 97.5 FM.

"Great!"

"Huh?" she asks, turning down the radio.

"Um, I have a *great* idea for dinner."

"What?"

"Burgers and fries."

"Yessss!"

I pull into the drive-through lane at Hardee's and tell A'Kyah to order anything she wants. During the drive home, I wolf down a burger and pray Preston calls.

It's true what people say about a watched phone never ringing. It's nearing midnight; Preston hasn't called. I pick up the phone and call Teresa for the sixth time tonight. "He hasn't called!" I whine when she picks up.

"Wh-what's up with that?" she mutters.

"You tell me!"

"He's gone call."

"When? It doesn't look like it's going to be tonight. It's eleven forty-five!"

"Whaaaat?" she screams. "Girl, you better get off this phone and"—she yawns—"go to bed."

"He waved at me, Teresa, and asked A'Kyah how I was! So why hasn't he called?"

Teresa yawns again. "I dunno. Willnetta did say that he's probably swamped right now."

"A phone call? He can't make *one* phone call?"

Silence.

"Wake up, Teresa!"

"Wh-what you say?"

"Wake up and talk to me!"

"I'm awake. I hear you."

"Why hasn't Preston called me?"

"Call him?"

"Uh-uh, I ain't chasing him." Mama warned my sisters and me about chasing men. She told us if we had to chase after a man to get him, we'd have to chase after him to keep him.

"You won't be chasing him by calling."

"And what will I say is the reason for my call?"

"You want to know why he hasn't called you," she replies, laughing.

"Oh, you got jokes! I feel awful, and you're making jokes!"

"I'm sorry."

"I feel like crying!"

"Eva, stop tripping! Preston's gone call you before the week is out, I betcha."

"You think so?"

"Girl, he sent you flowers. *Expensive* flowers at that. He's gone call."

Teresa is making sense. Why would Preston send me flowers and not follow up with a phone call? As difficult as it's going to be, I'm gonna have to be patient. But it's been so long since I've felt this way about anybody. I'm like a hungry dog after a bone. I'm ready, desperately ready, for love.

10

Revelations

"Mama, those flowers are beautiful!" Geraldine says, with a mouth full of trout. "Just beautiful!"

"So, when you and Mr. P. going out?" Mama asks. We're sitting out on her deck, eating fish, hush puppies, and baked potatoes. A'Kyah is present, so we're calling Preston "Mr. P."

"As soon as he calls," I reply.

"You haven't heard from him yet?" Mama asks, creasing her brows.

I shake my head and tell Mama and Geraldine what Willnetta told me about this being a busy time of the year for folks like Mr. P.

"Otis doesn't stand a chance now, does he?" Mama asks, laughing.

"No!" I cry.

"Eva, is Mr. P. a Christian?" asks Geraldine.

"According to what little I know about him, Geraldine, he is," I say.

"A lot of folks say they're Christians, but their lifestyles indicate otherwise," says Geraldine.

"Amen," Mama says.

"Don't let a good-looking sweet talker fool you. The Bible tells us to beware of wolves in sheep's clothing," Geraldine adds.

I love my sister, and I know she means well, but I don't want to hear a sermon right now. "I'm being *very* careful, Geraldine. Don't you worry."

"You're blessed with an ability to discern things. Don't ever turn a blind eye to what's revealed to you, even if it causes you unhappiness," says Geraldine.

"I won't," I reply.

"My baby got flowers!" Mama sings, dancing in her seat and snapping her fingers. "Wedding bells may not be too far off. Leon! Eva's finally got herself a boyfriend!"

Leon sticks his head out the back door. "Oh yeah?"

"Yeah!" cries Mama.

"I have an admirer, okay?" I say.

"Does admirer and boyfriend mean the same thing?" A'Kyah asks.

"Yes!" Mama replies, with a big smile and finger snap.

"I know who Eva's boyfriend is," A'Kyah says, giggling.

"Oh, you dooo?" Mama asks, opening her eyes wide.

"Yes, ma'am. It's supposed to be a secret, and I'm not to tell," A'Kyah whispers.

"Oh, really?" Mama asks, leaning forward. "Tell us, child. Who is he?"

Geraldine and I look at each other and burst out laughing. I can't believe Preston would tell A'Kyah he sent me flowers.

A'Kyah looks at me and grins.

Mama fills her glass with more lemonade. "Who is it, A'Kyah?"

"Okay, I'll tell if y'all promise not to tell," whispers A'Kyah.

"Cross our hearts," Mama says.

"Xavier sent the flowers," says A'Kyah.

Mama's forehead wrinkles. "Xavier?"

"Uh-huh!" A'Kyah replies.

Xavier. The only Xavier I know is . . . Uh-uh! Uh-uh! I fall back in the chair.

"Who is Xavier?" Mama asks, looking from me to A'Kyah.

"He in prison with my daddy," A'Kyah informs her.

"Jesus!" Geraldine hollers.

"Whoa!" Leon exclaims, stepping outside.

Mama pounds the table with her fists, sending several hush puppies airborne. "What? Eva! What is she talking about?"

I open my mouth, but nothing comes out. I'm speechless.

"Why is some *convict* sending you flowers, Eva?" Mama screams.

"Mama, I have no idea why!" I shriek.

Geraldine starts humming softly "Nearer, My God, to Thee." She always hums or sings hymns when trouble springs up around her.

Mama hits her with a dish towel. "Stop humming, and help me get to the bottom of this mess!"

Mama is turning into a wild woman right before my eyes. Her nostrils are flared now, and her eyes are big and round. A'Kyah is looking at her with sheer terror in her eyes.

I can't believe this! I am *so* embarrassed! And all this time I thought Preston had sent me those lilies. I feel like a fool, like a fool! *Lord, please don't let this get out.* All I need is for somebody like that big mouth Jo Ann to get wind of this. I'd never live it down.

"Mama, I honestly don't know why he sent me flowers! I'm just as surprised as you!" I cry.

"My daddy say he likes you," says A'Kyah.

"You," Mama says, pointing to A'Kyah, "go in the house! Finish eating inside!"

"Calm down, Rose," Leon says. "A'Kyah, let's go check on Miss Ida."

"Yeah! Go, go!" Mama yells. "Go!"

A'Kyah jumps up from the table and runs off the deck.

Geraldine has stopped humming and is sitting stone still, with her eyes closed. She's probably praying now.

"I don't believe this!" Mama cries, placing her head in her hands.

"Me either!" I cry. Joel was right. Show an inmate a smidgen of kindness and he becomes a predator.

Mama looks up and narrows her eyes at me. "Are you not telling me something?"

Geraldine opens her eyes and looks at me, too.

"Mama! I'm insulted! Do you think I'm *that* desperate for a man? Huh?" I say. I dare not tell her I had a conversation with Xavier. She'd flip out for real.

"Lord, I would hope not," Mama whispers.

"I'm not! Okay?" I say.

"Something happened on Saturday to cause that man to send you flowers!" hollers Mama.

Help me, Lord!

"Mama, calm down," Geraldine says softly. "You know how friendly Eva is. She probably smiled at that inmate one time too many, and he took it the wrong way."

Mama exhales. "I can see that happening," she says, nodding. "I can. She's too friendly, too nice. People take her kindness for weakness. I've seen it happen too many times."

"Now, just because the man is locked up doesn't mean he's not entitled to kindness," Geraldine says. "Hebrews 13:3 instructs us to remember those that are in bonds."

Mama narrows her eyes at Geraldine. "Some lowlife— a murderer or rapist for all we know—is sweet on your sister, and you gone quote me a scripture."

Geraldine looks off and starts humming again.

"I'm going to personally take care of this tomorrow. I'm taking A'Kyah to visit Tony. I'll get Xavier straight," I say.

"Why're you going back?" Mama hollers. "Gina'll be here tomorrow. Let her take A'Kyah. You don't need to go back to that prison!"

"Even if she wanted to, Mama, Gina can't take A'Kyah. Don't you remember me telling you her visitation privileges were revoked?"

"Revoked?" Geraldine asks, wide-eyed. "For what?"

"Acting like a fool!" Mama says.

Geraldine looks at me.

I nod. "When I told you Gina was upset with Tony for not being able to talk his mother or sister into keeping A'Kyah, I didn't tell you how upset she got."

Geraldine throws up a hand. "Don't tell me. I don't want to know."

"Umph!" Mama says. "Now wouldn't that have been something if they'd called the sheriff on her?"

"Jesus!" Geraldine exclaims.

"For A'Kyah's sake, I'm so glad that didn't happen," I say. "And while I'd rather spend my Saturday afternoon somewhere other than Hayesfield Correctional Center, I'm going to take A'Kyah tomorrow, like I told Gina I would."

"And make sure you get that jailbird straight. And don't be nice doing it!" Mama says, pounding on the table. "This *Xavier* needs to get the message loud and clear that you ain't thinking 'bout his sorry—"

"Mama!" Geraldine screams, throwing up her hands.

"Behind!" Mama yells.

Geraldine looks at Mama and shakes her head. "Don't be ugly, Eva. Remember, you're a Christian."

I look down at the crispy golden brown piece of fish on my plate. I can't eat it. I'm sick to my stomach, and my head hurts. I get up, go inside, and flop down in one of the recliners in the den. Screams arouse me at 10:25. Mama, A'Kyah, and Leon are sitting across from me on the sofa, watching *Jurassic Park*. When the movie ends, A'Kyah and I head home. After she's in bed and asleep, I take the lilies off my vanity and toss them in the garbage can outside.

11

Mixed Emotions

"What's wrong with you, Eva?"

I look over at A'Kyah. She's looking at me, frowning.

"You look like you mad," she says.

I am, but she doesn't need to know that. "I'm just thinking. That's all," I say, smiling.

"What you thinking 'bout?"

"Work," I lie.

"When I finish school, I'ma go to college."

"Oh yeah?"

"Uh-huh. I want to either be a lawyer so I can keep innocent people like my daddy from going to jail or a social worker like you, who is always helping people."

I smile. "Both are excellent career choices."

A'Kyah smiles back and looks out her window. She's dressed cute in a pink peasant T, white Capris, and blue jelly sandals. Determined not to entice Xavier further, I'm purposely looking like a bum in faded jeans, an oversized navy T-shirt with bleach spots on the front, and my scruffy gardening sneakers.

At 1:00 sharp, A'Kyah and I make our way through the administration building, to the crowded visitation check-in area
and then to the rec yard. I sit at a table next to three Latino
women and five small children. Just like last Saturday, most
of the visitors are Black women and children.

A'Kyah goes over to the water coolers, where a group of
children has gathered. A tall, slender, elderly Black woman
carrying a big brown paper bag walks over and speaks to her.
A'Kyah points in my direction. The lady looks over and
waves; it's Mrs. Dupree.

"Hello, Eva!" Mrs. Dupree yells, hurrying over.

I smile and throw up my hand.

"I brought us something to eat this time," she says, placing
the bag on the table. "I hope you and A'Kyah are hungry."

"Mrs. Dupree, you didn't have to do that."

"No, no, I wanted to. So please have some. I got fried chicken,
cabbage, yams, homemade biscuits, and chocolate cake!"

I smile back. "Sounds good!" I'm not hungry, and even if
I was, I don't know her well enough to eat her food.

"Will you help me set up?"

"Yes, ma'am."

Mrs. Dupree is a pitiful-looking thing. I can't image anybody ever looking into those hound-dog eyes of hers and
saying no to anything she asks.

As the correctional officers prepare to let the inmates into
the rec yard, I hand Mrs. Dupree the last item out of her
bag—tiny, burnt biscuits. She places them in the center of the
picnic table, next to her lopsided, two-layer chocolate cake;
stands back; and asks me how everything looks. "Delicious!"
I say, smiling.

The inmates enter the rec yard, smiling and waving white
lilies. Xavier explains that the lilies, which are grown at one
of the prison's nurseries, are Mother's Day gifts.

"I know you're not a mother," Tony says, handing me a lily.
"But this is for being A'Kyah's mom while Gina's gone."

"Thanks, Tony," I say.

Tony leans forward and attempts to embrace me.

I pull back and catch Xavier give him a cutting look. I know he's not tripping! *Lord, please let Mrs. Dupree leave early so I can have a word with her son.*

"Can a brotha get a handshake then?" Tony asks, laughing.

I smile and shake Tony's hand.

Xavier hands Mrs. Dupree a lily.

"Thank you, baby!" she cries, hugging him tightly. "I got a bunch from you yesterday."

"Here's one more to add to the group," Xavier says, kissing her on the forehead.

I wonder if he's really as doting as he appears.

He looks over and smiles at me. "Hi, Eva. How're you?"

"Fine. Thanks for asking." Out of respect for Mrs. Dupree, I'm going to be civil.

"All right now," Mrs. Dupree says, clapping her hands. "Let's sit down and eat!"

Tony plops down and reaches for a paper plate.

Mrs. Dupree hits him with her lily. "We're gonna say grace before we eat, Tony."

"Ooops, my bad!" Tony says, with a sheepish grin.

Neanderthal!

Xavier blesses the food, and Mrs. Dupree asks me to help her serve.

The only things A'Kyah says she wants are yams and cake; she doesn't like chicken. I marvel at that. She's the only Black person I've ever met that didn't like chicken. Mrs. Dupree piles yams on her plate and gives her a big slice of cake.

Xavier stares up in my face while I serve him. He smells good—fresh like Irish Spring soap. I inhale deeply and avoid making eye contact with him. From the corner of my eye, I see Tony and A'Kyah looking at us. They're nudging each other and grinning.

I haven't forgotten what Mrs. Dupree said last Saturday about not being much of a cook. But not to offend her, I take a chicken wing and small servings of everything else. Mama would have a stroke if she saw me now. From the corner of my eye, I see that Xavier is still staring at me. *Oh, you just wait till your mother leaves. I got something for you!*

"Mama Dupree, X-Man tell you," Tony says, smacking his lips loudly, "'bout his parole hearing?"

Mrs. Dupree gasps. "Xavier!"

Xavier smiles. "My hearing's Thursday, Mother."

My eyes rest on the dimple in Xavier's cheek.

"Wh-when were you going to tell me, son?" asks Mrs. Dupree.

"I," Xavier says, glancing over at Tony, "was going to tell you today."

"Sorry, man," Tony mumbles.

"This is the best news *ever!*" Mrs. Dupree cries. "The best news ever! Samuel is going to be so happy to hear this."

"If you're granted parole, when will you be released?" I ask.

"July eighth," says Xavier.

"That's almost two months!" Mrs. Dupree wails.

"He can do that time standing on his head," Tony says, reaching for another biscuit. "He's done one year and five months. What's two mo' months?"

Who would want to do one more day, let alone two more months, in prison except a maladjusted individual? I really wonder about Tony sometimes.

"Daddy, when is your hearing?" asks A'Kyah.

I narrow my eyes at Tony. *Now tell your daughter a lie. You're not going to have a parole hearing, recidivist. You'll do just about every day of your sentence.* I glance over at Xavier; he's looking at Tony with a sheepish expression on his face. Xavier catches me eyeing him. I roll my eyes and zoom back in on Tony, who, for the first time since he started pigging out, seems to have suddenly lost his appetite.

"Huh, Daddy?" says A'Kyah.

Tony clears his throat. "I don't know. I ain't heard yet."

The real question is: How long will he stay out when he's released? The statistics certainly aren't in his favor, or Xavier's, for that matter. Seventy percent of people released from prison are rearrested within three years of their release.

I wonder if first-time felon Dupree will defy such odds. I'm curious to hear what he plans to tell the parole board to gain his freedom. I hope it's not the same story he told me last week. I zoom back in on him; he's staring down in his plate.

"Xavier," I say.

He looks up and smiles at me.

"If you don't mind my asking, how will you convince the parole board to grant you parole?" I ask.

"I'm going to own up to the irresponsibility that led me here. I wasn't a very good businessman," replies Xavier.

"Don't say that, honey," Mrs. Dupree says, shaking her head. "You were just *too* trusting. You trusted the wrong person, that's all!"

Xavier sighs heavily and presses his lips together.

So he is going to tell them the same story.

"Eva, he hasn't been in any trouble since he's been locked up," Mrs. Dupree says, with pride. "The officers have nothing but good things to say to me about him."

I smile at her.

Mrs. Dupree continues. "He tutors other inmates, and he's even finished up two classes since he's been here. Tell her what they are, son."

"I've completed apprenticeship programs in plumbing and auto mechanics," says Xavier.

"That's great!" I say for Mrs. Dupree's sake.

Mrs. Dupree smiles. "Now tell her what you're going to do when you get out."

"Farm with Dad," mumbles Xavier.

Mrs. Dupree's smile widens. "And what else?"

Xavier sighs and smiles broadly. "Build that golf course I've been wanting to build for the longest, and open a nursery."

"A nursery?" A'Kyah asks.

"Not the kind you thinkin', baby," Tony says. "He's gone grow flowers and stuff like that. That kinda business is called a nursery, too."

"Oh," A'Kyah says.

"And, I want to mentor at-risk youth," Xavier adds. "Tony

tells me you're a social worker, Eva. Perhaps I can get some information from you on how to go about doing that. I want to do all I can to prevent another Black male from ending up where I am right now."

"That's quite admirable," I say.

"It is, isn't it?" Mrs. Dupree says.

"Yes, and I wish him well in all his endeavors," I say.

"X, how you gone have time to do all that?" Tony asks, frowning and sucking on a chicken bone.

"I'm gonna make time. I intend to make my parents proud of me again," says Xavier.

"Xavier, your daddy and I *are* proud of you. We always have been!" insists Mrs. Dupree.

"I'm sorry that you and Dad had to go through this, Mother," Xavier says.

"Don't worry about us, you hear? You just keep your mind straight for that parole hearing. We want you home in July!" says Mrs. Dupree.

"He's coming home, Mama Dupree! So stop worrying," says Tony.

"I hope so, Tony," Mrs. Dupree says weakly.

Poor Mrs. Dupree. I hope for her sake, Xavier makes parole.

"Too bad for me and a lot of other dudes in here," Tony says, looking at A'Kyah and then me. "The state did away with parole the year after Xavier got sentenced. So any inmate that came in after him gone have to practically do all his time."

"So when you getting out, Daddy?" A'Kyah asks pitifully.

"Next year," Tony mutters.

A'Kyah sighs and lays her head on his shoulder.

Poor child. Why can't Tony get himself together and be a positive influence in her life and the lives of his other children? He's sitting here barely literate, and I'll bet every dime I have that he hasn't taken advantage of any of the programs the prison offers.

"Tony, what're your plans upon release, *whenever* that may be?" I ask.

Tony cuts his eyes at me. "What you think, Eva? I'ma-I'ma get a job. A man's got to work, girl."

Interesting. With no education or marketable job skills, I wonder how he plans to do that. "What kind of job?"

"Whatever I can get," mumbles Tony.

"Whatever you can get?" I ask.

"I got skills, okay?" Tony says, sucking his teeth.

"You could work for Xavier, Tony," I say.

"Noooo, Mother," Xavier says, laughing and shaking his head. "I wouldn't hire Tony. He's not fond of outside work."

I look at Tony and shake my head. He's not fond of anything but loafing. When Tony looks at me, I roll my eyes.

"Eva, would you like some water?" Xavier asks.

"No," I lie.

"Get me some, son," says Mrs. Dupree.

"Sure, Mother," replies Xavier.

Despite how pissed off I am with Xavier for sending me flowers, I watch him walk up to the water cooler. He has such a confident, purposeful stride to go with his awesome physique. Not that sluggish, pimping strut that Tony and many of the inmates execute on the yard. When he turns back around, I look down at my food.

"I brought you some water, anyway," Xavier says, placing a cup of water in front of me.

I mumble, "Thanks," and continue to look down.

"Daddy, let's go walk around the yard," says A'Kyah.

"Okay, baby," Tony says, jumping up.

While Tony and A'Kyah stroll around the rec yard, Xavier and Mrs. Dupree chitchat about home affairs and their hopes for his parole. As I listen to the Duprees, I wonder, could what Xavier alleges about being set up be true? When Xavier tells Mrs. Dupree he'll be facing another year in prison if he doesn't get parole, she bursts into tears.

"C'mon. Get up, Mother," Xavier says warmly, rising to his feet. "Go inside and wash your face."

The crying exacerbated the dark circles and bags under Mrs. Dupree's eyes; she looks awful. *Please go, Mrs. Dupree. This will give me a chance to have a few words with your son.*

Mrs. Dupree stands and heads toward the administration building. The second she disappears inside, Xavier turns to me.

"Eva, what's wrong?"

I narrow my eyes at him. "Why did you send me flowers?"

"E—"

"You shouldn't have done that!"

Bewilderment, then sadness, clouds Xavier's face. He sits down as if knocked down by the force of my words. "I sent them because you said you like lilies."

"I did not appreciate what you did, okay? You were way off base!"

"I apologize for upsetting you, Eva. Please, please forgive me."

The sorrowful expression on his face causes me to look down. I look at my half-eaten piece of chocolate cake. Mrs. Dupree didn't lie. She can't cook some things.

"Are you upset because you still think I'm trying to run a game on you?" asks Xavier. "Because that's not the case. Please, believe me."

He really sounds sincere. Still, a nasty "Whatever!" flies out of my mouth.

"Eva, I'm serious. How can I get you to see that?"

I look up. "Listen, you don't have to get me to see—" I catch myself. I'm about to get indignant, and I don't want to do that. I take a deep breath to calm myself. "Xavier, please don't get any ideas. I'm not looking for a boyfriend in prison."

"I know you aren't," he replies, with outstretched hands.

I look back down and jab at the slice of cake.

"I also sent the lilies," he says softly, "to thank you for listening and talking to me last Saturday, because you didn't have to do that."

Have I overreacted? Are his motives for sending the flowers just as he stated? To keep from saying something unkind and later regretting it, I stuff a piece of the awful-tasting cake in my mouth.

Xavier stands and starts cleaning up the picnic table. The silence is almost unbearable. Why is it taking Mrs. Dupree so long to return?

"Eva?"

I look up.

"Did you throw the lilies away after you found out they were from me?"

I look back down. This isn't turning out like I thought it would.

Xavier goes on. "I wanted to bring a little sunshine to your day, like you did to mine last Saturday. Should I have to apologize for that?"

I can't bring myself to respond or look up. When Xavier walks away, I look up and watch him toss the trash into a garbage can and go stand by the door to the administration building. When Mrs. Dupree exits, he places his arm around her shoulders and leads her to another picnic table. Was I firm like Mama told me to be or nasty like Geraldine told me not to be? I'm not sure, but I certainly do feel real bad right now.

12

Another Lifetime Movie

"It's about time you got home," Stephanie says when I walk into the den.

"Why are you so late?" Teresa asks. She's lounging in my recliner, with the TV remote in her hand.

"Gina's flight was delayed," I say.

"How's her mom?" Stephanie asks.

I give Stephanie and Teresa an update on Mrs. Williams's remarkable progress.

Stephanie claps her hands. "Praise God!"

Stephanie is home for Mother's Day and is staying with me. Teresa is hanging out with us, and the three of us plan to pig out and watch TV.

"God is still in the miracle-working business," I say. "Gina, poor thing, won't be here for two weeks, like she'd hoped. She was unable to reschedule some job interviews until after A'Kyah finished school, so she's flying back to St. Louis next Sunday."

"So, Miss A'Kyah will spend her last week in Fairview with you," Teresa says.

"Yep," I say.

"You gonna take her to see Tony before she leaves?" Stephanie asks.

"Oh yeah. Because only God knows when or if she'll ever see him again," I reply.

"Ain't that the truth!" Teresa says.

"So what're we watching tonight?" I ask.

"My vote is *Waiting To Exhale* on Lifetime," says Stephanie. "Teresa wants to see *Scream, Blacula, Scream* on TV–ONE."

"*Waiting to Exhale*," I say.

Teresa makes a face at me.

Speaking of exhaling," Stephanie says, "you heard from Principal Cooper?"

"No," I mumble.

"What's up with that?" Stephanie mutters.

I sit down next to Stephanie, on the love seat. "Ladies, I have a bit of shocking news to disclose."

"What?" they ask.

"Preston didn't send me the lilies," I admit.

"He didn't?" Stephanie asks.

I shake my head.

"Was it Otis, girl?" Teresa asks.

I sigh, then squirm with embarrassment as I reveal the identity of my secret admirer.

Teresa's and Stephanie's eyes grow large and round. Teresa lowers the volume on the TV. "The lilies are from an *inmate*?" she asks.

Stephanie smiles. "That fine one you saw that Sunday you picked up Gina and A'Kyah from the prison?"

"Yes, yes," I say.

Teresa throws her head back and moans.

"I'm beginning to think Preston is not interested in me," I say.

Teresa bursts out laughing. "Well, we know who is!"

"Teresa, that's not funny. I think it was really nice of that inmate to send Eva those flowers, as a gesture of gratitude," says Stephanie.

Teresa looks at Stephanie and frowns. "I know you're joking."

Stephanie laughs. "And I bet he's got a crush on Eva, too."

"Whatever!" I say.

"What's he doing time for?" Stephanie asks.

"Grand larceny," I reply.

Teresa scoffs. "A thief!"

"He says he was set up," I say in Xavier's defense.

Teresa scoffs again.

"News flash! It is a fact," Stephanie says, waving her hands, "that innocent people get caught up in stuff and wind up in prison."

"How sad," I say.

"It doesn't matter," Teresa says doggedly, "if that is what happened in this man's case. He's been labeled a criminal, and Eva's not going to involve herself with a man who has a criminal record."

"Even if he's been unjustly convicted and turns out to be a wonderful guy?" Stephanie asks.

Teresa looks at Stephanie incredulously. "Stephanie, prison has probably turned him into a sociopath. They don't call them monster factories for nothing!"

"You don't know that," Stephanie argues.

"I don't think that's happened to Xavier," I say.

"Well, if he hasn't become a *degenerate*," Teresa asserts, with a finger snap, "he's a nut case."

I burst out laughing. "Girl, you crazy! I don't think he's a nut, either."

"Don't tell me," Teresa says, wagging her finger at me, "that being locked up in prison doesn't do something to a person's mind."

"Teresa, give the brotha a break!" Stephanie pleads. "There are men who leave prison, whether they deserved to be there or not, and reenter society and become upstanding citizens."

"I don't know any, do you?" Teresa says.

"Well, personally, no," Stephanie admits. "But—"

"Case closed!" Teresa exclaims, rolling her eyes.

"He is some kinda fine," I say.

"Eva, let's say Xavier's story of being set up turns out to be true," Stephanie says, grinning. "Would you allow yourself to become *romantically* involved with him?"

"Yesss!" I squeal.

Teresa gasps loudly and glares at me.

I narrow my eyes at her. "Girl, I'm joking, okay? I ain't dating no man that's been to prison."

"Where're the flowers? You take them to your office?" Stephanie asks.

"No, I threw them away," I reply.

"Eva!" says Stephanie.

"I would have done the same thing," Teresa mutters.

Stephanie looks at Teresa and shakes her head.

"I do feel bad about what I did," I admit.

"You should," Stephanie says.

I shouldn't have thrown those beautiful flowers in the trash. *Lord, please forgive me for behaving so ungratefully.* When I take A'Kyah to visit Tony, I'll apologize to Xavier for my actions.

"So if the principal never calls, what're you going to do?" asks Stephanie.

"I don't know, Stephanie. What's left to do? And don't say, 'Try the Internet,'" I say.

Stephanie sighs and hunches up her shoulders. "What about trying a hookup line?"

"And how is that different from surfing the Net?" I ask.

"I don't think there is a difference," Teresa says.

Stephanie exhales. "Maybe there isn't."

"Have you tried a hookup line?" Teresa asks her.

"No, but I've given it some thought. All the major Black radio stations in DC have one now," says Stephanie.

"SOUL 93 just started advertising one," Teresa says.

SOUL 93 is a major R & B station out of Raleigh. I look at

them, jump up, and run down the hall to my bedroom. They take off behind me, laughing.

"I'll look up the number!" Stephanie yells, reaching for the phone book on the floor next to my nightstand.

"I don't expect this to lead to anything, either," I say.

"So why are we calling?" Teresa asks.

"I don't know. To amuse ourselves," I reply.

"Y'all might be surprised!" Stephanie says.

Teresa grunts. "Yeah, I'm sure we will be."

"Here's the number!" cries Stephanie.

I dial the numbers that Stephanie calls out, and when I'm connected to the station, I press the SPEAKER button. After following several prompts to the hookup line, I'm instructed to press number one to hear the male personals. I rub my palms together and press the number one button.

"Hello, Miss Bachelorette," a sexy, baritone male voice says. "There are twenty-one bachelors looking for love in the Raleigh-Durham area. Could you be the lady that one of these lonely bachelors is seeking? Press number two to hear the first ten personals. You may press the pound key at any time to end your call."

Teresa shoves me aside and presses the number two button.

Personal number one: "Hello, my name is Ronald. I'm forty-three years old, six feet one, and two hundred fifty-five pounds. I'm brown-skinned, laid back, and open-minded about things. I need a woman to pamper and love, who is willing to pamper and love me back. Age unimportant. Later!"

"Later for you, tub of lard!" Teresa says, rolling her eyes.

Stephanie and I burst out laughing.

Personal number two: "I'm five feet six. I go to the gym; I own my place and my car. I'm a divorcé who spends fifty percent of my time with my son. I'm affectionate, passionate, and I'm seeking an attractive female five feet to five feet five, 105 to 130 pounds, who is not into one-night stands."

"Why did he have to say he has his own place and his own car?" I ask.

"Because way too many brothas don't," Stephanie says.

"Next!" Teresa yells.

Personal number three: "My name is Darryl. I'm six feet two, one hundred eighty-five pounds. I'm easygoing; have a quiet personality; and love movies, dining out, traveling, and sports. I'm seeking a nonsmoking, intelligent, trustworthy female thirty-five to forty-five, slender to medium build, with similar interests."

"I wonder what he does?" Teresa asks breathlessly.

"Neither he nor the others have said a word about their education, profession, or if they're Christians," I note.

"Good point, Eva," Stephanie says, nodding.

Personal number four: "Hi, I'm Kenneth. I'm five feet eleven, thirty-one years old. No BS, no lies. I'm tired of the struggle and drama. I'm ready to settle down, get married, and have children. Serious inquiries only."

"I hear you, Kenneth!" Teresa says quite dramatically. "I don't want the drama, either, baby!"

Personal number five: "Hello, my name is Lawrence. I'm thirty-six years old. I'm light-skinned, with hazel eyes. I stand six feet and weigh one hundred seventy pounds. I'm average looking, with a curly fade, and I'm well endowed. Only serious calls, please. Time is too short for game playing."

"Did he say he was well endowed?" I ask.

Stephanie laughs. "That's what he said."

"Does he mean financially?" I ask.

"I don't think that's what Lawrence is referring to," Teresa says, opening her eyes wide.

I look at Stephanie and shake my head. "And you want to try this."

Personal number six: "What's up? This is Shawn."

Oh, brother! I feel like pressing the pound key.

"I'm nineteen but act twenty-five," pubescent-sounding Shawn says. "I like older women, someone to spend quality time with. I'm seeking a woman who knows what she wants, someone who is caring and is capable of giving one hundred ten percent. Feeling what I'm feeling? Hit me."

Stephanie scoffs and shakes her head. "That brotha is *seeking* somebody to take care of him. I bet he's still living with his mama."

Teresa and I give each other high fives.

Personal number seven: "Hello, ladies. My name is Walter. I'm an accountant."

"An accountant!" Teresa screams, jumping up and down.

"I'm easy to get along with," bachelor number seven says, with a chuckle. "I'm seeking a woman for discreet erotic adventures who wants to be dominated."

"Awww! He's a freak!" Teresa cries.

Personal number eight: "Hit me up if it sounds interesting. I'm every woman's fantasy, tall, dark, and handsome. I'm an ex-marine who raises rottweilers and pit bulls for a living. I'm six feet five, seeking the *total* package. Beauty, intelligence, goal-oriented, and romantic."

"Another freak," Teresa mutters. "Press the pound key, Eva."

Personal number nine: Instrumental gospel music starts off the next personal.

"Oooh, a Christian man!" I say and lean closer to the phone.

"My heart's desire is a wife," bachelor number nine says, breathing heavily.

"What's wrong with him?" Teresa asks.

Stephanie bursts out laughing.

"Shhh," I say.

"A man that finds a wife finds a good thing," bachelor number nine continues. "I'm six feet three, muscular build, and financially stable. I'm a churchgoer." There's a pause, followed by more labored breathing. "I am saved, sanctified, and filled with the Holy Ghost. I love the Lord. He is first in my life. May God bless you."

"He sounds sickly," Teresa says, turning up her nose.

"You want to hit him?" Stephanie asks me, giggling.

"I pass," I say.

Personal number ten: "I'm five feet nine, one hundred

eighty pounds, forty-five years old, bald. My zodiac sign is Taurus the bull. I'm often told I look like Samuel L. Jackson."

We look at each other and burst out laughing.

"I have a steady job, and I'm seeking a serene, sincere woman, medium to slender build," bachelor number ten says. "I'm waiting. Please don't make me wait too much longer. Call meeee."

"Y'all want to hear more?" I manage to ask between bouts of laughter.

Teresa and Stephanie are laughing too hard to answer.

I press the SPEAKER button to end the call. We head back down the hall, laughing hysterically, just in time for *Waiting To Exhale*.

13

The Ties That Bind

"Radio listeners! If you got a living mother, you ought to say, 'Thank you, Lord,' this Sunday morning!" Mr. T. says.

It's Mother's Day! *Lord, I thank you for my mama.* She's called twice to make sure that Stephanie and I are up and getting dressed. Geraldine is the Women's Day speaker at, according to Mama, a "storefront" church in Raleigh. Owing to her radio ministry, she gets numerous speaking engagements during the month of May. We're supportive of her evangelical efforts and accompany her and her family to many engagements. After the service, we're treating her and Mama to dinner at the Cheesecake Factory. They've been dying to eat there since it opened two months ago.

The phone rings for the third time this morning. I don't bother to look at the caller ID display. I turn down the radio and pick up the phone. "Yes, Mama."

"Hey, girl. It's me," says Willnetta.

"Hey, what's up?"

"I know you're getting ready for church, so I'm not going

to keep you," Willnetta says, talking hurriedly, "but I want to tell you what I found out last night about Preston."

A lump forms in my throat; I swallow dryly. "He's seeing somebody, isn't he?"

"Yeah," she says softly.

I shoulda known. "Is her name Diane?"

"No, Kelly. Kelly Walker. She's an assistant principal at a high school in Raleigh."

"Did he just start seeing her?" I ask, surprising myself at how pitiful I sound.

"According to what I was told, no. He's been seeing her for some time now."

"Oh, well," I say as tears fill my eyes.

"And get this!"

"What?"

"She's *White*."

"White?"

"White."

"Awwwww!"

"I'm sorry, Eva."

"Me too," I cry.

"You're going to meet someone, Eva."

"When, Willnetta? When?"

"Sooner than you think," she says cheerfully. "So stop crying. He's out there. Just keep the faith, girl."

"That's getting harder and harder to do."

"Listen, Joel's working late tomorrow night. Come by. I'll fix you dinner."

"Willnetta—"

"Don't Willnetta me. Dinner. My house. Tomorrow."

"Okay."

"And in the meantime, forget about Preston."

"Who?"

Willnetta bursts out laughing. I laugh, too, as tears roll down my cheeks. After we say good-bye, I fall across the bed and pound the mattress. That lying Preston Cooper! He had no intentions of ever calling me. "Big, fat liar!"

"What's wrong with you?" Stephanie yells from the bathroom.

"That was Willnetta. Preston is dating a White girl."

"Sellout!"

When Mama pulls into the driveway, honking her horn, I'm reapplying my mascara. Tears over Preston streaked my earlier application. I put Visine drops in my eyes, throw on a pair of dark lens sunglasses, and follow Stephanie outside. Mama's car is shining like new money, and she's already moved over to the front passenger seat. Stephanie, Miss Indy 500, volunteers to drive. Mama motions with her head for Stephanie to get in the backseat. I climb behind the steering wheel of the Lincoln and ease out of the driveway. When we get to Geraldine's house, she, Cleveland, Jalisa, and Cleveland Junior are sitting in their Avalon, waiting on us.

As the mini motorcade makes its way to Raleigh, Mama asks me why I'm so quiet. I lie and tell her I have a headache. I can't tell her my heart is aching because my love interest has absolutely no interest in me, and I'm beginning to wonder if I'll ever find love. When I pull behind Cleveland, into a parking space on a narrow one-way street in downtown Raleigh, Mama grunts. The words ZION TEMPLE CHURCH OF THE RE- DEEMED are painted in black letters on the front of what looks as if it once was a small convenience store.

"I told y'all, it was a storefront church," Mama grumbles. "And I bet the pews are raggedy! Lord, I hope I don't mess up my brand-new suit!"

Stephanie and I burst out laughing. We're all dressed in light-colored silk suits. Mama is wearing the ice blue suit that Geraldine, Stephanie, and I gave her for Mother's Day. Stephanie's suit is peach-colored; mine is yellow. When we exit the car, Geraldine, dressed in a white linen suit, asks us why we're laughing. Stephanie points at Mama. Mama tells Geraldine to pay us no mind.

We follow Geraldine inside Zion Temple. The sanctuary is dank and quite small. There are air-conditioning units in two of the four red stained-glass windows. The sun shining through the unsightly windows casts a pink glow in the humid room. The Ten Commandments and a picture of a White Jesus on the cross hang in the pulpit. Mama grunts real loud when she sees the old wooden pews and whispers that she wishes she had worn something else. Geraldine tells her to be quiet and to behave. A tall, robust woman wearing an usher badge approaches and welcomes us to the church. Geraldine makes introductions, and the lady promptly seats everyone but Geraldine on the front pew. She takes Geraldine by the arm, and they disappear behind a door that has PASTOR STUDY written on it.

"What's your mama's text?" Mama asks Jalisa.

Jalisa hunches up her shoulders. "I'm not really sure. She was reading Esther and Ruth last night."

After the emotionally charged devotional period of testimonials, followed by a morning prayer, scripture reading, announcements, four lengthy songs, and an offering, Geraldine finally addresses the congregation. Her message is virtuous women in the twenty-first century.

Geraldine identifies Deborah, Ruth, and Esther as virtuous women of ancient times who today's modern women should emulate. She encourages the largely female congregation to embrace the traits of her Bible heroines: to be wise like Deborah, loyal like Ruth, and courageous like Esther. Married women are reminded of their duties as wives and mothers. Single women are encouraged to keep themselves healthy, loving, and spiritually strong. Geraldine assures us that we will then become an irresistible magnet for the mate God has in store for us. When she exhorts the single women further to wait patiently on their Boaz and King Xerxes, the pastor and his wife shout, "Amen!"

I look around Zion Temple and count eight adult men and forty-one women. These numbers don't surprise me. Women outnumber men in my church, too, and every other church I've visited. I wonder how many of Zion Temple's women got up this morning and left husbands at home. The man I marry has to be a churchgoer, no ifs, ands, or buts about it. He won't

be lounging around the house on Sunday morning while I'm
in church, praying and praising God. We're going to do that
together. A family that prays together stays together. I'm still
a firm believer in that, despite my devout parents' divorce.

After the service, the pastor and his wife invite us to join them
and some of the members for dinner at The Golden Corral. We
politely decline and hightail it over to the Cheesecake Factory.

The Cheesecake Factory is crowded. Mama, who has a tendency to be impatient, doesn't grumble when the hostess tells
us the wait is an hour and forty-five minutes. We find seats
near the bar and order mozzarella sticks, nachos, and buffalo
wings. I'm trying to have a good time, but I keep thinking
about being rejected by Preston. When Mama asks if I've heard
from him, I shake my head; Stephanie explains why. Mama
shakes her head, too. "There's still Otis, baby," she says, pinch-
ing me on the cheek. My eyes water, and I hang my head.

Stephanie pulls into Daddy's driveway, waving and honking her horn. Daddy and Miss Elsie are sitting on the porch.
Miss Elsie gets up and walks down the steps to greet us. I
reach into the backseat of Stephanie's silver Chrysler Sebring
and hand Miss Elise two gift bags.

"Oh, thank y'all," Miss Elsie cries, running back up the
steps and into the house.

"How was the service?" Daddy asks, standing to hug us.

"Good," I say.

"How's your mother?" he asks.

"Mama's fine," Stephanie says.

"Look, James!" Miss Elsie struts outside wearing a lilac
hat, one of two gifts we gave her. The other gift, a lilac pocketbook, is tucked under her arm.

"Oh, my! That's a pretty hat and pocketbook, Elsie," he says.

"Yes, they are! Girls, thank y'all. I love them!" Miss Elsie exclaims, embracing Stephanie and me. "And I got something in the kitchen for both of you!"

"Something sweet?" Stephanie asks, rubbing her stomach.

"An apple pie for you, and brownies for Eva."

Stephanie and I dash into the house, behind Miss Elsie. When I return to the porch, Daddy gets up and walks down the steps. "It's getting late," he says, looking at his watch. "Stephanie going back today or tomorrow morning?"

"Today," I reply.

His brows crease together. "Stephanie!"

Stephanie sticks her head out the door. "Yes, sir."

"Shortcake, you need to head on back before it gets dark," he says, inspecting the tires on the Sebring. When he pops the hood, Stephanie tells him she had her car serviced before she came home. Daddy nods, closes the hood, and returns to his seat on the porch.

I sit down in the porch swing and gaze out across the road at the pond. *Aha! That's it!* I've been racking my brain for weeks now, trying to figure out what to get Daddy for Father's Day. Now I know—a rod and reel. A really nice one. He'd like that since he's taken up fishing as a hobby. I might even throw in a one-year subscription to one of those fishing magazines.

"What you thinking about, honey?" asks Daddy.

"Oh, nothing much," I say.

Stephanie exits the house, with a brownie in her hand. She plops down next to me in the swing.

"I was pleased with the way you girls handled yourselves at Willnetta's reception," Daddy says. "I overheard folks pestering you two about getting married."

"You did?" I ask, swelling with embarrassment.

Daddy nods and smiles.

"Daddy, is something wrong with me?" I ask.

"What do you mean?" he says.

"I'm being made to feel like there is. That I'm deficient in some way because I'm not married!" I say.

Miss Elsie throws up her hands. "Lord, have mercy!"

"I walk around pretending that being single at forty doesn't

bother me, but it does," I add. "I really wonder if I'll ever get
married. I don't want to grow old by myself."

Daddy smiles sweetly at me and gently pats me on the knee
like he used to do when I was a little girl and upset. "Honeysuckle," he says, staring into my eyes, "keep the faith."

The smile and loving gesture cause tears to well up in my
eyes. I swallow dryly and try to maintain my composure.
When I tell Daddy about Preston, and my hopes that he and
I would hit it off, I burst out crying.

"He wasn't the one for you, baby," Daddy says soothingly.
"He wasn't the one."

"No, he wasn't!" Miss Elsie cries, running into the house.
She comes back outside and hands me a tissue.

Stephanie scoffs and shakes her head. "You would think it's
a crime to be single these days! I came pretty close to telling
off some of them busybodies at that reception!"

"I know that's right!" Miss Elsie grumbles. "People need
to mind their own business!"

Daddy reaches for Stephanie's hand. "And don't you get
discouraged, either."

"I'm trying real hard not to," Stephanie says softly.

"Why is it so hard for us to find somebody?" I ask, dabbing at my eyes. "We're good women."

"Yes, you two are!" Miss Elsie says soothingly. "You're the
salt of the earth! James and I say that all the time."

"God will provide," Daddy says, looking from me to
Stephanie. "Just keep the faith."

I burst out crying again. "It's so hard not to get discouraged, Daddy. I haven't been on a date in months! Out of desperation, I went to a nightclub, hoping to meet someone."

Daddy clears his throat and takes my hand. "When a man
finds a wife, the Bible says he finds a good thing. It's not your
place to go looking, sweetheart. God will send both of you," he
says, squeezing Stephanie's hand and mine, "a mate in *His* time."

I look down at my father's large, gnarled hands. He worked
hard all his life—holding down two, sometimes three, jobs at
once—to see to it that my mother, sisters, and I didn't go

without. These same hands would effortlessly fashion daffodil and honeysuckle leis for me on late spring evenings after having gripped heavy machinery for twelve hours at the undergarment plant. I let the tears flow. Through them I can see that Stephanie is crying, too.

Daddy closes his eyes and bows his head. He thanks God for blessing him with beautiful, kindhearted daughters and prays that we don't stray from our moral upbringing. Miss Elsie shouts, "Do, Lord! Do, Lord!" while he prays. Daddy's last petition to God is to bless us with God-fearing husbands.

It's 6:30 when Stephanie finally leaves for DC. The backseat of her convertible is covered with enough food to last her a week. She has lived in DC for fifteen years and is thinking about moving back to Fairview after law school. She says she's tired of living in the nation's congested capital, where women outnumber men fourteen to one.

I return home, shower, crawl on my bed, and turn on the TV. I call Teresa to tell her the news about Preston. She's not home. I leave the information on her answering machine and tell her to plan on having lunch with me tomorrow. I dial Gina to see how she and A'Kyah are coming along with their packing. They're exhausted and are already in bed. We make plans to have dinner midweek.

The phone rings, waking me from a crazy dream at 10:47. It's Stephanie. After chatting with her, I call Mama, Daddy, and Geraldine to let them know she's safely back in DC. I turn off the TV, turn out the bedroom light, and recall my crazy dream. It involved Xavier, who was towering over Preston, with clenched fists, demanding to know why he lied to me. "You shouldn't have lied to Eva! You hurt her!" Xavier yelled at sniveling Preston. Preston hobbled over to me and begged for my forgiveness. I slapped him and walked away. *Lord, help me.*

14

Marching Orders

My heart is heavy. Tomorrow, after visiting Tony, A'Kyah is off to St. Louis. During the year-end assembly at A'Kyah's school today, I sat in the back of the auditorium and cried. She looked so glum as Mrs. Hodges called students from her class to the stage to receive their Perfect Attendance Awards. Every action has a consequence. I hope A'Kyah has learned that lesson. She says she has. An hour later, she was shouting and jumping for joy when I told her the pizza, soft drinks, and ice cream piled on Mrs. Hodges's desk were for a going-away party in her honor. She hasn't stopped thanking me yet. As we were exiting the school, we ran into Preston. I acted like I didn't see or hear him when he said hello to me.

I pour more chamomile oil in my bathwater and try to recall the name of the movie coming on Lifetime tonight at eight.

"Eva! Phone! It's a man," A'Kyah yells from the hallway. "He won't tell me his name."

"Okay!" I wonder who this could be.

I pick up the cordless phone from where it's lying on the

floor and press the TALK button. I hear heavy breathing and Barry White's "Can't Get Enough Of Your Love, Babe."

"Hello!"

"Eva?"

"Yes."

"Well, hel-lo!"

"Hello."

"Do you know who you're talking to?"

"No."

The man laughs. "Guess."

"I wouldn't know where to begin," I say good-humoredly.

"Awww, girl! You're no fun. This is Otis."

Nooooo! I take a deep breath and exhale. "Hi, Otis."

"Hi," he says, his voice dropping several octaves. I guess he's trying to sound like Barry White now. "Your mother said it would be okay to call."

"Oh, really?"

"Real-ly," he replies seductively. "The little girl said you were taking a bath. I could come over and wash your back for you if you like."

"Excuse me?"

"I'll even bring candles and massage oil."

He's gone make me throw up.

"Eva?"

"Yes."

"Baby, I'm just teasing. Don't get upset. But seriously, I am *quite* good with my hands."

"Listen, Otis."

"I'm all ears," he whispers.

"You kinda caught me at a bad time."

"I can call you later, or better yet, you call me when you get freed up."

"Sure. Okay." Why did I say that?

"Grab a piece of paper and something to write with. I'll give you my home and cell numbers."

"Hold on." I act like I'm getting out of the tub by splashing around in the water. I silently count to five and then ask, "Okay. What are they?"

Otis slowly gives me his home, mobile, and pager numbers. I pretend to write them down.

"Eva," he says, sounding like Barry White again, "I can't *wait* to talk to you again."

And you'll be waiting and waiting and waiting. "Good night, Otis."

"Bye, gorgeous. I'll be thinking of you," he sings.

Please! I end the call and speed-dial Mama's number; her phone rings one time.

"Hey, baby," Mama says.

"Mama, why did you give Otis my phone number and tell him he could call me?"

"I didn't give Otis your number. You're listed in the phone book. So he called?" she asks excitedly. "When y'all going out?"

"Never."

"What?" she yells.

"Mama, I'm not interested in Otis, okay?"

"You listen to me! You weren't interested in bald-headed Joel until he put that big diamond on Willnetta's finger and built her that mini-mansion outside of town! Give Otis a chance, girl! He's a nice guy, he works hard, and he's *crazy* about you."

"Uh-huh."

"Don't you uh-huh me!"

Lord, have mercy.

"You go on out with Otis!" Mama hollers.

"I'll think about it, okay?"

"You told me that before! How much thinking do you need to do?"

I'm fighting a losing battle here. In order to get Mama off my back—and, Lord, you know I'm sick and tired of arguing with her about Otis Reid—I'm gonna have to go out with him. One date won't kill me.

"If you weren't so picky," Mama rambles on, "you'd be married by now! Girl, you'd better go out with Otis!"

"Okay! I will!"

"Good!"

"And you'll be the first to know how it went!"

"Good! Keep me posted!" Click!

No, she didn't hang up on me? I burst out laughing, throw the phone on the floor, and slide down in the bathtub.

15

Good-byes

"My baby's leaving me," Tony says.

I'm so glad I have my dark lens sunglasses on so Tony and A'Kyah can't see the tears in my eyes.

"Daddy, you gone write and call me?" A'Kyah whispers.

"Of course, I am," says Tony.

"You promise?" asks A'Kyah.

"I promise," says Tony.

"When you get out, move to St. Louis," A'Kyah entreats him.

Tony hugs A'Kyah and tells her he loves her.

"I'm really going to miss her and Gina," I say, my voice cracking at the end.

"You've been a good friend to them, Eva. A real good friend," replies Tony.

A'Kyah starts whimpering. "Daddy, I don't want to leave you behind."

"Shhh, I know, baby," Tony whispers.

This is so sad. This child may never see her father again. I try to blink back the tears in my eyes; they slip through my lashes and slide down my face.

"Come with me to St. Louis," A'Kyah pleads.

"Sweet pea, I can't," says Tony.

"You could do your time there. They got prisons," A'Kyah argues.

I can't listen to any more of this. I excuse myself and walk back into the administration building.

"Ma'am, are you all right?" Lt. Rivers asks.

"Where's the bathroom?" I ask.

"Around the corner, down the hall," replies Lt. Rivers.

I dash in the direction the lieutenant indicated, and collide into a hard body. A pair of large hands catches me as I stumble backwards. My sunglasses fall from my face. I look up. The lifesaver that kept me from falling to the floor is Xavier. A slight smile forms at his mouth and quickly vanishes as concern clouds his handsome face.

"Eva, what's wrong?" he says.

I open my mouth to speak, but nothing comes out. My heart is racing, and tears are steadily streaming down my face.

"Eva," he says, holding me tighter, "what's wrong?"

"A'Kyah is leaving for St. Louis today."

"I'm sorry," he says softly. He releases me, picks up my sunglasses, and hands them to me. "Tell A'Kyah good-bye for me," he says, turning to leave.

"Xavier, wait!"

Xavier turns back around, and the concern that I saw seconds ago returns. "Yes?" he says, stepping up to me. He steps so close to me, in fact, we're touching each other.

"I would like to talk to you about last week. Please, I won't take up much of your time."

"Okay."

I run into the bathroom to clean my face. When I come out, Xavier is nowhere to be seen. I walk back to the visitation check-in area, hoping he's there. He is. He's standing at the desk, talking to Lt. Rivers.

"Miss Liles," Lt. Rivers says as I approach, "Inmate Dupree has informed me of your wish to speak with him."

"Yes, ma'am," I reply.

"Inmates are not allowed visits with people who are not on their visitation card."

"I'm not requesting a visit. I just want to speak to him briefly."

"We consider that a visit, ma'am," says Lt. Rivers.

"I see," I reply and look at Xavier. He's wringing his hands and looking down at the floor.

The lieutenant looks over at him, then back at me. "This is not *normal* procedure, but"—she sighs heavily—"given that you've been cleared by the department to visit another inmate housed here, I will grant your request to visit with Inmate Dupree."

"Thank you," I say.

"You will need to add your name and address to his visitation card," says Lt. Rivers.

"Okay. Sure," I reply.

Lt. Rivers hands me Xavier's visitation card. There are eleven names listed on the card, including those of his parents and a sister and brother-in-law that live in Houston. The other names listed have friend, uncle, aunt, or cousin written beside them. I write my name and address on line number twelve and indicate "acquaintance" beside my signature. I hand the card back, and Xavier follows me outside. When he heads in Tony and A'Kyah's direction, I stop him. "Let them have this time alone," I say. He nods and follows me to the only picnic table where there's an unoccupied bench: the one where Freda and Clarence are sitting.

"How's Gina's mother?" Xavier asks.

"She's doing remarkably well."

"That's good. Tell Gina hello for me."

"I will. Your mother's not coming today?"

"No. She and my father are in Raleigh, at a Memorial Day service."

"How's your father?"

"He tells me he's fine. How've you been?" he asks, smiling.

"Busy. And you?"

"Good. Thanks for asking."

I look over at Tony and A'Kyah. They're laughing now.

"Tony's really going to miss her," Xavier says.

Tears fill my eyes again. I blink them back. "It's going to be another hot day," I say, fanning myself with my hands.

"It already is. Let me get you some water."

"Thanks."

Xavier goes up to one of the water coolers and returns with two cups of water.

"I want to apologize to you for my behavior last Saturday," I say to him when he sits back down.

"Apology accepted," he says warmly.

"The lilies were beautiful. Thank you."

"You're welcome."

My conscience is clear! Hallelujah!

"Eva?"

"Yes."

"May I sit here a little longer and talk with you?"

The pleading look in Xavier's eyes causes me to say, "Yes."

"Thanks."

I take a sip of water and glance over at Freda and Clarence. They're holding hands and gazing into each other's eyes. They really look like they're in love.

"You smell that?" Xavier asks me.

"What?"

"Take a deep breath."

I inhale and catch a faint whiff of honeysuckle. "Oh, honeysuckle!" I say, inhaling again.

"You smelled like honeysuckle the first day I met you," he says, with a big, dimple-cheeked smile.

"I *love* the smell."

"There're vines everywhere here. There're some." Xavier points to the back fence. "We call the vines nature's air fresheners," he says, laughing.

"Huh?"

"They help cover up the stench that fills the air around here."

"Stench? From what?"

"The chicken coops."

"Chicken coops?"

Xavier nods and wipes his sweaty forehead. "There're two chicken houses here. We process and ship poultry, just like the crops grown here, to prisons throughout the state."

"I didn't know that. Nor did I realize there was a nursery here until last week. I like how my tax dollars are being spent out here."

Xavier laughs. "And I assure you, Miss Taxpayer, contrary to what you or others may believe, we don't watch TV, play basketball, or lift weights all day. We *work* every day of the week."

"That's good to know," I say, laughing.

Xavier laughs again. A deep, hearty laugh.

Why is he locked up?

"Tell me about your job at social services."

"I supervise a team of social workers in the agency's family support unit. We provide short-term intervention for families grappling with financial or emotional crises."

"Sounds like demanding work."

"It is."

"How do you handle the stress?"

"I pray *a lot.*"

"I do a lot of that in here," he says, opening his eyes wide.

"I don't doubt that. Where here do you work?"

"In the nursery from six thirty to four. After that, I clean up the administration building from five to six, and from seven to nine, I tutor inmates in the library."

"Wow! That's a *long* workday."

Xavier smiles broadly, and my eyes rest on the dimple in his cheek. "I stay busy. It makes my time here go by faster."

"Xavier, I'm curious. I hope this doesn't embarrass or upset you, but I have to ask. You don't have to answer if you don't want to."

"What is it, Eva?"

"Has anyone ever," I lower my voice and whisper, "propositioned you for sex?"

Xavier's eyes widen, and he leans close to me. "I'm *straight*, Eva."

"I've been told a lot of straight men engage in homosexual behavior in prison."

"Not me!" he says emphatically.

"That doesn't mean you haven't been propositioned, or worse, assaulted. You're a good-looking man."

"Thanks for the compliment," he says, flashing another dimple-cheeked smile. The smile quickly fades, and his brows crease together. "I've never been raped, thank God. But to answer your question, yes, I've been propositioned."

"How did you respond to that?"

"I said no and meant it. And if it meant fighting to defend myself from a sexual assault, I would've done it. I thank God that it has never come down to that. One fighting incident in my file would adversely affect my chance for parole."

"Speaking of parole, how did your hearing go?"

Xavier sighs and shakes his head. "I'm not sure. My counselor believes it went well."

"You have a lot going for you. I can't see the parole board denying you parole. I was really impressed with what you said last Saturday."

"I don't belong here, Eva. It hasn't been easy doing time for a crime I did not willfully commit."

Why does a big part of me want to believe him now? For some reason, I'm beginning to do just that. "I don't think you'll be here much longer."

Xavier looks around the prison yard, then back at me. "I pray not, because doing time in prison is not easy. If it weren't for Lt. Rivers and a few others, it would be impossible for me to have an incident-free record. I thank God every night for her and the other officers who have zero tolerance for misconduct."

"They're guardian angels with billy clubs, huh?" I say, laughing.

"Yes!" Xavier leans close to me. "Can you *really* keep a secret?" he whispers.

"Yes," I whisper back.

He glances over at Freda and Clarence. Their backs are to us, and they're preoccupied with a game of footsy. "Two of my mother's nephews work here as officers."

"Why does that have to be a secret?"

"DOC policy—"

"DOC?"

"Department of Corrections. The department forbids inmates from being housed where relatives are employed."

"Why?"

"To prevent them from receiving preferential treatment."

"Oh yeah. I can see how that would be a problem. Have you gotten preferential treatment?" I whisper.

Xavier winks and smiles.

"I won't breathe a word of what you just told me," I say.

His smile widens, and he stares deeply in my eyes.

Man, oh, man! If this sexy chocolate man were paroled tomorrow, I'd be tempted to go out with him if he were to ask. As lust gets the better of me, I entertain thoughts of lying against his broad chest as his long, muscular arms hold me tightly.

Am I hard up or what? I'm sitting in a prison yard, lusting over an inmate. *Shame, shame, shame!*

"Eva, I haven't forgotten what you said the other week. But can I see you when I get out?"

I look down.

"I'm sorry," he says. "Forget I asked that."

I look up at him and smile.

A breeze stirs, and I catch a strong whiff of honeysuckle. I close my eyes and take several deep breaths. When I open them, Xavier is staring in my face.

"You are so pretty," he says.

The compliment makes me feel good, and lust gets the better of me again. I place my sunglasses on and hope he can't see my eyes raking over his body.

"Do you work out?" I ask.

Xavier flexes his arm muscles and smiles. "A little. It helps release stress."

"How old are you?"

"Forty-three."

"Any children?"

"No. One day hopefully," he says, with a big smile.

Lord, why does he have to be locked up!

"When I open my nursery, will you patronize it?" he asks.

"Mmmm."

"I plan to have lots of lilies."

"Well, I may just have to pay you a visit then, Mr. Dupree."

"I'd appreciate the visit more than your business."

I smile and look off.

"Do you play golf?" he asks.

"No. Never have, but I would like to learn."

"Good. I'm a pretty good golfer. I'll be more than glad to give you lessons."

I smile again and look back at Xavier. "I'll keep that in mind."

Xavier sighs and looks serious. "Eva, could you see someone like yourself married to a farmer?"

"I don't know. Maybe."

"My wife couldn't see that for herself. I always knew I would be a third-generation farmer. I told her that when we met."

"Is that why your marriage ended?"

"That played a big part. And she didn't really enjoy being the wife of an army sergeant. She hated the reassignments I got, because each one took her farther away from her beloved Atlanta."

"Is that where she is now?"

"Yes. She's remarried and has two kids."

"So, your ex-fiancée had no qualms about moving to the country?"

Xavier shakes his head. "No. With an MBA and a degree in marketing, she had all sorts of ideas for the nursery and golf course."

"Sorry that didn't work out for you."

"I'm not. Not anymore," he says, gazing into my eyes.

"Stop that."

"What?"

"Staring at me."

"I can't help myself."

"If you keep it up, I'm going to get up and leave." Now that's the first lie I've told today. I'm enjoying the attention Xavier is showering upon me.

Xavier smiles and throws up his hands. "Okay, I'll try not to stare at you, Miss Liles."

"Still no word from the parole board?" Freda asks, looking back and standing up.

Xavier shakes his head.

"Good luck to you," she says, pulling Clarence to his feet. The two of them walk off.

"I can't fathom them denying you parole," I say.

Xavier sighs heavily. "I need to be home, Eva. My father looked so tired and worn-out last Sunday. He's ready to turn the farm over to me now."

"Farming sounds like *real* hard work."

"It's not as physically strenuous as it used to be years ago, thanks to advanced machinery." Xavier's brows crease together, and he shakes his head.

"What's wrong?"

"I failed once as a businessman, Eva. Poor judgment on my part landed my friend and me in prison. I can't afford to make a costly mistake like that again. There's so much more to lose if I do."

Xavier tells me that land developers are anxious to get their hands on the family's land—valued at 6.5 million dollars—where cotton, peanuts, soybeans, wheat, and corn are grown. Since the onset of his hypertension—triggered by stress, which Xavier believes his incarceration brought on—Mr. Dupree has been physically unable to manage the farm like he once did. Several relatives help him but lack the knowledge to successfully manage things.

"It's up to me now to step in and run things. My father's depending on me," says Xavier.

"Don't doubt yourself, Xavier," I say, swinging into social worker mode. "Whatever mistakes you made in the past, learn from them."

"I have."

"So stop worrying. You won't fail a second time. Believe that."

Xavier's handsome face relaxes into a smile. "Thank you, Eva, for such encouraging words."

"And, you're *going* to make parole. I'm sure of that."

"Eva!" Tony yells, hurrying in our direction. A'Kyah is lagging behind him, scowling and stomping her feet. "I-I'd like for you and A'Kyah to leave now," he mutters.

"Is something wrong?" I ask.

"Um, I just think under the circumstances," Tony says, sniffling, "it's best y'all go on and leave now."

"Okay," I reply.

"Tell Xavier good-bye, A'Kyah," says Tony.

A'Kyah looks over at Xavier and throws up her hand.

"So long, A'Kyah," Xavier says, waving good-bye. "You take care in St. Louis."

"Okay," A'Kyah mumbles. Tony takes her by the hand, and they head toward the administration building.

I stand up.

"So, the only way I can see you," Xavier asks, staring up at me, "is when I open my nursery?"

I take another sip of water and place the cup down on the table. "Good-bye, Xavier. I wish you all the best."

"Thank you," he says, extending his hand.

I shake his hand and feel both relief and shame: relief that this visit has ended, and shame over my lustful behavior.

"It has been my utmost pleasure to have met you," he says, slowly releasing my hand. "I won't say good-bye, because I do hope to see you again."

I turn and hurry toward the administration building. I sense that Xavier is staring at me, but I dare not look back. Instead, I pray to God to keep him safe and to answer his prayer for parole.

Tony and A'Kyah are huddled together in the visitation check-in area. They look so pitiful. Tony tells his weeping daughter that he will stay in touch with her.

"I don't want to leave you!" A'Kyah cries.

Tony pries her arms from around his waist and shoves her to me. "Go!" he mumbles, fighting back tears.

I place my arms around A'Kyah's shoulders and lead her out of the administration building. As I pull out of the parking lot, I look over into the rec yard. Tony and Xavier are standing at the fence. They wave as we pass. When I turn off the prison compound and onto the highway, I am thinking about Xavier's gorgeous smile and rock-solid body. I turn up the air-conditioning as far as it will go.

The hour and twenty minutes we spent in Circuit City cheered up A'Kyah immensely, but as I circle the airport lot for a parking space, her cheerfulness slowly gives way to gloom. From the corner of my eye, I see her fidgeting with her new CD player. I ask if she's nervous about flying. She says she's not, that she's just ready to see Gina and her grandma. After getting A'Kyah's ticket and a gate pass in order to escort her to the departure gate, I keep the conversation light during the forty-five minutes before she boards her plane. We reminisce about birthday parties, trips, and other fun times she, Gina, and I had together. When the flight attendant comes out to get her, I start bawling. A'Kyah embraces me and kisses me on each cheek. The flight attendant assures me that she's going to personally take care of A'Kyah and see to it that she arrives safely in St. Louis. I remain in the terminal until A'Kyah's plane takes off. When I get home, I find an artificial red rose and a sheet of pink stationery on my bed.

Dear Eva, I want you to know that I love you very, very much. Thank you for putting up with me. Thanks for coming to school on Friday and giving me a going-away party. You made me so happy. I will never forget that. Call me and Mommy tonight. Stay sweet! I love you, A'Kyah.

When my phone beeps at 8:20, I'm crying to Teresa about missing Gina and A'Kyah. I click over. It's Gina. A'Kyah is in St. Louis.

16

Suitors

When the postman arrives with the mail, I'm standing in the yard, trying to decide where to plant my white impatiens. I settle on the flower beds bordering the driveway, and after planting the impatiens, go get the mail. I toss the department-store flyers into an empty plant container and tear open the envelope from Gina. In a thank-you card, she's written that she's still looking for work, that Mrs. Williams is steadily making progress in rehab and sends a thank-you for the flowers I sent, and that she wants to know when I'm coming to visit. I haven't been to St. Louis in seven years. I flew out there then with Gina and A'Kyah for Mrs. Williams's retirement party. It's time for another visit now. If Stephanie and Teresa are game, I'll drive out there in August and surprise Gina on her birthday. I still find it hard to believe that she and A'Kyah are gone. I've had to stop myself several times from looking for them around town.

I stuff the thank-you card back in the envelope before I get misty-eyed and shuffle through the other mail. When I see the envelope neatly addressed to me from Hayesfield Correctional Center, I flinch. I can't believe my eyes. I kneel down next to the impatiens and rip it open.

10:33 PM
Thursday

May 30th
Dear Eva,

It was so nice to sit and talk with you on Saturday. To be in the company of a beautiful, intelligent woman like you is a rarity around here, believe me! (smile) Your optimism is so refreshing. I feel blessed to have met you, Eva. I HAD to write and tell you that. I will cherish every minute, every second that you spent with me on Saturday for the rest of my life. I didn't want the visit to end. I can't believe no one has placed a wedding ring on your lovely finger. What's wrong with the brothers on the outside? You're a prize, an unclaimed treasure, Eva. I knew it the second I laid eyes on you.

I've been told that confession is good for the soul. Eva, I have a confession to make. I realize what I'm about to say may cause you some uneasiness, or worse, anger you. Know that I'd never want to do either. Just forgive me for having to say what's on my heart. Here goes. Eva, I'm attracted to you. Is it infatuation? I don't know. Perhaps. Since the first time I saw you, I haven't been able to stop thinking about you. Your smile, your thoughtfulness, the graceful manner in which you carry yourself, and those beautiful brown eyes. You are captivating. You're on my mind first thing in the morning and last thing at night. The faintest whiffs of honeysuckle, a flower kissed by the sun, are constant reminders of you. If I could create a lily, I would create one just for you, because you are so deserving.

Eva, I don't believe in chance encounters. I believe there is a purpose for everything, and there's a reason why you and I have met. Is it wishful thinking on my part to think someone like you would give me, an inmate, the

*chance to show you what I feel for you? Please, don't
be angry with me for what I've written. I can't help that
I'm taken by you any more than you can help that you're
beautiful. I wish you could see yourself through my eyes.
You are a treasure to behold.*

*I would never want to cause you a moment of pain,
Eva. And I hope what I've shared hasn't distressed you
in any way. It's just that every time I had the pleasure of
being in your company and gazing in your lovely face,
I found myself wanting to know you more and more. It
pains me to think I may never see you again. And if that
is the case, know that you will forever be special to me.
I'll never, ever forget you. Thanks so much for the conversation, smiles, and prayers. I wish you love, peace,
and happiness.*

Sincerely,
Xavier

*PS: I'm not running a "game" on you. My feelings are
quite sincere.*

Wow! I read the letter again before placing it back in the
envelope, then look up at the sky. "Lord, why does he have to
be locked up? Why, why, why?"

I don't care what Mama said. I'm not dressing up for this
date; I'm keeping it very casual—denim skirt, white blouse,
and navy sandals. She's called three times to tell me what a
good catch Otis is and not to "blow it." I'll be so glad when I
get a man, because then she can get off my back. I'm amazed
I haven't suffered a stroke or heart attack from the stress and
agony I endure from punking out to her.

When Otis pulls into the driveway, I'm in the living room,
peeping out the window. He's driving his black Hummer.
Before he opens his car door, I'm outside on the front porch,
grinning and waving like a fool. "Hey, Otis!"

"Hel-lo, there," he says, exiting the Hummer. Well dressed

as usual, he's wearing a burgundy polo shirt, tan trousers, and burgundy, kidskin StacyAdams slip-ons. His big belly—he looks seven months pregnant—is protruding over his belt, where a pager is clipped. "You look great!" he says, with a big smile.

I fly down the steps. "Thank you, and you don't look bad yourself." Well, it's not a complete lie. If it weren't for his Jheri Curl and potbelly, he would score favorably on my Best-Looking Brothers Scale. He gets a mediocre score of five right now.

Three years older than me, Otis is a divorcé raising his only child, a son who's a junior and a basketball player at Duke University. A trustee in his church, he's college-educated and well off. According to the grapevine, the notorious playboy is approaching millionaire status.

Otis embraces me, and I roll across his big, flabby stomach. *Ugh!* Why can't he have rock-solid abs like Xavier? Maybe if I pretend he has a body like Xavier's, this date won't be so bad.

"I don't know why you aren't sashaying down the runways in New York and Paris with Naomi Campbell," he whispers in my ear.

I step back and smile at him.

He gives me the once-over and rubs his stomach. "I hope you're hungry. I sure am. I've made reservations for us at Guy's. Is that okay?"

"That's fine." Guy's is Raleigh's premier Caribbean and soul-food restaurant.

Otis opens the front passenger door of the Hummer and helps me inside. From the corner of my eye, I see that he's grinning and eyeballing my legs. The mellow sounds of Luther Vandross emanate from the audio system. Luther crooning, the musk-scented freshener in the SUV, and Otis's sensual cologne relax me, and I settle back into the soft leather seat. When Otis gets in the Hummer, he leans over and asks about my listening pleasure. I say, with a forced smile, that Luther is fine and compliment him on his ride. I've never ridden in a

Hummer before. As Otis backs out of the driveway, he reaches for my hand and interlocks his fingers with mine; I grit my teeth. I hope his fingernails are clean. A major turnoff for me is a man with dirty nails. I sneak a look. The nails are clean and neatly filed.

Otis talks nonstop about his possessions and aspirations during the drive to Guy's. I feel he's trying to impress me, so I stroke his ego by appearing overly impressed with his accomplishments. In addition to his Hummer, he has a Navigator and a Mercedes S500 Sedan; a custom-built, thirty-five-hundred-square-foot home, not far from Willnetta and Joel; time-shares in Florida and Nassau; a sailboat; and yearly earnings of almost a half-million dollars, and he plans to open his fourth funeral home next year. When he says he's seriously thinking about settling down and sharing all that he has with a special lady, I look over and smile at him. He squeezes my hand, leans close to me, and starts singing "Going in Circles" along with Luther.

When we pull into the parking lot at Guy's, Otis asks me to go with him to Nassau for a few days. If only I were attracted to him. I cringe every time I glance over in his direction and see that big belly of his resting up against the steering wheel.

The hostess seats us right away at the restaurant. She tells Otis that a jazz band from Memphis is performing tonight, and the band he's fond of from Atlanta will be performing next Saturday night.

"Thank you for that info," he says, grinning and winking at the woman.

"You're welcome, Mr. Reid," she says, walking off.

A waitress hurries over to our table. She, too, greets Otis by name and welcomes us to the restaurant. After she takes our drink orders and leaves, Otis leans across the table and grabs my hands. "You're gonna make me chase you, aren't you?"

I burst out laughing. "Why would you ask that?"

"Just a feeling I have."

Could it be because I'm not chasing him, like half the women in Fairview?

"Your mama says you're real picky."

I'm sure that's not all she said. "Did she?"

"Uh-huh. I'm very attracted to you, Eva," he says, squeezing my hands. "You're a classy, beautiful lady."

I smile and pretend to be flattered. If I were a gold digger, I would lead him on and spend his money. *Father, am I making another mistake by dissing him? Will I find myself years from now sitting on a church pew, sadly watching him say, "I do," to somebody else?*

"So tell me. What do you do for fun?" Otis asks.

"My mother didn't tell you?"

He laughs.

"I need to ask you something," I say playfully.

"Sure."

"Will you let go of my hands so I can look at the menu?"

"Ooops, I'm sorry," he says, releasing them.

I pick up the menu and flip slowly through it. I already know what I want; I just don't want Otis holding and caressing my hands. I look up at him and smile. "Do you already know what you want?"

"You," he whispers. "I want you."

I laugh and look back down at the menu.

The waitress arrives with our drinks—two sweet teas—and a basket of hush puppies. After placing our orders—smothered turkey wings for Otis and jerk chicken for me—Otis reaches for my hands again.

"If you don't mind," I say, reaching for a hush puppy, "I'm gonna have a few while they're still hot."

"I like brown, hot things, too."

Oh, brother!

"You work out, don't you?" asks Otis.

"Yes."

"Mmmm," he moans. "I would love to see you work up a sweat."

"Excuse me?"

Otis runs his tongue across his top lip and winks. "Mmm-hmm, you heard me."

If he keeps this up, I'm not going to make it through dinner and the jazz concert.

"I like a woman who takes care of her body," says Otis.

"And I like a man who does the same."

He laughs and pats his midsection. "You don't like my love handles?"

Please!

The waitress places our salads on the table. Otis says grace. I like that, a praying man. When I look up, he winks and blows me a kiss. I look down and start in on my salad.

"You gonna go with me to Nassau?" Otis asks.

"I have to pass on that. But thanks for the invitation."

"Why?"

Otis's pager goes off. He unclips it from his belt and looks at the display.

"Business or personal?" I ask.

He smiles and clips the pager back over his belt.

"Tell me, Otis, how does it feel to be Fairview's most eligible Black bachelor?"

"Awww, come on now," he replies, laughing.

"Come on nothing! Don't tell me you don't encounter an unending *throng* of women dying to be the next Mrs. Otis Reid."

"I don't mean to sound *conceited*," he says matter-of-factly, "but, yes, I do." He smiles and leans forward. "And I hope I'm talking to one right now. Tell me I am."

"Otis, this is our first date. You may not want to see me after tonight."

"Nonsense. I'm looking forward to us spending *lots* of time together."

"Let's not rush things, okay?"

He nods and sits back. "No problem. You're in the driver's seat, my dear. The ball's in your court. We can take things as slow-ly as you like."

I smile and start back on my salad.

"What're you looking for in a man, Eva?"

"Romance, honesty, good communication, and respect for starters."

"When was the last time someone held you close and made you feel like a queen?" he asks, jabbing at his salad.

It's been a long, long time. My pride won't let me tell him that. "My last serious relationship was six months ago," I lie.

"Were you in love?"

"Yes."

"Did this man love you back and make you feel special?"

"Otis, I'd rather not talk about it, okay?"

"Tell me. I want to know."

"Let's finish our salads, okay?"

He smiles. "Okay."

When our dinners arrive, I dive right into my meal. Otis follows my lead. Halfway through dinner, he lays his fork down and gently kicks me under the table.

"Let's skip the concert. How does a massage after dinner sound? You seem a little uptight," he says.

I shake my head and continue eating.

"We could go skinny-dipping in my hot tub afterwards," he adds.

I almost choke on a piece of chicken. I swallow with difficulty and shake my head.

"Come on, baby. Let me show you a good time," Otis pleads.

"I'd rather listen to the band or catch Denzel's new movie."

"Let's make our own movie."

"No."

"Come on, girl. Let me hold you tonight," he says lustfully, "and make you feel beautiful."

That's it! The date's over! I drop my fork, grimace, and lean forward.

Otis jumps up and rushes to my side. "Eva! Are you okay?"

I hear concern in his voice. Good. My dramatic performance is working. I moan softly and rub my forehead. "I-I'm coming down with a mi-migraine."

"I have aspirin in the Hummer," he says softly.

I shake my head. "Aspirin won't help. I'm sorry. I need to get home and lie down. Oh, I'm getting nauseous and dizzy!"

Otis looks hurt, or is that disappointment clouding his face? I don't care. I'm angry and insulted! Homeboy was banking on getting some booty tonight. What type of woman does he think I am? An easy one who is willing to exchange sex for flattery and a meal? Maybe he's testing me to see if I'm easy. If that's the case, I resent that, too! Potbellied, horny dog!

My head is beginning to ache for real now. I should tell Otis off and leave his pregnant-looking butt right here in the restaurant. And this is who Mama wants for a son-in-law! I can't wait to tell her about Mr. Otis Reid, and I want Geraldine to be around when I do. She'll be understanding and supportive of my decision not to go out with him again.

Otis motions for the waitress. When she asks if I want a carryout box, I shake my head and tell Otis I'll wait for him outside. When he joins me, he has two plastic bags in his hand.

Once seated in the Hummer, I lean my head against the headrest, close my eyes, and pray Otis doesn't talk my head off during the ride home. When he tells me he'd hoped to take me by his house to see his extensive jazz and blues collections, I hear major disappointment in his voice. I want to laugh out loud. Instead, I moan real pitiful like. When he pulls into my driveway, I quickly unbuckle my seat belt and open the car door.

"Wait! Let me help you," says Otis.

"I can manage."

"Here's your dinner," he says, reaching in the back for one of the carryout bags from Guy's.

That chicken was good, so I take the bag. "Thank you."

"Can we get together next week?"

No! I step out of the Hummer.

"Can we? How 'bout it?" Otis insists.

"Otis, I have to check my calendar."

"I'll call you."

I walk hurriedly to the porch, grimacing and groaning

along the way. Otis places an arm around my waist and helps me up on the porch. I turn to thank him and say good night. He kisses me on my lips. I push him off me and nearly fall back onto the porch. He grabs me and wraps both arms around my waist.

"Let me come inside?" he asks, grinding up against me. "I got a remedy for that headache of yours."

I should smack this horny fart across those juicy lips of his or, better yet, knee him in the groin.

"Don't make me beg," he whispers, his hot breath hitting me in the face. "You say you like romance. Let me show you how romantic I can be."

"No!"

Otis steps back and throws up his hands. "All right, baby doll. Calm down," he says, chuckling.

I unlock the front door and step inside.

"I'll call you next week," Otis says.

I look back, shoot him a phony smile, and slam the door shut.

17

Rebuke

See me after church!!!

Teresa and I burst out laughing.

"Girrrl, you're gonna get it," Teresa whispers. "Pastor McKnight gone be preaching your funeral next Sunday."

I look back down at the note Mama had the usher bring me and bite my bottom lip in an effort to stop laughing. Mama is pissed. I won't even look in her direction for fear she's looking back at me. She called at 6:00, 7:20, and 9:15 this morning. I didn't answer the phone once. I didn't feel up to being grilled and then chewed out about my date with Otis Reid.

"Look!" Teresa whispers, nudging me.

I look up and in the direction Teresa is looking. Strolling up the aisle, toward the front, like a newly crowned Miss America on her victory walk, is, according to Mama, another Community Baptist spinster. Alongside her is a fair-skinned man in an ill-fitting black suit. I nudge Teresa. "That doesn't look like the guy that was with her two Sundays ago."

"It's not."

"How long do you think that's going to last?"

Teresa scoffs and rolls her eyes. "About as long as the others."

The woman and man sit down on a pew up front, beside Community Baptist's next bride-to-be, thirty-three-year-old Monica Isaac, and her fiancé, a prominent local ophthalmologist.

"Maybe she thinks Monica's luck will rub off on her," Teresa whispers.

"I sure wish it would rub off on me," I whisper back, laughing.

I don't care how much Mama or the church mothers ride my back about not having a man. I'm not going to date just anything breathing with a penis, like this woman, the serial dater, so I can be spared the stigma associated with being single.

Willnetta's wedding was the third wedding I'd been in at the church in the last two years. "Forever a bridesmaid and never a bride, huh, Eva?" the serial dater had said to me the Sunday before Willnetta's wedding. The comment hurled me into a deep state of depression and angered me, too, because Lord knows she's a fine one to talk. The guy she was showing off at church during the Christmas holiday turned out to be a bigamist. When one of his wives tracked him down in Fairview, he abruptly left town, with six thousand dollars of the serial dater's money. She doesn't think anybody at church knows this and would die from embarrassment if she knew some of us did. Joel became aware of the matter because a detective with the Norfolk, Virginia, police department came to town to investigate her claim of being ripped off. He told Willnetta, and she wasted no time telling Teresa and me.

My cousin and her fine husband are sitting two pews behind the serial dater and Monica. I close my eyes and pray for a lifetime of happiness for them.

"Sister Isaac wants me to announce," the church secretary says, "that her fiancé will administer free glaucoma screenings for the seniors of our church next Thursday and Friday at his office."

Loud applause and praises to God ring out.

"His office, for those of you who don't know, is located on

the second floor of that brand-new brick building downtown, across from Dean's Florist," adds the church secretary.

I look over at Monica. She's smiling broadly.

"I'm urging *all* our seniors," the secretary says, peering over her glasses, "to take advantage of this, especially if you've never been tested for glaucoma before."

"Amen!" Pastor McKnight says from the pulpit. "Madam Secretary, do people need to call and schedule an appointment time?"

The secretary looks over at Monica and the doctor.

The doctor stands and nods. "Giving honor to God, my Lord and Savior Jesus Christ, the fine pastor of this church, its officers, and the church family, let me first say, I'm glad to be back visiting at Community Baptist one more time."

"Glad to have you, son!" someone from the Deacons and Trustees Corner says.

"Thank you," the doctor says, nodding, with a big smile. "In response to your question, Reverend McKnight, no appointment is necessary. We will take people on a first-come, first-served basis."

More applause and praises to the Lord ring out. The doctor sits down, and Monica leans over and smiles up into his face. *Why can't I meet somebody like that?*

"He's a fine young man," someone sitting behind me says.

"Monica sho' is lucky," someone else says.

"I sho' hope the choir sings something to lift my spirit," I whisper to Teresa.

"Amen!" she whispers back.

"Will all our visitors please stand at this time?" the secretary asks warmly.

Several people throughout the church stand, including the guy that came in with the serial dater.

The secretary continues. "On behalf of Pastor McKnight and the officers of this church, I extend to each of you a warm welcome. And if there's anything we can do to make your visit with us more enjoyable, please let us know. Because we would love nothing more than to have you visit with us again."

"Amen!" Pastor McKnight and some of the deacons and trustees say.

"The doors to Community Missionary Baptist swing open, wide open," the secretary says, smiling, with outstretched arms, "on welcome hinges. Again, you are welcomed!"

Applause and shouts of "Amen" ring out.

The visitors sit down, the secretary returns to her seat, and the senior choir rises. While they do injustice to "What a Fellowship," I take a trip down memory lane. My thoughts turn to a former love and the Sunday we sat here in church. I sat on the pew, close to him, and imagined the two of us standing at the altar, exchanging wedding vows. If I hadn't followed Mama back home and stayed as long as I did, I believe my last name would be Donovan now, and I would be the mother of several children.

It was a bone-chilling, wintry January night, January 19, 1986, to be exact, and approaching midnight when sweet, sweet Troy Donovan and I met. I was thirty minutes from my apartment when my 1974 Toyota Celica broke down on Delmar Boulevard. I had just gotten off my part-time job as hotline counselor at a battered women's shelter and was trying to make it home before the snow started falling. My life flashed before my eyes that night as I shivered and cried in my car, fearing I would freeze to death. I didn't start bawling until I had thoughts of my parents, back in North Carolina, hearing on the evening news the following day that a Black, twenty-three-year-old, second-year, female grad student attending Washington University had been found dead in her car, and that the cause of death was hypothermia.

As I sobbed and prayed not to become a human icicle on the side of the road, I heard tapping on the driver's window. Through the light blanket of snow on the window I saw a concerned face.

From the time we met, Troy and I rarely went a day without seeing each other. Three years older than me, he had moved to St. Louis from New York and was working at McDonnell Douglas as an aerospace engineer. My graduation present from him was a weeklong trip to the Bahamas. We were to leave the Sunday after my graduation, and while away, we were going to talk about the next step of our relationship.

The day of my graduation proved to be one of the happiest and also one of the saddest days of my life. Hours after I received my master's and graduated with honors from a prestigious university, with my family in attendance, Mama told my sisters and me that when she returned home, she was going to leave Daddy. The news floored me. I followed her back to North Carolina, weeping and wailing, thinking I could help Stephanie and Geraldine talk some sense into her.

A week after returning home, Mama packed up her things and moved out. Daddy was heartbroken. I couldn't bring myself to leave him, and I grew more determined to get him and Mama back together.

The days at home became weeks and then months. When Troy came to visit that Sunday we sat in church together, me grinning like Monica, he asked me to go back to St. Louis with him. I refused, because I was still trying to get Mama and Daddy back together. A month later, I was standing at the altar, crying my eyes out. Troy had called off our seven-month relationship. He said it was for the best, seeing that I could not say when I would be returning to St. Louis, and he had no desire to be in a long-distance relationship.

Since Troy, there have been two other guys that I've cared deeply for. Unfortunately, they both turned out to be commitment-phobic.

I sigh heavily and look over at Teresa. Summer is weeks away, and it looks like she and I are going to end up on another cruise with Stephanie. When it's time for altar pray, we join fellow parishioners at the altar and petition the Lord for boyfriends.

"Amen" is barely out of my mouth when someone taps me hard on my shoulder. I look back; it's Mama.

"Meet me at my car," she whispers hoarsely.

"Okay. What's up?" I ask, with a cheery smile.

Mama narrows her eyes at me and walks off. I wonder if she's talked to Otis.

I slowly make my way to the front exit, dreading the tongue-lashing she's gone give me when I tell her she has to abort her plans for a Liles and Reid wedding. Pastor McKnight and Mrs. McKnight are in the vestibule, bidding farewell to congregants.

"Sister Eva, what's this I hear?" Pastor McKnight asks, grabbing my hands.

"Sir?" I reply.

"Wedding bells next year!" Mrs. McKnight exclaims, with a big smile.

"Wedding bells? For who?" I ask.

"You!" she says. "I hear you and Otis Reid are an item now."

Oh, Lord, what has Mama gone and done?

When the shock of what Mrs. McKnight said to me wears off, I'm standing in the middle of the church parking lot, not knowing how I made it out of the church and down the front steps.

"Eva! I'm parked over there!" shouts Mama.

I take off for Mama's car. I beat her and Miss Ida getting to it.

Mama brushes past me, unlocks the car doors, and tells me, with a finger and a grunt, to get in the backseat. Miss Ida climbs up front. When I close the door behind me, Mama starts the car, locks the doors, and turns the air-conditioning up full blast. *Oh yeah, it's about to be on now.*

"How're you doing today?" Miss Ida turns and asks me.

"I'm fine, Miss Ida, and—"

"I don't believe you!" Mama yells, lowering her sun visor. She glares at me in the rearview mirror. "What is wrong with you?"

"Nothing," I reply coolly. "And did you tell Pastor and Mrs. McKnight that Otis and I were *dating*?"

"Isn't that what you call what you two did last night?" cries Mama.

"No! Don't get it twisted, Mama," I reply. "That was a *date*. A date and dating are two different things."

Mama hits the steering wheel. "Don't get sassy with me!"

"Rose, calm down," Miss Ida says softly. "If she don't like Otis, she just don't like him."

"Ida, please!" says Mama. "If you had daughters, *single* daughters at that, you'd understand what I'm going through."

"My great-nieces, Regina and Lynette, are like daughters to me," Miss Ida says, with a big smile. "They aren't married."

"And what man would want to marry either one of them, Ida, with all them babies they got?" asks Mama.

Miss Ida sighs softly and looks out her window. Granted, she and Mama have been friends for as long as I can remember, I don't see how she puts up with Mama's insensitivity sometimes.

"Am I to assume that you and Mr. Reid have talked?" I ask.

Mama glares back at me in the rearview mirror. "Yes, you can."

"I'm curious. Who called who?" I ask.

"You didn't answer your phone this morning, so I called him," says Mama. "I didn't know where you—"

"You thought I'd spent the night at his house!" I cry.

"You didn't answer your phone, so what was I supposed to think?" says Mama.

"Be for real, Mama!"

"You get real! You want to grow old by yourself? Huh? Is that what you want?" shouts Mama.

I look out the window.

"You gonna let this good man get away, too?" Mama murmurs.

I laugh. "What makes you think he's such a gonna man? Huh? He tried to get in my bed last night!"

"My goodness!" Miss Ida shrieks.

"He's a man," Mama says coolly. "What man ain't gonna get frisky with a woman? It's *your* job to keep him in his place."

"I think it's downright disrespectful," I say.

"It is," Miss Ida says.

Mama scoffs. "You don't think your daddy didn't try to have his way with me the first time we went out?"

I narrow my eyes at Mama. "Let's not go there, okay?"

Mama looks over at Miss Ida. "Ida, you see. She just like her sisters. She thinks the sun rises and sets on her long-legged daddy. She doesn't like to hear *anything* unbecoming about him."

"I 'spect she don't," Miss Ida says.

Mama looks back at me in the rearview mirror. "Eva, men are mannish. It's their nature. If Otis hadn't gotten fresh with you, you'd think he was funny. Like you did Deacon Jones's grandson."

"Deacon Jones's grandson is gay, okay?" I say.

"I heard the same thang," Miss Ida says, looking back at me. "Heard, too, he shacking with an old man in Durham."

"Say what, Miss Ida? Who told you that?" I ask.

"Will you two stop it?" Mama yells. "We're not talking about Deacon Jones's prissy grandson!"

"You brought him up," I mumble.

Mama narrows her eyes at me. "Daughter, you're really stressing me out now."

I exhale and rest my head on the back of my seat.

"When are you going out with Otis again?" asks Mama.

Never! "I don't know, Mama."

"Whatcha mean you don't know?" Mama says. "You're forty years old. When I was your age—"

"Otis said he would call me. We'll see," I say.

Mama sighs loudly and turns the air-conditioning down. "Help me, Jesus!"

Yes, please help her, Lord.

"You coming by for dinner?" asks Mama.

"No, Teresa and I are going out," I say.

"Well, I'll fix you something to take to work. Stop by later to get it," says Mama. "Geraldine's speaking next Sunday somewhere in Hayesfield. Leon's working, so I want you to take me and Ida."

"Okay," I say and unlock my door and get out.

"Bye, sweetheart," Miss Ida says.

"I wave good-bye.

If Mama thinks I'm stopping by later so she can badger me again about Otis Reid, she can think again. I burst out laughing and hurry to my SUV.

18

The Blues

"You still at work, I see."

"Yep, still here," I reply.

"You coming by?"

"Naw. I'll be here a while."

"Don't work too late."

"I won't, Mama."

"Bye."

I hang up the phone and listen as my female coworkers ramble on in the hallway about weekend plans with their significant others. I feel so left out. *Lord, will I ever be able to join in on these Friday afternoon conversations?* Tears fill my eyes again. I get up and close my office door.

Unlike scores of working folks, I've never experienced a case of Monday morning blues; I suffer from what I call the Friday afternoon blues! My spirit, without fail, plummets Friday afternoons around quitting time over not having someone special to spend my weekends with.

"Eva? Can I come in?"

I blink back the tears and take a deep breath. "Come on in, Rhonda," I say cheerfully.

The door opens, and blond, hazel-eyed Rhonda Pearl enters, flashing her picture-perfect all-American girl smile.

"Hey, girl. Whatcha doing?" she asks, walking up to my desk.

"Signing off on mileage reimbursement requests."

"Oh."

Rhonda works down the hall, in the child abuse and neglect unit, as an investigator. Attractive, smart, and personable, she appears to have it all.

"This weekend is going to be *gorgeous*! Steve and I are going to the beach," she says.

"Wonderful!" I manage to say, with a smile.

Steve, Rhonda's current beau, is an assistant district attorney.

"We packed last night, so when Steve picks me up"— Rhonda looks at her watch—"in about twenty minutes, we're heading straight to South Carolina."

"Myrtle Beach?"

"Naw, Hilton Head."

"Nice."

"So, what're you doing this weekend?" she asks, with raised eyebrows. "And don't tell me, 'Nothing.'"

"Well, I don't have anything fun planned like you," I say, laughing.

Rhonda sighs heavily.

I sit back and wait for what typically comes next—an update.

"I saw this cute guy down at the courthouse this morning. Girl, he was fine. But I couldn't see if he had a wedding ring on. He got on the elevator before I could."

"He probably did," I say, sighing.

Rhonda and Delores, the receptionist, have been trying to hook me up for the longest. I used to find their man-hunting antics funny; now they're wearisome and quite depressing.

"Judge Melville asked about you."

I roll my eyes. Good-looking, flirtatious, Tom Selleck–looking Judge Melville is always asking Rhonda about me.

Whenever he runs into me at the courthouse, he smiles and makes small talk. The last time I bumped into him, he was bold enough to ask me out to dinner.

"You're beautiful and smart, Eva. There's somebody out there for you," says Rhonda.

And if I had a hundred dollars for every time she has said that, I'd be wealthy.

"We're gonna find him, girl. We are," she promises.

Easier said than done. Rhonda hasn't a clue. Most professional White women I know are married or dating. Rhonda is no exception. When she broke up with her last boyfriend—an IBM programmer—three months ago, it wasn't long before she hooked up with the ADA. I'm a firm believer that no other group of women has it as bad as the sistas when it comes to finding love.

"Well, let me go finish up a few things before Steve gets here," says Rhonda.

"Okay."

"You have a great weekend."

"Thanks. You too."

Before Rhonda closes my office door, I overhear someone in the hallway say she's heading to the mountains for a romantic getaway.

When I pull into my driveway, the Jenningses' puppy runs over, barking ferociously. Mrs. Jennings's grandchildren run outside in their pajamas, yelling for him to come back. He takes off running down the street. I park and walk back to the mailbox.

"Sorry 'bout that, Eva," Mrs. Jennings says, stepping outside. "He will not stay in this yard when we let him out. He ran over there this afternoon and almost bit that man from Dean's Florist."

"Dean's Florist?" I blurt out.

"Yes." Mrs. Jennings smiles. "There're some pretty flowers on your porch."

My head jerks around, and the rest of my body follows. Even though it's dark outside, I can see the yellow lilies next to the geraniums on my porch.

"Good night, Eva," Mrs. Jennings says, hurrying down the street.

"Good night, Mrs. Jennings."

Xavier has sent me lilies. I know they're from him. I hurry to the porch to find out.

Roses are red, violets are blue, neither flower is as lovely as you. Take care, Eva. Xavier

I burst out laughing. Corny, but very sweet. I place the card back in the envelope, pick up the lilies, and head inside.

19

Surprise!

"Good mornin', Miss Liles! And thanks for breakfast!"

"You're welcome, Mr. Terry, and good morning to you!"

Whenever I bring in breakfast for the unit, I always extend an invite to Harvey Terry. The chatty sixty-seven-year-old Black security guard is well liked by staff, and is good about keeping me and the other Black supervisors abreast of what's going on in the building. I can tell he's in a talkative mood by the way he's leaning up against Delores's desk. She's grinning broadly and tossing her Fashion Fair make-up into her pocketbook. When I became supervisor of the family support unit eight years ago, Delores was one of my first hires, and she has yet to disappoint me. Loyal, hardworking, proficient, hands down, she's the best receptionist slash secretary I've ever worked with. And despite my itching ears, I'm not going to mosey over to chew the fat with her and Mr. Terry right now. Six new cases have been transferred to my unit; I need to review and assign them to social workers before the end of the day.

I dart around the corner and down the carpeted hallway to

my office to finish watering my plants. When my computer boots up, I sit down at my desk to check my e-mail. I have four new messages. The first one is from Stephanie. She e-mails me every morning.

Morning, girl,
Have you and Tee made up your minds about the cruise? If we're going, don't you think it's time we made reservations?!
I talked to Mama last night. Hee, hee! She's still pissed at you about Otis. Ooooh, imagine that!

I click the reply icon.

Hey!
Teresa and I haven't talked any more about the cruise. Since Mrs. Williams is ill, I've been toying w/the idea of driving to St. Louis. Sound like fun? I would want you and Teresa to go w/me. We could even drive up to Chicago for a few days! Let me know.
Yeah, Mama is still a little warm w/me. She didn't even cook yesterday! Girl, I had to eat at Daddy and Miss Elsie's.
Later!

The second e-mail is from the agency director. It's a reminder about the supervisors' staff meeting this afternoon.

E-mail number three is from the dean of the arts, humanities, and social sciences department at the community college. She wants to know if I will teach the social work and child welfare course again this fall.

I reply. Be glad to.

I click on my last new e-mail.

Good morning, Beautiful,
I was thinking of you first thing this morning, like most
days, and wanted to say hello. I think of you often, Eva.
I do. You'd be surprised to know how often. By now
you should have received a letter from me. Everything
I've written is sincere. I hope to change your mind
about me.
Hope you liked the lilies.
Xavier
PS: My e-mail to you has to be another one of our
 secrets. ☺ Inmates are prohibited access to the
Internet.

I sit back hard in my chair and stare at my laptop screen.
What in the world? How did he get my e-mail address? Loud,
rapid knocks on my door pull me from my bewildered
thoughts.

"Come in," I reply, sitting up.

Delores walks in, rolling her eyes and sighing heavily. It's
just a few minutes after eight, and she's already worked up
about something. I close Xavier's e-mail.

"Misty Neville and those hyperactive boys of hers are in
the waiting room. They smell terrible!" Delores rolls her eyes
again and exhales loudly. "I told her that her worker wasn't in
and to come back after one. She tells me she'll wait. I heard
one of the boys say he was hungry. Eva, I don't want them sitting up front with me until one! Neither my nerves nor my
stomach can take it!"

"I'll get someone to see Misty."

"Thank you!" Delores says, hurrying out of my office.

I pick up the phone and dial the extension of a social
worker in the unit. When she answers, I explain my need for
her to meet with one of her coworker's clients. After ending
the call, I try to figure out how Xavier got my e-mail address.
Then it dawns on me. He must have logged on to the agency's
Web site and perused the employee directory. That information is accessible to anyone with access to the Internet.

"Got something for you!" Delores says, sticking her head into my office.

"What now?"

"Oh! I think you're going to like this," she sings, stepping inside.

"No!"

"Yes! Where do you want them?"

I can't bring myself to speak.

"I think they'll look pretty right here," Delores says as she places the bouquet of multicolored lilies on my desk, between the five-by-seven photos of my niece and nephew. She then looks at me and smiles. "You got a boyfriend?"

"I wish."

"Who's sending you flowers?"

I smile at Delores. "What was Mr. Terry talking about this morning?"

"Uh-uh!" she grunts, shaking her head. "You answer *my* question."

Delores removes the yellow envelope from the card caddy and hands it to me. I take it from her and pull out the card.

Thinking of you. Xavier

"What's it say?"

"Thinking of you." I tuck the card back in the envelope. "So, what was Mr. Terry talking about?"

Delores smiles and places her hands on her hips. "You didn't tell me you'd started seeing somebody."

"I'm not seeing anyone."

"So what's this?" she asks, with a wave of her hand.

"Nothing."

"Nothing? I beg to differ! This looks like a whole lot of *something* to me!"

"Believe me when I say, it's nothing."

"Now what's wrong with *this* man? He don't make enough money? He short? He ugly? What?"

He's in prison! Okay? Lord knows I ain't about to tell her that!

Delores looks back at the door, then back at me. "Is he married?"

"No!"

"So why you being secretive then?"

"Girl, will you get out of here so I can get back to work. And close the door behind you. Thank you."

Delores smacks her fuchsia-colored lips. "You gone tell me who this man is," she says, backing out of my office.

When Delores exits, I reopen Xavier's e-mail. My eyes rest on the words *I hope to change your mind about me.* I minimize my e-mail page, log on to the Internet, and then click on the FAVORITES icon. I stroll down to the North Carolina Department of Corrections Public Access Information System link and click the mouse button. This Web site provides pictures, demographics, and sentence information on persons actively serving time in North Carolina prisons. I access it from time to time in search of absentee parents whose children come through the family support unit. Gina and I used to peruse the site for information on Tony during his stints behind bars.

After typing in Xavier's name, sex, and race, and clicking on SEARCH FOR OFFENDER, one "Dupree, Xavier S." pops up on the screen. I click on the name. A head shot of Xavier appears. The demographic information notes that he is forty-three years old, six feet four inches tall, and weighs 225 pounds.

I scroll down to the incarceration summary. He was convicted two years ago of grand larceny, and his total sentence is five years. He has no infractions and is considered a low escape risk. His parole eligibility date is July 8 of this year.

I scroll back up to Xavier's picture and stare at his face. I see what I believe to be sadness in his eyes. I click off the screen as tears fill mine.

I flip through my Rolodex with one hand and pick up the

telephone receiver with the other. When I find the number I want, I pray that the person I'm calling is at her desk.

"Probation and Parole."

"Trenise Johnson, please," I say.

"Just a moment."

Trenise, a family support unit success story, worked her way off welfare. A single, young mother of two, she's employed full time as a clerk typist in the pre-sentence reporting section of the Department of Probation and Parole. Whenever I need information on someone in the corrections system, she's the person I call.

"Hello, this is Trenise."

"Hey, Trenise. How are you?"

"Miss Liles, hey! I'm fine. How're you?"

"Doing well. How're the kids?"

"They're fine."

"Good. You busy this morning?"

"Kinda. You need me to look something up for you?"

"Yeah, a pre-sentence report."

"No problem. Let me grab something to write with. Okay. What's the name?"

"Xavier S. Dupree. Inmate number 046693."

"Got it. You in your office?"

"Yeah. Think you can get back to me this morning?"

"Yes."

"Thanks, Trenise."

I hang up the phone and try real hard to direct my attention to the six files piled on my desk.

At 11:37, my phone rings. I'm hoping it's Trenise.

"Eva Liles."

"Hey, Miss Liles."

"Trenise, whatcha got?"

"Well, there's not a whole lot in this man's pre-sentence report. He's never been arrested or convicted of anything until this incident."

"Really?"

"Uh-huh."

"What do you have?"

"Authorities found stolen clothes with a street value of seventy-five thousand dollars in a Raleigh store owned by Dupree and another individual, identified as his business partner. The clothes were stolen from a New York clothier. Dupree denies any wrongdoing. He claims he did not know the clothes were stolen and provided authorities with the name of a witness who could corroborate his claim. Authorities were never able to locate the witness at the time of this report. Oh, get this."

"What?"

"The name of the supplier he gave the authorities turned out to be that of a man who had been dead ten years."

"What?"

"Uh-huh," Trenise says, laughing.

"My goodness! He was set up big time."

Trenise stops laughing. "You think he was set up, Miss Liles?"

"Yeah, I do. Any mention of a wife or children?"

"Ummm, yes. Married once, currently divorced, and no children. At the time of his arrest, he was living in Charlotte. You want me to keep going?"

"Yes, read everything you got. Everything."

"In addition to the clothing stores, he is part owner of a sixteen-unit apartment building—"

"Sixteen-unit apartment building?"

"Yes, ma'am. And . . ." Trenise exhales loudly.

"What, Trenise?"

"He is also part owner of two McDonald's."

"McDonald's Restaurants?" I yell.

"Yep, *and* a laundromat."

"Dang!" I spin around in my chair and look out my fourth-floor office window.

"Dang is right!" Trenise says earnestly. "He's banking

mega bucks, 'cause I know them Mickey D's are bringing in big money."

Wow! To have accomplished all that and to end up in prison. "Anything else?"

"Member affiliations include Charlotte Black Businessmen, Inner City At-risk Youth Initiative, North Carolina A&T State University Alumni Association, and the North Carolina Rural Farmers' Bureau. Twelve years in the military, achieving rank of sergeant. Two college degrees. One in business and the other in agriculture science, both from A&T. He reports a close-knit family, has one sister living in Houston, and plans to live in Hayesfield, North Carolina, when released, where his parents, Samuel and Ann-Marie Dupree, reside. And that's it."

"I don't understand why he didn't get probation. No prior record, not even a speeding ticket. I don't get it."

"The probation officer that did this pre-sentence report recommended probation."

"Say what?"

"Uh-huh. I guess the ADA and the judge thought otherwise."

"That's a shame!"

"Miss Liles, I know for a fact that there are people walking the streets who have committed more serious crimes than grand larceny, and they've never spent a day in prison."

"Sometimes justice is truly blind."

"When it comes to people of *our* color, it often is."

I thank Trenise, say good-bye, and click back on Xavier's e-mail.

Good morning, Beautiful,
I was thinking of you first thing this morning, like most days, and wanted to say hello. I think of you often, Eva. I do. You'd be surprised to know how often. By now you should have received a letter from me. Everything I've written is sincere. I hope to change your mind about me.

Hope you liked the lilies.
Xavier
PS: My e-mail to you has to be another one of our secrets. ☺ Inmates are prohibited access to the Internet.

I click REPLY.

Xavier
Surprised to hear from you. I did get the flowers, BOTH bouquets. They're lovely. Thank you.
Eva

I take a deep breath and click SEND.

20

Social Work

"Get out! Get out!" Rhonda exclaims, rushing up to my desk. "They're beautiful!"

"See? What I tell you? And she still hasn't told me who sent them," Delores says, sitting down on the edge of my desk.

"Give it up, Eva," Rhonda orders.

"Welcome back, Rhonda! Looks like you got a lot of sun. You have a good trip?" I say.

"I did," Rhonda replies, eyeing and fingering my lilies. "But I don't want to talk about that," she says, batting her black, heavily coated eyelashes. "I want to know who sent you these lovely flowers!"

"Get her, girl!" Delores says, with a neck roll.

I burst out laughing.

"Now when I last saw you, you gave me the impression that you were going to be spending another weekend home alone," says Rhonda.

"And I did," I say.

"You did?" Rhonda asks, narrowing her eyes at me.

"I did," I repeat.

Rhonda looks at Delores, then back at me. "You didn't meet anyone this past weekend?"

I shake my head.

"You would tell us if you did, right?" says Rhonda.

"Of course, I would," I reply.

Rhonda looks at Delores and hunches up her shoulders. "This must be somebody she met prior to this past weekend and never bothered to tell us about."

"You think?" Delores asks.

"Will you two get out of here so I can finish looking over these court reports!" I interject.

Rhonda gasps loudly, and her eyes grow large and round. "Judge Melville?"

"Judge Melville? Heck, no!" I yell.

"Judge Melville?" Delores asks, looking from me to Rhonda.

"He's *crazy* about Eva," says Rhonda.

"Say whaaaat?" Delores exclaims.

Rhonda nods. "Cra-zy about her."

I sigh heavily and fall back in my chair. "What courtroom is he in this week? Please don't say 4D."

"Courtroom 2B," Rhonda says.

I exhale and wave my hands in the air.

Rhonda and Delores look at me questioningly.

"I have to be in 4D this morning," I say.

"And when you leave there, go down to 2B," Delores says, grinning.

"I don't think so," I mumble.

"Why not?" Delores asks.

Rhonda grunts. "He's too old for Eva."

"No, he's not!" cries Delores.

"Yes, he is. He's old enough to be her father," Rhonda argues.

"He's old enough to be *your* father, not Eva's," says Delores.

"Hey! Enough about Judge Melville, okay?" I say. "And to

answer your question"—I look at Rhonda—"he did not send me the flowers."

"Who then?" Delores asks, wide-eyed.

"Some guy, okay?" I reply.

"Duh! I figured that much out by myself," mutters Delores.

Rhonda plops down in the chair across from my desk. "Who, when, and where?"

I look down and start reading the court report in front of me.

"Hel-lo!" Rhonda yells, tapping her knuckles on my desk. "We're not leaving until you tell us something."

I sigh and look up. "If I tell y'all his name, will you leave?"

"Yes," Rhonda replies, smiling and bobbing her head.

"His name is Xavier," I say.

Rhonda's smile widens. "Mmmm, nice. Xavier. That's a strong, *sexy* name. When did you meet him?"

"No more questions! You agreed to leave after I told you his name," I say.

"I lied," adds Rhonda.

"What does he do?" Delores asks.

"Yeah, and what does he look like? Is he tall? I know you like 'em tall," adds Rhonda.

"I'm not saying any more," I reply.

"Oh, Eva!" Delores grumbles.

"Why won't you tell us something else about him?" Rhonda asks, pouting.

"Because it's not going to materialize into anything, that's why," I mutter.

Rhonda sighs and shakes her head. "And why not?"

Oh, brother! "Listen," I say. "He—"

"He what?" Delores asks, standing up and placing her hands on her hips.

"He has a few issues that I'd rather not talk about," I mumble.

Delores throws up her hands. "Who don't have issues? You got issues, Rhonda got issues, I got issues, all God's children got issues!"

"Amen, sista!" Rhonda shouts.

"Ain't no perfect man," says Delores.

"I know that, Delores," I reply.

"Do you?" Delores asks.

I look down.

"This man likes you, Eva," Rhonda says. "These flowers say, I want you."

I burst out laughing and look up at her. "Girl, you so silly."

"You're the envy of every woman on the floor, including me," Rhonda says, pouting.

"I have to be in court at ten. Good-bye!" I shout.

Rhonda and Delores sigh and shake their heads.

"At least we know his first name," Delores says.

"This conversation is not over!" Rhonda says, wagging a finger at me. "We'll be back. Count on it."

"And don't count this man out so fast," Delores advises.

When Rhonda and Delores clear my office, I reopen the e-mail I was reading when they barged in.

Good morning, Eva,
Thanks so much for replying to my e-mail. I was afraid you wouldn't. It made my day. You have no idea how much it did.
I'm glad you like the flowers. Did you get my letter? You didn't mention having so. I want to know your thoughts. Share them with me.
Will you help me w/something? I need the names and addresses of local agencies that provide mentor services to at-risk youth. One of the things I intend to do at my golf course is open an academy. I want to introduce the game of golf to at-risk youth. Any help you can offer will be greatly appreciated. Thanks!
Take care,
Xavier

If I respond to Xavier's request, it will give him a reason to e-mail me again. Do I want that?

I minimize my e-mail page and log on to the county's directory of resource providers in search of agencies providing services to at-risk youth. After discovering a Web site with links to numerous agencies, I log off the Web site and reopen my e-mail page and Xavier's e-mail. I click REPLY.

> Xavier,
> Your desire to help at-risk youth is admirable. You can find the names and addresses of several agencies that work w/this population at ncsaveouryouth.org
> I did get your letter, Xavier. I honestly don't know what to say or think. I wonder if it's all a con. And, I'm curious, although I think I know. How did you get my e-mail address?
> Eva

I hit SEND, close my e-mail page, and stare at the lilies.

"How was court?" Delores asks. She's sitting at her desk, completing a crossword puzzle.

"I didn't run into Judge Melville, if that's what you're asking."

Delores laughs. "Where'd you go for lunch?"

"The mall. Here's a cinnamon bun for you."

"Thanks! What did you buy?"

"Shoes, a bag, and this." I stick out my arm for Delores to smell my wrist.

"Nice! What is it?"

"Romance by Ralph Lauren."

"Oh, how fitting! New man, new perfume. Go on with your bad self!"

"Delores, Romance has been out awhile."

"You've worn it before?"

"No."

Delores grins. "No reason until now, huh?"

"Oh, please!"

"Oh, please, my foot! I think you like Xavier," Delores says, giggling and following me to my office.

I look back at her. "Have you had lunch yet?"

"No. I was waiting for you to get back."

"Why? What's up?"

"That's what's up," she says, pushing open my office door.

I gasp out loud. There, on my desk, is another bouquet of lilies. Red and white lilies.

"Eva, this man is se-ri-ous about you."

I walk over to my desk and remove the envelope from the card caddy.

Thinking of you, like always. Xavier

21

E-mails

Who am I fooling? I am worried. I didn't sleep well last night, and I couldn't concentrate at work today. Xavier hasn't e-mailed in two days. I fear it's because he got caught e-mailing me.

"Dear God," I pray, "please let him be okay. Father, wrap your arms around him and keep him safe. And Lord, I ask for your forgiveness now. I know it's wrong to lie, but if someone from the Department of Corrections contacts me and asks if I've received e-mails from him, I will deny having so, because he doesn't deserve to be in prison in the first place. Lord, why did he get sent there? Like Trenise said, there are people who've blatantly committed more serious crimes than his, and they've never seen the inside of a prison cell. Where is the justice in that? Where, Lord?"

I open my eyes and reach for the printed copies of Xavier's e-mails on my nightstand. I lie back on my bed to reread them.

Wednesday, June 12:

Eva,
I'm not conning you. Please, please believe that!
Inmates that con women do so for two reasons: they
want money sent to them while they're locked up,
and they need someplace to stay when released. I
don't want to come off like a braggart, but I don't
need either of those things from you or anyone. I
have a home to go to when I get out of here, and I
have money. What I want from you . . . Well, I'll
settle for your friendship for now. But know I'm
longing for more.
Thanks for the info. Regarding your e-mail address, I
got it off the employee directory on your agency's
Web site. ☺
Have a safe and wonderful afternoon.
Xavier

Thursday, June 13:

Good Morning, Eva,
I'm no druggie or alcoholic. I experimented with
marijuana once in high school, and I rarely drink.
And no, no, no! I've never, ever willingly or
unwillingly engaged in ANY homosexual behavior.
NEVER! I'm a heterosexual Black man partial to
tall, slim, long-legged Black women. Does that
description remind you of anyone? If not, look in
the mirror. ☺
No, I've not pursued a relationship with anyone
since being locked up. Haven't had a desire to, until
now.
Still no word from the parole board. ☹ My frat
brother's wife wrote me the other day. He is waiting
on a decision, too.

Eva, I never would have thought anything good could come out of me being in prison. Nothing could be further from the truth. Meeting you has been the best thing. Gotta go. Off to work. Take care.
Xavier

Friday, June 14:

Good Morning, Beautiful,
So you like the golf academy idea? Great! Any ideas on how I can get that going? I welcome your input. Who knows, Dupree Golf and Country Club could give birth to the next Tiger Woods. ☺ Plans for it and the nursery will begin as soon as I get out of here. If I'm released this summer, my goal is to open them next spring.
The businesses that I co-own, in addition to the clothing stores, are two McDonald's restaurants, a laundromat, and a sixteen-unit apartment building. All are doing well. My frat bro's wife & a management firm in Charlotte are overseeing things. I also own property in St. Lucia.
How're your flower gardens? The weekend's forecast is hot and humid. Please be careful if you work outside.
Have a wonderful weekend. I look forward to Monday morning, when I can e-mail you again. I enjoy e-mailing you and reading your e-mails. Tony is still Tony. I haven't given up on him yet. I think I've convinced him to get his GED. Time will tell how successful I am with that.
Take care,
Xavier

Monday, June 17:

Good Morning, Beautiful!
Hope your weekend was restful. Did you work
outside in your gardens? I wish I could see you, you
smart, gorgeous thing. I feel like a lovesick kid. Do I
sound like one? ☺ Not a day goes by that I don't
think of you, Eva, and pray that God keeps you in
His loving care.
St. Lucia is about a hour and a half from Jamaica.
It's a beautiful, small island. I traveled there for the
first time four years ago and fell in love w/the place.
Are you vacationing this summer?
Xavier

Tuesday, June 18:

Good Morning, Beautiful,
Still no word from the parole board. If you, your
sister, and girlfriend decide to go to St. Lucia, you're
welcome to stay at my house. It has four bedrooms.
Plenty of room!
We had a shakedown this a.m. The first in a long
time! Tension between several groups of inmates
is running high. Yesterday twenty new inmates
arrived. All Black. They're getting younger and
younger, Eva. That saddens me. Like Tony, they
lack direction and purpose for their lives. I thank
God every day for my father. He's been a positive,
constant presence in my life. Many of the inmates
in here I realize don't have that. Speaking of Tony,
he got reprimanded yesterday for slacking off on
the job. If it happens again, he'll probably get
transferred.
Take care,
Xavier

Wednesday, June 19:

Morning, Beautiful!
Can't write much today. Please keep me in your
prayers. Still no word regarding parole. And, yes, I'm
serious about you using the place in St. Lucia.
Xavier

"Dear Lord," I pray again, "please keep him safe."

22

Distressing News

Avoiding problems doesn't always make them go away. It's been two weeks since the dinner at Mama's, and Otis has not stopped "chasing" me. I don't answer the phone now when he calls or return his messages. Why can't he take a hint? I spotted his Hummer at D & L Barbecue twenty minutes ago and called to see if he was there. Uncle Lee said he was having dinner with the mayor and some of the county commissioners. I pick up the receiver and dial his home.

After Otis's Barry White–sounding greeting, I apologize for not returning his calls, sigh heavily, and say that I don't think it will work out between us. I wish him well and hang up. That was painless and quick. *Lord, help me when Mama finds out what I've done.*

The phone rings. I jump, and my bowl of popcorn falls to the floor. *Doggonit!* I peep at the caller ID and yank up the receiver.

"Hello, St. Louis!" I yell.

"Hello!" Gina yells back. "Guess what?" she yells louder.

"What?"

"I started a job todaaay!"

"You did?"

"Yes!"

"Congratulations!"

"Thanks! I didn't want to call and tell you about it until after I started."

"Where're you working?"

"At Missouri Liberty, as a bank teller."

"That's great, Gina!"

"I think I'm gonna like it. The people seem nice, and the pay is okay."

"Those things are important. I'm so happy for you, Gina."

"You're happy? Girl, I'm so, so glad to be finally making some money! And thanks for the loan. I'll pay you back as soon as I can."

"Not a problem. How's Mrs. Williams?"

"God is so good, Eva! Mama's walking a little now. Can you *believe* that?"

"Praise God!"

"Can't nobody tell me God don't answer prayer!"

"Amen! Tell her hello for me."

"I will. She keeps asking me when you're coming to see her."

"Tell her before the summer ends."

"For real?"

"Yes."

"All right! When?"

"I'm not sure. I'll keep you posted."

"Mommy!"

"Hold on, Eva. What, A'Kyah? I'm on the phone."

"Who you talking to?" asks A'Kyah.

"Eva," Gina says.

"Hey, Eva!" calls A'Kyah.

"Tell A'Kyah hi," I say.

"Eva says hi. Don't turn that TV on! Here, you and PaQuita go get some ice cream," Gina tells A'Kyah.

"Okay! You want some?" she asks.

"No!"

I hear retreating footsteps and then a door closing.

"Okay, Eva. I'm back." Gina sighs and starts giggling. "I got sump'n else to tell you!"

Instinctively, I feel what she is about to tell me has sump'n to do with a man. I stretch out on the bed. "What?"

"I met somebody! And, girrrrl, he's *fine*!"

I knew it. "Who is he?"

"His name is Darnell," she says, giggling. "He's thirty-three, and he lives in University City."

"He works at the bank with you?"

"Naw."

Gina tells me she met Darnell last week while walking home from the corner store. He was "hanging out" with his "partnas" at the neighborhood park. He complimented her on her cute hoochie mama outfit and walked her home.

Déjà vu! When she met Tony, he was hanging out with a bunch of guys. I bet this man ain't got no job. "So where does Darnell work?"

"He used to work at McDonnell Douglas. He was making good money, too."

"Used to work? What happened to his job at McDonnell Douglas?"

"Girl," Gina says, sighing heavily, "some mess went down in his department over some missing airplane parts."

"He was stealing airplane parts?" I yell.

"Naw! They tried to *accuse* him of that. He said to hell with it and quit." Gina smacks her lips. "I don't blame him, either. Do you?"

Help her, Lord.

"Does Darnell work now, Gina?"

"He works with an uncle, mowing lawns."

"That's all he does?"

"Yeah."

Lord, has my counseling with her been in vain? Why is she aligning herself with what seems to be another shiftless, irresponsible man? "Gina, let's look objectively at this situation. Does Darnell remind you of anybody?"

"Noooo," she replies slowly.

"Let me help you out here. Hanging out on the street, not gainfully employed, and a *possible* thief?"

"He ain't no criminal, Eva. And I told you he works!"

Poor thang. She's sprung already. "Gina, listen to me. Doesn't Darnell remind you of *Tony*?"

She gasps. "Uh-uh! Hell naw! Darnell ain't never been to prison. He's only been on probation one time," she says, like that's something to be proud of.

"Probation?"

Silence.

"Gina!" I yell.

"Huh? What?"

"Nothing." I see right now AT&T is going to make a whole lot of money off her. Soon she'll be calling me, crying over what is bound to be another topsy-turvy, disastrous love affair that she's foolishly rushed into and will have a hard time walking away from. "Please, all I ask is that you take your time and not fall in love so fast, okay?"

She laughs. "Don't worry, girl. I'm not gone make another mistake like I did with A'Kyah's *father*."

"I hope not."

"I'm not!"

"Have you heard from Tony?"

"He called last night. I didn't have much to say to him."

"Holding a grudge is unhealthy."

Gina smacks her lips and sighs. "I know. He told me he's studying for his GED."

"That's good."

Gina smacks her lips again. "It's about time."

"Is Xavier tutoring him?"

"Yeah. You remember Xavier?" Gina asks, sounding surprised.

"Uh-huh."

Gina laughs. "He's fine, ain't he, girl?"

"He is easy on the eyes."

"Yes, he is!" Gina clears her throat and sighs heavily. "His dad had a *massive* heart attack."

"What?" I yell, sitting up. "When?"

"I don't know. Tony said Xavier's mother didn't tell him right away. He just found out this week."

I bet this is why I didn't get an e-mail from him yesterday and today.

"How's he doing? Did Tony say?"

"Tony says he's taking it real hard. Poor thing can't even go see 'bout his daddy. Can you imagine how he feels? I would've lost my mind if I couldn't have made it out here when Mama got sick."

Poor Xavier! I don't tell Gina about the flowers or e-mails I've gotten from him, because she'll get all excited and tell me I'd better snag him. "Is his dad at the VA hospital?"

"I dunno. Is he a veteran?"

"Yeah."

"Xavier is a nice guy. Don't he seem out of place at Hayesfield? Unlike"—she sighs—"my child's father."

Perhaps it's because he doesn't deserve to be there. "Yeah, he does." Poor Xavier! Poor Mrs. Dupree! I'm sure she's a wreck!

"Mommy!" calls A'Kyah.

"I'm still on the phone, A'Kyah."

"Mr. Darnell is outside," says A'Kyah.

"Eva, I gotta go! I'll call you next week."

"Okay."

"And I'll tell Mama you're coming out here this summer."

"All right."

"Later!"

"Bye."

I step over the spilled popcorn and hurry to my home office. Poor Xavier! Will he lose it if his dad dies? He'll jeopardize his chance for parole if he does.

I flip open the phone book to the white pages. Five Duprees are listed in Hayesfield. I recall that Xavier's father's name is Samuel. S. Dupree is the fourth listing. I dial the number. No one answers after seven rings. Assuming the other Duprees listed are relatives of Xavier, I hang up and dial the first listing. No answer. I hang up and try the second one. After two rings, a lady answers. I quickly explain the nature of my call. She tells me she's married to Xavier's uncle and that her husband and Mrs. Dupree are at the veterans hospital in Durham. I thank her and hang up. My phone rings as I'm writing Mrs. Dupree's home number on a Post-it. I look at the caller ID; it's Willnetta.

23

Benevolence

It's 10:00, the sun is shining, and I'm raring to go. Willnetta and I haven't hung out since she got married, and we're planning to spend the day at the mall. Teresa would be hanging right with us, but she's away at a conference in Las Vegas. I pick up the phone and dial her mobile and hear a beep. I end the call to Teresa and click over.

"Evaaa!" yells Willnetta.

"Hey, you on your way?"

"I can't go!"

"Willnetta, don't tell me that!"

"Mama needs help at the restaurant."

"Please tell me you're joking."

"I'm not. I'm sorry!"

Darn!"

"Let's reschedule. I don't want you to go shopping without me," Willnetta whines.

"I won't. It wouldn't be that much fun, anyway."

"Let's go next Saturday."

"We can't. We got the bazaar meeting, remember? And it's no telling when that will end."

"Shoot! I'd forgotten about that."

"And the Saturday after that is the bazaar."

"Hey, why don't you and Teresa come over after the meeting Saturday? Joel and I will fix lunch. We can schedule another shopping date then."

"Cool!"

"Oh, hold on. I got a beep. It's probably Mama."

"Go on. Call me later."

"Okay, bye."

Now I've got to regroup. I'm not staying home, that's for sure. I hang up the phone, grab my keys and my pocketbook, and exit the house. I hop in my SUV and head to Raleigh. I don't have a special destination in mind until I see the sign for I-440. I swing over into the left lane, exit onto the interstate, and head to Durham.

I thank God that I've never been confined to a hospital bed. Good health is a blessing. I stare at the name on the door: Samuel Dupree. I take a deep breath and push the door open.

Mrs. Dupree is sitting in a chair next to the hospital bed. Her eyes are closed, and her frail left hand is resting on the edge of the bed, where a handsome, dark-skinned, broad-chested, gray-haired man lies. Xavier is the spitting image of this man. Various machines beep and hiss throughout the room where the comatose-looking man lies. I clear my throat, hoping to rouse Mrs. Dupree; she doesn't stir. A lump forms in my throat, and I wonder if coming here was such a good idea. I turn to leave and drop my keys.

"C-can I help you?"

I turn back around. Mrs. Dupree is staring at me.

"Hello, Mrs. Dupree," I say softly.

"Hello," she says, sitting up in the chair.

"I'm Eva," I whisper. "I met you last month at the prison."

Mrs. Dupree's brows crease together. "E-va? Oh yes, yes!"

she exclaims, standing up. "Forgive me, honey. I know exactly who you are."

"I heard about what happened from A'Kyah's mother. Tony told her. I'm so sorry, Mrs. Dupree. I'm praying for all of you."

"Thank you," she says, looking over at her husband.

I pick up my keys and step forward. "How's he doing?"

"Each day that he's here is a miracle. He's not out of the woods yet."

"I hear Xavier is taking this real hard."

Mrs. Dupree moans and shakes her head. "He's blaming himself for this, Eva. I keep telling him that what's happened to his daddy is not his fault."

"He needs to talk to his counselor or the chaplain at the prison. They can help him deal with this."

She looks over at me. "I'll tell him that," she says, nodding. "It would help if you did also."

"Ma'am?"

Mrs. Dupree smiles and walks over to me. "He's quite fond of you, honey. And I know he e-mails you," she whispers.

I smile and avert my gaze to Mr. Dupree.

"And he's right," she says, embracing me. "You are sweet." Mrs. Dupree releases me and stands next to the hospital bed. "I haven't seen Xavier since Samuel's heart attack. I couldn't face him Sunday. I just couldn't tell him his daddy was . . . Dear Lord, help us!"

Yes, Lord, please help them!

"I want to see him, Eva. I know I need to," adds Mrs. Dupree.

"I think that would be good for both of you."

"I just hate to bother folks about taking me too many places," she says, shaking her head and looking back at me with those sad, hound-dog eyes. "They're so good about bringing me here every day. I hope Xavier understands that."

"I'm sure he does." I thought she drove.

"My daughter feels bad about not being here. She's expecting her third child any day now and is in no condition to come home."

"Is something wrong with your car, Mrs. Dupree?"

"Sweet Jesus!" she cries, throwing up her hands. "I've wrecked it."

"Ma'am?"

"I was leaving the hospital last Wednesday night and fell asleep at the wheel."

"Oh, my goodness! Are you okay?"

"I'm fine."

"Thank God, you're okay," I say. Xavier would have been *devastated* if he had received word that his mother was also in the hospital.

"Eva, when I got home that night, I fell down on my knees and thanked God that I was still alive and didn't run into anyone."

"Yes, ma'am."

"The accident, however"—Mrs. Dupree pauses and wipes her eyes—"resulted in me losing my license."

"I'll take you to see Xavier," I say, not believing I said it.

"Eva. Nooo," she says, shaking her head.

"He needs to see you."

Mr. Dupree stirs in the bed, as if aware of what I just said. Mrs. Dupree leans over and rubs his forehead. "I-I can't ask you to do that," she says.

"Mrs. Dupree, it won't be a bother." She turned down my charitable offer, so why don't I drop it? "As a matter of fact, I'll be in Hayesfield tomorrow."

She looks back at me. "You will?"

"Yes, ma'am."

"You sure it's no bother, Eva?"

"It's no bother. I assure you."

A young Black nurse with burgundy highlights enters the room and greets us with a wide, sparkling smile. I count three gold teeth in her mouth. Mrs. Dupree introduces me as a "special friend" of the family. I nod hello. The nurse responds with another wide smile, squints, and gives me that I've-seen-you-somewhere look. "You live in Hayesfield, too?" she asks.

"No, in Fairview," I say.

While she checks Mr. Dupree's vitals and engages in small talk with Mrs. Dupree, I run outside to phone Geraldine.

Geraldine agrees—not that I thought she wouldn't—to give Mama and Miss Ida a ride back home after the service tomorrow, but being nosy like Mama, she inquires about my plans tomorrow afternoon. I tell her I plan to visit a distressed friend in Hayesfield. She suggests scriptures of comfort that I can share with my friend. Before ending the call, I solicit her support of my decision to diss Otis. She says she doesn't blame me for not wanting to go out with "carnal-minded" Otis, and that she'll get Mama straight on the matter tomorrow. I almost hate having to miss that.

When I return to Mr. Dupree's room, the nurse has gone. Mrs. Dupree is smiling down at her sleeping husband and gently stroking his forehead. I get directions to her house and tell her to expect me tomorrow between 1:00 and 1:30. I'm writing down my home and cell numbers when the phone in the room rings. Mrs. Dupree picks up on the second ring. "Hi, sweetheart!" she soon exclaims. She looks back at me. "It's my daughter, Carla!"

I hand Mrs. Dupree the paper with my numbers on it, wave good-bye, and leave. As I head down the hall, toward the elevator, the young nurse with the burgundy highlights exits another patient's room. She stops and smiles at me. "You go to church at Fairview Baptist, don't you?" she asks loudly, wagging her finger at me.

"No, Community Baptist."

She snaps her fingers. "That's where I've seen you! Yeah, I've been to your church quite a few times, too."

I don't recall ever seeing the lady at church, but that's not to say she hasn't been there. The pews at Community Baptist are packed every Sunday.

"That gospel choir of yours can sing!" she says, with a big, gold-toothed smile. "And that short preacher of yours can preach!"

I'm about to ask her who she knows at Community Baptist

when another nurse rushes past and tells her she's needed down the hall "pronto."

"The next time I'm there," she says, rushing off, "I'll holla at you."

I smile and head for the elevator.

Coming back through Raleigh, I stop at the new Home Depot on Martin Luther King, Jr., Boulevard. I buy ferns, zinnias, lantana, and vinca; new flowerpots for my patio; bags of potting soil; and mulch. When I get home, I dress in shorts and a tank top and head outside. An hour later, Willnetta calls and says she'll drop off some food from D & L on her way home. When she arrives two hours later, I'm sitting out back, enjoying my handiwork and talking on the phone to Teresa.

"Girl, I'm beat!" Willnetta says, placing two plastic bags and a half gallon of Aunt Della Mae's homemade lemonade on my patio table.

"And you look it." I tell Teresa bye and reach into one of the bags. "Thanks for dinner!"

"There's a sweet potato pie in the other bag."

"Thanks!"

"I keep telling Mama that she and Daddy need to hire more folks, 'cause I can't keep playing fill-in on the weekends." Willnetta laughs and throws up her left hand. "'Cause I's married now!"

I laugh, too. "I hear ya, Shug!"

"Girl, I'm telling you. Being a wife and working an eight-hour gig, wipes me *out* most days."

"Are you taking your vitamins?"

"I'm out."

"Willnetta!"

"I'm gonna get some more, so don't fuss. I see Dr. Chambers next Friday."

"You okay?"

"Yeah. It's just time for my yearly exam."

"Well, you know how anemic you can get sometimes. You need to stay on those vitamins."

"I know."

"I was really looking forward to us hanging out today."

"Me, too. Whatcha end up doing?"

I don't think it's wise to mention the Duprees; it'll require too much explaining. "Oh, nothing much. Yard work mostly."

"It looks good out here," Willnetta says, looking around. "I want you to help me start a perennial garden next to my deck."

"No problem. I'm ready whenever you are."

"Cool." She points to the bags from D & L. "Enjoy!"

"I will, and thanks again."

"I got some chitlins in the car for Joel," she says, turning up her nose. "I need to take them on home before they really stink up my ride."

I laugh and walk Willnetta around front. I feel pangs of loneliness and depression when she backs out of my driveway in her beautiful, shiny Mercedes. When Mrs. Jennings pulls into her driveway, honking loudly, I'm still standing in the same spot, looking out at the street.

"Eva! I got some of your mail by mistake!" she yells. "I discovered that last night. I'll have Keisha bring the letter over. It's in the house."

I walk over to the row of hedges between Mrs. Jennings's yard and mine and wait for Mrs. Jennings to park and go inside. When Keisha emerges from the house, she's giggling and talking on the telephone. I take the white envelope from her and am surprised to see that it's a letter from Xavier. It was postmarked on the nineteenth. My last e-mail from him was on the nineteenth.

8:17 p.m.
Wednesday

June 19th
   Dearest Eva,
   I'm in the library, helping some guys write letters home, and couldn't resist writing you. I've said it before, and I'll say it again: the best thing that's come out of me

being locked up has been meeting you. I want so desperately to see you again, Eva. Your smile, your lovely face, the way you smell, everything about you is unforgettable. I can't sleep nights for tossing and turning because you've crept into my dreams. During the day, you invade my thoughts, because the wind whispers your name over and over again. Eva, know that you're constantly thought of, because you're too lovely to forget.

Warmest Regards,
Xavier

"Who writing you from *prison?*"

I look up. Keisha is peering over the hedges, down at Xavier's letter. I'd forgotten she was standing there. I stuff the letter back in the envelope. "Um, nobody you know."

"Hold, hold on," she says into the phone. She looks at me and grins. "You got a prison pen pal?"

"Girl, no!"

"So who is Xavier Dupree?" she asks, with the phone still up to her mouth.

"A friend of A'Kyah's father."

"Why he writing you?"

"A'Kyah's father is illiterate, so Xavier writes letters for him. They want me to get a message to A'Kyah and her mother."

"Oh, okay," she says, slowly nodding her head.

I turn and head inside the house. I don't need gossipy Keisha Jennings in my business. She's got just as much mouth as that Jo Ann Outerbridge. I read Xavier's letter two more times before placing it in my vanity drawer, on top of the other one and the copies of his e-mails.

24

Covert Activity

"Who're you visiting in Hayesfield?" It's 1:52, and we're just getting out of church. I'm sore from where Mama kept hunching me in the side, grumbling about the long-winded pastor and the horrible singing of the choir.

"Nobody you know, Mama," I reply.

"You'd be surprised to know who I know. So where you going?"

"Maybe she got a date," Miss Ida says, chuckling.

Mama grunts. "Wouldn't that be something? Speaking of *date*," she says, grabbing my arm, "when you and Otis going out again?"

I slip free of Mama's grip and increase my pace. *Lord, please don't let Geraldine forget to talk to Mama, like I asked her to!*

Joel, Willnetta, and Aunt Della Mae cruise past, waving good-bye; Daddy and Miss Elsie are behind them. When they wave at us, Miss Ida and I wave back; Mama turns her head. After they pass, she grunts and comments that Miss Elsie is "one ugly thang."

I sprint to my SUV to call Mrs. Dupree. Poor woman is probably thinking I'm not coming. The phone rings ten times. No answer. I double-check the number and redial. Still no answer after seven rings. Where is she? I look at my watch; two more minutes have gone by. I need to go! But I can't take off and leave Mama and Miss Ida in the parking lot. The big babies don't want me to leave until Geraldine and Cleveland come outside. I trudge over to the Avalon to unlock the doors.

"Hello, ladies!" a slim, balding, middle-aged man dressed in a gaudy burgundy suit and two-tone black-and-white shoes yells at us.

We nod hello. I recognize the man from the choir; he sung a solo during altar call. He unlocks the doors to a pretty black Seville, tosses a choir robe in the backseat, and walks over.

"That was a beautiful song you sung this morning," Miss Ida says, extending her hand.

"Thank you, ma'am," he says, shaking her hand.

"Yes, it was," Mama adds. "But the service was a little *long*, thanks to your pastor."

Miss Ida grunts and gives Mama a disapproving look.

"I apologize for any inconvenience that may have caused you," Mr. Burgundy Suit says.

"Young man, don't *ever*," Miss Ida says sternly, "apologize to *anyone* when the Lord's work is being done!"

Mama sighs softly and rolls her eyes.

Mr. Burgundy Suit smiles and nods. "Yes, ma'am." He looks over at Mama. "Your daughter delivered a *fine* message this morning."

Mama smiles. "Yes, she did. Thank you."

"Is this young lady in the ministry also?" he asks, eyeing me.

"She's not an evangelist like her sister, if that's what you're asking. But she's good about bringing me and my dear friend here along with her to hear her big sister spread God's Word," Mama replies piously.

"She's real good about that. Yes, Eva is," Miss Ida chimes in.

Oh, brother! I unlock the Avalon doors and plop down in the driver's seat. I try Mrs. Dupree's number again. No answer. I'm getting antsy now as two grim thoughts run through my head: Has Mrs. Dupree been summoned to the hospital because Mr. Dupree has taken a turn for the worse? Or, is she lying on the floor of her home, unconscious, having succumbed to the stress and strain of everything and suffered a heart attack or stroke? I close my eyes. "Dear God," I pray, "please don't let either be the case."

"She doesn't have the responsibility of caring for a husband or children yet," I hear Mama say quite loudly.

As often as Mama does it, I still get embarrassed and angry when she advertises me to men she thinks are single and are prospects for a son-in-law. I hope this man is married. I remove my jacket and lower the car windows.

"And where's your wife, Mr. . . . . I didn't catch your name," Mama says.

"Decker. My name's Wade Decker. And, I'm not married," he says, with a silly grin.

Awww shucks! That's music to Mama's ears.

Mama laughs. "Well then, come meet my *single* daughter, Mr. Decker."

"My pleasure," he says, smiling and bobbing his head.

"And it's so nice to meet you," replies Mama. "I'm Rose Allen. This is Ida Truelove, and *this* is my daughter Eva Liles."

Wade extends his hand through the passenger window. "Nice to meet you, Sister Liles. I noticed you from the choir," he says softly, giving me the once-over.

I smile and shake Wade's hand.

Mama opens the car door behind me and sits down. She's grinning like a Cheshire cat. "Did you come to church *alone*, Mr. Decker?"

"Yes, ma'am," he says, with another bob of his head.

"Single and alone. Hmmm," Mama moans. She clears her throat and gently kicks the back of my seat. I look up in the rearview mirror at her. She nods and winks at me.

"You can do more work for the Lord single than you can married," Miss Ida says doggedly.

The big grin disappears from Mama's face. She looks over at Miss Ida. "Ida, please!"

I burst out laughing.

Wade laughs, too.

I glance at my watch. It's 2:05 now. I have got to go! I'm thinking about going inside to get Geraldine and Cleveland when they emerge from the church. *Thank you, Lord!* I start the engine and turn on the air-conditioning.

"I enjoyed meeting you, ladies," Wade says warmly. "Please come back and visit us again."

"Thank you!" Miss Ida says.

"And feel free to come visit us one Sunday at Community Baptist," Mama says, with a big smile. "Eva, why don't you tell *Wade* what time we have service."

"Eleven," I say flatly.

Mama kicks the back of my seat.

Wade laughs. "She's not very talkative, is she?"

"Um, sh-she's a talker," Mama stammers.

When Geraldine and Cleveland approach, Wade steps back and waves good-bye. I raise the car windows.

"Now what's wrong with him?" Mama asks, jabbing me in the shoulder. "He ain't fat like Otis."

"Are you blind?" I say. "Maybe he did blind you with that *loud* suit he has on, looking like an extra in the movie *Superfly*!"

"My goodness, Eva! You're forever making excuses for why this one won't do and that one won't do," grumbles Mama. "I wonder sometimes if you really want to get married."

And I'm so thankful I don't have to ride back home with you! I open the car door. "I love you, too, Mama."

"You coming by for dinner?" Mama asks.

"Yep!" I reply.

As I'm closing the car door, I hear Mama say to Miss Ida, "She's gone end up an old maid."

* * *

I make it to 1616 Charity Chapel Road in ten minutes. The Dupree home is a sprawling brick rancher down a wide, paved driveway lined with elm trees a quarter of a mile from the highway. The lawn is well manicured, and the grass is a lush Kentucky bluegrass green. Small flower beds and boxwood shrubs adorn the front of the house. A porch—half of which is screened in, with wicker furniture and two white rocking chairs—runs the entire length of the house. Cement planters with red geraniums sit on opposite ends of the top porch step. Yellow and red rose bushes and budding crepe myrtle line one side of the house, and huge magnolia and maple trees the other side. Far off in the distance are barns, farming equipment, and two cab pickup trucks. Beyond the barns are a pond and gazebo and farmland as far as the eye can see. I called Mrs. Dupree again when I left church, and she answered, thank God. She was just getting in from worship service at her church.

I park and open my car door. Two German shepherds race from behind the house, barking loudly; I slam the car door shut. They don't have to worry about me getting out; I'm terrified of dogs. I toot my horn. Mrs. Dupree exits the house and yells at the dogs to "hush up!"

"When I told Xavier you were bringing me, Eva," she says, getting into my SUV, "he got so excited."

"When did you talk to him?"

"Last night."

"How's he doing?"

"Not good. He's still worried about Samuel."

"And how is Mr. Dupree?"

"He's steadily making progress."

"Praise God!"

"Yes, praise God! My sister and her husband are taking me to the hospital when I get back."

I start the SUV and ease back down the driveway. "You have a pretty place, Mrs. Dupree. It's beautiful. Very picturesque. Looks like something out of *Better Homes and Gardens*."

"Oh! Thank you. Xavier did all of the landscaping."

"Wow! He's talented."

Mrs. Dupree smiles proudly and nods.

"What kinds of fish are in the pond?"

"Catfish and trout."

"They're two of my favorite."

"Mine, too. Do you fish?"

"No, ma'am. My father and stepmom do. They've taken it up as a hobby since their retirement."

"Aha," Mrs. Dupree says, smiling and nodding.

I pull out of the driveway and onto the highway. "How's Carla?"

Mrs. Dupree chuckles. "Ready to have that baby."

"Does she know what she's having?"

"A girl, and it will be her first."

I look over at Mrs. Dupree and smile.

"She wants to move back home. I'd love that. Houston is so far away," says Mrs. Dupree

"How long has she lived there?"

"They moved there after Michael, that's my son-in-law, finished medical school. That's been well over ten years now."

"Your son-in-law's a doctor?"

"An ear, nose, and throat specialist."

Go ahead, Carla!

"My daughter is blessed. She's married to a good man," adds Mrs. Dupree.

A Black man in a silver, banged-up, old Mercedes, smoking and talking on a cell phone, zooms past, nearly sideswiping us.

"Low-down, dirty, rotten, drunken scoundrel!" Mrs. Dupree mutters.

"He needs to get off the phone!"

"Vulture! Snake in the grass!" Mrs. Dupree yells, wagging her finger at the speeding car.

I look over at her. "You know that man?"

"Umph! Yes, I know him!"

"Who is he, if you don't mind me asking?"

"That *man*, if you want to call him that," she replies bitterly, "is Charles Glover, Xavier's half brother."

"What?" I hear myself yell.

Mrs. Dupree moans and slowly shakes her head.

"Forgive me, Mrs. Dupree. I didn't mean to yell out like that."

"That's all right, honey."

"I didn't know Xavier had a half brother."

"He doesn't talk about Charles much now."

My curiosity antenna shoots way up. I hate to pry, but I got to know. "Is there bad blood between them?"

Mrs. Dupree sighs and tells me that Charles Glover is a "conniving, bitter, jealous individual." Four years older than Xavier, he tricked Xavier into buying what later turned out to be stolen merchandise from a man he introduced as a friend and reputable businessman from Philadelphia.

"Charles has always felt that Samuel favored Xavier over him," says Mrs. Dupree. "And when he's had a little too much to drink, he tells his daddy that and how much he resents him for not marrying his mother."

Oh, my goodness!

Mrs. Dupree continues. "Samuel and I have gone out of our way to welcome Charles into the family, and we never once thought he'd return our love with such hatred. I know I'm supposed to forgive," Mrs. Dupree says, shaking her head, "but it's so hard to do. He's caused me so much pain!"

"I'm so sorry, Mrs. Dupree. I know this has been awfully hard on you."

"It has! The day Samuel had the heart attack, Charles was at the house, demanding what he feels is his rightful share of the farmland."

"Oh no!"

"I don't want Xavier to ever find that out," she says, touching my arm.

"I won't say a thing. I promise."

"Samuel gave Charles three hundred acres five years ago.

And don't you know, he only has two acres left. Two! What he didn't lose to creditors, he sold."

From the corner of my eye, I can see that Mrs. Dupree has worked up a sweat; I turn up the air-conditioning.

"Xavier used to think the sun rose and set on his older brother," she says, with outstretched hands. "He could see no wrong in him. It was not until the day Charles took the stand and testified against him in court that Xavier finally saw him for what he was. I thought Samuel was going to have a heart attack right there in the courtroom."

My mouth flies open, but nothing comes out: I'm at a loss for words. I can't believe what I'm hearing. This sounds like something straight out of a TV movie.

"Xavier had *never* been in a courtroom for anything other than his divorce! Now my son has a criminal record!"

"I'm so sorry, Mrs. Dupree."

"I just can't understand how a person can hate another person so badly!"

Your own flesh and blood, at that! This Charles Glover has ice water running through his veins! "So jealousy drove Charles to do this *despicable* thing?"

"No, honey. It was greed."

"Ma'am?"

"God's word is true, Eva. The love of money is the root of all evil."

I glance over at Mrs. Dupree.

"In his sick, twisted mind, Charles was trying to disgrace Xavier in Samuel's eyes. You see," she says, turning to look at me, "he thought Samuel would disown Xavier when he got arrested and, in turn, would make him sole heir to the farm."

"No!"

"Yes. The farm is worth more than six million dollars."

"Xavier told me that."

"Charles wants it so he can sell it."

"Land that's been in your husband's family for generations?"

"Yes, but it'll never happen. Not as long as there's breath in my body."

"And Xavier's, too," I say, recalling how proudly he spoke to me about his family's land.

"My heart aches for my husband and son."

"I know it does," I say softly.

Mrs. Dupree bursts into tears. "Xavier is a good son, Eva. Samuel would *never* disown him. He loves Xavier. And I don't believe God could have blessed us with a better son."

Oh, how sweet! Tears fill my eyes.

"When he lived in Charlotte, he would come home twice a week sometimes to help out around here. Charles stays right here in Hayesfield, down the road from us, and the only times he comes over is to ask Samuel for money. And he has the *nerve*"—Mrs. Dupree hits the dashboard—"to demand more land from my husband! He'll never get another acre. You hear me? Not another acre!"

I nod and almost miss the turn to the prison for the tears in my eyes. I console Mrs. Dupree by saying God will see her family through this difficulty. For the life of me, I can't recall any of those scriptures Geraldine told me yesterday.

When I pull into the prison parking lot, Mrs. Dupree has calmed down and dried her eyes. She insists that I accompany her inside. I decline, assuring her it's best that she and Xavier have this time alone. She smiles and takes off toward the administration building. It's 2:26.

I lower the windows and reach for the radio. My cell phone rings. I retrieve it from my purse and look at the display; it's my niece. I flip open the phone. "Hey, sweetie."

"Hey, Auntie. Grandma says you're in Hayesfield. What time you coming home?"

"Within the hour. What's up?"

"I got an extra ticket to the Yolanda Adams and Kirk Franklin concert and was wondering if you wanted to go."

"Yeah, love to!"

"Cool!"

"What time is the concert?"

"Seven thirty."

"Okay." I hear Mama in the background tell Geraldine to

get the turkey and stuffing out of the oven. "Sweetie, are you in the kitchen?"

"Yes."

"Does your grandma seem to be in a good mood?"

"I guess so. Why?"

"Just wondering."

"Mama was at her earlier about something," Jalisa whispers. "I don't know what. I did hear Grandma tell her she was through with it."

"Uh-huh."

"You wanna talk to Grandma?"

"No! But do your auntie a favor."

"Name it."

"Keep your ears open, and let me know if you hear my mother or sister say anything about me."

Jalisa laughs. "Okay."

"Thanks, baby. See you in a few."

"Bye."

"Buh-bye."

I place my phone back in my purse and look over at the rec yard; it's crowded as usual. From where I'm parked, I don't see Xavier and Mrs. Dupree. I wonder how their visit is going. I close my eyes to pray for the Duprees and hear my name called out. I open my eyes. Mrs. Dupree is running across the parking lot, waving her hands.

"Eva!" she shouts.

I hop out of my SUV.

"Xavier wants to see you!" she yells.

My heart starts racing. I retrieve my driver's license from my wallet and take off behind her.

When I step into the rec yard, Xavier is the first person I see.

"Hello, Eva," he says, walking up to me. "A part of me feared I'd never see you again, and here you are."

My knees buckle.

"Thanks for bringing my mother," he says.

"You're welcome," I say. Worrying about Mr. Dupree has clearly taken a toll on Xavier. He's lost weight, and there're bags and dark circles under his eyes. "I'm so sorry about your father."

"Thanks," he replies.

"Come. Let's sit down," Mrs. Dupree says.

Neither Xavier nor I move. I can't stop staring up into his face.

"You look beautiful," he says, smiling down at me.

I stare at the dimple in his cheek and imagine his luscious-looking lips locked with mine in a steamy kiss. Wait a minute! Didn't I just leave church? And isn't he grieving over his father? *Lord, forgive me.* I step back and walk over to the picnic table where Mrs. Dupree is sitting.

"Eva, Xavier got a letter from the parole board," says Mrs. Dupree.

"It's good news I hope," I say.

Mrs. Dupree sighs and shakes her head.

Xavier sits down next to her and places his arm around her shoulder.

Oh, Lord, no! He's been denied parole!

"They haven't made a decision," Mrs. Dupree says tearfully.

I exhale.

"They still have time, Mother," Xavier replies.

"They were supposed to let you know something within thirty days!" says Mrs. Dupree.

"Well, they haven't said no. That's good news," I say, hoping to shed some positive light on the situation.

"You're right, Eva," says Mrs. Dupree. "I'm just ready for him to come home. The thought of him being locked up another year—"

"Shhh, Mother. I'm coming home. Don't worry," whispers Xavier.

"I believe he has a very good chance at parole, Mrs. Dupree. This is his first conviction, and what he's been charged with is nonviolent. Surely, the parole board will take those things into consideration," I say.

Mrs. Dupree scoffs. "They don't have to! They don't have to let him out!"

That's true. They don't. But this is a miscarriage of justice. Xavier doesn't belong here. The thought of him having to spend another year in prison brings tears to my eyes. I look down so no one can see them.

"I just pray," Xavier says softly, "that Dad hangs on."

I want to say something to comfort him, but I'm too choked up. *Lord,* I pray silently, *please restore Mr. Dupree to good health, and let Xavier make parole.*

"Your father's a fighter," Mrs. Dupree says, chuckling. "He'll pull through. You'll see. So stop worrying."

"If I could just be by his bedside for *five* minutes!" says Xavier.

"I know, son. I know," whispers Mrs. Dupree.

"Escaping has crossed my mind," Xavier mumbles.

My head jerks up.

"God forbid!" Mrs. Dupree cries.

"No, Xavier! Please don't!" I plead. "There's too much at stake. You'll be home soon."

"Listen to Eva, son!" Mrs. Dupree begs.

Xavier looks up at me. The tears in his eyes move me to tears. "Are you rooting for me, Eva?"

"Yes," I say as tears roll down my cheeks.

He reaches over and gently wipes the tears away. "Thank you. That means a lot to me," he says, staring deeply into my eyes. "You have no idea how much."

"Promise me, son," Mrs. Dupree cries, "that you won't do anything foolish!"

"I promise, Mother," replies Xavier.

"Promise *me*, Xavier," I say.

A slight smile appears at his mouth. "I promise."

"Visiting hours are over! Inmates remain seated! All visitors exit the visitation area!"

The shout from the correctional officer could not have

come at a better time. I could literally shed a bucket of tears for the Duprees.

Xavier embraces Mrs. Dupree and kisses her on the cheek. He looks up at me and blows me a kiss.

My heart starts racing again. I help Mrs. Dupree to her feet and follow her out of the rec yard, wondering what is happening to me.

I decline Mrs. Dupree's invitation to have dinner with her, her sister, and her brother-in-law. After dropping her off, I head to Mama's, hoping Geraldine has talked to her about Otis, and that she will in turn stop badgering me about him. Who knows, maybe she'll even forgo her relentless pursuit of a husband for me altogether. Now that would be dandy. Just dandy.

25

Confessions

Monday, June 24:

Dear Sweet Angel,
Good Morning! I pray that you're well. Thank you, Eva,
for bringing my mother to see me. Thank you! Thank
you! I'm convinced more now than ever that you are an
angel. Please forgive me for the comment I made
yesterday about escaping. It was a stupid thing to say.
God knows, I don't intend to subject my parents to
more misery and embarrassment. They've endured
enough. Each day I pray and ask God to strengthen
me so I can handle however many more days I have
here, and to restore my father to good health.
Still nothing from the parole board! July eighth is two
weeks away. To think I could be that close to freedom.
Enough about me. You looked great Sunday. Wow!
You are so beautiful.
Tony was involved in an altercation this morning in the
cafeteria. Infractions of this nature automatically result

in transfers and at least thirty more days added to an
inmate's sentence.
Love,
Xavier
PS: I won't be able to e-mail you again until the end of
the week. My boss here in the nursery is one of my
cousins. He just told me the warden is sending him to a
three-day workshop. Needless to say, I'll be glad when
he returns, so I can communicate once more w/you.
Angel, I will e-mail you first thing Friday morning.

I click REPLY.

Xavier,
It's so good to hear from you. Stay strong and don't
despair. You should be hearing something from the
parole board any day now. So hang in there! Okay? ☺
I look forward to hearing from you Friday.
And please know that I am still praying for you and
your father.
Sorry to hear about Tony.
Eva

I look over at the multicolored lilies Xavier sent me this
morning and smile.

Friday, June 28:

Eva,
I have great news. Great news! I've been granted parole!
I've been granted parole! I got the news minutes ago. I'll
be a free man in ten days. Ten days, I'll be FREE! Praise
God!! Will you be one of the first people I see when I get
out? Please, I would like that so much.
Eva, I know now that it's not infatuation that I feel for
you. It's something much deeper. It's love. I love you,
Miss Eva Liles. I started loving you the first time I saw

you. Angel, you occupy a special place in my heart.
When you walked into the rec yard Sunday, you
literally took my breath away. Am I being presumptuous
when I ask, is there chemistry between us? Has my
wish come true that you now have feelings for me?
I have been labeled a criminal, and it's a label I will
carry to my grave. That label, however, does not define
who I am, Eva. I am an intelligent, responsible man
willing and capable of loving you and giving you all that
you deserve and long for, and even that which you've
never dreamed of. May I have the chance to prove to
you that I'm worthy of your love? This is a promise: I
will love you the way God expects a man to love a
woman. I pray He sends you into my waiting arms.
Love,
Xavier

Tears stream down my face. Xavier has made parole! I'm
so happy for him. I close my eyes and place my head in my
hands. He wants to see me. Is that wise? Should I see him?
Loving him comes with *too* high a price. I can't subject myself
to the ridicule bound to come my way if I were to love him.
My family, for goodness sake, might even disown me. I've
said I'd never settle or lower my standards. I'll be stooping if I
involve myself with an *ex-con*. But could I unknowingly be
passing up a chance at love?

"Eva!" Delores yells, knocking on my door.

I open my eyes and dry my face. "Yes, Delores. Come in."

The door opens, and Delores steps in, smiling with a bouquet of red roses.

The red roses towering over the geraniums on my front
porch catch my eye the instant I pull into the driveway. I turn
off my engine, gather my pocketbook, and hurry to the porch.

The bouquet is identical to the one I got this morning at

work. I sit down on the porch and remove the envelope from the card caddy.

Forever indebted to you. Love, Xavier

I burst into tears. *Lord, what am I going to do?* My conversation with God is interrupted by my ringing cell phone. I reach into my purse to get it. I can't make out the caller's name on the display for the tears in my eyes. I flip open the phone. "Hello."

"Hel-lo, Eva."

Noooo!

"Eva?"

"Hi, Otis."

"You sound tired or surprised to hear from me." Otis laughs. "Which is it?"

"Both," I reply, laughing.

"You had dinner yet?"

"No."

"Miss Rose gave me your cell number. I just ran into her, and she said you were probably heading home. Soooo, I thought I'd give you a call to see if we could meet up for dinner somewhere."

"I'm already home."

"Cool. How 'bout I come pick you up and bring you to my place? I'll throw some steaks on the grill."

"No, thanks."

"Girl, why you giving me such a hard time?"

Didn't you get my message? "I'm not trying to give you a hard time."

"You seeing somebody, aren't you?"

"What?"

"Don't lie now. I know Dean's Florist made a visit to your house this afternoon."

A lump forms in my throat. *Oh nooo! What does he know?* I swallow the lump. "Really?" I ask coolly.

"Really. I was in the neighborhood and saw the van in your driveway."

I breathe a sigh of relief.

"So who is he?" Otis asks.

"It's not what you think," I lie.

"Tell me anything."

How about good-bye? "Otis, you called me at a really bad time," I say, faking extreme weariness. "I'm just getting home. I've had a rough week. I'm tired."

"Okay," he says slowly. "I'll let you go. The ball is still in your court. You know where to reach me when you're ready to play."

I hang up and hurry inside. The number to Dean's Florist is on the envelope that came with the roses. Being the only Black-owned florist in Fairview, it gets most of the Black business. I misdial the number twice before finally hearing, "Good Afternoon, Dean's Florist." I don't know any of the store employees, but paranoia causes me to disguise my voice, anyway. I ask to speak to the owner in a curt Northern accent. When Erma Dean comes to the phone, I question her at length about the store's confidentiality policy. Mrs. Dean assures me that neither she nor any of her employees disclose information to third parties regarding the senders or recipients of flowers. I hope she's not lying, and that Otis doesn't know more than what he's letting on. Reid Funeral Homes is one of her biggest clients. I thank Mrs. Dean for her time and hang up.

I sit down on my bed and stare at the roses. I wish I could be happy about getting them. I pick up the phone and call Mrs. Dupree; she doesn't answer. I try the hospital. After I'm connected to Mr. Dupree's room, the phone rings one time. "Hello," Mrs. Dupree answers cheerfully.

"Hi, Mrs. Dupree. This is Eva."

"Eva! I've been meaning to call you. Xavier made parole!"

"I know. He e-mailed me. I'm so happy for all of you."

"Thank you, honey."

"How's Mr. Dupree?"

"God is still blessing! Samuel's doing good!"

"Looks like you'll have both of your men home soon," I overhear a woman say.

"Mrs. Dupree, you have company?" I ask.

"No, honey, it's just the nurse. She's changing Samuel's IV."

"I won't keep you. I just called to say congratulations."

"It's so sweet of you to call. You're such a lovely girl. I can see why Xavier's so taken with you," she says, laughing.

I thank Mrs. Dupree for the compliment and feel special as she tells the nurse how much she appreciated me taking her to see Xavier on Sunday.

"That was nice of her," I hear the nurse say. She then asks Mrs. Dupree if she spoke with Mr. Dupree's doctor today.

I feel it's time to hang up, so before Mrs. Dupree answers the nurse, I bid her good-bye. I speed-dial Stephanie's number and tell her to hold on while I get Teresa on the line. "Hello, spinsters!" I say when we're all connected.

"Who you calling a spinster?" Teresa asks.

Stephanie laughs.

"Y'all want to go to St. Lucia?" I say.

"St. Lucia?" they both ask.

"Yeah. Instead of going on a cruise, we could fly to St. Lucia. I have access to a four-bedroom house."

"For real?" Teresa asks.

"Yep," I say.

"What about the trip to St. Louis?" Stephanie asks.

"We can still do that," I say.

"Cool!" Teresa says.

"When we leaving?" Stephanie asks.

I laugh.

"When we leaving?" Stephanie asks again. "I'm ready to go now!"

I sigh heavily and lie back on the bed. "I didn't call to talk about going to St. Lucia or St. Louis. I need to talk to y'all about something else."

"What?" Stephanie asks.

"Don't pass judgment on me, okay?" I ask, growing hot with embarrassment. "It's not easy for me to tell y'all this."

"We're listening," Stephanie says.

"What is it, Eva? You're scaring me," Teresa says.

"I don't know how to say it," I whisper, covering my mouth.

"Girl, don't make me come through this phone," Teresa roars. "What is it?"

I sit up and take a deep breath. "I know it's gonna sound crazy, 'cause I can't believe it myself." I close my eyes and take another deep breath. "I've developed feelings for Xavier." There, I've said it. I've told two people that are dear to me that I have feelings for a man in prison. I'm relieved and so ashamed.

My confession is met with profound silence. I can't even hear Stephanie or Teresa breathe. Someone finally exhales; I can't tell who. I clear my throat, hoping to prod a response from one of them.

"Whoa! Hold up! Wh-what you just say?" Teresa asks.

"Crazy, huh?" I murmur.

"Repeat what you said," Teresa says slowly.

"I've developed feelings for Xavier," I repeat.

"The inmate?" Stephanie asks hesitantly.

"Uh-huh," I say.

"O-okay, I-I'm missing something. When did this happen? Are you visiting him?" says Stephanie.

"Well, I did take his mother to see him, Stephanie." I lower my voice. "On Sunday."

Teresa gasps. "Naw, you didn't!"

"He's written me letters, sent me e-mails and *lots* of flowers. I got two dozen roses from him today," I tell them.

"What?" Teresa yells.

"What do I do?" I say.

"Oh, my goodness!" Teresa yells louder. "Help her, Lord!"

"He says he's in love with me. What do I do?" I say.

"Are you for real?" Teresa asks, with condemnation hanging on every word.

"I-I'm speechless," Stephanie mutters.

"Well, I'm not!" Teresa hollers.

"Calm down, Teresa!" Stephanie hollers back.

"Calm down? Your sister is pining over a damn *inmate*, and you're telling me to calm down?" Teresa yells.

"There's nothing wrong with her liking him, I guess," Stephanie blurts out.

"You guess? Yes, there is! It's absurd!" Teresa yells in a strained, nasty voice.

"Stop yelling, Teresa!" I say, then switch the phone to my other ear. "You gone bust my eardrum!"

"Pleeease, stop yelling!" Stephanie pleads.

"He'll be paroled on July eighth," I say.

"What that got to do with you?" Teresa asks coolly.

I fall back on the bed. "He wants to see me when he gets out."

"No!" hollers Teresa.

"What're you going to do?" Stephanie asks.

"I don't know," I murmur.

Teresa moans loudly. "You don't know? I don't believe what I'm hearing. You need to have your head examined!"

"Teresa, please! What harm is there in Eva befriending Xavier? Sounds like he caught a bad break," says Stephanie.

"Bad break my ass!" shrieks Teresa.

"He has a lot going for him, Teresa," I say. "He's educated. He's been in the military—"

"I don't care if he was a former university chancellor and a four-star general! You don't need to befriend him!" shouts Teresa.

"You can be so cold sometimes," Stephanie says.

"I don't care what you say," Teresa snaps. "Eva, let me ask you a question."

"I'm listening," I reply.

"What woman with as much going for her as you would want to be romantically involved with a *convict*? Don't you think you deserve better?"

"His half brother set him up," I say.

"Half brother?" Stephanie asks.

I share what Mrs. Dupree told me about Charles.

"Wow!" Stephanie exclaims.

"The family farm, according to Xavier, is worth six and a half million dollars," I say.

"Six and a half million dollars?" Stephanie yells.

"Yep," I reply.

"He's lying!" Teresa yells. She lets out an exasperated sigh. "He's a *convict*, Eva. You do know what *con* means, don't you?"

"You don't know if it's a lie," Stephanie argues.

"Nor do you," Teresa fires back.

"Eva, do you pity him? Is it pity that you feel for Xavier?" asks Stephanie.

"No, Stephanie, it's not," I insist. "Don't get me wrong, though. I do feel sorry for what's happened to him—"

"Don't be so gullible, Eva! Xavier deserves to be in prison!" shouts Teresa.

"You don't know that, Teresa!" Stephanie replies angrily.

"Eva, do you know what people are going to say about you if you involve yourself with an inmate?" asks Teresa.

My stomach muscles tighten. "That I'm hard up," I whisper.

"Bingo! And they'll say much worse," says Teresa. "You could barely hold your head up at church after Jo Ann spread that lie about you and Joel. Now you're talking about involving yourself with a convict! Whatcha gone do when Jo Ann crucifies you this time? Huh?"

"Screw Jo Ann." Stephanie smacks her lips. "Eva," she says softly, "you've always been a very good judge of character. Do what *you* feel is best. People are going to talk regardless."

So true, baby sister, so true!

"Just don't rush into anything," Stephanie adds. "What does he plan to do when he's paroled?"

"Manage the family farm. He also plans to build a golf course and nursery. *And* mentor at-risk youth," I reply.

"How honorable," Teresa says facetiously.

"Be quiet!" Stephanie yells.

"Don't encourage this, Stephanie," warns Teresa.

"I'm not encouraging anything," snaps Stephanie.

"Then tell her to forget about that inmate!" Teresa yells.

"I can't tell her that!" shouts Stephanie.

"You're gonna let your sister make the biggest mistake in her life!" screams Teresa.

"How do you know it's a mistake?" Stephanie shrieks.

The fiery debate is on. My stomach hurts, and I've got a headache and an earache. I burst into tears. Through my hic-cupping sobs, I listen as Stephanie and Teresa go at each other. Like Stephanie said, bottom line, I've got to do what I feel is best, regardless of what anyone else thinks.

26

Dreams

"Ladies, I believe this year's bazaar will be our biggest one ever!" Mrs. McKnight sings. "And I want to thank all of you," she says, with a wave of her hands, "from the bottom of my heart for making it so!"

"Yes, thank y'all!" Aunt Della Mae adds. She cochairs this event with Mrs. McKnight and provided breakfast for everyone this morning.

"Mother Della Mae and I met with the men last night, and they're raring to go!" Mrs. McKnight exclaims, clapping her hands.

"Mmmm," I moan, rubbing my stomach.

Mama and Teresa look at me and laugh.

Community Baptist men can cook! Under Uncle Lee's supervision, they'll be frying fish and grilling sausages, hot dogs, ribs, and chicken. I can't wait!

The bazaar is a week away now, and everyone on the committee is eagerly looking forward to next Saturday. Like always, I'll be overseeing the sale of home accessories; Teresa, clothing; and Willnetta, baked goods. Mama and Geraldine will distribute health-care packets and administer free vision and blood pressure tests. Mama, Teresa, and I, along with Miss Ida and Geraldine, are sitting at the same table, wishing this meeting would end. Mrs. McKnight's painstaking attention to detail always results in long, drawn-out meetings. It's almost 1:00; we've been meeting since 8:30.

"Ladies, do you think one more meeting would be in order before next Saturday?" Mrs. McKnight asks.

"No!" the outspoken, opinionated church secretary hollers.

Teresa kicks me under the table and bursts out laughing.

"I would like *everyone's* opinion on the matter, thank you," Mrs. McKnight says, opening her eyes wide. "With a show of hands, how many are in favor of meeting one more time? We wouldn't have to meet too long."

People start squirming in their seats and looking down. Three hands finally go up; there are seventeen of us present.

"Well," Mrs. McKnight says, clearly disappointed, "I guess we'll have prayer and adjourn."

"You've covered everything quite nicely, First Lady," the church secretary says pleasantly. "Don't y'all think so?" she asks, looking around.

Heads bob throughout the fellowship hall.

Mrs. McKnight smiles. "Thank y'all. I just want this to be like it's always been, an organized and *grand* affair. The children want to go to Myrtle Beach and Disney World this summer."

"Don't worry. We won't let you or the children down," the church secretary says, with a big smile.

"Amen!" several of us say.

"Before everyone leaves, I want to make an announcement," Willnetta says, rising to her feet.

"Ahhhh! Thank you, Jesus!" Aunt Della Mae shouts, bursting into tears.

"I found out yesterday afternoon that Joel and I are going to be parents! I'm *two* months pregnant!"

Cheers fill the room, and Willnetta is bombarded with hugs and kisses. Teresa and I burst into tears and jump up and down like cheerleaders. Aunt Della Mae, grinning from ear to ear, passes around several issues of *Jet* featuring Willnetta and Joel in the Society World section of the magazine. The caption under their wedding picture is INSEPARABLE.

It's 1:42 when Teresa, Willnetta, and I leave the church. As I tail the Mercedes and Porsche, my thoughts drift toward Hayesfield. I didn't sleep much last night for thinking about Xavier. Despite all that Teresa said yesterday, I still find myself longing to be with him.

When I pull into Willnetta's driveway, I push thoughts of Xavier to the back of my mind and follow her and Teresa to the rear of the house. Joel is on the deck, grilling steaks. After we exchange hellos and congratulate him on impending fatherhood, Willnetta ushers Teresa and me inside.

"Oooh, I love that!" Teresa exclaims, running over to the sixty-gallon saltwater aquarium in the great room. "This is beautiful!"

"I love it, too," Willnetta says. "Ever since we've been back from our honeymoon, Joel has been *dying* to have one. It's been up a week now."

"It is beautiful," I say.

"What else you got new?" Teresa asks.

"Follow me," Willnetta says, smiling.

Teresa and I take off behind Willnetta, oohing and ahhing at the new black art and the posh-looking, contemporary dining-room and living-room furniture. When we get to an empty, small bedroom upstairs, painted in soft yellow, Willnetta tells us, with a big smile, that this will be the nursery. Aunt Della Mae is going to furnish it as a gift to her and Joel.

"Does that mean you'll *have* to name the baby Della Mae if it's a girl?" Teresa asks, narrowing her eyes at Willnetta.

Willnetta and I burst out laughing.

Teresa shakes her head. "Please, please don't do that. One Della Mae in this family is enough!"

Willnetta and I double over laughing.

"I'm serious, Willnetta. Please don't do that," says Teresa.

"Hush!" Willnetta hollers.

I'm laughing so hard, I can't say a thing.

"Fairview's not ready for another Della Mae," Teresa says.

"Hush, Teresa!" Willnetta begs. Tears are streaming down her face, and she's stomping her feet and holding her stomach.

When Joel sticks his head in the room, the three of us are laughing hysterically.

"What's so funny?" he asks.

Willnetta points at Teresa.

"Teresa, are you misbehaving?" asks Joel.

"No, Joel," Teresa replies innocently. This sends Willnetta and me into another fit of laughter. It's been a long time since the three of us laughed like this. I miss it.

Joel laughs and shakes his head.

"Are the steaks ready?" Willnetta asks.

"Not quite, baby. Give me ten more minutes," replies Joel. "Anybody want hot dogs?"

Teresa and I throw up our hands.

"You got it!" Joel says, dashing back downstairs.

I lean up against the wall. "A boy or girl? What're y'all hoping for?"

"A *healthy* baby. We don't care what the sex is," says Willnetta.

"What about baby names?" Teresa asks.

"If it's a boy, he'll be named Joel," Willnetta replies, blushing. "But if it's a girl, her name will be La'Netta Noel."

"That's pretty!" I say.

"I'm so happy for you," Teresa cries.

"I'm blessed," Willnetta says, throwing up her hands. "Truly blessed. And, Eva, you have no idea how many times I've thanked God for you sending Joel my way."

"Oh, I'd guess a million times," I say.

Willnetta places a finger up to her mouth. "Don't y'all say anything, but the trustee board is considering him for a trustee."

"That's great!" I say.

"Sure is," Teresa says.

"Daddy said they would be voting on the matter at their next meeting," says Willnetta.

"Cousin, our lips are sealed," I say.

"Unseal yours, and tell her what you told me and Stephanie last night," says Teresa.

I shoot Teresa a dirty look. Granted, the three of us share everything with each other, but I don't want to tell Willnetta about Xavier, not yet. Not until I figure out what I'm going to do. Besides, I don't expect her to think much of the idea, anyway, or her husband, the ex-correctional officer.

"What?" Willnetta asks.

"Nothing," I say as matter-of-factly as I can.

Teresa folds her arms across her chest and glares at me.

"All right. What is it?" Willnetta asks.

"I had a run-in with Jo Ann not too long ago," I reply.

Teresa gasps.

I cut my eyes at her, then look back at Willnetta. "She was talking about Aunt Della Mae, Uncle Lee, and your *expensive* wedding."

Willnetta places her hands on her hips and starts tapping her right foot. "What she say?"

From the corner of my eye, I can see that Teresa is still glaring at me. "She implied that Aunt Della Mae and Uncle Lee were going broke, girl. Broke! On account of your extravagant reception and expensive dress."

"What?" Willnetta yells.

"She also said, they would probably jack up prices at the restaurant to keep from going bankrupt," I say.

"That pop-eyed heifer!" Willnetta hollers.

"I got her straight," I say.

"Good! And when I see her, I'm gone get her straight!" Willnetta yells.

"Was that *it*, Eva?" Teresa asks, smirking.

"Is there more?" Willnetta asks, looking from me to Teresa.

"No, that was it, Willnetta," I say. I'm about to kick Teresa on the sly when Joel yells upstairs, asking if anyone wants baked beans.

"Let me get downstairs," Willnetta says, throwing up her hands, "and help my baby so we can eat." She smiles and pats her stomach. "I don't know about you two, but we're hungry."

"I'm starving," I say. I won't even look at Teresa. "Y'all need any help?"

"No," replies Willnetta.

"Anybody want baked beans?" Joel yells again.

"I'm coming, honey! And let me tell you," Willnetta yells, hurrying down the stairs, "what the church gossip has said about my mama and daddy!"

Before following Willnetta, I grab Teresa's arm and plead with her to keep her mouth shut about Xavier. She throws her hand up in my face, grunts, and walks out of the room.

It's nearing six o'clock when Teresa and I leave Willnetta's. My cousin hit the jackpot; Joel can cook! When I get home, I give myself a workout by washing and waxing my SUV. It's nearing ten when I crawl into bed. I fall to sleep dreaming about Xavier and me lying on a beach in St. Lucia. While the stars twinkle overhead, he caresses and kisses every inch of my body, and tells me over and over again how much he loves me.

I awake at 3:13 a.m. from a perplexing dream. I dreamed that Xavier and I were living in a beautiful, big house like Willnetta and Joel's. We were playing tag out on our spacious green lawn, and I tripped and fell. When I looked up, Mama, dressed in a correctional officer's uniform, was standing over me, screaming and swinging her arms. I couldn't make out what she was saying, because of the police sirens in the background. Xavier ran over to calm her, and she started beating him with her billy club.

I kick back the bedcovers and turn on the TV. When I awake again, it's 9:10. I jump out of bed, shower, and dress quickly so I can make it to church.

* * *

I hear very little of Pastor McKnight's sermon. I can't even recall his sermon topic. Xavier is occupying my thoughts. He'll be a free man in eight days. I look over at Mama. She's glowing because Leon is in church with her today. I couldn't be happier, because this means I won't have to chauffeur her and Miss Ida around this afternoon.

Despite their thirteen-year age difference, Mama and Leon are a vivacious, amorous couple. I never saw this side of Mama when she was with Daddy. Their marriage lacked passion and romance. It makes me wonder if either of them were truly happy and in love with each other. What a sad thing if they weren't.

When I avert my eyes back to the front of the church, I discover Jo Ann, who is perched on her usual pew—the fourth, center section—looking back at me, grinning. I catch myself; I almost roll my eyes at her. *Help me, Lord, not act ugly in your house.* Jo Ann leans over and whispers in her sister's ear. She looks back at me and turns up her nose. I close my eyes and start humming "Yield Not to Temptation."

As soon as the benediction is given, I head out the door. I take off my peach-colored linen suit jacket and sprint to my SUV. I lower the windows, open the sunroof, and take off for Hayesfield.

27

Yielding

There's a different lieutenant manning the visitation check-in area today, a middle-aged White man. A young Black male officer is working with him. The lieutenant greets me, with a big smile, and tells me I look and smell "wonderful." I thank him, hand him my driver's license, and state whom I wish to visit. The young officer gives me the once-over before looking in the file box for Xavier's visitation card.

"Inmate Dupree," the lieutenant says, "has been a model prisoner since the day he arrived here."

"You his *lady*?" the young officer asks, giving me the once-over again, much slower this time.

"No. A friend of the family," I reply.

The lieutenant looks over at the officer. "Sergeant, Inmate Dupree will be leaving next week."

"Is that right?" the officer says.

"Uh-huh," murmurs the lieutenant.

"And this young lady is?" asks the officer.

The lieutenant looks back at my license. "Eva Liles."

"All right, Miss Liles," the officer says, "sign in and you may enter."

I quickly sign my name on the visitation sheet.

The lieutenant hands me back my license. "Enjoy your visit, ma'am," he says, winking his eye.

"Thank you," I reply. From the corner of my eye, I see him and the sergeant turn and watch me exit the room.

I sit down at the first empty picnic table I come upon. I can't imagine running into anybody I know, but paranoia causes me to put my sunglasses on. My heart races as an array of emotions war against each other inside me: shame and pride versus compassion and love, and honesty versus deceit. Hopefully, after this visit, these feelings will subside. I close my eyes and take several deep breaths. When I open them, Xavier is staring down at me, with an incredulous look on his face.

"Eva? Wow! What a surprise! I-I couldn't believe it when the lieutenant said you were here to see me."

That makes two of us. I don't believe I'm here, either.

"If this is a dream," he says, sitting down next to me, "I don't want to wake up."

My eyes shift to the yellow lily in his hand.

"This is for you," he says, placing the lily before me.

I wonder if I look as stupid as I feel. Have I unconsciously undergone some type of trauma? Why can't I open my mouth and say something? I can't even will my hands to leave my lap to wipe the sweat trickling down the side of my face.

I take a deep breath and catch a whiff of Irish Spring soap. I look up into Xavier's face. My eyes travel slowly across every inch of it. When he smiles, they rest on the dimple in his cheek.

"Mmm, it's so good to see you," he says softly, looking deeply into my eyes.

Lord, have mercy! I start fanning myself with my hands. I'm overheating.

"Let me get you some water," he says, rushing to his feet.

I should get up, too, and walk right out of here, but I can't;

I don't want to. So far, my feelings for Xavier have not subsided, but have mounted with each passing second.

Xavier smiles at me all the way from the water cooler to the table. He places the cup of water next to the lily. "Here you are, beautiful."

"Thank you," I hear myself say. "And thanks for the lily. It's lovely."

"Not as lovely as you are," he says warmly.

I reach for the cup with a trembling hand. The cool water helps calm my frayed nerves and lower my soaring body temperature.

"Eva," Xavier says, leaning toward me, "may I ask a personal question that I've been afraid to ask until now?"

"What?"

"Are you seeing anyone?"

"No."

He sighs and smiles. "I would like to see you when I'm released. Can I?"

I take a sip of water.

"Please?" he says.

"Xavier, let me first congratulate you on making parole."

"Thank you."

"And I wish you all the best with the farm, golf course, and nursery. I know you're going to do well with those."

"I want you to be a part of all that," he says, leaning closer to me.

"I don't think I can."

"Tell me why not?"

I sigh and look off.

"Tell me," he says.

"Even though I believe now that you did not intentionally break the law, you—"

"Bear an ugly label?"

I look back at him and nod.

"And that's something I cannot change. If I could, Lord knows, I would. But please don't let that stand in the way of what you feel for me."

"This would all be so perfect if you weren't here!"

"We don't live in a perfect world, baby."

I sigh and shake my head. "No, we don't."

"I'm in love with you."

Help me, Lord!

"You've been to church today?" he asks.

"Yes."

"I've heard a lot of good things about your church. I'd like to come visit when I get out."

I laugh.

"And why are you laughing? Did I say something funny?" he asks.

"No, you didn't. I'm sorry. I'm just nervous."

"What are you nervous about?"

"Being here, talking to you."

Xavier grabs my hands and smiles. "Don't be."

I stare at the dimple in his cheek, then look away. "You want to know what I find so attractive about you, more than your *stunning* good looks?"

"What?"

"Your fortitude. I have a ton of admiration for you," I say, smiling at him.

"Thank you."

"And I'm not going to sit here and pretend I'm not fond of you. I just don't think it's wise for me to act on those feelings."

"Don't be afraid, Eva."

"I sneaked out here today!"

Xavier winks. "I won't tell anyone you came."

I laugh.

"Give me a chance, Eva."

"I—"

"Give *yourself* a chance. Darling, this I promise you: I will help you weather the storms of disapproval and scorn that will come your way for loving me."

I shake my head. "There's a storm in my family called Rose, and she's a force to reckon with."

Xavier laughs. "This, no doubt, is your mother?"

"Yes. She hit the *roof* when A'Kyah told us you sent those pink lilies."

"If I remember correctly, so did you," he says, opening his eyes wide.

Oops! "I did, didn't I?"

"Uh-huh."

I close my eyes. *What do I do? What do I do?*

Xavier squeezes my hands. "Give us a chance, Eva. Please."

I open my eyes and look into Xavier's. "My mind is saying one thing, my heart another. I came out here today hoping the feelings I have for you would lessen."

"Have they?"

"No."

Xavier smiles. "I'm glad. Say yes. We can take this"—he rubs the backs of his hands gently down my face—"as slow as you want."

I remove my sunglasses. "If I say yes, can we keep this between us for right now?"

"For as long as you like," he whispers. "For as long as you like."

Lord, what do I do?

Xavier leans forward. "You won't regret it." He kisses me gently on the lips. His lips are like I'd imagined: luscious.

"Yes!" I hear myself say weakly.

I can't fully take pleasure in what Xavier and I are beginning, because I can't share it with the people that mean so much to me. I've never kept secrets from my family or best friend, so this is going to be hard. But for now, it has to be this way. If Mama and Teresa knew what I was up to, they might try to commit me to the nearest mental health facility, with Geraldine outside maintaining a prayer vigil. So it's for the best that I say nothing to them right now.

Besides, my mind's made up. I'm going to see Xavier when he gets out, and there's no need to stress myself out right now defending that decision to anyone. Time is a revealer. I'll

know in the upcoming months if what Xavier and I feel for
each other is destined to soar to higher heights. If it does, then
Xavier's love will help me weather Hurricane Rose and Trop-
ical Storm Teresa. And they will in time, I pray, out of their
love for me, accept my decision to love Xavier. On the other
hand, if this budding romance falters, they're no more the
wiser.

"Xavier, what about Charles? How do you feel about what
he did to you?"

Xavier chuckles. "So my mother's told you about my cun-
ning half brother?"

"Yes, she has."

"I've come to terms with what Charles did to me *and* my
family. I've forgiven him."

"You have?"

"Yes, I have. And even after being in here, a tiny part of me
still doesn't want to believe he did this."

"It's ironic, isn't it?"

"What?"

"He's the criminal, but you're the one doing time."

Xavier sighs. "Yeah, it is," he says slowly.

"Do you still love him?"

"Yes, I do."

Would his love change to hatred and rage if he knew
Charles had been arguing with his father prior to the heart
attack? I reach over and take Xavier's hands in mine. "Tell me.
What's the first thing you're going to do when you get out?"

"Go see my father!"

"What next?"

"Take a long, hot shower, and then spend some time
with you."

I smile and grow warm all over. *Lord, I think he's the one!*
Each time I look into his eyes or behold his beautiful smile,
I grow fonder of him. I am smitten. Funny thing is, two
months ago I would have never imagined this possible, me
sitting in a prison yard, in love with an inmate. Have I found
love where I *least* expected? I think so. And when Teresa asks

me again why a woman like me would get involved with a convict, I'll tell her: I'm a woman who has learned an invaluable lesson about judging a book by its cover, and who is not so quick anymore to diss someone who could turn out to be the man of her dreams.

When it's announced that visiting hours are over, Xavier kisses me again and wraps his arms tightly around me. "You feel so good!" he moans. "I miss you already, and you're not even gone."

I exhale and nestle in the warmth and strength of his loving embrace. And each time the inquisitive sergeant from the visitation check-in area yells that visitation is over, I hold Xavier tighter.

28

Lies

I see Mama has let herself in again. I'm tempted to drive right on by. Here I was thinking I had the afternoon to myself, and Leon's Navigator is parked in my driveway.

"Hello!" I yell loudly, entering the den.

Leon throws up his hand. He's stretched out on the love seat in front of the TV, flicking through the sports channels. Mama is nowhere to be seen. She's snooping no doubt. I spot the copy of Xavier's last e-mail to me sticking out of this month's *Essence*, which is lying on the end table, next to the *TV Guide*. I was reading it last night and forgot to put it back in my vanity drawer, where all the others are safely tucked away.

"How long have y'all been here?" I ask.

"About five minutes. Rose! Eva's here!"

Mama pops out of my bedroom. "Who gave you those roses?"

"The girls at work, for being a *sweet* boss."

"I raised you well, didn't I?" she says, smiling and patting me on the cheek.

"Yes, you and Daddy did."

"You left church before I had a chance to speak to you. Where you rush off to? Teresa called. She didn't know where you were. We couldn't reach you on your cell phone."

I stroll over to the end table, pick up the *Essence,* and discreetly push the e-mail down inside. "What Teresa want?" I ask, thumbing through the magazine.

"She didn't say. So where were you?" says Mama.

"Running errands," I lie.

"What kind of errands? You've been gone almost two hours," replies Mama.

"Rose, please!" Leon yells, looking over at us. "Eva's grown. Stop questioning her like she's a little kid."

Mama sighs softly and rolls her eyes. She's putty in Leon's hands. If Daddy had ever spoken to her like that, she'd have gone ballistic.

"Honey," she says, with a big smile, "why don't you tell Eva about the new assistant manager down at the supermarket?"

"He's not Eva's type," mutters Leon.

"Does he look like this man?" I ask breathlessly, pointing to the picture of Denzel Washington on the magazine's cover.

"There ain't but *one* Denzel Washington, and he's already spoken for, okay?" Mama says, glaring up at me. "Now Gary, that's the assistant manager's name, he's fairly attractive, but what's more important," she says, snatching the *Essence* out my hand and throwing it down on the end table, "he's single."

"No kidding," I say.

Leon bursts out laughing.

"Don't get sassy," says Mama.

"I'm not sassing you, Mama," I say, laughing.

"I'm only trying to help," Mama says.

And I wish you would stop. Lord knows, I wish you would.

Mama goes on. "Gary's brown-skinned, about six one. He goes to church at Fairview Baptist—"

"Okay, okay," I say. "I'll swing by the supermarket this week to *check out* Gary, all right?"

Mama smiles. "Good."

When will I get up enough nerve to stop giving in to her? And where is my integrity? I've got to stop lying! I have no intentions of going by Fairview Foods.

"When did you last talk to your father?" asks Mama.

"Friday," I say.

"Is that when they left?" says Mama.

"Huh?" I reply.

"For Myrtle Beach?" Mama says.

"No. They left yesterday morning," I say. It amazes me how Mama keeps up with what Daddy and Miss Elsie are doing. "You wanna know when they will be back?"

Leon bursts out laughing. I try not to, but I laugh, too.

Mama rolls her eyes at both of us. "Leon, let's go. I need to make another stop before we go home."

"I love you, Mama," I say, giggling.

"Just make sure you go to the supermarket," she says, exiting the house.

Leon looks at me and shakes his head. He's still laughing when they back out of the driveway.

I kick off my pumps and head down the hall. I'll call Teresa later, much later. I'm in no hurry to lie to her about my whereabouts this afternoon, should she ask. And knowing her like I do, she's gone ask.

I wake up with a cramp in my neck and discover that the CBS Sunday Night Movie is on. Shoot! I missed *60 Minutes*. I wanted to see Mike Wallace's interview with Aretha Franklin. I click off the TV, ease out of the recliner, and hurry to my office. I have a long list of people to call this evening regarding the bazaar.

By ten, I've added eighteen names to my sponsors list. When my phone beeps, I'm on my twenty-fifth and last call for the evening. I glance at the caller ID display; it's Teresa. I put my sponsor on hold and click over. Before Teresa says anything, I tell her I'm on the phone, soliciting donations for the bazaar, and will call her later. She tells me she'll hold on, and to hurry up and finish the call. Shoot! I reconnect with my sponsor and purposely drag out our conversation for another five minutes. When we say good night to each other, I press the FLASH button, praying that Teresa has hung up.

"Teresa?"

"I'm here."

"What's up?

"Negro, where've you been? Miss Rose tell you I called?"

"Yeah."

"Why didn't you call me back?"

"I—"

"You went to see that convict, didn't you?"

"Te—"

"Don't lie to me!"

"Can I get a word out?"

"Go right ahead," she replies calmly.

"I had to take care of some business for Gina."

"Gina?"

"Yes, Gina."

"What kind of business?"

"I had to pick up a check from this guy who bought her car."

"Eva?"

"Huh?"

"Stop lying."

Oh, Lord, here we go.

Teresa bursts out laughing. "I can't believe somebody bought Gina's old, raggedy car."

I exhale.

"I know she's not getting much for it," adds Teresa.

I don't respond.

"Tell her hi for me the next time you talk to her."

"I will."

"So how many donations you . . . Hold on. I got a beep."

When Teresa clicks over to her call, I rub my nose.

"I'm back," she grumbles seconds later.

"You gotta go?"

"No. Girl, that was William. Can you believe that?"

"William?"

"The professor. The guy from the singles club!"

"Whaaaat? What he want?"

"He wants to *see* me."

"No!"

"Yes!"

"You gone see him?"

"No! I told him that last night when he called! I also told him to lose my phone number."

"You seem a little agitated. What's wrong?"

"I got cramps, girl."

"Sorry. Whatcha doing the Fourth?"

"Taking Grandma to her sister's in Durham. You?"

"Spending the afternoon at Daddy's."

"Let's do lunch one day this week."

"Okay."

Teresa and I make lunch plans for Tuesday. After saying good-bye, I hurry to the bathroom mirror and stare at my nose to see if it's grown long like Pinocchio's.

29

Bliss

The bazaar is two days away, and the donations continue to pour in. My garage floor is covered with pictures, lamps, bedding, towels, drapes, dishes, pots, pans, and a few toaster ovens. I've been sorting through and tagging items since 8:00 this morning. I hear someone pull up in my driveway. More donations I hope. I head to the front door. My heart starts racing when I see the vehicle in my driveway. It's a van from Dean's Florist.

A young man exits the van and walks up on my porch. He smiles and hands me a bouquet of red roses and white lilies. Through the tears in my eyes, I count twelve roses and twelve lilies! I remove the envelope from the card caddy.

Can't wait to hold you in my arms again! Love, Xavier

When I return home from dinner at Daddy and Miss Elsie's, there are donations on my porch. I drag them to the garage and head straight for bed. I have to get up real early tomorrow. Mrs. Ida and I have a busy, full day ahead of us.

Miss Ida and I have been at it all day. We spent the morning at the Home Depot, purchasing clay pots, potting soil, and flowers; and the afternoon, filling one hundred tiny flowerpots with zinnias and marigolds. We're hungry and tired now. When Mrs. McKnight stops by, we're packing the flowerpots in cardboard boxes under Miss Ida's carport.

"Hello, Mother Truelove! Hello, Eva!" Mrs. McKnight yells out the passenger window of her Mercedes.

Miss Ida and I wave hello.

"Trustee Jones will be by *early* tomorrow to pick up the flowers!" shouts Mrs. McKnight.

"Aw right!" Miss Ida yells, nodding.

"Don't forget to be at the church no later than six o'clock, and pray for good weather!" adds Mrs. McKnight.

"Aw right!" Miss Ida yells again.

"Eva, do you have enough people helping you transport the home décor items to the church?" yells Mrs. McKnight.

"Yes, ma'am," I shout.

"Good! I'll see you ladies in the morning! Bye!" hollers Mrs. McKnight.

We wave good-bye.

Mrs. McKnight speeds off and pulls into Mama's driveway. Mama's in the back, cooking fish. When Miss Ida and I go over fifteen minutes later, Mrs. McKnight's gone.

"Our First Lady is a bundle of nerves," Mama says, shaking her head. "I pray everything goes smoothly tomorrow."

"It always does," Miss Ida says, fanning herself with her straw hat. "Poor thang just worries unnecessarily."

Mama grunts. "You can say that again."

"Mama, please fix me something to eat. I'm hungry!" I whine.

"Okay, baby. Ida, you ready to eat?" says Mama.

"Yes, chile!" replies Miss Ida.

Mama goes into the kitchen and comes back out with two Styrofoam plates. She fills mine with shrimp, two pieces of catfish, hush puppies, and a baked potato.

After a second baked potato and another piece of catfish, I say good night and hurry home, envisioning the aromatherapy bath I intend to indulge in.

When I get home, I find a black, plastic trash bag on my porch. A note is pinned to it: *Donations from Jo Ann Outerbridge.* I look inside. There're two faded, red twin comforters and some dingy white sheets in the bag. My blood starts boiling. Is it her sole purpose in life to be difficult? Mrs. McKnight announced not once, but several times, at church that we would not be accepting any used items for the bazaar. Jo Ann heard the announcement; she was at church the Sunday it was first made. And when she approached Mrs. McKnight after the service and asked if "gently used items" were acceptable, Mrs. McKnight told her in no uncertain terms they were not.

I drag the bag to the garage, wondering why there are people like Jo Ann in the world. Sunday I'll take her "gently used," funky-looking bedding to church and get a lot of satisfaction out of returning it to her.

When my phone rings at 9:17, I'm about to step into the bathtub. I pick up the cordless phone; UNKNOWN is on the caller ID display. I press the TALK button, praying it's someone calling about the bazaar, and not a telemarketer.

"Hello."

"Eva! How are youuu?"

Shoot! It's neither; it's the chatty next bride-to-be at Community Baptist. "Monica!" I say cheerfully, "I'm fine and you?"

Monica sighs heavily and says she's weary from planning her fall wedding. When I inquire about her fiancé, the ophthalmologist, her mood brightens and her complaining ceases. I sit down on the edge of the bathtub and let her ramble on about this "wonderful man" that God has blessed her with and pray that someone calls so I can get off the phone.

"Honey won't tell me where he's taking me for our honeymoon," says Monica.

"No?"

"He wants to surprise me at the reception."

"Ahhh, how sweet."

"The reception is going to be at D & L, you know?"

"Uh-huh."

"We're gonna use the *same* interior designers that Miss Della Mae used for Willnetta's reception."

"Uh-huh."

"Willnetta's wedding reception was something *else*, wasn't it?"

"Yes, it was."

"I want mine to be just as lavish!"

"I'm sure it will be." *Somebody call me, please!*

"I've settled on my dress. It's a Vera Wang gown."

I'm happy for Monica, and I love her dearly, but she's not gone talk my ear off about her wedding. I'm thinking real hard about getting my cell phone and dialing my home number, and then Monica asks if I'm seeing anyone. I cough.

"You all right, Eva?"

I continue to cough.

"Eva?"

"Monica," I say weakly, breathing heavily. I clear my throat. "Can I get back to you?"

"Sure. I'll let you go. I called to find out if you were coming to my wedding," she says quickly. "I was going through my RSVP list and discovered I hadn't heard from you."

"I wouldn't miss your wedding for anything in the world."

"Great! Now you go take something for that cough."

"I will."

I hang up, feeling sad about not being able to share my good news. But, it has to be this way for now. My relationship with Xavier has to remain secret.

I step into the bathtub, stretch out, and send sweet thoughts his way.

30

Humiliation

God does answer prayer! We couldn't have prayed for better weather. The sun is shining, a light breeze is stirring, and today's expected high is eighty-two degrees. I'm raring to go, and from the looks of it, so is everyone else. We're all looking sharp in our new white t-shirts. Community Missionary Baptist Church is printed in bold black letters across the front. Mrs. McKnight is all smiles as she and Aunt Della Mae bounce from one "department" to another, distributing plastic shopping bags. They issue everyone name tags and remind us to wear "warm smiles."

Gospel 680 AM will broadcast live from the bazaar. Mr. T and two other radio personalities are set up at the entrance, under a big tent bearing the station's slogan, "Gospel all day, every day!"

I wave at Teresa. She's up near the entrance, across from Mr. T, arranging shoes on a long folding table. My department is in the rear of the parking lot, down from where the deacons and trustees have arranged the grills, deep fryers, and fruit and vegetable stands under the oak trees. Two of the deacons are making homemade lemonade, and Uncle Lee has already fired up one of the grills. My mouth is watering now from the smell of sizzling smoked sausage.

Willnetta has *nine* tables to the left of me, covered with all kinds of mouthwatering goodies. Every woman on the deaconess and mothers board, on the pastor's aid committee, and in the women's choir was asked to provide one dessert. Naturally, many, including Mama and Aunt Della Mae, donated more. Mama baked five cakes, all from scratch. A smile and a "bless you, Sisters" from Pastor McKnight were all it took to ignite the bake-off.

At 7:30 sharp, Mrs. McKnight and Aunt Della Mae, assisted by Cleveland, remove the barricade from the parking lot entrance, and Mr. T announces that the Seventh Annual Community Missionary Baptist Church Summer Bazaar is underway. People out on the street flood the church lot.

By noon, my department has pulled in $625. This is two hundred dollars more than what we earned by noontime last year. It seems the turnout for the bazaar gets bigger with each passing year. Mrs. McKnight, I know, is elated about that.

I'm enjoying my third hot dog when I see Mama and Aunt Della Mae through the smoke from the grills, walking briskly in my direction. Mama is scowling, and Aunt Della Mae looks like she just lost her best friend.

"Eva! Eva!" cries Mama.

"What, Mama?" I say.

"That lying Jo Ann is at it again!" Mama mutters, snatching the hot dog out of my hand.

"It's a lie, Rose," Aunt Della Mae cries. "Don't waste your time asking Eva about that dreadful lie!"

"What in the world is going on?" I whisper, a little embarrassed and irritated.

"Jo Ann told me you seeing some man in the *pokey*," Aunt Della Mae whispers, with indignation in her voice.

"The pokey? What's that?"

"The penitentiary!" Mama spits out.

My body reels, and I grab my head. Nooo, uh-uh, she didn't say what I thought she said. *Oh, Lord! Please, Lord, no!*

"I'm sick of that lying, troublemaking wench!" cries Mama.

"Rose!" Aunt Della Mae yells, tugging on Mama's arm, "you at church!"

"I'm sick of her, Della Mae! And this is it! I'm bringing her before the church! You hear me?" shouts Mama.

I look down at my feet as my heart performs flip-flops in my chest and pray earnestly for the earth to open up and swallow me whole. A hard lick from Mama ends my fervent prayer.

"C'mon! We're going over there to confront that big-mouthed, pop-eyed liar!" cries Mama.

"Ignore her, Mama!" I yell.

"I will not! And nor will you! Not this time," says Mama.

"She does nothing but sow seeds of discord, and I'm gone have her removed from the premises!" Aunt Della Mae exclaims, spinning around. "Lee! Somebody! Go get Pastor and Deacon Jackson!"

Jo Ann, her sister, and a woman wearing a red baseball cap are chatting with Mr. T and looking at CDs. Despite Mama's insistence that we go confront Jo Ann, I don't budge. I can only stare at Jo Ann and wonder how she knows about Xavier and me.

"What's going on?" Willnetta asks, running over.

"Jo Ann going 'round here telling folks Eva's messing with a convict!" Aunt Della Mae blabs rather loudly.

Several oohs, along with Willnetta's, ring out around me.

"Where's Pastor McKnight?" Mama asks, breathing fast and hard, and looking like a certifiable lunatic.

The church lot is packed now because the men are selling fish, barbecued chicken, and ribs. I've lost my appetite, and the aroma of the food is making me sick to my stomach.

"I made it, Eva!" Mrs. Jennings yells, running up to me. "I hope y'all still got towels and bed linen!"

Aha! Now I know. It was that mouthy Keisha Jennings!

She's responsible for this drama unfolding before my eyes. Who else? Jo Ann heard directly or indirectly from Keisha about the letter I got from Xavier that was mistakenly mixed in with Mrs. Jennings's mail, and she has concocted this story—an accurate story, but she doesn't know that—about my involvement with him. Now, in order to spare myself utter public humiliation, I've got to counter it with a *lie*.

I zoom back in on Jo Ann and watch her and her entourage strut over to the clothing department. Being the idiot that she is, she walks right up to Teresa and taps her on the shoulder. I hold my breath. This all seems surreal. Even as I watch bug-eyed Jo Ann duck an airborne pump and sprint across the parking lot in my direction, with Teresa at her rear, I don't know whether to laugh or cry.

"Eva!" Jo Ann yells, running up to me. "Tell Te—"

"Shut your lying, filthy mouth!" Mama screams, throwing the hot dog she'd snatched from me at Jo Ann.

Mustard, ketchup, and chili splatter across the front of Jo Ann's pink cotton shirt. She gasps, and the shocked expression on her face quickly changes to rage. "You gone pay for this, Miss Rose!"

"Like hell I am!" Mama yells.

"Go get Pastor!" Aunt Della Mae whispers hoarsely to Willnetta.

"Young lady, you shouldn't tell lies about fellow church members," Miss Ida says, peering from underneath her straw hat. "Lying is a sin!"

"She's a demon!" Mama yells, swinging her fists. "And we all know the devil is a liar!"

"Amen, Aunt Rose!" Willnetta yells.

Aunt Della Mae turns to Willnetta. "Baby, go get Pastor McKnight now! Because I want *this* woman," she says, pointing at Jo Ann, "removed from these premises!"

"I got a right to be here!" Jo Ann hollers.

"Uh-uh. You leaving here, troublemaker!" Aunt Della Mae hollers back.

"I ain't causin' no trouble!" shouts Jo Ann.

Mama steps up to her. "Every since you've been at Community Baptist, you ain't done nothing *but* cause trouble!"

"Amen! Amen!" several people shout.

"I'm bringing you before the church," Mama declares, jabbing Jo Ann in the chest. "For spreading this bald-faced lie about Eva! I'm *sick* of you scandalizing my daughter's good name!"

Jo Ann steps back and throws up her hands. "Whatever!" She cuts her eyes at me. "Don't y'all get mad at *me* 'cause Eva is so *hard up* that she had to go to prison to get a man!"

"Shut up!" Teresa screams, lunging toward Jo Ann.

"Fight! Fight!" someone in the crowd yells.

Jo Ann stumbles back onto the table where the miniature flowerpots are displayed. The table collapses, burying her beneath soil, flowers, and clay pots. A group of children from the orphanage standing near us burst out laughing.

"Pastor! Pastor! Somebody hurry up and get Pastor!" Aunt Della Mae hollers, jumping up and down like a jack-in-the-box.

I could just die! My secret is out! I grab my throbbing head and look over at Teresa. She's eyeing poor, pathetic Jo Ann, who is babbling and twitching frantically on the ground, with contempt.

"Pastor McKnight!" Mr. T's booming voice, with urgency in it, rings out. "You're needed on the church grounds, near the barbecues! Pastor McKnight, to the church grounds, near the barbecues!" Mr. T turns up the volume on his stereo; "Show Up," by John P. Kee, is playing.

The deacons and trustees abandon the grills and fruit and vegetable stands and run over. Two deacons help Jo Ann to her feet, while the others, along with Uncle Lee and the trustees, try to disperse the thickening, murmuring crowd. Jo Ann, clearly embarrassed, starts whimpering. Her tears effortlessly slide down her dirty face, leaving thin trails under her bulging red eyes. Covered in dirt, leaves, and flower petals from her waist up, she stoops and picks up her blond wig, which came off during her fall, while her sister brushes away the debris from her clothes. The woman with them glares at me. I've seen this woman before but can't recall where for the life of me right now. The children from the orphanage are laughing hysterically now. Several adults are snickering, too.

"You still standin' there, not sayin' a doggone thing," Jo Ann mutters to me. "You know I ain't lyin' on you!"

"Shut your damn mouth!" Teresa yells.

Bowlegged Deacon Jackson, chairman of the deacon board, rushes over to Teresa and admonishes her for cursing. When Pastor McKnight and his bewildered-looking wife charge through the crowd, Mama is about to lay into Jo Ann again.

"What in heaven's name is going on?" Pastor McKnight asks, looking from Mama to Aunt Della Mae to Deacon Jackson.

Mama and Aunt Della Mae, talking over each other, tell him what has transpired and demand that Jo Ann be removed from the premises.

Tears fill my eyes. How did this beautiful day, within a matter of hours, end so badly for me?

"Don't you cry, Eva," Mama says. "It's time you stood up for yourself!"

"Sister Eva," Pastor McKnight says, walking up to me, "don't fret over the lies people tell." He hugs me and smiles. "Remember, Jesus was lied on."

I burst into tears. *I can't keep lying. I just can't.* "It's not a lie, Pastor."

"What she say?" I hear someone ask.

"Ha! I told y'all I wasn't lyin'!" Jo Ann yells defiantly.

"What did you say?" Mama asks, grabbing my arm.

I can't bring myself to answer Mama or look at her. I'm embarrassed for her, Aunt Della Mae, Teresa, and Willnetta. I hope Daddy is not out here. He and Miss Elsie told me they would stop by around one for something to eat.

"Let's go inside," Pastor McKnight says softly to me.

"What did she say, Pastor?" repeats Mama.

"Sister Rose!" Mrs. McKnight cries, "let's go inside. Please!"

"She said it's not a lie!" Jo Ann yells.

Gasps fill the air.

My eyes rake the crowd. The children from the orphanage are still laughing.

"His name is X-a-vi-er!" Jo Ann sings, with malicious glee. "And he locked up over there in Hayesfield!"

Mama's and Aunt Della Mae's mouths fall open, and their eyes widen in horror.

Teresa throws a sneaker at Jo Ann.

Jo Ann ducks behind her sister and the woman who is still glaring at me.

"Ladies!" Pastor McKnight shouts. "Stop this ungodly behavior!"

"You got it bad, girl!" Jo Ann sneers. "Baaad!"

"Sister Jo Ann! That's enough, I said!" Pastor McKnight says.

"Well, she do got it bad!" Jo Ann says, rolling her big eyes.

"Deacon Jackson!" says Pastor McKnight.

"Yes, Pastor?" replies Deacon Jackson.

"Escort Sister Outerbridge off the premises!" demands Pastor McKnight.

The woman with Jo Ann and her sister curls her lips into a malicious grin, exposing three gold teeth. Oh, my goodness! Now I know who she is! She's the nurse I met in Mr. Dupree's hospital room!

The will to flee overpowers me; I start running to my SUV. I hear Mama, Aunt Della Mae, Teresa, and Willnetta running behind me, yelling for me to stop.

31

Hurricane Rose

My head feels as if it's going to explode! I stumble to my bedroom and fall to the floor, on my knees. Shame and fear cause me to clasp my trembling hands together. "Dear God, help me!"

A car screeches to a stop in the driveway. I crawl to the window and peek out. It's Mama. My heart starts beating wildly, and I break out in a cold sweat. She's the last person I want to see or talk to. I can't face her, or anyone for that matter, right now. I spring to my feet, hoping I dead-bolted the front door.

Mama is in the living room before I make it down the hall. "Have you lost your mind?" she screams, throwing her car keys at me.

I duck and run back to my bedroom.

"Come back here!" Mama shouts.

I try to close and lock my bedroom door, but Mama manages to slip in before I can do either. She pushes me back and shakes her fists at me. "I asked you a question! Answer me!" she shrieks.

Another car screeches loudly to a stop outside; it's probably Teresa. *Lord, help me, please!* Mama is standing in the doorway, with her hands on her hips. Her nostrils are flared, and she's turned a pinkish red. I try to pass her and leave the room.

"You're not going anywhere!" she screams, pushing me back.

The front door opens.

"Mama! Eva!"

It's Geraldine. I'm sure Teresa is not far behind. I plop down on the bed and place my head in my hands.

"She's lost her mind!" Mama yells to Geraldine when she enters the room. "You hear me? Lost her *damn* mind!"

"What's going on?" Geraldine asks, breathing fast and loud.

"They didn't tell you at the church?" Mama hollers.

"I couldn't make sense out of what Aunt Della Mae was saying," replies Geraldine. "Pastor McKnight told me you and Eva left upset and to go find y'all."

"Your sister is seeing an *inmate* over there is Hayesfield!"

"What?" says Geraldine.

"Eva is seeing some *convict* at the prison in Hayesfield!" Mama shouts.

I massage my temples. The pain in my head intensifies with each of Mama's outbursts.

Geraldine walks over to the bed, sits down next to me, and places her arm around my shoulders. "Eva, is that true?"

"Pastor McKnight said she told him it was!" screams Mama.

"Mama, calm down. Let me talk to Eva, okay?" says Geraldine.

"Calm down? Don't you tell me to calm down! How can I be calm after learning about this awful mess!" shrieks Mama.

It suddenly feels as if my bedroom is closing in on me. I inhale and exhale deeply, and pray for Mama and Geraldine to leave. The phone rings, causing the pain in my head to skyrocket. I massage my temples again.

"It's probably Della Mae! Pick up the phone, Geraldine!" snaps Mama.

Geraldine snatches up the receiver.

"Hello! Hello! Eva! Is this you?"

"It's me!" Geraldine yells into the phone.

"Is Eva there?" Aunt Della Mae yells back.

"Yessss!" Mama yells from across the room.

Help me, Lord!

Geraldine tells Aunt Della Mae that I'm okay and that it's not necessary for her to come over.

"This mess is all over town now!" Mama whispers angrily after Geraldine hangs up the phone. "Aren't you the least bit embarrassed about that?"

I swallow the lump in my throat and nod. "I'm sorry, Mama. I'm sorry you had to find out this way."

"You sorry? Is that all you got to say? I want to hear you say, 'Mama, Jo Ann is lying on me.'"

I look up at Mama. "I can't say that."

Mama gasps loudly and clutches her chest.

Lord, please don't let my mama have a heart attack!

"Is-is it the inmate that sent you those flowers, the ones we thought A'Kyah's principal sent you?" Geraldine asks softly.

"Yes," I reply.

"You told us there was nothing going on between you two," says Geraldine.

"There wasn't at that time," I say.

"Awww!" Mama screams, falling up against my vanity.

Geraldine turns my face toward her and peers into my eyes. "When did things change?"

"After I got to know him," I reply.

I tell my bewildered sister and distraught mother how my attraction for Xavier grew after A'Kyah's last visit with Tony. When I tell them about the flowers, letters, and e-mails from Xavier, and the visits I've made to the prison, Mama screams for God to help me.

"So," Geraldine says slowly, as her eyes grow large and round, "you *like* him?"

"Yes," I whisper.

"Ro-romantically?" Geraldine asks.

"Yes," I whisper again.

"Get up, Geraldine!" Mama screams.

Geraldine doesn't move. She presses her lips together and closes her eyes. I expect her to start singing or humming any second now.

Mama pushes her back on the bed and slaps me. "I don't want to hear any more of this!" she yells. "You made me look like a fool today. What's *worse*, you made yourself look like some foolish, hard-up woman!"

I'm stunned. Speechless. Horrified. And if it were not for the excruciating pain in my right cheek, I wouldn't believe Mama just hit me. I reach up to nurse my cheek, and Mama smacks me on the other one. Geraldine pushes her back, and I jump off the bed and run out of the room. They charge behind me.

"I will not be the laughing stock at church or in this town, and neither will you!" Mama yells. "This foolishness is going to end *today*!"

I run into the den and bump into the end table.

"You will not see this man anymore!" Mama yells, jerking me around. "I forbid it!"

Geraldine pries Mama's hands from my T-shirt and steps between us. "Stop it! Stop it, Mama!"

Mama smacks Geraldine. "Get outta my way!"

"It just happened, Mama!" I cry.

"You're crazy," Mama mutters.

"I'm not crazy!" I yell.

"Don't you raise your voice at me!" shouts Mama.

"Xavier is a good person," I say.

"He's in prison, Eva. He broke the law!" Geraldine cries.

I don't attempt to defend Xavier's innocence. They wouldn't believe it, not now. But in time, I hope they will. "He's paid his debt to society. And he's committed to being an upstanding, law-abiding citizen, just like us."

Mama scoffs. "Do you hear how foolish you sound? I don't

know *any* crooks that stayed clean once they got out of prison. They right back in the jailhouse just as soon as they get out!"

"Not Xavier," I say.

Mama lets out a sarcastic chuckle. "You hear her, Geraldine? Not Xavier."

"How can you be so sure of that, Eva?" asks Geraldine.

"It's a feeling I have, Geraldine," I reply. "Xavier is different. He's been a model inmate since he was locked up. I heard one of the lieutenants say so the other day."

"Is that right?" Mama asks, turning up her nose.

"He's educated. He has plans to—"

"Shut up! I don't want to hear *nothing* about this man!" Mama yells.

"He's different, Mama," I whisper.

"Are you willing to bet your reputation on that?" Geraldine asks tearfully.

I look away.

Geraldine grabs my arm. "Huh? Are you?"

"I don't believe this," Mama whispers hoarsely. "An inmate, an *inmate!* How many more lies were you planning to tell to keep this mess secret, Eva? Huh?"

I can't bring myself to answer Mama.

She narrows her eyes at me and shakes her head. "Daughter, lies have a way of catching up with you."

I expect Geraldine to follow that up with scripture; she doesn't.

"I apologize for lying," I say.

"What is Xavier in prison for?" Geraldine asks hesitantly.

"Grand larceny," I reply.

Mama lets out another sarcastic chuckle. "A thief! My daughter's in love with a thief, robber, burglar, rogue!" she sings. "And he's gone take everything you got, just mark my word!"

"Eva, are you feeling desperate now that you've turned forty?" asks Geraldine.

"Aha!" Mama exclaims. "That's got to be it, Geraldine!"

"Don't let loneliness cause you to do something irrational," says Geraldine. "God said He would never leave or forsake you. He knows what's best for you, and He will supply *all* your needs. Just trust and believe. Don't—"

"Geraldine, I don't want to hear a sermon right now, okay?" I say.

"You listen to your sister!" cries Mama.

"I bet there's a nice guy right here in Fairview that would love to date you," says Geraldine.

Mama throws up her hands and exhales loudly. "There is! The new assistant manager down at Fairview Foods is a nice, churchgoing man. Did you go to the supermarket like I told you to, Eva?"

"Ye—" I begin and catch myself. I'm about to tell another lie. Haven't I suffered enough for being deceitful? "No, Mama, I didn't."

"You told me you would," cries Mama.

"I lied. I told you what you wanted to hear," I reply.

Mama reaches across Geraldine and tries to hit me. Geraldine pushes her back. "I'm going to have Pastor McKnight talk to you!" she yells over Geraldine's shoulder. "You need counseling!"

"Eva, rethink what you're getting yourself involved in," Geraldine pleads. "You don't really know this man. And I don't want to see you hurt, or worse, in trouble because of him."

"And that's where she's headed! That scumbag's gone take her down with him!" screams Mama. "And if she thinks I'm gone bail her out of trouble or come to the penitentiary to visit her, she's wrong!"

"Consider what we're saying, Eva. I don't think"—Geraldine pauses and clears her throat—"this is a good idea, either."

"Does James know about this?" shouts Mama.

I shake my head.

"Well," Mama says, rocking her head from side to side, "your *beloved* father will know within the hour. Because I'm going to his house when I leave here. You can count on it!"

Geraldine hugs me. "Think about what we're saying, Eva, please!"

"Soooo, did the lowlife send you these flowers?" Mama asks, walking over to the dining-room table, where the roses and lilies are.

"He's not a lowlife. And, yes, Xavier sent me the flowers," I say.

"This is what I think of him and this sordid affair!" Mama screams, snatching the lilies and roses out of the vase.

"Stop!" I scream, running over.

Mama knocks the vase on the floor and stomps on the flowers.

I manage to retrieve one unharmed rose and two lilies from the crushing blows of Mama's mules. She tries to take them out of my hand. I push her back. My entire body trembles with anger. "Get out!" I shriek.

Mama's eyes widen, and shock registers across her face. She blinks, and the shock slowly gives way to a scowl. "What did you just say to me?"

Geraldine starts humming "I Need Thee Every Hour."

Mama steps up to me. "What did you say?" she whispers hoarsely.

I swallow and take a deep breath. "Go home, Mama."

"Naw, uh-uh, I'm not going anywhere, not until I hear you say you're not going to seeing that convict anymore."

I shake my head.

Mama reaches up and tries to hit me. I block her swing with the hand that has the rose and lilies in it. She snatches them out of my hand and throws them across the room.

"Mama! Stop it!" Geraldine cries. "Please, stop it and let's go!"

Mama bursts into tears. "You gone talk to Pastor McKnight whether you want to or not!" she cries, shaking her fists at me.

Through the tears in my eyes, I watch my mother weep bitterly. I reach out to hug her; she pushes me away and heads outside.

"We only want what's best for you," Geraldine cries, hugging me tightly. "Please, think about what you're doing, okay?"

I'm too choked up to say anything. I nod.

"I'll call you later," she whispers.

I don't move until I hear the last car back out of the driveway. As hot, salty tears stream down my bruised cheeks, I kneel and pick up the flowers from the floor.

I'm going to be the talk of Fairview for a good, *long* while. Surprisingly, the fear and humiliation I feel haven't lessened the fondness I have for Xavier. But is loving him worth losing my family? I need them in my life, too. Their love and approval have always and still do mean a lot to me, and I don't want anyone or anything to ever come between us. Yet, I deserve to be happy, and I won't be happy if I don't act on what I feel for Xavier. I know Mama and Geraldine want what's best for me, but maybe they're wrong about this, Or, am I?

The need to flee rises up inside me again. I grab my SUV keys and exit the house.

The German shepherds run around my SUV, barking loudly. The more I honk the horn, the louder it seems they bark. *Lord, please let Mrs. Dupree be home.* Here I know I can find the solace I so desperately need right now.

My prayer is not answered; the front door to the rancher remains closed. Mrs. Dupree is probably at the hospital. *Darn!* I start the engine and head back down the driveway. I'm not going back home to face more condemnation and ridicule right now, that's for sure. Like Mama said, this is all over town now. And she'll make good on her threat to tell Daddy, if it means having to track him down in the farthermost corner of the earth.

The clock on the dash shows that it's 2:57. Visitation is about to end at the prison. In only two more days, Xavier will be free. Tears fill my eyes. I pull out of the driveway and onto the highway and head to the lake.

The motion lights over the garage pop on when I pull into my driveway. It's almost ten. I don't think anyone will come over now, but I can't put anything past Mama and Teresa. I press the garage door opener, pull inside, and lower the garage door.

The phone is ringing when I enter the house. From the hallway, I hear, "Call me, Eva, please!"

"And what will you say to me, Teresa, when I do? Berate me like Mama?" I cry.

I kick off my shoes and flip on the hall light on the way to my bedroom. From the doorway, I see the message display light on the answering machine blinking in the darkness. I walk over and press PLAY.

Message one: "Eva, it's me, Geraldine. Why didn't you come to me about this? I feel *awful*, because you obviously didn't feel you could. I would've helped you sort through this." Silence. "Eva, you're a beautiful, kindhearted person. You deserve the love of a good man. I know he's out there. Just be patient. Be patient. I, I will call you later. Bye."

Message two: "Eva! Pick up! Your father wants to talk to you. Here, James!"

"Hello, Eva. It's Daddy. Pick up the phone, honeysuckle, if you're there." Silence. "Pick up, honey." Silence. "I don't think she's home, Rose."

"She's there! I just left her house!"

"Honeysuckle, call me and let's talk about what's going on. Bye-bye."

Message three: "Eva, Willnetta and I are on the way. I can't believe that big mouth Jo Ann! Ooooh, I can't stand her ass. Bye."

Message four: "Eva, pick up the phone! It's Mama!" Silence. "Ooooh, I have a *terrible* headache. I'm going home to lay down. When I get up, I hope this all turns out to have been a bad dream."

Message five: "Honeysuckle, me and Elsie just stopped by. You call us just as soon as you get in, okay? We love you."

Message six: "I can't rest. I can't rest knowing my child is making the biggest mistake of her life! You cannot be serious about seeing this convict, Eva! Lord knows, you can't be! I hope you've thought about everything Geraldine and I said."

Message seven: "Where are you, Eva? Teresa and I just left your house. *Please* call us as soon as you get in. You can reach us on our mobiles. Bye."

Message eight: "My phone has been ringing off the hook! You mark my word, I'm bringing that Jo Ann Outerbridge before the church!" Silence. "Della Mae said to tell you she's praying for you. I . . . That's somebody beeping in. I'm not gone answer. I'm sick of talking about this mess. I'm gone pray it'll all go away."

Message nine: "Sister Eva, this is Pastor McKnight. I'm here if you need me. You can reach me at home. The number is 555-2127."

Message ten: "Girl, where are you? Willnetta and I are worried. Call us!"

Message eleven: "I guess you still not answering your phone. I'm too weary to drive over there. I've asked Pastor McKnight to call you. He said he would. You pick up the phone when he calls, you hear me? I'm going to bed now. I'll call you first thing in the morning. Night night."

Message twelve: "Eva, I just got off the phone with Mama and Geraldine. I'm coming home tomorrow. Bye!"

I turn off the ringer on the phone and on every other phone in the house. I then dead-bolt the front door to prevent any unannounced visitors. I kneel beside my bed. I'm not talking to anyone tonight, but God.

"Dear God, I need guidance. You, and only you, can clearly see what lies ahead for me. I'm in love with a man who happens to be in prison, and I believe with all my heart that he loves me and that he's a good man. Mama and Geraldine disapprove of me seeing him, and so does Teresa, and perhaps everybody else that's dear to me. Should I walk away from what I believe is my long-awaited chance at love? Please, God, help me make the right decision. In the stillness of my home, speak to me. I'm listening."

32

Resolve

"Why weren't you in church this morning?" Mama asks, barging into my bedroom, all out of breath. She obviously rushed over from church, because she still has on her purple choir robe. Geraldine is with her. "You didn't even return our phone calls from yesterday or this morning."

"You're gonna have to face Jo Ann and everybody at church sooner or later," Geraldine says. "No need to hide out at home."

"I'm not hiding," I reply.

"Oh, you went to church with Daddy and Miss Elsie?" Geraldine asks, eyeing the lilac silk dress I'm wearing.

I don't answer Geraldine's question; I address Mama's instead. "Mama, after y'all left yesterday I went out for a drive, and when I got back in, I didn't feel like talking to anybody."

Mama smiles and runs the back of her hand down my face. "I understand. You feel better? You look like you do. You're glowing!"

"She sure is!" Geraldine exclaims.

Tears fill Mama's eyes. "I apologize for hitting you yesterday.

Please forgive me, baby. You know I only want what's best for you. Forgive Mama, okay?" she asks, kissing and hugging me.

I smile and kiss her on the forehead. "You're forgiven."

"I cooked all your favorites. Come over for dinner," Mama pleads.

"Okay," I say.

"Jo Ann wasn't at church," Geraldine says. "Pastor Mc-Knight plans to speak to her."

"Not a bad idea," I say, sitting down at my vanity. I catch Mama and Geraldine cutting their eyes at each other. They're dying to know what I've decided to do about Xavier. I clear my throat.

"And," Geraldine says, with a big smile, "he's going to call you."

I smile back at her in the mirror.

"And please call Teresa and Willnetta. They're worried about you," adds Mama.

"I will," I say.

"Soooo," Mama says, unzipping her robe, "what have you decided to do about this convict?"

Before I can answer, Geraldine places her hands on my shoulders. "You did think about what we said yesterday?"

"Yes, and I've prayed about it, too," I reply.

"Good," Geraldine says, patting me on the shoulders.

"I've never doubted for a second that y'all didn't want anything but the best for me," I say.

They both exhale. Mama claps her hands. "Thank you, Lord, for hearing my prayer!"

I turn around and smile at her. "What prayer was that, Mama? That He help you accept the decision I've made about Xavier and me?"

Gasps and groans fill the room.

I turn back around and reach for the Romance perfume.

"You-you on your wa-way out?" Geraldine stammers.

"Yep," I say.

Mama starts flailing her arms, looking like a big bird. "Don't tell me you going to that prison?"

"Eva, where're you going?" Geraldine asks, sounding like a little kid.

I spray perfume behind my ears, on my neck, and on my wrists—places I want Xavier to kiss. Our behavior today may rival that of Freda and Clarence. I smile at the thought.

"Eva, where're you going?" Geraldine asks again.

I get up and walk over to the closet and slip on my black stilettos.

"Mama, I love you and would never want to do *anything* that would cause you or Daddy shame. But, I can't deny what I feel. I'm fond of Xavier, and I'm going to continue seeing him."

"Lord, have mercy!" Mama cries, falling down on the bed.

Geraldine closes her eyes and shakes her head.

"I'm happy," I say, walking back over to the vanity to look in the mirror. "Real happy. Xavier will be paroled tomorrow."

"I don't approve," Mama mutters. "I don't approve!"

"You made that quite clear yesterday," I say.

"An *inmate*?" asks Mama.

"You can't handpick who I'm to love, Mama."

"An *inmate*?" Mama asks again.

I smile. "An *inmate*. I *never* would have thought that possible."

"Naw! Uh-uh!" Mama cries, shaking her head. She looks over at Geraldine. "Say something, Geraldine! She didn't hear a thing we said yesterday!"

"What're you trying to do, Eva?" Geraldine asks, with outstretched hands. "You can't save the world, honey. Don't confuse the pity you feel for this man with love."

"Geraldine, I know the difference between the two," I reply.

"Well, then, it must be sheer desperation causing you to do such a foolish thing!" cries Mama.

"No, Mama, it's not desperation," I say flatly. "It's me choosing to live my life as I please, doing what makes *me* happy. This is no different from what you did when you left Daddy and married Leon."

"Hush, Eva!" Geraldine cries, waving her hands.

"Was it love or desperation that drove you into the arms of a younger man?" I ask.

Mama's lips quiver, and tears stream down her face.

Geraldine starts singing "Come By Here, Lord."

"So you're doing this to hurt me? To get back at me for leaving your father?"

"No, Mama," I say. "I'm doing this because I want to. And it feels good." I grab my keys and pocketbook.

"Stop singing, Geraldine," Mama mutters, "and pray."

I look over at Geraldine. "Big sister, you teach a lot about forgiveness and compassion. Is Xavier to be condemned for the rest of his life because he's been to prison?"

Geraldine looks down at the floor, then back up at me. "No."

I squeeze past her and exit the room.

"Come back here, Eva!" Mama cries, staggering behind me down the hall.

I look back and smile. "See ya later, Mama."

Mama falls up against the wall. "Evaaa!"

I pick up singing "Come By Here, Lord" where Geraldine left off as I head out the door. "Someone's crying, Lord, come by here . . ."

Epilogue

Nine Months Later

"You two want more lemonade?"

"No, Mrs. Dupree, we're fine," I reply.

"Okay. We'll see you later," she says, following Mr. Dupree to his Ford F-150.

Xavier takes my hand and leads me down off the porch when they drive off. The German shepherds get up from where they've been lying near the steps and follow us. Last year this time, I was helping Willnetta prepare for her wedding, and now she's helping me prepare for mine. I look down at the four-carat, platinum, emerald-cut diamond ring on my finger and swell with happiness.

Things, although a little rocky at first, have gone well for Xavier and me. True to his word, he has helped me weather the criticism I've faced for loving an ex-con.

Mama and Teresa have finally come around. Mama no longer refers to him as "the convict." She's picked out her dress for the wedding and is helping me select light fixtures for my new home.

Xavier's ex-fiancé made an unsuccessful attempt to win

back his heart. His alcoholic half brother was the victim of a single-car accident and now lies in a semi-vegetative state at the convalescent center where Mama and Geraldine work.

Since Xavier opened his nursery three months ago, business has been great. The grand opening of the golf course is next month. Our wedding reception will be there. D & L will be catering it.

Beginning this year, July, the month Xavier was released from prison, will hold more sweet memories for him. Because that is the month that I will say, "I do," to him.